The Demon's Ring

Amara Bea Glavin

ISBN: 978-1-7372455-4-4

For information address Kindle Direct Publishing

PROLOGUE:

May 24th, 1937

Elise's Antique Shop was about to close for the night. The warm, spring evenings were usually the slowest times of the year. Therefore, Elise assumed it would be okay to lock up a few minutes early. The night was indeed an evening to enjoy. A moonlight walk would be an ideal way to end such a day.

The past year had been a rough year for Elise's shop. Sales were dropping. Fewer customers. The previous week, a customer came barging into the store, claiming that Elise had sold him a broken clock. Elise must have spent at least ten minutes explaining to him that when a customer drops an item in a puddle moments after they buy it, it's not her fault. Luckily for Elise, she still had a few satisfied regular customers who cherished the shop and many of the items it contained.

There were a few antiques in the shop that Elise herself treasured so greatly that they weren't for sale. She only kept them in her shop hoping that customers would ask the story behind them.

One was a porcelain elephant that was given to her by her son. It stood on top of a miniature grandfather clock behind the cashier desk. She always made sure to dust it off daily.

The second was a handcrafted chest the size of a piano bench. The base color of the trunk resembled the pigmentation of grass: deep, smooth, and blended. Gibberish, gold markings were written all over the masterpiece. Its shimmering presence was stunning, and breathtaking even though nobody ever bothered to guess what they meant, or where the trunk was from.

The third was a blue crystal necklace, but she always wore it around her elderly neck. She often told her friends and her son that the necklace kept so many secrets that even she didn't know them all.

Almost every citizen of Pembina, North Dakota, knew about her shop. It was a small town on a busy road. It was easy for pedestrians to pass by it daily, but rarely did she make a true connection with a customer. They had to be passionate and a wonderful listener.

As she was leaving, she made a checklist in her head. Was everything clean? Did she count the money? Everything was checked off, and she was ready to go. Her heels clapped on the floor as she made her way to the door. Her handbag was under her arm, and she was fiddling with her keys when all of a sudden, a fancy automobile pulled up in front of her store.

Whether or not this was a potential customer, Elise wasn't sure. She looked outside the window to see a dark-haired woman in a luxurious red, wool jacket stepping out of the driver's side. The woman grinned as she elegantly glanced up at the sign entitled "Elise's Antique Shop." Now, Elise knew she was about to come in. As excited as she was to go home, this woman clearly exemplified wealth. She could, of course, spare a few more minutes for a good sale.

"You're still open, aren't you?" asked the woman as she entered the store. She had pale skin with rosy cheeks that complimented her dark brown hair and deep gray eyes.

"Yes, of course!" said Elise, realizing now that she was awkwardly staring. "What are you looking for today, ma'am?"

"Something for my son. It's his birthday next week." She looked deeply intrigued by everything surrounding her. Her head was jotting from side to side not missing a single item in the shop.

"How old is he?"

The woman hesitated in answering the question, but she slowly turned around and smiled to eventually say, "Ten." Her eyes even started to wander behind the counter. "I was thinking of something porcelain."

A surge slithered down Elise's spine. Was it a warning sign from her instincts? She was beginning to feel an uncomfortable tension from this woman. But why? Was it the woman's gray eyes that looked into Elise's soul as if she wanted something that she couldn't have?

"What's his name?" Elise nervously swallowed. "I must say, I've never heard of a ten-year-old boy wishing for anything porcelain, but maybe he'll enjoy a porcelain animal?"

"Yes, well, he's special." The woman gave her a crooked smile that made Elise feel as if she just helped this woman steal thousands of dollars from a bank.

"Okay," Elise croaked and showed her to the shelf where she kept the small animal figurines, which she definitely already had seen, but Elise thought it would be best to just go along with it. After all, there was still a possibility Elise was simply overreacting. Plenty of customers came barging in with flabby frowns all the time. It usually persuaded Elise to keep an extra eye open until they came to the counter and gave her compliments about the store. Some would even offer to pay more than what she was asking. It wasn't often, but it did happen occasionally.

"Right here, we have a few dogs and cats. Most of the cats are curled up in sleeping positions. Quaint and adorable." Elise was trying her best to make her voice sound as natural as possible. She didn't want to let this woman acknowledge her discomfort, but the woman let the energy fade away from her eyes as the corners of her mouth pulled to the floor. None of these was what she was looking for.

"What about bigger...other animals?" asked the woman. Finally, it clicked. Somebody must have told her about the elephant that she put on display, but wasn't for sale. This aristocrat seemed like she wasn't going to take no for an answer, so Elise replied with "No. I apologize. I don't have anything like that." She did her best to keep the woman's back turned, so she wouldn't catch a glimpse of the elephant.

"Really?"

"That's correct." Suddenly, the tension shifted. Was this woman faking her wealth and trying to rob the store? Did she know how valuable some of these items were?

Elise turned to look at the clock and prayed it was time for her to close up. It was two minutes until six o'clock and that was close enough for her.

"Well! I am so sorry, but we are closing up for the night." But the woman saw right through her.

She eyed the glossy elephant, cracked another crooked smile, and whispered the words "Got you."

"I'm sorry?"

"How long have you been here, just out of curiosity? How long did you think you could hide?"

Everything went silent. Elise could hear the sound of her own heartbeat. She would have been able to hear the sound of the woman's breathing too, but she was too calm. Her neck was long and her jaw was relaxed. This woman held no strain as she slipped off her leather gloves.

"Do I know you?"

"No, but this would have been a hell of a lot easier if you did."

Elise was utterly confused, but everything made sense to her once the woman forcefully threw her arm forward and a small beam of blue light materialized out of the tips of her fingers. In the blink of an eye, the light raced toward Elise, but halfway there the light transformed. It transformed into the most reflective, smoothest dagger Elise ever laid eyes on.

No, Elise thought as she ducked and avoided the sharp weapon. *It can't be.*

She wasn't an aristocrat after a valuable gift. This woman was a spy working for somebody whom she had been hiding from for decades.

"Where is it?" screamed the woman.

"I don't know—" But before she could finish, the woman shot four more daggers along the lining of Elise's body, pinning her wool dress to her wooden desk.

"Don't play daft with me." Her raspy voice stayed quiet as she grabbed a hold of Elise's neck. Her youth and strength overpowered Elise. "Your son's petty little elephant gave you away. He knows where you are now. There's no point in protecting them, and there's sure as hell no point in fighting me. Now, where are they?"

Elise could barely breathe, but she noticed something odd about the woman's hand. Her left arm was upwards, prepared to shoot more daggers if needed, but on her palm, was the strangest looking scar Elise had ever seen. It was round, with dashes pointing inwards around the circle just like a clock. Only one dash extended from the center of the circle to the end, pointing towards her middle finger. Was it a burn? Did she have this on purpose? Elise had no idea what this meant, but she knew she couldn't play games anymore.

"If he—wants—to kn—so bad. Why doesn't he come here himse—?" she stammered, fighting for control.

"There we go." The woman released her choking hand and brushed it off on her coat. "Pardon me for that nonsense, but as you can see, it *was* necessary." There was a smoothness to her tone of voice. She revealed no regret whatsoever from her actions. "Where are you hiding them?"

"You didn't answer my question."

"You didn't answer mine." The woman stood there with tense patience, making little movement and barely blinking.

"I've been protecting them for decades. You'll never find them. Why do you want them anyways? What value do they have for you? Who are you?"

The woman gave Elise a small chuckle and asked "You really have no idea, do you?"

Elise felt dazed and confused, but then it hit her like a lightning bolt.

"You already have some of them, don't you?" Elise shivered. "You found our other hiding spots!"

"Your little friends aren't quite as brave as you are, and they sure are terrible secret keepers." She took a few steps toward Elise and looked deeper into her eyes. "And you also should probably know; I unfortunately...um...had to take care of them." A lost puppy dog look came about her face, mocking the shock and despair Elise's body language presented.

"Why was that necessary?" Elise demonstrated the fury in her voice, waiting to be released. "No. You're lying."

"Alright, fine. Don't worry I only had to take care of one. But don't look at me. It was his idea." Clearly the thought of this amused her. Who was this magical psychopath?

"Which brings me back to my original question? Why didn't he just come and interrogate me himself? Is he still too weak to come to Earth?"

"Oh, did I not mention? I was just coming in first to see for certain that we had the right place. He hates his time being wasted."

Elise stood there unable to move. Not because of the daggers still pinning her clothing to the desk, but because of the shock racing through her veins. What was this woman going to do to her? She needed information. Therefore, killing her couldn't be the answer.

Suddenly, a rush of burning hot wind came pouring through the store. The woman stood there untouched by it. The doors burst open. The windows cracked from edge to edge before they exploded and shattered throughout the air. When Elise thought the worst was over, a haunting, dark figure flew before her and proved her wrong.

It was covered by a black cloak with what looked like steaming red lava pouring out of its skin. Only after it presented itself and stepped in front of Elise, did it transform into a tall, handsome man. Elise knew exactly who it was.

"How did you find me?" asked Elise.

"Don't flatter yourself," said the man. "Unlike you, I've maintained my sovereignty. People who believe in me. People who agree with me."

"Well, I was just telling your little follower here that you can tear this whole universe apart, and you'll never find them."

His deep, raspy voice chuckled as he stepped so close to her that she could smell his burning breath.

"You know. Out of the kindness of my heart, I sent Kali in first to give you a chance. Just telling her where your hiding spot is would have saved your life." He grabbed her necklace and tore it from her chest before he dangled it in front of her eyes. "But at least you'll let me have this, right?"

Elise's face shifted from fearful to hopeless. How did they know what the necklace contained? Without it, she had nothing. They didn't need her.

"I know what you've been thinking," said Elise. "But I promise you, you're wrong. People might agree with you now, but they won't soon. They value their lives.

"Exactly," the man responded. "I will save them, and they will thank me for it."

The man slowly turned around to Kali, handed her the necklace, and spitefully nodded his head. There was nothing that Elise could do except struggle and squirm, hoping that she could free herself. She tried to reach for at least one of the daggers, but her sleeves were pinned down. It was too late.

Kali expressed such power and pleasure holding one palm in the air to materialize a dagger that was even longer and more reflective than the other ones. It was lined with a shiny silver color, and both ends were sharper than a sewing needle. Without hesitation, she threw the dagger straight into Elise's heart. It was a perfect piercing.

Elise took one last gasp of breath and collapsed backward onto the desk. Kali watched the blood quickly seep through her dress.

"I am so, deeply sorry about this. It's really nothing personal, but we are going to save countless lives. Besides, you had a chance to save yourself...Maya."

1:

"EVERYBODY OUT! THERE'S A BUILDING ON FIRE ACROSS THE STREET!"

Shani Simons and Asher Rodriguez pulled up to their senior year apartment a few blocks away from their college: Boston University. Class of 2018. It was their first time not living with their parents or in a dorm. They had been roommates ever since freshman year, and senior year wasn't going to be any different. They grew up together. Next door neighbors since birth.

They rented a small van that mainly contained Shani's cultural decorations. She was tall with dark skin and was adopted by two dads; one, an immigrant from Japan, the other from India. Shani had been exposed to so many different cultures her whole life that her decorations never reflected just one. She had everything from South African serving plates, which she repeatedly had to remind Asher that they were not to be used for morning pancakes, to old Bollywood film posters, but her favorite type of decoration was anything that had to do with the sea.

Shani and Asher both grew up in Cape Cod, and her favorite part about being there was the beautiful, big, Atlantic Ocean. She knew she wanted to be a marine biologist practically from birth because of living there. Anything even remotely sea-related, she collected, and she almost always kept her favorite small, gold, seashell beads in her cornrows.

Asher, on the other hand, was a minimalist. He unloaded his bed, two bins of clothes, a full-length mirror, a desk, and a dresser from the truck. As a psychology major, his philosophy was "The less things you own, the more room you have for relationships and other experiences in your life." It was the only useful thing that his high-class, Puerto Rican mother taught him. The only exception to this rule was his collection of glasses. He had a pair for every shade of gray, black, and pastel color. His wardrobe didn't expand far beyond that section of the color wheel, but he did like to look put together, even though he only needed his glasses to see what was on the board in class.

On the other side of town, Logan Kwan unloaded his 9x36 truck into the Sigma Chi frat house. He was the new president of the fraternity and quarterback of the school's football team. His brothers helped him carry in his king-sized bed in the hot, late summer afternoon. Together, they all stripped down to their shorts to show off their sweaty, muscular bodies. Logan was especially proud of the six-pack he had maintained over the summer, and despite all of the heat and heavy lifting, Logan could not be happier. He spent his entire summer working at his father's law firm outside of Boston, which caused him more misery than all of his high school classes combined.

Logan was a graphic design major and had zero interest in law, but his father insisted it would give him "real life experience." He put up with it mainly because he valued not arguing with his father too much. Logan's mother died when he was just a baby, and he knew his father was just trying to give Logan the best life he could since he couldn't do the same for Logan's mother.

The brothers of Sigma Chi spent most of their afternoon hanging up their BU Terriers merchandise and preparing for their first rush, while the students moving into the dorms didn't have the luxury of time.

On-campus housing was so busy on move-in day, it took each student about an hour and a half just to park and unload. Brex Everly was lucky and parked her car at her friend Jenna's house, which was only a fifteen-minute walk from the single that she had in her new residence hall.

Brex was also a senior, or at least she thought she was. About a year and a half ago, she took an incomplete for the semester and disappeared. She deleted all of her social media, and as far as her classmates were concerned, she only ever spoke to Jenna. No one knew what happened, but this year, she was returning to finish her degree in photography. She wasn't exactly sure when she was going to finish, but she figured it was going to happen eventually.

A few dorm halls down, Lexi Flannagan and her father carried nothing but clothes, flower headbands, and her newly stringed guitar. Lexi's thick, curly, blonde hair and long Woodstock skirt stood out like a sore thumb. Everybody around her could tell that she was a freshman and not from the city, but she never cared. She didn't have the time or effort to.

Lexi spent her summer singing and playing her guitar at numerous bars and restaurants. She was popular back in Portland, Maine, so it was a great way to raise money for college. Ever since her mom left, Mr. Flannagan had trouble paying the bills. Lexi helped out as much as she could, and she knew she was going to have to pay for all of her college tuition.

It was a bittersweet goodbye that Lexi had with her dad. Just like most parents when they drop their children off at college, they shared a tearful and memorable moment together. Although Mr. Flannagan had plenty of reasons to be worried about Lexi, Lexi was more worried about Mr. Flannagan. For the first time in a long time, he was going to be alone.

.....

When it was time for their first class of the year, the five of them all had the same tedious gen. ed. class: Philosophical Debate. Whatever that meant. They casually trickled into the lecture hall taught by Professor Morialsa. Almost every student in his classes agreed that his name sounded like he belonged at Hogwarts. It didn't help that he also spoke with an English accent. Although, most of the women tried not to complain about him. He was, after all, quite easy on the eyes.

It was a massive lecture hall that sat at least 350 students. The ceilings were around forty feet high, and instead of having a carpeted floor in front of the seats for the teacher to stand on, there was a stage. A big, wooden, brown, polished stage. The school could have put on full Broadway musicals there, but as everyone trickled in, they realized that it was going to be a smaller class than usual. All of the students took their seats as Professor Morialsa made his grand entrance into the classroom.

"GOOD MORNING STUDENTS!" the professor operatically sang, thinking it was going to encourage positivity at eight o'clock in the morning. A few students almost jumped out of their seats while most of them were silent, and then there were a few casual groans from the tacky-looking sophomores who were still in their pajama pants and most likely already stoned. "How are we all doing this fine morning?" Still, absolutely no response.

Being a gen. ed. class, it was mainly filled with freshmen. The young women were stunned when they saw him, and even more flustered when they heard him speak. They kept their googly eyes locked on him while the rest of the students kept the "just wait until you hear his lecture" look on their faces.

Brex, being visually unamused, kept her chin resting on top of her left fist and her eyes locked down on her notepad. Logan couldn't help but notice the long, pin-straight, black hair diagonally in front of him. Was Brex really back? What happened to her last year? Where did she go, and why did she leave? He could also see the dark denim jacket wrapped around her that Brex always used to wear. It had to be her.

The longer Logan's gaze lingered, the more Brex could sense someone staring at her. She slowly turned her head around, preparing to uncomfortably glare at whatever pervert was checking out the back of her head, but Logan snapped his chin away just in time for her to not notice. She slowly turned back around to return to her doodling, trying not to think anything of it.

Both Logan and Brex had had a few of the same classes together. She was a photography major, and he was a graphic design major. Logan always admired her art. He had enjoyed scoping out her photography Instagram page before she deleted it the year before. Bugs. That was 90% of her photography. Dragonflies in particular. Why? Nobody in their department knew, but they usually did get a lot of likes on her page.

Shani and Asher sat next to each other, also not paying any attention to what Mr. Wizardwhatever had to say. This was their second class with him. The first was Philosophical History. It wasn't always boring, but most of his students did find his obsession with Socrates a bit odd.

"Are those socks on his tie?" Shani asked Asher, squinting her eyes.

"Looks like it. For some reason, I'm low key obsessed," Asher shamelessly responded as the two of them exchanged quiet, excited laughs.

"And those are all the basics of the syllabus...really all you need to know." Professor Morialsa's voice suddenly got louder as he realized half of the class was not listening.

BAM!

The classroom door swung open and books fell everywhere within a ten-foot radius. The entire classroom gave a quiet giggle as the short, blonde, hippie-looking girl gathered up her books and continued to confidently walk to her seat.

"And you are...?" Professor Morialsa asked.

"Alexandra Flannagan, or Lexi, sir. Sorry I'm late. I got really lost," she responded while frantically pulling out her books and notepad.

"Freshman, no doubt" Logan's friend, Adam, whispered to him, laughing and nudging his arm.

Logan started to laugh back under his breath until he spotted Brex leaning her head back to give him and Adam the death glare.

"Yeah, and you're a senior, no doubt? Didn't get your gen. eds. done sophomore year, bud?" Lexi asked. No one responded, leaving Adam awkwardly silent. He didn't realize how loud his senior cockiness was.

"I think you two would get along just fine," Asher whispered to Shani. She was going to respond with a deathly stare, but instead acknowledged the accuracy and agreed by subtly nodding her head. After all, she didn't finish her gen. eds. sophomore year either.

Professor Morialsa took a deep breath with his eyes stuck to the floor and gave a long, scornful "Okaaaay," which caused all of the students to sit up in their seats a little straighter.

"So, a lot of you are new to this school," said the professor, changing the subject. "But we are, for some reason, lucky to have a lot of upperclassmen this semester. So, I'd like you to just start off by getting to know one another. We're going to be discussing a lot of personal stuff in this class, and I want everybody to get comfortable with one another. Why don't you start by introducing yourselves to the people around you? Let's do uhhh name, favorite color, where you're from, and list any artistic talents you have. Go!"

The class slowly filled the room with a blended sound of voices. Students slowly got up to shake their peers' hands.

Brex took a break from staring at and scuffing around her beat-up Converse sneakers and turned to her right to exchange pleasantries with a tall freshman boy, who had rainbow hair and was sitting a few seats over from her. Then, looked around to see who was next. The only person unoccupied and in her reach was a tall, familiar man with black, thick rimmed glasses, and dark olive skin.

"Hey, Brex right?" Asher asked, shaking Brex's hand.

"That's me."

"As in Brexit?" Asher gave himself a mental pat on the back for coming up with a joke so quickly.

"You're totally the first person to make that joke." Brex gave him a sarcastic grin and finger gun while Asher snorted and dropped his chin to his chest. "You're Asher, right?"

"You got it. Was it Creative Writing that we had together freshman year?"

"Yeah. Oh, and Career Development with Dr. O'Donnell."

Asher thought for a moment about the accuracy of that statement, but nothing rang a bell.

"It was that class that you showed up to about maybe three times," Brex said. "And one of those times you came in clearly still wasted from the night before. You fell off your seat halfway through an exam."

He wasn't sure whether to laugh or to be embarrassed, but he miraculously remembered it vividly.

"I got an 'A' in that class actually," Asher responded.

"Don't flatter yourself too much now. A monkey twice as drunk as you were could have gotten an 'A' in that class."

They exchanged laughter and turned to meet new people. Shani had a three-way conversation with two freshman girls both from California and both named Katelyn, but they made it clear that one was spelled "K-A-T-E-L-Y-N" and the other "K-A-I-T-L-I-N." But Shani immediately forgot which one was which. They both had long, straight blonde hair with thin waists, identical noses, and large perky breasts. She tried to cut their conversation as short as possible.

Two rows in front of her was the short, curly-haired girl who awkwardly burst into the class late.

"Hey!" Shani quietly shouted to Lexi, catching her attention. "I'm Shani."

"Hi! Lexi, as you probably heard. What's your favorite color? Where ya from? And what's your favorite art form?"

"Well," Shani giggled. "Dark green, Cape Cod, and singing. What about you?"

"Really?" she perkily responded. "I sing too! And my favorite color: Lilac. Also, I'm from Portland. Portland, Maine."

"Ahh, the home of Stephen King himself."

"And Anna Kendrick," Lexi added.

"Oh, how could I forget? How are you liking B.U. so far? Meet any interesting people?"

"Well, I've been around a few restaurants to look for places to play music, and I managed to get a gig for tonight at Pete's Pub downtown."

"Really?" Shani was completely taken off guard. A few of Shani's old friends and local musicians constantly tried to get into that pub, but it was usually at least a five-month waiting period to get a spot to perform.

"They had a last-minute cancellation," said Lexi.

"You should tell everyone," Shani added. "That place is usually filled with B.U. students. Mainly on the weekends, but I'm sure a lot of people will come for a bit, if they know there's gonna be some good music."

"Okay." Lexi stood up straight and turned towards the majority of the class. "Hey! Everybody! My favorite color is lilac. I'm from Portland, Maine, and I like to sing. Along with that you all should come to my gig tonight at Pete's Pub, eight o'clock sharp. My specialty is early 2000's pop music, and I know you millennials love your throwbacks, so you're welcome!"

The class was dumbstruck, but only for a moment. Lexi made quite a first impression. But at the same time, the class showed no ignorance of the early 2000s.

"Thank you, Lexi. Great ice-breaking," said Professor Morialsa who was hardly paying attention to what was happening in his own classroom.

Brex couldn't help but quietly laugh. She admired Lexi's confidence and appreciation of everything. It made her feel a little bit more confident and settled into the new school year.

.....

The warm, summer evening approached. The streets of Boston were crowded and filled with more people and exertion by the minute. Lexi walked into the popular restaurant "Pete's Pub" with her guitar in one hand and set list in the other. The place was filled with mainly forty-year-old men who stared at her as she walked through the door. She had a new headband and skirt on, which she bought specifically for this gig. The outfit made her everyday combination look like a potato sack. The flowers were brighter. The skirt was more colorful, and it was certainly not something that these men saw every day.

The restaurant was courteous enough to give her all the equipment she needed: a microphone, speaker, and a few footlights to give her a soft yet intense gleam.

Lexi took one look at the long, thick cord and whispered "The hell is this?" Everything was different and more complicated from what she was used to.

She searched for the correct outlet on the back of the speaker when she heard a soft, deep voice behind her say, "Need help?" Lexi turned her head around to see Logan right behind her.

"Well." She paused, trying to remind herself that she wasn't the type of person who wanted to ask for help, but she needed to be smart about her lack of technological knowledge. "Yeah, I do." She gloomily handed over the cables.

"Don't you do this all the time? I thought you would be an expert at this by now." Lexi shot him a look that clearly said, "Well that was rude."

"I mean...I'm sorry. That came out wrong," He shamefully said, trying not to make eye contact with her. "I'm not trying to mansplain anything to you either. I'm just good with electronics."

"No, it's fine. These cables, they're always different! It's confusing! And I don't always have lights. And besides, my dad usually handles that part. He just talks a little bit less than you do."

He let out a slight laugh and said, "Fair enough. My name's Logan by the way. I'm sorry, again, and I'm sorry about Adam this morning in class. He was the one that made that dickhead freshman joke. I promise you. He's usually a lot nicer than that. He just really likes the fact that he's a senior this year, and it's clearly going to his head."

"It's okay. This place just has a different feel to it than my hometown does, but it's fine. It's just different."

"College will do that to you, but don't worry. You'll adjust in no time," said Logan warmly, throwing his hand in the air like it was no big deal. "Where are you from again?"

"Portland, Maine. It's a city just like this, but in my part of town, everybody knows everybody. You know what I mean? I just hope I don't have a panic attack from culture shock." They exchanged a quiet laugh that only consisted of a single chuckle. Lexi felt slightly odd about sharing this much with him.

"Nah, I think you'll be fine. I mean you already got a dope gig, right? It'll be just like home."

"Well, I hope you're right. Thanks. So, what are you doing here?" Lexi asked.

"What do you mean? You said eight o'clock, right? And don't worry, I made sure more people are coming. You better be playing some Kelly Clarkson too!" He finished up the lights and stepped off stage before heading toward the bar and looking for a good seat. That was the answer she was hoping for. A familiar face in the audience was never a bad thing.

Lexi had a few more minutes before it turned eight o'clock. She tried to kill some time by tuning her guitar and fixing the flowers on her headband. She looked around to see if there was anyone in the audience whom she knew, but no other familiar faces yet besides Logan's.

The time finally came, and Lexi decided to start off by playing the 2002 hit *Complicated* by Avril Lavigne. Logan was sitting at the bar ten feet away from the stage, smiling and already on his second beer. Lexi began to play the first few bars, and right as she took a breath to sing the first note, Asher and Shani walked through the doors.

Lexi could see Shani looking at Asher and pointing in her direction. They looked around to find a good seat and sat down at a little table in the middle of the room.

The first song was perfect. Lexi's confidence didn't drop once, and every little note flowed flawlessly. She finished strumming the last chord of her first song and everybody there politely clapped except for the one elderly man in the corner trying to hide the fact that he was falling asleep. But as for Shani, Asher, and Logan, the three of them decided to stand up, holler, and cheer like they were at a football game. It made Lexi feel like she was playing at home again.

As the applause continued, Brex walked in through the front door. She looked around for a moment as she caught Logan's eye. He tried not to panic.

Really? Brex? She came out? Logan thought to himself. She took a glance over to him which made him realize that he had been staring at her this whole time. Just like before, he snapped his head back over to Lexi as she began to play her next song, and out of the corner of his eye, Logan saw Brex wave to a guy before she headed towards him on the other side of the restaurant. She was on a date.

Logan suddenly felt a popping discomfort in his stomach but tried his best to ignore it and just enjoy his night out, but he couldn't help feeling confused. Brex was a catch, but she didn't seem the type of girl who would be on a date the first night of school, especially when she had been gone for so long. Logan turned around on his bar stool and drank a little bit faster.

The night continued on. The sky faded into darkness, and the lights shining on Lexi grew in intensity. She played more and more as people continued to trickle in and become more engaged in her voice and guitar. She finished playing an acoustic version of the song *Invisible* by Clay Aiken, which caused Shani to shout out "Wooooo! Girl! Let's hear some Taylor Swift!"

"Really?" Lexi asked. "People are still into her?"

"Hell yeah! Do you remember *Teardrops on My Guitar*? It's a classic!"

"Actually, I'm not sure."

"Alright, let's duet then!" Shani shouted as she jumped up and immediately began to walk up to the stage, and left four empty beer bottles on her table.

Lexi shrugged as she said, "Alright, sick!" It felt nice for someone to be this invested in her performance.

Shani pulled up the lyrics and chords on her phone as people were buying another round of drinks to prepare for the next song. One of the bartenders brought up an extra bar stool for them to put Shani's phone on.

"Okay. Here we go!" Shani said and continued to clear her throat and fix her curly hair. Lexi changed picks, tuned two strings, and began to strum. Both of them started gracefully bobbing their heads and rocking from side to side.

"*Drew looks at me...*" Shani began to sing. Her voice sent a meditative calmness throughout the room. Asher loved watching Shani sing. He was always her biggest cheerleader whenever Shani felt like belting out her favorite tunes. Logan, on the other hand, was about 60% invested in Lexi's and Shani's performance, and 40% invested in Brex's date. Logan didn't even recognize this guy, but he was tall, charming, and blonde. Did he go to school in the city? Was he older? The curiosity was bothering him.

The song came to the chorus where Lexi and Shani were harmonizing with each other. *"He's the reason for the teardrops on my guitar..."* they both sang. Their voices were a match made in heaven. The richness in Shani's dark voice and the raspiness of Lexi's alto vocals rang peacefully together like the bells of Notre Dame.

Asher didn't even bother to hide the fact that he and Shani had done some hardcore pregaming before they came out. He finished his third beer, slammed it down on the table, and gave out a holler and a little dance to go along with it. He put his hands down on the table to help himself get up and get another beer before he stood up and turned around too quickly to realize that there was someone directly behind him.

"Whoa, sorry!" the familiar voice said. Asher shook his head to look at the person in front of him to realize that it was Adam, Logan's friend.

"It's okay. That was my bad, man," Asher replied with a slight slur. "I was just going to get another drink. Do you need anything?"

"Nah, I'm good. You seem like you've had a lot to drink though," Adam chuckled. "You okay? Why don't you get some water for now?"

"Uhhhhhh," Asher thought for what felt like all four of their college years. "Yeah, good idea." He began to walk but immediately tripped over his own foot.

"Why don't I get it?" Adam said while helping Asher sit back down. He started towards the bar when he spotted Logan.

"Hey, Man!" said Logan, already tipsy. "What were you doing talking to that kid, Asher? I've never seen you two talk before."

"Oh, I'm just getting him some water. He's drunker than I was at our first frat party." He chuckled as he took the waters and brought them to Asher's table.

Adam gently and carefully handed Asher the water as he sat down next to him.

"You didn't have to do that," Asher said after he took a sip. A good amount of the water missed his mouth and went straight onto his shirt.

Adam tried hard not to laugh, but it was becoming more and more difficult.

"Okay, now you're just trying to show off and be funny," he said, trying to wipe at least a little bit of the water off him.

Shani and Lexi finished their song, and the whole place cheered. Many of the boys in the restaurant, who were clearly teenagers with fake IDs, slowly migrated to the edge of the stage where they could get the best view.

Shani nodded her head, acknowledging her and Lexi's obvious stardom. She leaned down to hug Lexi in her chair and said "Thank you!

We will have to do this again soon!" Shani hopped right off the stage and immediately initiated a conversation with the only boy in the front row who was taller than her.

"Alright I got a few more songs for you all tonight!" Lexi yelled into the microphone. She strummed the first few chords of *Hey There, Delilah*, and half of the crowd started to whistle while the other half looked like they couldn't care less and had gotten over the hype of this song fifteen years earlier. Lexi didn't mind. She performed the song like she performed the rest, with passion and soul, like she always did.

"Oh, hell yeah. I love this song! You know, I could play this on the guitar. Well...Guitar Hero," Adam exclaimed.

"You know that Logan is over there, right?" Asher asked, pointing to Logan, sitting at the bar.

"Well, you looked a little lonely, and the only other person I've ever seen you talk to was rocking her face off on stage, so I thought you could use the company. Plus, he's more of a 'leave me alone. I'm trying to look like a sensitive, closeted poet and musician, so I can pick up girls at bars' kind of guy."

"You can also be kind of a dick sometimes, though. No offense," Asher stated, laughing into his water.

Adam chuckled with his head down and said, "Yeah, well...my girl-friend broke up with me over the summer. Something about me being too much of an asshole."

"Oh. You don't say?" Asher jokingly replied. Adam instantly chuckled and rolled his eyes.

"Well, Lexi just kind of reminded me how right she was, and I should be less of a dillhole and probably get some new friends. Logan is the only one of my friends that isn't a complete asshole. Just a little."

"Hm. That doesn't really explain why you're sitting here drinking water though." Asher tilted his head down, glaring into Adam's eyes with a goofy frown on his face.

"Oh, yeah, I don't drink the night before football practices. I've made that mistake before and learned my lesson the hard way. I basically only drink on Saturday nights after the games. I know, it's a rough life I have."

A few drops of water burst out of Asher's nose and mouth so fast, he almost didn't realize that Adam's joke was not that funny.

"Oh, noooo," Asher gasped in his longest, deepest voice.

"Oh, yesssss," Adam teased.

Shani came up behind Asher and threw her arms around the back of his neck.

"DID YOU SEE THAT? HOLY MOTHER, I MISS SINGING!" Shani screamed directly into Asher's ear.

"You sounded amazing!" Both Asher and Adam humorously yelled back in her face.

Logan glanced over at his friend and laughed in admiration. His eyes happened to drift over to see what Brex was doing only to realize that her date was no longer with her. She was simply enjoying the night by herself, drinking her beer and watching Lexi.

Logan tried desperately to resist the temptation to go over and talk to her, but he knew that it would be bizarre for her if she was on a date with one guy and then another guy came up and started talking to her directly afterwards.

But what if she started talking to me? Logan thought. That wouldn't be as awkward. He was aware that Brex was not the type of person to initiate a conversation, but he thought he might give it a shot anyway.

On the other side of the bar, Shani, Asher, and Adam were all laughing hysterically while a few people were shushing them, trying to hear more of Lexi's music.

"Alriiiight!' Lexi chuckled as she strummed the last chord of her previous song. "I have just one more song for you all tonight. I think you're reeeally going to like it. You ready?"

The whole bar cheered, but Shani overpowered the entire bar with her deafening vocal encouragement. It even made Brex laugh for the first time all night.

"I'm gonna take that as a yes," said Lexi ironically.

She picked up her hand to pluck the first string—

BAM!

Everyone went dead silent and jumped out of their seats. The thud was so loud and intense, it felt like a bomb went off, but no one had a clue as to what was going on. Was the city being attacked? Was it an earthquake?

Everyone could hear screaming coming from outside. Half of the patrons in the bar were frozen, not knowing what to do. Was it too dangerous to go outside? The other half ran up to the windows to see what catastrophe could possibly be disrupting their night.

Logan and Asher both ran up and pressed their faces against the window, trying to see through the foggy night. All of the pedestrians were running as fast as they could to the left. Asher pushed his way through the crowd of people, crushed up against the windows to get to the door. He had to see what these people were running from, and he feared that it was coming from close by.

He got to the door and pushed open the hefty piece of metal. He raced out of the building with his heart thumping and his hands quivering beyond control. He took one glance over to the right across the street to see the tall, red, brick building in flames.

The fire was blazing orange and shimmering yellow. If anyone got too close to it, it would be like staring into the sun, if the sun was only yards away from them. More and more people were fleeing from the building by the second. There was a brief moment of complete petrification all over Asher's body, but he quickly had to snap himself out of the trance and get everyone out of the bar.

He could feel his heart beating again, and with every ounce of force in his body, he pulled the door back open and screamed "EVERY-BODY OUT! THERE'S A BUILDING ON FIRE ACROSS THE STREET!"

One second, there was complete silence, and just like a light switch, everyone began screaming and pushing each other out of the way to get to the door. Asher held the door open for every last person racing to save their lives. He repeatedly looked back to see if the building was going to collapse on them.

The sirens grew louder and louder by the second. The intensity of the sound waves vibrated against the pavement. First, there was one fire truck. Seconds later, there were four. Police cars were piling up on the sidewalk and grass. Ambulances were spitting out stretchers and paramedics almost as fast as the fire hydrants were spitting out water.

Finally, everyone was out. Shani and the bartenders were the last ones to escape. She flung herself towards Asher and reached for his hand.

"Are you okay? Is that everyone?" Shani asked frantically.

"Yeah I think so," He responded, breathing heavily.

They could both hear a fireman or a paramedic scream something from the burning building that sounded like a warning, but they couldn't make out what. They both snapped their heads towards the fire to see the section of the building that already fell off and continued to crumble down in massive pieces. Only this time, it was coming towards them.

Their eyes were locked, staring at the building that was beginning to cascade for what felt like a lifetime. Their sweaty hands were still glued together. Shani recovered from the fearful trance just a moment before Asher did and began to pull him away, sprinting from the scene.

"C'mon!" Shani screamed. She tried not to look back. She knew that it would only slow her down. They saw Brex, Logan, and Lexi running away in the distance. Brex and Logan struggled to maintain their speed, probably from all of the alcohol. Lexi was struggling to keep up with the rest because of the long skirt and flimsy shoes she was wearing. She kept hiking up the multi-layered skirt to keep from tripping over it until—

"AH!" Her sandal snagged onto a rock stuck in the pavement. Before she could stop herself, Lexi fell forward and scraped her hands on the black tar. Her staccato, high-pitched scream caught Brex's and Logan's attention. They instantly turned back around to help her stand up while trying to pull her away at the same time.

Shani and Asher caught up with Brex, Logan and Lexi before the bricks finally collided with the pavement and shook the ground like an earthquake that was never going to end.

Asher felt the sweat spraying off his face. He wasn't sure if the alcohol was helping his adrenaline or hindering it.

They all kept running, thinking at any moment they were going to be able to stop because they would be safe. Their escape began only seconds earlier, but the conclusion was still ongoing.

Shani turned her head to look back while still pumping her legs as fast as she could. The fog made it difficult to see, but she never saw anything so powerful, so overwhelming. She couldn't help but keep worrying about Lexi, or anyone else falling again. If anyone did, they might get crushed or burnt to a crisp. She refused to stop looking back to make sure they were all still there.

The fire looked like it was about to stop spreading until sparks jumped into the tree close by. It only took a few seconds for the leaves to burst into flames. Unfortunately for every living being surrounding it, the fire spread to the tree next to it, and the tree next to that. It continued spreading at an atypical speed. It wasn't normal. Not even dead trees could carry fire that quickly.

The five of them continued their run towards the park, but the flames in the trees migrated over to the entrance of the park and caused them all to stop in their tracks.

Dead, flaming branches fell before their feet. Asher jumped back and put his arms out to prevent the rest from running into the fire.

"THIS WAY!" Lexi screamed looking and pointing towards their right. She saw a clear path, leading them to safety, and they all dashed towards it. Their heart rates were still increasing, but their breath intake was significantly decreasing.

It only took a few moments for them to slow down and realize the fire had stopped spreading. They eventually eased up on speed and began to walk instead with their jelly legs fighting to stay strong.

"What just happened?" Asher hollered while trying to treat his violently painful runner's cramp. They all turned back around to see nothing but gray with orange, prying its way through the darkness. Out of nowhere, they suddenly saw giant arches of water, shooting towards the building in all directions. The flames were finally dying down.

"That goddamn building almost killed us!" Logan screamed.

Lexi crouched down in a fetal position with her hands clutching her skull. "No, no, no, no, no, I don't even wanna think about how many casualties there were." Shani and Brex both went over to console her gently, placing their hands on her shoulders.

"We all need to keep moving!" Brex exclaimed. "Who knows if this fire is gonna start spreading again?" They all agreed and began to walk slowly in a clump, still catching their breath.

Asher couldn't help but scratch his head and knit his eyebrows together. "How did that fire spread so quickly? And how did that brick building catch on fire anyway? It practically exploded!"

"What if it was a terrorist attack?" Logan cried out.

"No." Shani shook her head "Any terrorists wouldn't have blown up an office building with probably nobody in it in the middle of the night. They would want as many people there as possible."

None of them could deny it. How could a building that was mostly made of solid brick burn down that quickly, and how did the fire spread that fast on trees that were still alive? It down poured practically half of the summer. Something didn't add up.

They kept walking until Lexi pointed out, "Um guys, we're not walking the right way." They all stopped in their tracks.

"Oh right," Shani said quietly with little emotion. "Let's walk through the park."

Asher looked at her as if she just asked them all to directly walk through the burning building, which to him, she might as well have.

"Are you nuts? That holy demon magic fire just spread through those trees like crazy. I'm not taking any risks by walking next to more trees."

"Oh, come on, we'll be fine. Look, they're not spreading anymore. The fire is almost out. They have every fire truck in Boston there now. Besides, we should all stick together. I got a weird, creepy feeling, and I don't like it."

"Shani's right," Brex lethargically said. "Let's just go." They all headed toward the entrance to the Boston Common. Everything was still. There was no wind. No voices. Everyone had safely returned to their homes, except for them.

They walked in complete silence for over five minutes, but it felt more like fifty. What was anyone supposed to say anymore? The shock wasn't going to wear off anytime soon.

"Boston isn't always like this, right?" Lexi said, breaking the silence. Her question made Shani snort with laughter. Then, she remembered this was Lexi's first night of college classes.

"No. I promise. But from now on, you have people to go to in case that changes." An ounce of relief poked Lexi hoping to get through, but something caught her attention instead.

Lexi thought her eyes were deceiving her when she saw a silhouette of a head in the trees. Attached to that head was a piece of fabric with what looked like a shimmering sun on it. It was on the bottom of what was probably a coat, but she couldn't be sure. She only caught a glimpse of this figure for a fraction of a second, but it made her think, and it made her shiver even more.

"Somebody had to have done this on purpose," Lexi said. "Just wait, I'm sure the police will find alcohol dumped all over the trees. They'll put together a profile and figure out who the main target was and all that. It will all be fine."

"You watch a lot of crime shows, don't you?" Asher asked her.

"I've seen an episode or two of *Criminal Minds*," she said, trying to break at least a little bit of the tension. Lexi decided not to say anything about what she saw. She was sure she was just hallucinating.

"I mean, what I just don't get is—" She was interrupted by a quiet but deep growl coming from a patch of trees just a few yards in front of them. It didn't sound like a dog, and that's what made the vibrations in their fingertips and feet so overwhelming. Something about that sound was much darker than any dog could make.

"What was that? Do you guys see anything?" Logan asked, cautiously looking around.

It was too dark to make out a silhouette of the trees, let alone an animal. Shani pulled out her phone, but the flashlight on her phone only went so far.

The growl continued, and its volume began to increase. Whatever it was, it was getting closer. They all squished together, trying to make as little noise as possible. All of a sudden, they heard a loud *CRACK* come from the edge of the woods. A twig snapped in half. Someone or something had stepped on it.

Their eyes were locked, and their bodies were stiff as statues. They stood there, waiting and preparing for any sudden movement. But instead, two giant, glowing, gold eyes slowly pierced through the dark and made their way towards the five students.

"Guys," Brex whispered "Run."

In the blink of an eye, they all gasped for breath and sprinted in the opposite direction of the creature with the glowing gold eyes. They didn't dare to look back as they all ran in a clump, but they could hear deep breathing and paws hitting the ground. Whatever it was, it was running after them, and it was gaining on them fast.

They were coming up to a small hill with a truck-sized ditch in it. Asher spotted a red door against the side of the hill, and all of a sudden, he stopped in his tracks.

"GUYS OVER HERE!" he screamed, and ran towards the wooden door. Without any hesitation, they all followed him. Within a fraction of a second, Asher feared the possibility of the door being locked, and they would be trapped outside in more danger than they were in before.

Asher reached his hands out as he frantically threw himself against the door. His right palm slapped the middle of the dust-covered wood while his left palm and fingertips jiggled the handle. It was locked, or maybe it was stuck. Asher couldn't tell, but the four-legged predator was getting close.

They all crowded around the door, regretting their impulsive decision to follow Asher.

"C'M ON! C'M ON! C'M ON!" Shani spat out. They could hear the creature make some vocal outburst that resembled the sound of a bull when it sees a red flag. It gave them chills to hear such a disturbing sound getting stronger and more deafening. Now, it was getting so close that Brex could have sworn she saw saliva spray on the door.

Asher kept frantically turning and wiggling the handle until he heard a loud *SNAP!* The handle broke. It felt like his heart stopped for a full three seconds, but Logan felt no hesitation.

"OUT OF THE WAY!" Logan screeched, and with every ounce of force he possessed in his body, he kicked open the door. Dust flew into their faces as the door swung forwards. They all grabbed one another and pulled each other inside to their safety. Shani was the last one to run inside and slammed the door behind her.

"Come on. We gotta hold it!" she said, getting into her runner's position and pushing her palms up against the door. The rest of them prepared for the dangerous creature to try to break through the wooden door, but nothing happened. Everything was still. They could no longer hear the sound of a dog breathing with every throat muscle. They could no longer feel the ground shaking every time the mysterious creature slammed its paws down. Everything was silent. There was nothing there.

They all stood still for a few moments, hoping that their dangers were at an end.

"Do you hear anything?" Brex asked as quietly as possible.

"No," said Shani. "I don't know how or why, but I think it's gone." They all slowly took their hands away from the door. Lexi and Logan both crouched down to the ground, trying to get their heart rates back to normal. Shani looked at Asher and said, "Well that was hella risky bringing us in here." Asher shrugged and turned away from her. He wasn't in the mood to be ridiculed or bossed around for what he instinctively thought was the best option.

Lexi noticed there was something odd about the floor. It took her a second to realize how cold she was, but before she said anything, she heard Asher say, "Guys...where are we?" They all looked back at the room they were in, and every inch of the place was covered in thick, white ice.

"I don't think this is a crypt," said Logan.

"It's only fall. How is this frozen? And where is the light coming from?" Shani asked.

"I think the ice is the light," Brex answered before she could stop herself. "It's kind of...glowing."

"I think we should get out of here."

"What?" Brex asked, breaking from her trance. "What if that thing is still out there? We could all get eaten alive. We should wait at least a little longer and come up with a plan just to be sure, so we can all get home safe."

"What was that anyway?" Lexi asked "And why was it chasing us? I know it was too dark to see, but it was way too big to be a dog."

Shani rubbed her forearms and biceps as her goosebumps got bigger. Asher wrapped his arms around her, hoping his body heat would help keep her warm, but the temperature continued to drop.

Logan couldn't stop his jaw from vibrating, but he kept trying to keep his body heat up by pacing back and forth. Eventually he came to an abrupt stop when he heard something unusual. Bubbles. More specifically, bubbles that one would hear come from a hot tub.

He looked around, squinting his eyes to see if he could spot where the sound was coming from. It didn't take him long before he saw small streaks of steam coming from the other end of the icy cave.

He turned around to catch everybody's attention, but stopped himself before he opened his mouth. Did he really want to worry anybody? He just wanted to see if it was anything they should stay away from, or if it was something that would prevent them from freezing to death.

Logan took a few slow steps towards the peculiar sight. The sound of the boiling bubbles grew stronger, and the steam seemed a little higher than it was a few moments before, and there were little animated patches of blue and green that moved along with the streaks of steam. It was almost like a miniature sighting of the Northern Lights.

Brex's eye caught Logan creeping toward the pool of the unknown substance, and a bad feeling immediately stabbed her in the stomach. She looked back and forth between whatever it was that the steam was coming from and Logan. It didn't take her long to notice that the steam popped louder and the colors shined brighter as Logan got closer to it.

Logan figured he should keep a safe distance away from it, but he got close enough to admire the thick, dark-green liquid swirling around in the ice like a whirlpool. Something wasn't right. Along with them being in an underground ice cave at the end of the summer, there was a green boiling substance giving off blue and pink colors.

Brex couldn't take it any longer. She decided to step in and say, "Hey, Logan, I really don't think you should—" and without any warning, the pool of boiling liquid exploded quicker than a bomb.

The only thing that the five of them could see was a burst of bright green lights before they were knocked off their feet and left unconscious on the ice-cold floor.

2:

"WOULD EVERYONE JUST SHUT UP?"

None of them had any idea how long they were unconscious for. Everything was white and blurry. Their pounding headaches were too severe to worry about how cold it was. Asher tried to lift his head, but felt an intense pain in his back instead. He tried to wiggle his fingers to regain control over his limbs, but every bone and muscle in his body felt like it instantly aged over a hundred years.

Brex lay flat on her back. Oxygen quickly reentered her lungs. Her eyes twitched open, and she clenched her body in pain. The memory of the explosion was rushing back to her. All she wanted to do was make sure everybody was okay, but the throbbing ache in the back of her skull made it hard to sit up. That wasn't even the worst pain she felt. There was an excruciating sting in the palm of her left hand.

A scratch from the fall, she thought.

Her vision cleared up, and she flipped over her hand to reveal a dark, circular, clock-like mark scarred into her palm. It almost resembled a tattoo with a hint of red in it. The skin was peeled. Not in an infectious way, but rather as if it was making room for the permanent, dented mark.

"What the hell?" she mumbled under her breath. There was no way. No way that a scratch of ice made this perfect circle. Dashes surrounded the edge of the circle pointed in towards the center like markings on a gas gauge, and one perfectly straight bleeding line was engraved into her skin pointing twelve o'clock sharp.

"Is everyone okay?" Logan cried out, trying to find the strength to stand.

Shani was the first one to retrieve enough energy to stand up and run to Lexi, who hadn't yet moved. She scraped the back of her hands against the icy floor to scoop up Lexi's upper body and placed her on her lap.

"Arrrahhhh, Shani I'm fine. My shoulder just hurts a little. I think I landed on it, but my palm, it kills. I think I scraped it." She wiggled her fingers, trying to make the stinging go away. Brex overheard, and her adrenaline immediately kicked in. She pulled herself up and stumbled over to help.

"Let me see," Brex tried to say as her throat cracked and croaked, but after flipping over Lexi's left hand, she wasn't sure if it was help that Lexi needed.

Lexi's palm reflected Brex's perfectly. Whatever it was, the scar-like shape was the exact same size and color as Brex's. The longest point that stretched from the center of the circle to the end both pointed towards their middle fingers. The rest of the notches were evenly spaced, pointing inwards along the inner circumference of the circle. Just like Brex's.

"It's okay, Lex," Brex, once again, tried to articulate, although she was speaking to herself more than Lexi.

Brex reached her shaky hand to gently touch Lexi's palm, but even holding her fingertips an inch away from Lexi's palm made her flinch.

"Do we all have this?" Brex turned to Logan, who was trying to help Asher stand up. They all exchanged pale, frightened looks before the rest of them slowly lifted their left arms to reveal the same perfectly circular, fiery-red, aching tattoo.

"Guys," Asher said, breaking the tense silence, "What just happened? Where are we?" His voice grew louder, trembling with fear that was growing stronger with each and every syllable. "What is that?" He pointed towards the smoking body of liquids in the ice with his shaky finger.

"Shani," said Brex. Shani snapped her head to exchange looks with Brex. It was only two syllables, but she didn't like the way Brex said her name. "You've got a giant piece of ice in your leg."

The rest hurried toward her as Shani looked down to see her jeans covered in blood and a long, thick piece of ice sticking out of her thigh.

"Holy shit, holy shit, holy shit, holy SHIT!" Shani tried and failed to not panic.

"Lay down. Come on. We have to get it out," Asher said. Lexi sat up from Shani's lap, and Logan started ripping up the bottom of his shirt.

Shani's entire body shook. Her adrenaline was pumping so rapidly, she didn't notice how much it hurt until Brex pointed it out.

"I could barely feel it a minute ago," she said. "Damn, it's cold."

"You're in shock," said Logan. "Your body is going to feel weird, but this is definitely going to hurt. Are you ready?" Shani nodded her head, but refused to burst into tears.

Asher reached out his hand, so Shani could squeeze it. She took it, and Logan yanked out the piece of ice as hard and as fast as he could.

"BITCH!" Shani screamed. Logan immediately put pressure on it with his ripped-up t-shirt. For a moment, he was almost afraid of her. Brex couldn't help but close her eyes and look away. Blood was not her thing.

The ice lay there on the cold floor, covered in blood. It was thicker than they predicted. Logan became concerned that it had almost touched her femur. He wasn't sure what kind of medical procedures that would require.

"I think I'm okay," Shani said, trying to stand up. "I swear it feels better now. I can stand." She grabbed onto both of Asher's arms and hauled herself up.

"Whoa, whoa, whoa, easy! Take it slow. You may have lost a lot of blood."

"Asher, calm down. I'm fine." She wobbled around, trying to stay balanced. "We need to all stay calm."

"That might be a little hard, considering the door is gone," Logan said as if nothing could get any worse. They all turned towards him to see him facing a flat, icy, doorless wall.

"Okay we must have been passed out for a while then. Someone's probably trapping us in here!" Asher screamed.

"Okay, how could somebody possibly freeze ice over a door?" Brex asked. "Does anybody have a signal? We gotta try calling someone." She pulled out her phone, which now had many cracks on the screen and, of course, no signal. Not even 4G, but the time on her phone read half past two.

"Shit. It's two-thirty in the morning," said Brex.

They all spent a few minutes walking around the cave, lifting their phones as high as they could to get a signal, but hope was nowhere to be found.

"Great. Now what?" said Asher.

"Come on. We all gotta—" said Shani.

"What was that bla—" Brex interrupted.

"We can't get out of here if we—" Asher chimed in.

"What the hell was that giant dog thi—" Logan wondered out loud.

Each voice piled on top of one another. Nobody could understand what anyone was saying. Every word jumbled into one out-of-tune orchestra. A truck could have plowed through, and none of them would have noticed.

They were getting nowhere. Lexi's head started pounding from all the stress, confusion, and yelling. Brex became so overheated, she had to wipe the sweat off her forehead. For a moment she had to stop yelling and think; why on Earth was she sweating? She was trapped in an ice cave. There was nothing but cold, thick, solid water surrounding her. Something wasn't right.

After a few minutes of continuous shouting, it was mainly Shani who was trying to overpower Logan and Asher. Lexi was staring at them, rolling her eyes and realizing that arguing was pointless.

"We should have just gone around the park. Why did we have to listen to you?" Asher complained, while trying not to explode with anger.

"Me?" Shani exclaimed. "Why did we listen to you? You led us in here!"

Logan's fists clenched like he was about to punch a bully on the school playground.

"WOULD EVERYONE JUST SHUT UP?"

And just like that, his body let out a shock wave of bright blue lightning. For a brief second, the thick bolts of electricity covered almost the entire interior of the cave. They all jumped back. Crouched down and away from Logan. Finally, there was silence.

"Um...what?" Lexi mumbled. She stared at Logan's smoking hands with her wide, blue eyes. Logan stood there frozen with his hands still propped up like he was carrying a tray in each hand. His hair stood straight up, and little, lingering shock waves of electricity continued to zap through his fingertips.

They all suspiciously turned around to look at the pool with the smoking, mysterious liquid.

"What the hell is in that stuff?" Shani asked with a trembling, airy voice. "Do that again."

"What? I don't know how! I don't even know what I did!" he said in a slightly squeaky and high-pitched voice.

"Okay, can we just try and get out of here before Logan tries to electrocute us again?" Brex asked, heading toward where the door used to be. "It couldn't have just disappeared. There must at least still be an opening."

"And what are we gonna do? Chop it down with all these tools we have?" Shani asked sarcastically.

"Well, we can at least try and use our body heat to melt it."

"That'll take hours."

"Do you have a better idea?" None of them ever heard Brex speak so loudly before.

Shani gave an exhausted sigh before walking over to Brex. They both headed toward the icy wall until they heard—

"Heads up!" Asher hollered from behind, throwing a giant chunk of ice directly at the wall, almost hitting Shani and Brex. They both crouched down so fast they almost lost control of their legs.

"DUDE!" Brex and Shani screamed at the same time.

"You asked if there was a better idea, and I found one." They all looked back at the wall where the block of ice hit. It wasn't much, but they were able to see tiny indents where the ice had collided.

"Alright, let's go," Lexi said, finally able to pull herself up. She took the biggest block of ice she could find, turned towards her target, pulled her arm back, took two steps forward, and as she was about to aim, "WHOA!" She slipped.

Everything would have been fine if she hadn't thrown the chunk of ice directly into the air. It was inches away from hitting the ceiling, and on its way back down, it headed directly towards Brex.

Brex used her best instincts and jerked her arms in front of her face. She expected to feel a sharp pain in her forearm, but nothing happened. All she noticed was that her hands felt a little hot, and something was cracking. She uncovered her face to see the others staring at her with wide eyes and dropped jaws. Her hands and forearms had thick, black smoke drifting from them just like Logan's did. It took Brex an entire breath to realize what had happened.

"My hands just caught on fire. Didn't they?"

"Yup," Asher responded.

"Of course, they did," said Brex, trying to stay calm.

Logan tried to examine the mark on his hand. "All this crap has something to do with these marks on our palms."

"Was it the fire or lightning that gave it away?" Lexi asked, still recovering from her fall. "Can we just focus on getting out of here before we try and unmask whatever voodoo shit is going on here?"

"Brex, do you think you could do that again?" Asher asked.

"What? Make my arms catch on fire again? Why don't you throw more ice at me again and see what happens?" she responded sarcastically.

Asher, not caring if she was serious or not, said, "Okay," and reached down to pick up another block of ice.

"NO!" they all yelled. Asher immediately dropped the ice and put his hands up by his head, trying to demonstrate his innocence.

"I can do it. Just give me a second." She cautiously walked over to where the door used to be, took a deep breath, and gently placed her hands on the ice. Her eyes shut tight. She was trying her hardest to relax all of her muscles, so her brain would only focus on the thought of fire and power. She took one more breath and realized she had absolutely no idea what she was doing, and nothing was happening.

Her arms collapsed by her side before she took a step away from the wall and stared at it questioningly.

Why wasn't it working? Brex thought. *Where was this fire even coming from? Was it magic? Or supernatural science?*

"It's okay," said Shani. "Try it again. You can do it."

Brex took a moment to think. What did she need to do differently? She focused hard on the ice and stepped back in front of it. She closed her eyes again, reached for the wall and flexed every muscle in her body. Her fingertips slowly started to sweat, and then came smoke. Suddenly, there was a spark, followed by popping and sizzling. Her eyes slowly opened to see bright orange flames covering all the way from her scuffed-up nails to her wrists.

A part of her felt scared. Another part of her couldn't help but absorb the power and pride. The ice was melting, and it was melting fast.

"Guys," Asher interrupted "what if we all got superpowers? I mean, we all have these weird looking circles on our palms."

"We are not calling them superpowers," Shani said, glaring at him. "We can call them literally anything else but superpowers."

"Okay, you come up with something."

"This cannot possibly be what you are fighting about right now," Logan intervened. He stood there with his arms crossed, unamused.

"Easy for you to say, Percy Jackson," Asher sassed.

"Percy Jackson wasn't the lightning thief. It was that Mr. Sexy Pants guy...Austin Butler."

"Jake Abel," Lexi corrected.

"Yeah, the other Mr. Sexy Pants."

"Jesus Christ," Shani said, scraping her fingernails through her hair.

Brex was putting all her strength into melting the barrier and didn't appreciate the obnoxious distractions. "If you want your 'not called superpowers' so bad, why don't you just try doing something to figure out what they are? And maybe you can help us get out of here."

Asher shrugged his shoulders and scanned the room. He thought that if he snapped his hand toward an object, it might blow up. He started jumping around and kicking the air, mocking what he had seen in the *Ninja Turtles* movies that he still watched religiously.

Shani and Lexi both decided to take a more meditative approach and "listened to their inner voices." They both stood still with their eyes closed and palms toward the sky. Lexi was guiding Shani through her usual vinyasa yoga routine, but nothing was happening.

Brex continued to melt the ice, but was fatiguing quickly. "Hey guys," she said, trying to get their attention, "What if my fire is sucking all of the oxygen out of the air? What if we suffocate before I get through this?"

"Don't worry. The ice and water should give us enough oxygen, or at least I think that's how science works." Logan chuckled, but Brex didn't return the laughter. Logan saw her eyes drooping and her skin covered in sweat. He was worried she could lose consciousness at any moment.

"Hey, why don't you let me try?" he asked.

"What are you gonna do? Zap it, so it shatters?"

"Wouldn't hurt to give it a shot. You just look like you could...use a break. We can take turns."

"Yeah. Okay." Brex backed away with her head down and her hands rubbing together. She didn't feel any pain, but they felt oddly firm, and she didn't trust it.

Logan placed his hands on the deathly cold ice and closed his eyes. He flexed all of the muscles in his body just as he saw Brex do. For a few moments, all he could feel was the burn of the ice, but as he focused his mind toward the energy coursing throughout his body, he felt the smallest vibration buzzing in his fingertips.

"Hey," said Brex, "You're doing it." Logan opened his eyes to see bright, little bolts of electricity covering his hands so beautifully it looked like a photoshopped picture with three Instagram filters. His heart began to beat a little faster as his excitement continued. The blue and white bolts of lightning grew larger and almost touched his elbows, but nothing was happening to the ice. Not even a tiny crack.

"I think you need a little bit of leverage," Asher called out. "Just like we did with throwing chunks of ice at it."

Logan looked at Asher like he was trying to ride a unicycle with no training wheels. "You want me to chuck a ball of electricity at the wall? Like the Flash?" Logan asked.

"Yeah! I mean it is a physical matter. It should do some damage."

"He's right," Lexi said, shivering on the ground. "The electric shock waves and the intensity of the blow should make it crack right open."

Logan couldn't remember the last time he felt this hopeless. He knew that wasn't going to happen. He could barely make the little lightning bolts cover his forearms. How was he going to make a giant ball of electricity big enough to bust down a thick wall of ice?

"Come on," said Shani, "Just think of it like you're on the football field and you're throwing a touchdown or whatever."

Logan rolled his eyes but also felt a slight bit of relief. He knew exactly how to throw a football and who he became when he did. It was something that he was comfortable with and made him feel unstoppable. He cupped his right hand, pulled his arm back, and tried to take a swing before Brex grabbed his arm to stop him.

"Hold on there," she said. "I think you need to try and like...I don't know...channel your energy first. Take a deep breath. Focus."

Logan took a second, closed his eyes, and tilted his head down. He imagined himself on the football field. A specific memory came to his mind. The day before an important game in high school, his uncle had made fun of him for getting a "C" in his chemistry class. Logan remembered him asking, "How weak are you, boy?" He couldn't even remember what he said back to his father's brother. All he remembered was how he felt the next night after he crushed his rival team. It made him feel like he could prove anyone wrong.

He kept that feeling in the pit of his stomach. He opened his eyes and focused on the wall. His pupils were so dilated, they were almost fully black. His fingers were flexed like claws and as close together as they could be without touching. Sparks crept along his skin towards his knuckles, spinning into spheres.

A bright blue and white sphere of energy extended through the creases on his fingertips. It slowly expanded larger and larger. From the others' point of view, it looked like one intense jolt of electricity shooting through his blood and out through his skin. When it grew to be the size of a giant beach ball, Logan pulled his right arm as far back as it could go, and threw his electric sphere directly at their escape route as hard as he could.

The energy left his electrocuting body and hit the wall faster than any MLB pitcher threw a fastball. The ice ruptured like a miniature volcano as the two matters collided. Both small and large pieces of ice rapidly dispersed from what was now a deep dent in the wall.

Everyone stood there in amazement, but not surprised. He was the quarterback after all.

"Do it again!" Lexi yelled, full of excitement. Without any hesitation, Logan got right back to it. His energy continued to radiate through his skin. This time, it was a breeze for Logan to create such power.

He once again readied his body to throw an even faster and bigger collection of energy. His muscles were tense but in a strong and powerful way. He now knew how to latch onto that and use it to his advantage. As he threw his next pitch, the blue and white streaks left his arm so quickly he could barely see them flying through the air. The next thing he saw was another chunk of ice missing from the wall.

Logan kept heaving and throwing like rapid fire. Ice was flying off the wall in every direction. The rest kept ducking for cover as shards of ice bounced off the floor and ceiling, but that didn't stop them from cheering him on. He was on a roll and not fatiguing any time soon.

A small patch of the red door peaked through the ice. It was much broader than they thought. Logan cracked a relieved and cocky smile as more of the door was revealed. He kept breaking the ice harder and sharper with every thrust, but in the blink of an eye, he was interrupted.

All of a sudden, Logan stopped, and the rest went quiet. He thought his eyes were deceiving him when he saw a bulky ball of fire snap towards the red door and take a lump of ice out of the wall that was twice the size of any dent Logan made. He turned around to see Brex with smoke coming from her upper limbs.

"I think I'm done taking a break now," she said. Logan could see the eagerness shimmering from her eyes. He cracked that same cocky smile, beckoned her with a slight head tilt, and they returned to demolishing the ice like robbers breaking into a bank.

Red, orange, yellow, blue, white. That's all anyone could see, but not for long. Brex and Logan added their left hands into the mix, making the digging go by at immense speed. Only a few bits of ice were left frozen over the door when they finally stopped. Lexi was the first one to try to open the door by jerking it back and forth, but the handle and lock were still frozen.

"After you," said Logan, gesturing to Brex. She gladly accepted and held her fire up against the handle until Lexi was finally able to bust it open.

Shani and Asher gave out their loudest "WOOOO" while they all rushed through the door helping each other back up the ditch.

It was still pitch black out. The air was fresh and had a slight breeze. Not a soul was in sight.

"Is everyone okay?" Logan asked once again. There was a moment of silence where everyone collected themselves and thought about how to give a genuine answer.

Asher shook the shreds of ice from his clothes and said, "I guess I just have a lot of questions."

3:

"I need to show you guys something."

The five of them scanned their surroundings to make sure that the mysterious, vicious creature was gone. Nobody checked what time it was, but they couldn't hear a single thing. Not even a cricket echoed through the park.

"We need to keep moving," said Shani, already walking. The rest didn't argue and immediately followed.

"What time is it now?" Lexi asked. She pulled out her phone. It was almost dead, and it was about to be three o'clock in the morning. They had been stuck there for almost four hours.

"Okay, I know I need to keep my voice down," said Asher, "but can we please talk about what just happened?" It all dawned on everyone at once. They weren't in the cave anymore. It wasn't just a dream. The clock-like scars were still carved into their skin. It was all real, and they needed answers for their own protection.

Shani opened her mouth as if she was going to say something, but stopped herself before she did.

"Well, we know all of the weird stuff that happened," said Logan. "The big dog thing. It sounded like a bull and had big, bright eyes. We also know the ice cave had a big ditch of weird liquid that gave us these marks and magical powers...or some of us...or...I don't know, and we know that the fire probably had something to do with it."

"What could all of these things possibly have in common besides being extremely fucking random and impossible?" Brex asked.

"They all seemed like they were trying to hurt somebody," said Lexi. "But do you think it was us specifically? Or just one of us?"

"Or maybe somebody else," said Logan. He stopped walking and stood still, pensively looking down. "I think we should call everybody we know on campus just to make sure it wasn't some sort of distraction." Everybody stopped to look at him.

"Well, that would be one hell of a distraction if it was," said Brex.

"Okay, well it wouldn't hurt, would it? Just to be safe. I haven't heard from Adam yet. I'm worried."

"Fine, but we need to keep walking," said Shani, pulling out her phone and continuing to walk.

For the next few minutes they called, texted, and Facebook messaged all of their friends to see if they were safe. Shani messaged her classmates and her friends from the Aquarium Club. Asher messaged his teammates from intramural soccer. Brex messaged Jenna, Lexi messaged her roommate, and Logan sent out a safety check mark to the group chat with all of his brothers.

They were all fine. Even Adam sounded, for the most part, normal on the phone.

"You still shaken up?" Logan asked Adam.

"Yeah. I mean they haven't reported anyone hurt or dead on the news yet. It's crazy this happened on the first day of classes, but I'll be fine. Aren't you in your room right now?"

"Uh, yeah. I mean no. I, um, went to get food."

"At three in the morning? Don't you have food here?"

"Yeah, I wanted...pizza," Logan sounded highly unconvincing, but Adam bought it anyway.

"Okay, just be careful, man. Hey, have you heard from that kid, Asher?" Adam asked. "Do you know if he's okay?"

"Uh no, but I think he's probably alright." Logan knew there would be questions if Adam found out they were together. The last thing he wanted was for his best friend to worry. His instincts told him to just keep Adam in the dark. For now, at least.

"Okay, well I'm glad you're alright. I might see you in the morning, or in class or whatever, but I honestly don't even know if we'll have school."

"True. Yeah I'll be home soon." Logan hung up the phone. "Well, everyone I know is okay. What do we do now?"

They all pondered the question for a moment.

"I think we need to go to the police," Asher proposed. The others made it perfectly clear they did not agree, and not just by the disappointing looks they couldn't help but display.

"Are you crazy?" Shani yelled. "What would we tell them? There's a giant ice cave under the Common's hillside and there's a magic potion in there that gave Brex and Logan superpowers?"

"I thought we weren't calling them superpowers?"

"AAAAAAAAARE YOU KIDDING ME?" Her volume increased so quickly, they all had to shush her. "Asher, you have been a pain in my ass all night! You can be so immature sometimes!"

"What? Well, I'm sorry. What did I do?" Asher stood there confused and defensive, but he knew that Shani was just exhausted and stressed out.

"Nothing. Whatever. We're going home."

"I think we should go back to the fire," Logan interrupted. Shani and Brex both looked at him like they were about to say something, but they didn't. They all knew that that was most likely going to give them the answers they were looking for. "But, Shani and Asher, why don't you guys just go home? The rest of us can look." They both nodded.

"Yeah, we'll let you know what we find tomorrow," said Brex. "Just get home safe."

Shani and Asher agreed and quietly left. Logan, Brex, and Lexi headed to the scene of the fire.

.....

Everything was brown, gray, or black. Bricks were crumbled everywhere. The air was still immersed in smoke, and there were even more firefighters and police officers than there were before. Luckily, no flames were in sight. Even at one hundred feet away, the three of them could spot at least ten reporters.

"Tonight, on Fox News..."

"This evening, a fire in Boston..."

"Good evening. We have here…"

The three of them tried to get any information they could get. Was it an accident? What was the cause of the fire? Was someone caught and arrested for arson? They meandered around the crime scene tape until they finally heard a reporter say, "Fortunately, as far as anybody knows, nobody has perished or been injured in this tragic event."

It felt like somebody grabbed the tension right out of their heads and wiped it away in one clean swoop. That was at least one thing they could stop worrying about. They also happened to notice none of the other buildings were affected, including Pete's Pub. Although it nearly was.

"Okay, is there anything that you guys see that looks weird in any sort of way? Is there anything that you see that could connect the giant dog thing to this place?" Logan asked.

"Well, I don't think that dog would come out in plain sight while there were a whole bunch of people here," Brex stated. "So, that might not be the best lead to follow unless the dog can transform or something. Or unless it was…ya know…an actual dog." Logan bit his lip as he couldn't resist the cringe since he had no idea if she was making a joke or not.

"I can't believe nobody was hurt," said Lexi. "None of us were hurt, or at least stayed hurt. If somebody is trying to harm us in any way they did a shitty job by giving us these…um…abilities…or whatever. And thank God no other buildings were burned down. I'm gonna go see if I can get my guitar."

"We'll go with you," said Brex. They headed toward the restaurant, still keeping an eye out for anything that seemed out of place.

The smoke in the air was so thick, they almost didn't recognize where they were going. Shards of glass and broken pieces of brick were smothering their pathway. It almost didn't seem safe to walk through, but no one was stopping them.

The restaurant was completely untouched. The ground surrounding it needed a hefty sweep, but when Lexi opened the door to the big empty room, the only things that seemed out of place were a few broken beer glasses on the floor. Although, for a Boston bar, that wasn't unusual.

"Here it is. It's all good," said Lexi, heading towards the platform which held her guitar. She grabbed it and began walking away until she suddenly heard a voice coming from the back.

"Who's there?" the voice said. The owner, Pete, came out from behind the kitchen door to see the three of them standing there. "Oh, Alexandra. I'm sorry about all of this. You kids alright?"

"Yeah, we're okay," Lexi responded.

"Here. I'll go get you your hundred bucks. I'll be right back," said Pete. They noticed he was all alone. The bartenders weren't even there with him.

Was he going to clean this whole place up by himself? Lexi thought.

"No. It's fine. I don't need it. Do you want help cleaning up?" Lexi asked.

"Yeah, we can all help, and we can pay our tabs too," said Brex, pointing to herself and Logan. Although he thought it would be a nice gesture, he knew he had about three dollar bills in his pocket. He looked at Brex with uncertainty before she held her hand out and mouthed "It's fine."

"Thank you," said Pete. "That would be great. I'll get some trash bags." He sounded touched and relieved.

Between the four of them, they cleaned up quickly. Brex and Logan swept up the broken glass, Pete fixed the broken chair, and Lexi went outside to wipe off the smoke residue from the window. Brex kept noticing Logan's freshly drawn tattoo on his palm and she repeatedly pointed to her own scar to remind him to be subtle, unaware that she was drawing attention to hers, but Pete didn't seem to notice or care.

Lexi hauled a bucket of soapy water with some Windex to scrub the windows. The caution tape was still up, and the firemen were still hosing down what little was left of the fire. More reporters came and started interviewing people who were still lingering and getting as much video as they could on their phones.

Lexi managed to clean the walls until they were crystal clear, but as she started to bring all of her supplies back into the restaurant, she heard an odd noise coming from behind a pile of bricks a few feet away from her. The sound resembled a leaf fluttering in the wind. It wasn't loud, but it was noticeable. The pile was too small to be hiding an injured human, but she was afraid it was crushing an animal.

She rushed over to uncover whatever was under there, but she didn't find anything like what she expected. Underneath the bricks was a small clump of thick liquid with a glow-like essence, almost like the liquid substance in the cave, but it was deep red. It wasn't a lot, but it continued to make cracking, bubbling noises.

Lexi carefully and slowly reached out her hand to touch it, but when her fingertips came within an inch of it, she felt a sudden, powerful wave of tension push through her body. Whether it was a negative tension or positive, she couldn't tell, but she pulled back her hand anyway as fast as she could. Her lungs pulled in so much oxygen at once, she almost passed out. After she put herself back together, she noticed her scar starting to sting again. She rubbed it and tilted her head down to look at it. For a moment, she thought her eyes were playing a trick on her. It was glowing. She looked away and turned her palm over, hoping that it would stop, and she was right. It turned back to its normal, black pigmentation when she looked at it again.

"What the hell is this stuff?" Lexi whispered to herself.

"Hey!" a voice said behind her. She whipped around, and a cop was coming straight for her. She jumped in front of the pile of magic goo, hoping the cop wouldn't see it.

"What are you doing, miss?" the cop asked.

"I was just helping the owner of this restaurant clean up. I was wiping down his windows," Lexi responded nervously, even though she was telling the truth.

"Yeah? Then why are you playing around with those bricks?"

Lexi understood that she looked a lot younger than she was, but her fists always clenched and her fingernails dug into her skin when people in authority talked to her like she was a little kid.

"I was just trying to clean them up off his sidewalk," she said. "I wasn't playing with them. I'm just trying to help."

"Okay, fine...just don't go behind the caution tape," the cop mansplained to her.

"Oh, really? Okay, good to know." She mockingly saluted him as he walked away. Lexi didn't want to be outside anymore. She pulled out her phone, took a few pictures of the red mush, and headed back inside.

"Thank you, kids, for helping me. You really didn't have to do that. Normally, I would say leave it till the morning, but we open for breakfast in less than five hours." Pete chuckled. "It was a lot worse before all o' you came in. I had a few broken lights, picture frames were shattered, and the police were shining their flashlights at me and interrogating me, like I was some sort of criminal."

Brex and Lexi exchanged looks, knowing what each other was thinking.

"What'd they ask you? What'd you tell them?" Lexi asked.

"Oh, nothing. They think somebody sprayed some sort of gasoline onto the trees, and that's how the fire spread so quickly. I told them I didn't see anything, but they probably don't believe me since they know I'm here all the time."

This man looked anything but guilty. The loneliness and stress in his eyes said everything. He knew and saw nothing. Whoever set those fires probably did it without anybody seeing them, and that was something the five of them had to look into.

"Is there anything else that we can do? We can help more in the morning," said Brex.

"No, no. You kids have done enough. Thank you again. Come play here again soon, Alexandra."

"Thank you, sir. I will."

Brex, Logan, and Lexi exited the building. Lexi let the door fully close before she started talking.

"I need to show you guys something," she said, pulling out her phone. She brought up the pictures she took of the glowing red liquid.

"That looks like blood mixed with glitter and Cool Whip," said Logan.

"I know, and when I tried to touch it, it felt like...I don't know, like a lot of pressure just jolted through my entire body. It was really weird."

"You're okay now, right? Not still feeling weird?" Brex asked.

"Yeah, no, I'm fine."

"Okay. That might be something to go off of, but we should all get home. We have class in the morning. We'll figure this all out later."

Before they headed back toward campus, they managed to get close enough to the caution tape to pick up a few burnt twigs and leaves. Lexi said she would try to run tests on them if she could get into her botany lab by herself.

Logan walked them both home and helped Lexi carry all of the stuff she was juggling, including her guitar case. They kept their eyes wide open the entire walk home. To their knowledge, no one was following them. They stayed under the street lights as much as they could.

"This is me," Lexi said as they approached her dorm.

"You're in Danielson Hall? I am so sorry," Logan chuckled.

"Unfortunately, yeah, but that's not even the worst part." Lexi kept a look on her face that was jokingly suspenseful.

Brex laughed and asked, "What's the worst part?"

"The extent of me and my roommate's interaction includes an awkward handshake and an even more awkward 'hello'...that's it."

"Different from where you're from?" Logan asked.

"Yeah. Well, people from Portland are definitely friendlier than she is. I barely know anything about her. She took one look at me and then just had no interest in knowing who she's living with."

"That's secretly a good thing," said Brex. Lexi cocked her head back. She didn't follow. "You annoy her to the point where she moves out, and then you get a room to yourself. They always say that they'll replace them with someone else, but it never happens. That's how I ended up with a single for almost all of my freshman year, and then my parents finally let me move in with my best friend, Jenna."

Logan looked at Brex, hoping she would continue with her story, but it stopped there. He was tempted to ask her where she had been, but he knew he wasn't going to get the answer, and now was the absolute worst time to ask.

"That's really clever," Lexi chuckled. "I'll think about it." She turned around and headed toward the dorm entrance, but stopped and turned around before she reached the door. "We're gonna figure this out, guys." She cracked a promising smile.

"Yeah," Brex mumbled. "We're gonna be okay." Lexi scanned into her dorm with her key card. Brex turned to Logan and said, "You don't have to walk me home, you know. My dorm is just a few more blocks."

"I can spare a few more blocks. And what if I need someone to protect me?" Logan joked.

"Yeah. I'd buy that," she said in a way that, once again, made Logan question whether she was kidding or not.

They walked in silence for a few moments before Logan asked, "Does your hand hurt at all?"

"I mean, I can feel it. It's kind of weird. What about you?"

"Same. It kind of looks like a speedometer on a car." They both smiled.

"Yeah, you're right. This is one hell of a way to come back to school." The look on her face and tone in her voice shifted. "And now we're just supposed to act like nothing happened, right? We shouldn't tell anybody this, 'cause they'll think we're crazy. We still have school to go to while we're probably trying to avoid somebody killing us or coming for us. I gotta cover whatever this shit is, and on top of that, I have to look for a job."

Logan had no idea what to say next, but he blurted out the first thing that came to his mind.

"We don't know if anyone is out to hurt us."

"Isn't that how it always works?" Logan acknowledged that she wasn't wrong with an eyebrow raise and tiny head tilt.

"It's not like we don't have whatever these things are to protect us." He wiggled his fingers to try to make her laugh again.

"Yeah, exactly." Brex didn't laugh, and she turned to face him and stopped walking. "If people know that there's this magic cave with magic powers, we could be terrorized. Do you know what people would do to have abilities like this? And what if there are people out there that already know who we are? What the hell are we gonna do if they hunt us down? You and I are the only ones that can do anything so far. What if the rest can't do anything and have no way of protecting themselves?"

Logan stood there and stared at her with a blank face. "There's gotta be an answer," he said after taking a deep breath. "This didn't just happen for no reason. When there are no more firemen near that building, we can go figure out why it burned down. We have an advantage, knowing things that the police won't. We're smart kids, and I'm sure we will find other people that wanna help us." He took a step closer to her and looked even deeper into her eyes. "Between the five of us, we can and will protect each other."

"But we can't protect everybody." Brex shook her head. "No matter how hard we try." Logan broke eye contact and looked down and saw smoke coming from her wrists and fingertips. She was getting tense and wound up.

"Hey, hey, hey, hey." Logan took her forearms and looked around to make sure nobody was watching them, but then the smoke from her pink hands almost burned the skin on his wrists.

"Ah! Shit! I'm sorry! I shouldn't have done that." He rubbed and scratched himself, trying to heal his wounds. Brex looked at him like he was a four-year-old walking into a wall.

"Uh...Are you okay? Sorry," Brex asked. He made a few little grunting noises and tried to laugh it off.

"I'm good." His voice went up almost a full octave.

"Yeah, we're in great hands," she said sarcastically. "Good pep talk, Logan. This is me." She pointed to her dorm and started working her way toward it.

"Okay! See you in class!" Logan screeched, still cradling his arms. Brex gave him a little salute, but didn't turn around or stop walking. "Nice...nice."

.....

Shani and Asher took a cab home and barely spoke. Asher spent his five-minute ride scraping the peeling skin from his scar. Shani kept shoving his hand away, so he would stop.

As the cab pulled up to their apartment, Shani pulled out her wallet, which had spots of blood on it. She swiped her dad's credit card and scampered out of the car. Asher had a hard time believing that that didn't hurt her leg. He was surprised that she could walk at all, but she didn't even limp.

"Are you sure you don't want to go to the hospital?" Asher asked for the fifth time.

"I'm fine. I can barely feel it. It was just ice, not a rusty knife, and I'll just pour some alcohol on it and re-wrap it."

"Okay. Fine." Asher opened their door, and Shani pushed them both into the apartment. "Shani, I highly doubt anybody is following us."

She ignored him and bolted the door.

"I'm not taking any chances." She didn't even look at him and headed straight for the refrigerator. Ice cream was usually her form of comfort.

"So, what do you think our powers are?" Asher quietly asked.

"Hunny, I love you, but I really don't wanna talk about this right now. I also asked you not to call them that."

Asher tilted his head down, looked at the floor, and softened his voice even more before he said "You said not to call them *super*powers."

"Oh, my God." She slurred her words together and walked away with her ice cream.

"Oh, come on! I'm sorry. I'm just as scared as you are. Can we just talk about this?"

Shani turned back around, took a deep breath, and leaned her hip up against the counter with her arms crossed.

"Yes. Of course, we can talk about it, but I have absolutely no idea what there is to talk about. I don't know what's going on! None of this is possible. There's never been any sort of scientific evidence that this is real. OH! How could I forget? WE HAVE A GODDAMN GIANT DOG THAT WANTS TO EAT US!"

"I know, I know, I know, but we have people that can help us."

"What do you mean? The police?" Shani was fairly certain that they already went over this. They were by no means going to the police.

"Maybe not the police, but...I don't know. Somebody!" Asher started pacing back and forth, trying to think of people who would have resources to help them and wouldn't put them in a mental facility. It wasn't easy.

"We live in America. If anybody sees us doing whatever we can do, they could pull out their goddamn guns and shoot us down, and I don't think that any amount of special, magical abilities is going to protect us. And our dark skin most certainly doesn't help us."

There was a tense, but silent moment between them. That hadn't even crossed Asher's mind, but she was right.

"Then we need to find somebody who can," he said. "We just need to be really careful and do our research."

"No," Shani said with no hesitation. "Everything...anything could be a trap." She took a moment to think before she said "We're just going to have to figure this out on our own."

Asher knew exactly what that meant. Shani didn't mean "we." She was talking about herself. Controlling was her other super power, but she didn't call it that.

"Really? So, what exactly is it that you plan on doing?" He was hoping that this question would stump her, but instead, her voice just got louder and her words came out faster.

"Well, my plan is better than whatever crap you're planning!" She began mocking him by saying, "'Oh, I'm just going to go tell somebody that I have magical powers now.' 'Okay, Sir. What are your powers?' 'Umm I don't know yet.' YEAH! THIS ALL MAKES COMPLETE FUCKING SENSE, ASHER!"

He made a noise that alternated between a scream and a yell. Shani shushed him, so he wouldn't wake up the neighbors, but just like Asher usually did, he ignored her. He always made it a point to never yell at anyone.

"Can we just talk about this in the morning or whatever?" Asher asked.

"Fine, but I'm not going to change my mind."

"Maybe the rest will agree with me."

Shani held up her hand, indicating that she wanted him to stop. "Again. Morning." She turned around to head to her room when Asher mocked her by jiggling his head from side to side and putting up his hand just like she did.

What did she know? Until now, she didn't believe in anything mystical. Not God, not ghosts. How was she going to know what was best?

Asher knew he wasn't going to be able to sleep, so he flopped down on the couch in their tiny living room. He turned on the T.V. and scrolled to look for any news channel. The fire wasn't hard to find. The first one that he came across had the headline plastered on the screen.

"UNEXPLAINED FIRE IN BOSTON!" The reporter, Karen Kropowski, was sharing the story.

"We come to you live from the streets of Boston," she began, reading from the teleprompter. "The students of Boston University expected to celebrate their first night back at college, but instead, the Romanov office building burst into flames. And unfortunately, when I say burst, I mean burst. Some witnesses are giving statements saying they saw part of the building explode, which is unusual, considering the firemen and police have found no evidence of any explosive device. The other pressing question we have tonight is: how did this fire spread so rapidly? According to Andy Kremmer, the Chief of Boston P.D., 'If anybody spread something flammable all across the border of the park, somebody would have seen it. We'll catch 'em.' Well, Officer, I hope you're right. We now go to—"

Asher practically punched the "off" button on the T.V. remote, spread out his arms and legs on the couch, and stared at the ceiling. Maybe he could tell his dad. He wouldn't try to lock Asher up, would he? That is, he might have to wait until he was sober first, which could probably be a while, but still, it was probably worth a shot. He wasn't particularly close with his mom, so she probably wouldn't do anything. He could count the number of times he had talked to her on one hand since he came out to her. She didn't care, but it's not like she asked to be back in his life after that.

He pulled out his phone to see that the battery was on two percent, and the time was now almost five o'clock in the morning. Was there any point in sleeping? His mind was still racing at three hundred miles an hour.

Then, his phone buzzed. He received two notifications from Facebook. One: a friend request from Lexi, and then two: a message request from her. He unlocked his phone to confirm the friend request, then opened up Messenger to see what she had sent him.

At first, he had no idea what he was looking at. If he squinted hard enough and held it at a certain angle, it almost looked like bright red Greek yogurt. Then he read her caption; "I found this behind some fallen bricks at the fire. Any ideas? I put it through a Google picture search, but of course, nothing came up. Not sure where else I could look. Lemme know what you guys think!"

Asher spent a few minutes zooming in and out of the picture. Whatever it was, it looked like it belonged in a lava lamp.

Lexi sent this in a group chat, but he messaged her back privately.

"Whatever it is, we'll figure it out! Good work, Lex. Thanx for the pic!"

He took off his glasses and rubbed his eyes. He didn't like fighting with his best friend, but he was going to do this with or without Shani's help.

·····

A few hours later, over in Shani's room, she lay on her bed flat on her back with headphones on, but no music playing. She couldn't concentrate hard enough to decide which song to play. Every time she reached for her phone, she got distracted and rekindled her scratching session with the scar on her palm, which, by the spreading color of red on her palm, her skin clearly didn't appreciate.

"A YouTube video," she whispered to herself. "That's what I need."

Once again, she sat up and reached for her phone. Only this time, something changed. She had an idea.

"Damn it, brain," she quietly yelled to herself. Her laptop was nowhere to be seen, but now her sleep would permanently leave her until she found what she was looking for. "Where are you, where are you?" Under a pile of books on her desk was her sea-shell-covered laptop that she slammed open the second she found her chair in the dark. She could have turned on a light, but the amount of sleep she had already lost persuaded her to lose no more time.

In the Google search bar read "unexplained fires that spread abnormally rapid" after she typed it in. She wasn't sure what else to include so she could only hope Google understood what she was trying to say.

"No...no...no." There were countless articles that read anything from "Gas Fire Unexplained!" to "Rapid Fire Arsonist Caught!" Google wasn't doing its job. Shani was about to try a different search until her eye caught something unusual.

"Well, well, well."

The link must have been from a website that archived newspapers from the previous century since the article was from May 25th, 1937.

NO HOPE AS FIRE SPREADS FASTER AND FASTER BY THE MINUTE, BUT WHY?
May 25th, 1937
By Analise Jeanette

Last night, three hundred acres of land in Pembina, North Dakota were set to flames, but this was unfortunately no ordinary fire. More than five anonymous sources gave statements saying that they saw the fire spreading rapidly from one part of the land to the next. The grass, the trees, bushes, and fences are still being put out as this newspaper is being published. Almost every fire truck and carriage in the state of North Dakota is present and working to save what they can.

One source claimed that they saw the fire spread ten blocks within five seconds, but the police have found no traces of gasoline or any chemical that would cause flames to spread at this speed. Another source claimed that a singular line of fire extended across their meadow "faster than a police horse chasing after a robber." They also claim to be certain that their grass was alive, fed, and well. There was no reason for this outbreak.

Only one casualty has been reported as we hope and pray there are no others. Elise Patel was reported dead in her local antique shop where the fire unfortunately spread.

The police believe that this was an act of vandalism, but some of the attendees of the local churches believe this was a

punishment from God or a sign that an unknown tragedy is coming our way. There will be more stories to come regarding this catastrophic event. We advise the people of our beloved town to stay safe and pray for whatever is to come.

Shani let herself push back into her chair in thought. This was as close as she was going to get. Was it helpful yet? She wasn't sure, but if she were to find any more evidence, at least she could try to make a connection.

Her fatigue slowly returned, but she still wasn't sure if she was going to sleep. What she craved was telling the rest about her discovery, but that would have to wait. Instead, her fingers tapped against her thighs, trying to find a way to pass the time.

"Bandage," she whispered to herself before slowly making her way to the bathroom.

Trying to avoid waking Asher up, she tip-toed down the hall and slowly opened the creaky bathroom door. No matter how badly she wanted to pass the time, she still wasn't in the mood for a confrontation with Asher.

After checking her smooth skin and shiny hair in the mirror as she always did, she put her leg up on the toilet seat to unwrap the sticky bandage. But instead of seeing a bloody mess, the only thing that was under that bandage was her smooth, brown, unscarred skin.

4:

"Stop that!"

The weekend finally came. Lexi still didn't feel or notice anything different about herself, which in general was a rarity for her. But if one more person asked her where she was during the night of the fire, she was going to sacrifice her guitar and hit them over the head with it. It was only a reminder that she was stuck with an ugly scar, but no abilities.

As Lexi sat in her room, humming along to an unnamed tune that she was strumming, her phone rang before her dad's cheeky face popped up on the screen.

"Hi, Dad!" she answered. He was holding his phone like he usually did; low and at an angle where the camera only caught the top half of his face. The typical way of the older generation.

"Hi, honey!"

"Dad, I can barely see you."

"Oh, sorry. How's this?" He brought the camera so close to his face, she could almost see every pore on his nose.

"God, Dad. No! Further away. Further away. Thank you. I'm surprised you remembered how to do that after I taught you."

"It took me a few times, but I wasn't going to give up on seeing my little girl." He kept walking around the living room, holding his phone. Lexi noticed a few things were different in the background.

"Dad, why is the China cabinet on the other side of the room? And what's that painting next to the couch? Did you redecorate?" Rearranging furniture or other decorations in the house was something he only did when he needed a distraction. A few years before when he got laid off from his job, Lexi caught her dad rearranging the entire basement. Not a single box or bin stayed in its original place, and there was now a library down there that was filled with books about fishing that he never read.

"I know what you're thinking, but I promise you, I'm fine." He seemed like he was telling the truth, but that didn't stop Lexi from proceeding with her investigation.

"Oh, really?" she doubtfully asked.

"Yes. Actually, I was calling to tell you something." There was a serious tone in his voice that didn't reflect his normal goofy self.

"Yeah? What's up?" Lexi asked.

"Well, you know that woman who also works at the warehouse that I told you about? She's new. Tall and brunette."

"Yeah. Isn't she like thirty?" She knew where this was going, and she wasn't sure how she felt about it.

"She's thirty-eight, thank you very much, and, well, we got to talking, and we had dinner the other night, and she's coming over later this evening. I thought that I would just fix a few things to make the place look a little nicer."

Lexi felt relieved that her dad wasn't going mad again. The one thing that worried her about going to school three hours away was that her dad was going to be lonely. She knew she needed to be supportive if this is what made him happy.

"I'm happy for you, Dad. I'm glad to hear that."

"Thanks, Kiddo. So, how's school going for you?" So far school had been pretty uneventful for her besides almost getting burned alive and possibly getting magical voodoo powers, but she managed to scoop up a few other things to talk about.

"Well, my roommate, Anika, is roughly twice my height and has almost as much muscle on her as Serena Williams. I can't tell if she likes me yet though, but it's okay. I've made other friends."

"Yeah? That's awesome. What are their names?"

"Shani, Logan, Asher, and Brex. They're all seniors, but I've been getting really close to Shani."

"Seniors? Wow! Don't let them push you into doing anything stupid."

"I know, Dad. Don't worry. They're great. They all came to my gig the other night. Logan even helped me set up my equipment since you never actually taught me," Lexi teased.

"Hey! You can't blame me for wanting to be needed. Were they all okay after that fire?"

Lexi paused to think of a response that wasn't a complete fib. "Oh yeah, they were totally cool. Listen, Dad, I love you, but I have a lot to do before next week. I gotta go."

"Okay, Honey. Call me soon?" He gave her a puppy dog face with a teddy bear tone in his voice.

"Of course. Bye!" She hung up and dropped her phone on the bed. She hated lying to her dad. At this point, Lexi was sure she was the only person in his life whom he could trust.

She glanced at her hand to admire her scar. It was still red, but it wasn't peeling anymore. She wondered if it was ever going to completely heal and turn white like most scars. So far, she was using her bike gloves to cover it up, which was weird because she didn't bring her bike to school.

Lexi picked her guitar back up to continue practicing until Anika busted through the door without looking up from her phone.

"Hey," Lexi asked before she could stop herself. "How was your week?"

"Eh, Fine," Anika responded, still not looking up from her phone.

The two of them hadn't quite clicked yet. Lexi barely knew anything about her except that she kept to herself, she was freakishly tall and fit, with gorgeous long Indian hair, and that her parents were born in India. She didn't even know what Anika's major was.

Lexi's side of the room was filled with tiny plants, fluffy faux pillows, and one large dream catcher. Anika's side of the room consisted of posters of older male actors that she didn't know the names of and gym bags. Lexi wasn't certain how they got paired together, but maybe the residence directors were pursuing the "opposites attract" theory.

Anika pulled out her largest gym bag from under her bed. She zipped it open, and Lexi caught a glimpse of the school's mascot and logo.

"Do you play a sport here?" Lexi asked.

"Yeah. I got a full ride here for cheerleading. I'm a physical education major, but I think I got the full ride mainly 'cause I skipped a grade. Did I not tell you that?" Anika still barely made eye contact with her, but had a tone in her voice that made it sound like Lexi was an idiot for not knowing this information.

"Whoa. No, you didn't, but that's awesome!"

Anika responded with a lethargic "Yeah," and then came dead silence. Lexi had already made friends at school, but she was hoping not to have a terrible relationship with the person she lived with. Although, there was *one* thing that they did have in common.

"Hey, I really like your eyeshadow palette. I'm a fan of Morphe myself," said Lexi. To her surprise, Anika looked at her with a somewhat engaged expression on her face.

"Thanks."

"I have their small palette that they came out with last year. It's about to expire, so I'm trying to use it as much as I can." Lexi went to reach for her palette on her desk to show her.

"Hey, what's that on your hand?" Anika asked. Lexi snapped her head to look at her left palm. She had forgotten to put her gloves back on.

"Nothing. It's just some...henna." Anika gave her the dirtiest, most suspicious look yet. Lexi realized that if she had just said that in a normal tone and not jerked her arm behind her back, then her lie would have been somewhat believable.

"Man, you are weird, Flannagan."

Lexi was used to hearing people say things like this, but she knew her roommate didn't mean it in a funny, teasing sort of way. The vibe between them was getting more uncomfortable with every word exchanged. What was Anika's problem, and why was she so miserable all the time?

Lexi was trying to not be awkward, so her eyes naturally drifted toward her phone. The classic millennial reflex. Her screen said that it was almost ten in the morning and the dining hall was about to run out of all the good breakfast food.

"Oh, shit. Still haven't eaten. I'll be back later." She grabbed her bag, jumped into her Birkenstocks, and ran out the door.

Anika felt relieved to have some peace and quiet with no one to bother her. She wasn't always the best with sharing, or patience of any sort.

After packing up her duffel bag for practice, she heard something ping from Lexi's side of the room. It was her laptop that was left open on her desk. She looked over and realized that Lexi's iPhone was connected to her MacBook, and the best part of all; it didn't look like she had a password. How careless could she be? Anika thought it would be the perfect time to invade the personal space of the person whom she was sharing space with.

Why not? Anika thought. It would be funny to find something weird or embarrassing that she could tease Lexi with.

She waited a few moments, just in case Lexi came running back for something, before she rubbed her fingertips on the mousepad. The background picture was of Lexi and her dad, standing in front of the school's entrance on move-in day. The gushy daddy-daughter stuff made Anika laugh, almost in disgust.

"Man, she really needs someone to hold her hand, doesn't she?" she said underneath her breath.

She clicked on the notification in the upper right-hand corner of the screen. It was a message from Shani that read:

> Hey! So last night I found an article that might possibly explain something, but we're not sure. We found some really weird ones and absolutely nothing that explains what that cave was all about or that dog thing, but I sent you the article. You should def read it. Let me know what you think! <3

Immediately after she was done reading the text, another notification bell rang. It was the article. Anika read the title and was dumbstruck. She knew what this Shani person was talking about when she referred to the fire, but what was this cave that they were talking about? And what "dog thing"? She figured "Logan" was Logan Kwan, the cute quarterback that all the cheerleaders talked about, and that intrigued her even more. What were they up to? She took a picture of the screen with her phone and closed the messenger application, hoping that Lexi wouldn't notice that she was there.

·····

Later that morning, Shani went into her first day of her new internship at the New England Aquarium. The position included feeding the fish, cleaning a few of the tanks, taking notes on how to train the seals to do tricks or something of the sort, and cutting up pieces of meat to feed to the baby sharks.

These were the tasks that the biologists called "paying their dues." It was the basic internship, but that didn't make Shani any less nervous. Her favorite part about marine biology was the aquatic aesthetics. Beautifully colored coral, bright patterns on fish scales, opening up a clam shell to find a perfectly polished pearl. Those were all her favorite parts about her major, but the thought of shark feeding sometimes made her go into panic mode. She always knew it was something she was going to have to eventually do and get used to, but she wasn't sure how prepared she was for it. How could that day already be here?

The aquarium was busy when Shani walked into the building. Girl scout troops were giggling as they watched the African Penguins play with one another. Moms and dads were helping their small children reach over the tanks to pet the sharks and rays in the touch tank before they cried and screamed.

In her hand, she held her purse, a three-inch thick notepad, a daily calendar, and four newly-sharpened pencils. Being overly prepared was something she always took a lot of pride in. She arrived at the office in her best stretchy, black dress pants, casual blazer, and all with twenty minutes to spare. That was the normal arrival time for her, regardless of how long she'd been at a job for. It was something people always admired about her. She wasn't about to give that up.

Her scar was covered up by a thick, square Band-Aid. It was the most efficient solution that she had come up with so far. Nobody was going to ask questions, but she came up with a back story anyway. "It's just a big paper cut." Simple, really.

"Hello!" Shani said, gently knocking on the door. A short, plump woman dressed in a fluffy, purple blouse sat at her desk and turned around to see Shani nervously standing at the door.

"Oh! Hello...um..." the lady said, holding her finger to her chin.

"Shani."

"Yes! Right! I'm Dr. Carter. Follow me!" The doctor led her down the hall where they had the offices and meeting rooms. They passed the Freshwater Gallery, the Yawkey Coral Reef Center, and then finally, the best part about the aquarium: The Giant Ocean Tank. It was filled with almost a thousand animals such as moray eels, barracudas, and loggerhead sea turtles.

It was a sight like this one that made Shani want to be involved in anything with the sea. There was a special on the Discovery Channel when she was a kid called *Undiscovered Creatures of the Ocean*. After she saw that, she begged her dads to bring her into the ocean to see the fish underwater. They weren't sure if that meant scuba diving or becoming a mermaid, but they decided to bring her to Aruba instead where she could see plenty of beautifully-colored fish in popular semi-submarine rides. When she was a little older, they went another time, so Shani could swim with the little fish in their "Baby Sea." They bought her the best snorkel, flippers, and frozen fish food they could find. It was, by far, one of Shani's best memories as a kid.

The moment she saw a fish that looked like Dory from the movie *Finding Nemo,* she knew she wanted to work with sea creatures. She was only seven. The ocean was only a five-minute drive from their house, so it was convenient for her dads to hop in the car and bring her there when she insisted on "checking up on the fish."

The Giant Ocean Tank was four stories high, but the best view was from the first floor. It was where most of the artificial coral and sea turtles liked to hang out. Shani felt right at home when the doctor led her straight there.

"When was the last time you were here, Shani? Do you basically know your way around?" Dr. Carter asked.

"Not since my interview last semester, but I used to come here as a kid. I know my way around pretty well." She couldn't stop staring at the view above her head. They had repainted it since the last time she was there, or maybe it had been there for a while. She wasn't sure. Last semester, when she came in for her interview, she was too nervous to look around and enjoy being in the Aquarium. Now, she felt confident. Dr. Carter seemed nice so far. Shani felt hopeful about this experience. Everything was going to be a smooth ride. She could feel it.

"Where did you grow up, dear?" Dr. Carter was rummaging through her folders for Shani's resume, looking a little unorganized.

"I grew up in the Cape, but my dads have been taking me to tropical islands when I told them that I was interested in marine biology. I came here a few times, of course, but they really like to travel."

"Two dads? Okay, lovely!"

Shani was used to that sort of reaction. It didn't bother her. She was just glad she was making a good impression on Dr. Carter. She needed all of the recommendations she could get for graduate school.

They continued to stroll around the first floor. Shani made sure she was writing everything down that Dr. Carter said. Whether it had to do with schedules, future plans for the aquarium, or people she needed to know, it was in her notebook.

"So, you'll start off your first twenty hours shadowing me and a few other employees, but mainly the other employees because you'll be doing a lot of the dirty work. How does that sound?" Dr. Carter made a noise that sounded both like laughter and a shout. Shani wasn't sure if she was to laugh, act nervously excited, or both. Without overthinking it, she went with both.

"Ah! Here it is!" The doctor pulled out a single piece of paper with a long list of what were probably Shani's responsibilities. The print was so small, she could barely catch a glimpse of what was on it. "This is a checklist for you, but only for your first ten hours. Then we will knock a few things off and add a few things on, but we will get to that—"

"Stop that," came a muffled voice out of nowhere. Dr. Carter didn't notice it, but it sounded like it was coming from right over the doctor's shoulder.

"Stop that!" it said again. Shani attempted to look around while Dr. Carter continued to speak. It wasn't like Shani at all to be ignoring her superior, but she was heavily drawn to this voice for some strange reason. Where was it coming from?

"Really? I'm just trying to get some sleep in *my* cave," she heard the same voice shouting. "This is *my* spot. Now would you please leave me alone?"

That was an odd thing to say in an aquarium, Shani thought. *It was probably some dad doing a silly bit for his toddler.* Shani was able to redraw her attention back to her new boss for a brief moment until—

"Oh, come on!" Shani leaned over Dr. Carter's right shoulder to see a little girl, giggling and tapping on the Giant Ocean Tank's glass. A three-foot-long eel was staring straight at her as if it were about to pounce on her if he could. The voice. It was coming from the eel.

Shani's jaw dropped without thinking, and before she could stop herself, she let out a slow and long "WHAT THE—?" The relief she felt about the fact that she didn't finish that sentence was indescribable. Dr. Carter was staring at her with pure confusion. Shani, again, felt an incomparable relief that she somehow remembered what the doctor's last words were.

"What the...yeah...I mean, I can come into the facilities *whenever* I want without *paying*? That's insane, I tell you. INSANE!" That last word made Dr. Carter jump with a hint of fright, but Shani kept the nervous grin plastered on her face. She felt one drop of sweat roll down to her eyelid. The doctor's facial expression did not change, but that gave Shani a leeway for her response.

"Oh, I'm so sorry. I—I'm withdrawing from coffee, and I'm just feeling a little loopy! Ha—ha." Luckily, she managed to break a little bit of the tension.

"My dear!" she chuckled. "I did the same thing years ago. Let me tell you, it wasn't pretty. Don't worry. You'll be fine."

"Oh, thank goodness. I—I really have been worried." Shani mimed wiping sweat from her forehead before she realized she actually needed to do so.

"Come! Follow me, we'll continue with your training." Dr. Carter beckoned Shani and led her toward the food lab on the first floor.

Shani tried her best to continue listening to Dr. Carter, but how on Earth was she able to interpret eel language into English? That. That was her special ability. If one could even call that a special ability. What use was that? Maybe she should check the help wanted ads. Brex could make her skin catch on fire, and Logan could carry electricity through his entire body. But Shani? She could talk to fish. On the other hand, it gave her a theory. It sounded crazy, and a little cheesy, but was it really a coincidence that she'd been studying fish for as long as she could remember, and now she could talk to them? It wasn't much to go on, but it was a start...maybe.

Fortunately for her, Shani was good at letting pestering thoughts escape from her mind when she needed to work. It was her first day, and she didn't want to act any more eccentric than she already had. Dr. Carter showed her how to operate all of the filters, how to make the fish food, and how to do the rest of her responsibilities. So far, everything went great. It was a good shift, but a slow one, especially in the last hour. She kept looking at the clock to see how much longer she had left, so she could go back to the Giant Ocean Tank and attempt to pry some answers out of that eel.

The clock struck three, and Shani was able to leave. She signed her internship hours form, washed her hands, collected her belongings, and headed to the tank.

She knew she needed an excuse. An excuse as to why she was still there, after work, waiting by the same exhibit. She figured she would say something like, "I have nowhere to be, and I just need to clear my head." or "I couldn't fall asleep while trying to take a nap, so I decided to count fish." Neither of those sounded sane to her. First of all, biology majors always had somewhere to be. Second of all, what kind of twenty-one-year-old takes naps and then comes back to work for any reason? She figured she would just worry about that if she got caught. She had been able to lie on the spot to Dr. Carter before. She felt confident in her ability to do it again.

Shani started circling the tank, looking for the eel. The problem was, all of the eels looked exactly the same, and there were a *ton* of them. But did she need to speak to the same eel she had heard before? Maybe if she could get some aquatic species' attention, she could possibly get some answers.

"Um...hello?" She whispered underneath her breath. There were still a significant number of people around her, and someone was bound to catch her trying to talk to a fish tank.

"My phone," she whispered again. She could pretend to talk on her phone and act like the person on the other line couldn't hear her. "Hellooo?" No response. "Hellooo...again!" Plenty of fish were swimming right by her, but none of them were acknowledging the fact that she was trying to get *their* attention. Why would they? When was the last time a grown human thought they could talk to fish? This wasn't New York City.

Shani put her phone away and took a second to think. The little girl who was tapping on the glass before got the eel's attention by, well, tapping on the glass. The answer was obvious. All she had to do was find that little cave that the eel was hiding in. Easy.

She circled the tank one more time before she found it. It was tiny, but dark, a nice place to hide and rest for an eel. There were still people around her. Turning around with her back to the glass was the best option to hide her tapping. She did work there, but did that make her tapping more or less acceptable?

Nobody seemed to be watching. Her knuckles gently tapped against the tank behind her back while she tried to keep an inconspicuous look on her face. No response. Gentle wasn't going to do it. She tried again, only this time, she knocked as hard as she did on Asher's door whenever he refused to wake up for their 8 a.m. classes together.

"ARE YOU KIDDING ME??" The voice made her jump. She wasn't expecting him to be so loud. "I thought you left al—" He came out of his cave to see Shani standing there instead of a four-foot-tall blonde girl. "Oh, great. Another one. What's a grown woman tapping on my glass for? Seriously? How immature *are* you?" He was, of course, speaking as if she had no clue what he was saying.

Shani only looked at him in a daze unsure of what to say. Her head naturally tilted to the side as her jaw and eyes opened a little wider. There was no connection from her brain to her mouth at the moment.

"What the hell is up with you?" the eel asked.

"What?"

"AHHHH!" And the eel darted back to his hideaway.

"Wait—oh—shit, wait! I'm sorry. I promise you, I'm not going crazy, and you're not going crazy. But at the same time, I can't really explain it."

The eel's scales complimented his movement so elegantly, it was mesmerizing. He slithered back out from behind his cave and asked, "What are you? How are you able to do that?"

"I was hoping you could tell me."

"Oh, hell no! I stopped being a little snitch a long time ago!" He began to swim away from her again, but she followed right behind him along the side of the tank.

"So, you do know something."

"I didn't say that."

"But you implied it."

"No, I didn't."

"Oh, come on! You're obviously hiding something. What do you know?" The eel looked at her, not knowing what to say next. It wasn't *that* big of a tank. He couldn't hide from her forever.

"Who are you, anyways?" the eel asked.

"You didn't answer my question."

"You didn't answer mine."

"Fine. My name is Shani. I work here now. My friends and I—" She paused to look around to see if anybody were listening or watching. She remembered the promise they had made to one another to not tell anyone about what happened, but she figured sugarcoating it might be okay. "Well, something happened, and now we all have these...abilities."

He gave her a suspicious and distrustful look and asked, "What happened?"

"Does it matter? Look, has anything like this happened before? Have you ever been able to talk to humans?"

"Not that I can recall. Unless you're not actually human."

"What's that supposed to mean? Of course, I'm human."

"Never mind." There was something about the way that he turned away from her. It made Shani want to dig deep into the possibilities. What if that blast somehow made them all not human anymore? Could that be possible?

"What's your name?" Shani asked.

"Ilisa," he responded.

"Is there anybody else who might know why I can speak to fish, Ilisa? Since you don't want to be a 'little snitch'."

"Well, I don't know about anybody here, but there was someone I knew a long time ago, but I haven't seen her since maybe the seventies."

"The what now? Wait. How old are you?"

Before Ilisa could answer, he looked down at Shani's waist level. His eyes quickly widened, and he swam away as fast as he could.

"Wait! What—" Shani looked down at her left hand. Her Band-Aid had fallen off. The scar had scared him away. There was no use trying to get his attention again. He was gone, but now she knew there was somebody out there who could help them, and this scar meant something powerful. There had to be others like them with the same scar. The only problem was, they didn't know who. But that was enough to run home to Asher to tell him what she learned.

5:

"Okay. One, two-"

That Saturday night was the first football game of the season. It was the Boston University Terriers against their number one rival: The Holy Cross Crusaders. Boston had been leading in their rivalry for the past ten years, and Logan was determined to keep his team on top.

The football team had the most diverse demographic out of the whole school. Students, teachers, parents, and even grandparents would show up in full gear. Growing up in the Boston area, Logan would come to the Boston University games frequently. His dad would take him and buy him a chili hot dog and a doughnut for dessert if every bit of the hot dog was eaten.

The night was cool with a light breeze. Almost every student's favorite football weather. Hoodie season was always the best time of year in New England. Everybody had their favorite Terriers merchandise. The bleachers were full, and from a bird's eye view, the crowd looked like a square clump of dark red.

Logan gathered up his team in the locker room to give them the pregame speech.

"Alright!" He belted with a growl in his voice. "First game of the season, and we are not going to disappoint this school!"

"YEAH!" They all yelled in their deepest octave.

"This team. Our team has been kicking our rivals' asses for a decade now! WHOSE ASSES ARE WE GONNA KICK ONCE AGAIN TONIGHT?"

"CRUSADERS!"

"WHO'S GONNA WIN THAT CHAMPIONSHIP?"

"WE ARE!"

"LET'S GOOOOOO!" They all joined together, hollering and cheering.

The cheerleaders' pompoms were shaking with glitter as the football players darted through their white paper sign. Their supporters roared. Asher sat in the middle of the bleachers, keeping a space open next to him just in case Shani was able to show up. She texted him a few minutes before, saying she was going to be late, but she didn't say why.

He sat there with his large popcorn and Coke and searched for Logan's and Adam's numbers, #14 and #55. He spotted both of them in their huddle on the field.

Adam was a talented linebacker. The crowd always roared whenever either of them had the ball, even if it was only for a second. Asher was more of a baseball and soccer guy, but he, for the most part, knew what their jobs were on the team.

Asher's phone buzzed as the players were getting into their positions. It was Shani.

"I don't know if I'm gonna make it. I'll explain later," she wrote. He knew what it was about. She either had found out something about the cave, discovered what her powers were, or deciphered the hidden meaning behind their scars. He just didn't know which one yet.

Brex and Jenna walked up the bleachers, looking for seats.

"You've been more quiet than usual. You doing okay?" Jenna asked Brex.

"Yeah. It's just weird being back. I guess it hasn't settled in."

"Okay. I just wanted to make sure you weren't traumatized after that fire."

"Yeah...I mean it was crazy," Brex was calm, hoping it would convince her that it was no big deal, "but I promise, I'm fine. I guess it's just kind of weird not being able to talk to other people about it."

"Yeah, that sounds normal."

Asher spotted Brex and Jenna looking around for seats.

"HEY, BREX! JENNA!" He pointed to his extra seats and held up his large popcorn with a cheesy, animated grin on his face, hoping it would beckon them to him. Both Brex and Jenna chuckled.

"Asher's got seats over there. Let's go," said Brex. She led the way as they pushed through to the middle of the bleachers where Asher was sitting.

"Hey, Shani didn't come with you?" Brex asked as she sat down next to him with her cheese fries.

"You know, contrary to popular belief, I do have other friends."

"Oh, really?"

"A few!"

"Okay, okay, but aren't you two usually attached at the hip?"

"Yes, but she's still kind of being snippy with me. And I don't know if you've caught onto this yet, but that's pretty much just her being her usual bossy self. Plus, she just texted me, saying she probably isn't gonna make it, and that she will 'explain later.' We shall see how well that goes."

Brex looked back at Jenna, who was sitting next to her, not paying attention at all. Her eyes were, instead, glued to the game. Brex scooched a little closer to Asher to make sure no one could hear them and asked, "You think she figured something out?"

"Probably. It's Shani. She always wants to be the one to unmask everything. I mean we all know she probably will, but we'll text you if she did."

"See, that's what I mean."

"What?"

"*We'll* text you. It only takes one person to text. You guys are literally the same person." Asher laughed and playfully nudged her. She wasn't completely wrong.

The game carried on. Surprisingly enough, for most of the game, the two teams were neck and neck. Luckily for Boston, they took back the lead shortly after the marching band went on for the halftime show.

Asher, Brex, and Jenna devoured all of the food they had. Jenna bought all of them doughnuts after they were finished with their snacks, which they called "dinner."

Asher chose to wear gloves to hide his scar. He ended up getting more butter on them than he put in his mouth, but he didn't care. They were keeping him warm too. Brex wore the usual athletic jacket with thumbholes in it to cover hers up. Not that anybody was going to notice besides Jenna, but each time she lifted a plate of food to her mouth, she tried her best to pull her sleeve down as far as it would go.

"Damn. Logan's ass looks fine in those pants," Jenna said, taking a seductive bite into her doughnut.

"His ass literally looks exactly the same as half the team," said Brex.

"Yeah, but it's Logan Kwan. Come on."

Brex took a second to think and said, "Okay, I guess you have a point."

"Look at that!" Jenna's voice suddenly shot up three octaves higher than usual. "Brex thinks a boy is cute again! She's getting back in the game!"

"And that's as far as I am going for a while," she responded, clearly wanting the subject to change.

"I don't know, Brex," Asher cut in. "I think Logan likes you, and if I were you, I'd get on that real quick." Brex laughed and threw a tiny piece of doughnut in his face. She didn't deny it. Ever since they had started going to college together, she could sense him staring at her. Nothing that made her feel uncomfortable, but she didn't feel interested. "Hey, what about that guy you were with at the bar last week? The tall handsome one that made Logan's face go pale."

"You might not believe me when I tell you this, but he was a blind date that this one set me up with." She shoved her thumb towards Jenna. "It was weird. I have zero interest."

"Okay. I believe you."

She sounded like she was telling the truth, and he could already tell that she was the type of person who wouldn't put up with something that even remotely pissed her off.

"What about the guy that *you* were at the bar with last week?" Brex teased.

Asher knew exactly what she was talking about. He took a moment to answer, but finally said, "Adam and I are just friends too." He nodded his head with a slight smirk on his face. Brex wasn't sure if she bought that, but she knew it wasn't any of her business.

"Okay. I believe you too," she said.

All of a sudden, the BU crowd roared. Logan had scored another touchdown. They were in the fourth quarter, and only two minutes were left on the clock. The Terrier's streak was bound to continue.

Asher stood up to cheer so fast, he knocked over what was left of his popcorn. Kernels flew everywhere, hitting people in the back of the head, but they were all too distracted from Logan's big score. He sat back down, and in doing so, his phone slipped out of his back pocket and fell through the bleachers.

"Dammit!" Asher cursed.

"What? What happened?" Brex asked.

"My phone. It fell through the bleachers. I gotta go get it." Asher looked around. There was no getting out. They were stuck in the middle of the crowd. He looked down to see how far of a drop it would be.

"Alright, guess I'm going this way." He crouched down, preparing himself to be as graceful as he could. The drop wasn't too bad. The bottom was grass, and he was skinny, so sliding through the bleachers wouldn't be much of a challenge.

"Oh God, please don't hurt yourself," Brex begged.

"I'll be fine. I've jumped from worse heights before."

"Shockingly, that doesn't make me feel any better."

Asher tried his best to plan out how he was going to fluidly drop down from the bleachers, but six months of karate at seven years old wasn't going to help him.

The moment his legs slid off the foot plank, his hands remained grasped onto it, and his legs swung from side to side so intensely, one of his hands almost came loose.

"You good there?" Brex asked sarcastically as she watched him struggle.

"Yeah, yeah, I just gotta stop swinging first." He waited a moment before he started to count down. Brex couldn't watch, so she turned away and covered her eyes. It was only about a six-foot drop from his feet to the ground, but he remembered in that moment that he was scared of heights.

"Okay. One, two—" His sweaty hands slipped off the foot plank before he was ready, and he shot downwards, but only for about a half a second. Something stopped him. He didn't hit the ground, but there was some sort of noise that sounded like fabric ripping instead. Then, he heard something flapping, like a bird. He turned his head to see the back of his jersey torn and a white figure moving from side to side that was attached to his back. It was dark under the bleachers and hard to make out what it was, but then he looked on his other side to see the same thing. It all happened so fast, it took him a moment to realize that he was controlling them. They were wings, and he was flying.

"Asher?" Brex called out before she looked down through the bleachers.

"Uhhh," Asher responded. He wasn't sure what he was supposed to say.

Brex crouched down to see Asher floating midair with two giant wings gracefully flapping in the wind.

"Holy shit," she said.

"What?" Jenna asked from above. Brex snapped back up to stop her from looking down.

"Nothing! Asher just...um...landed on his feet, and I'm just really impressed."

"Nice! Prouda you!" Jenna chuckled as she yelled down without looking.

Brex nervously laughed with her and then crept her head back to Asher to quietly yell, "Asher, cut it out before someone sees you!"

"Umm, I'm not sure how to do that," said Asher, nervously looking around to see if he could find a solution to the situation.

"Just relax all your muscles. You'll just fall to the ground."

"Why would I—"

"Oh, just do it!" said Brex, frustrated.

Asher, not finding any other solution, released all of the tension in his muscles, and a few seconds later, dropped to the ground. He had been only a few feet from the grass, but he still managed to not land on his feet. Instead, he fell straight onto his back. The fall would have been a lot softer if his tailbone hadn't smashed onto his phone.

"You good?" Brex asked.

"Yup! I'm fine." Asher looked like he was an intoxicated old man who had just fallen and broken his back, but too drunk to realize what had just happened. He looked beside him to realize his wings were gone. He reached back to touch his shoulder, but there was nothing there, only two giant tears in the back of his shirt. He reached underneath him to pull out his phone.

"Hey! At least there are no cracks on my screen!"

·····

Shani sprinted home that night. She didn't care what Asher had to say about her powers. She had a lead. Another lead, that for all she knew could be worthless, but her ego told her that it didn't matter.

Her stomach growled so loud, the people walking on the other side of the street probably heard it. She had forgotten to eat. That happened frequently whenever she was stressed.

She expected to see Asher lying on the couch, playing video games like he usually was, but when she busted through the door looking for him, he wasn't there. The game must have ended by now. Where was he?

She texted him a few times, but no response. It wasn't anything to worry about just yet, but she was getting anxious. She made two peanut butter and jelly sandwiches to make her stomach stop growling and checked her watch every thirty seconds. Shani didn't deal with waiting well. There was a lot of homework that she had to do, but she knew she wasn't going to be able to concentrate, so she didn't even bother to try.

The clock finally struck nine o'clock, and Asher casually walked through the door.

"Where were you?!" Shani yelled in his face. Asher jumped so far back, he almost knocked himself over.

"Jesus, Shani! What's the matter with you?" Asher asked, trying to bring his heart rate back down. They were still in their bickering stage, and this was not helping Shani's cause.

"I've been home for an hour, dying to tell you what happened at my internship today."

"Okay, okay, okay. After you go, I'll tell you my news."

"You have news?" Shani asked, confused.

"Yeah."

Without knowing whose turn it was to speak, at the same time they both said, "I found out what my powers are." And then there were a few brief seconds of silence with blank expressions on their faces.

"Wait, really?" Shani asked. "What are yours?"

Asher took a few steps back and took his already-ripped shirt off.

"What are you doing?" Shani asked.

"Just wait for it." Asher took a deep breath, flexed every muscle in his body, and jumped up in the air as high as he could, but nothing happened.

"What?" Shani asked. "Did you just poop?"

"What? Shani, no! Hold on. Let me try again." And so, he did...four more times. However, on the fifth try, his bright white wings sprouted from his upper back and held him hovering in the air.

"WHAT THE—?" Shani almost fainted. That was the last thing she was expecting.

"You're a freaking bird!" she hollered.

"What? No, Shani. I'm not a bird."

"Then what the hell are you?"

"Dude, how am I supposed to know?"

"BUT YOU HAVE FEATHERS!"

"I KNOW I HAVE FEATHERS!" Asher tried to come down from the air gracefully, but he forgot how big his wings were, and they knocked Shani's framed picture of the Eiffel Tower off the wall.

"Nice," said Shani, going over to fix it. "How did you find this out?"

"Well. I kinda dropped my phone and—" Shani held her hand up to stop him.

"Let me guess, you fell trying to do something ninja-like?" Asher's facial expression answered the question for her. "Of course, you did. Shocker."

"I'm sorry I've been so difficult lately." There were silent but empathetic expressions exchanged between them.

"Me too," Shani quietly replied.

"It's just, this is not how I pictured our senior year. And not knowing what's going on is scary, but I'm also scared to find out what's happened to us. We've got so much going on and a lot going for us, but what if we have to put our lives on hold for this?"

"I know." Shani walked over to hug him and gave him a long, tight embrace.

"So, what's your power?" Asher asked. Shani hesitated answering so she could figure out how to phrase her reply without sounding like a complete dork and psychopath. Who was she kidding? Of course, she cared what Asher thought of her pathetic powers.

"Um...I had a conversation...in English...I think...with...a fish." Her eyes dropped to the floor, and Asher burst out laughing. The tender moment was long gone.

"You can talk to FISH? HAHAHA! Of course, that would happen to you! Why would the universe give you something useful?" Asher hunched over and began losing his breath.

"Hey! Technically it was an eel, but you know what? I think it'll be very useful at work! I can communicate with all of the aquatic creatures and see what they need and—I don't know! It could be useful!" She sat on the couch and pulled out her stuff from her bag and pretended to do work.

"Just wait until the rest hear about this. I bet Lexi can like blow things up or something like that, and then you'll be at work, talking to the wittle fish." Asher crawled around the room with his hand over his head, imitating a baby shark.

Shani glared at him and said, "I'm going to dump water over your head...once we get rid of these powers, so you can't fly away from me when I do!"

She continued to talk, but the moment Shani said the word "water," it made Asher think.

Water...

He turned around to see a fresh vase of flowers on the kitchen counter. While Asher was impulsively taking them out of the pot, Shani kept mumbling about how mad she was, and didn't even notice that he had left the living room and came back. Asher stood in front of her, and without giving her any warning, he threw the pot of water at her.

Luckily for Shani, she looked up right before he threw it and put her hands up to block the water from getting on her face. She expected to feel water splash on the front of her body and to scream at Asher afterwards for unjustifiably throwing water at her when she had homework on her lap, but the water never came. She uncovered her face to see multiple bubbles of water floating midair. Asher's theory was right.

"Shani, I think I know where our powers come from."

6:

"Okay, there's no way this is a coincidence."

Brex spent her Sunday morning lying in bed and avoiding doing homework. She was planning on going outside and taking some pictures, but for now, all she wanted to do was watch YouTube videos and try to master sliding tiny fireballs through her fingers.

The tiny dot of light sped over and under her knuckles. It was the size of a pea, and she had been practicing tricks with it for hours. She figured if she tried to make anything bigger, somebody would smell the smoke, and she would get written up.

Her photography assignment was to photograph something up close in nature and swap out every color in the photo for a different one. It was a fairly dreary day, which meant it was perfect lighting for outdoor pictures.

She finally gathered up the energy to collect all of her equipment. There was nothing like sliding a new, expensive SIM card into her favorite camera. She threw on her thirty-pound backpack and headed for the hallway. As she opened up her room to leave, there was Asher standing in the doorway with his fist held up as if he was about to knock, with Shani standing right next to him.

"Whoa, GEEZ!" Brex jumped.

"Sorry! I was about to knock," said Asher with a somewhat guilty look on his face.

"It's okay. Wait, how did you know which room I was in?"

Shani butted in before Asher could speak and said, "We didn't. We just knocked on the last four dorms, but luckily you live on the first floor. You also don't have any social media, so it was impossible to get a hold of you."

"Ah. Remind me that we need to exchange phone numbers." Brex used her head to beckon them inside. She looked around the hallway before she closed the door to make sure nobody was spying on them.

"What's up?" Brex asked.

"First of all, remember how I have wings?" Asher asked.

"Yes, Asher. That was literally last night," Brex responded.

"Yeah, I know. I just really wanted an excuse to talk about that again, but anyways...check out what Shani can do!"

Shani looked around for something with water in it and spotted a half-filled water bottle on the floor right next to Brex's backpack. "I'm just gonna unscrew this if you don't mind," she said, not giving Brex a chance to respond. She unscrewed the cap and started to pour the water over her hand, but instead of it dripping all over her skin, Shani was able to make the water float in the air, preventing it from spilling everywhere.

"Whoa. Hell, yeah, Shani," Brex cheered. "How'd you figure out you can do that?"

"I threw water at her," said Asher.

Brex squinted her eyes and paused before she responded with, "Okay, then." Shani struggled with making the water float where she wanted it to float, but she was miraculously able to get the water back into the bottle.

"Anyways, we did some thinking, and we think our powers come from—"

"Greek mythology?" Brex interrupted. "Like Hades and Zeus and all that. Didn't we already make a Percy Jackson joke?"

"Well, yeah." Shani and Asher looked at each other, feeling marginally relieved that Brex was thinking the same thing, and they weren't being stupid.

"I was thinking that last night when angel-looking wings sprouted from Asher's back," Brex continued. "I don't know. It all just seemed more like characteristics to me rather than superpowers."

"That's kinda what we were thinking," said Shani. "But, I mean that's really all we know so far. We still don't know what our scars are, or what Lexi's abilities are, or why Boston, Massachusetts, has the powers of gods from Athens, Greece, just randomly chilling here."

"I have no idea, but we do know that Shani has the powers of Poseidon. Logan has Zeus, Asher has Hermes, and I have Hades. So, where is that going to leave Lexi?"

"I don't know," Shani responded. "That's more than just the big three. That's not really much of a pattern."

Brex's eyes widened as she realized something.

"What? What are you thinking?" Asher asked.

"The dog," Brex replied. "I think...wait, let me show you." She went to her laptop and pulled up pictures of mythical-looking canines on Google. "What if that thing was a hellhound? Remember those dogs in Hercules and Percy Jackson?" They all took a look at the drawings and old photographs. Each one looked different from the other, and none of them looked exactly like the dog they saw chasing them. None of these artists knew what a hellhound looked like. Maybe it was possible.

"Yeah, yeah, yeah. Aren't those, like, that Persephone person's pets, or whatnot?" Shani asked.

"I think so. So, what was it doing near that fire?"

Asher noticed many of these hellhound paintings had fire somewhere in the portrait and asked "What if the dog was the one that started it?"

Brex and Shani doubtfully looked at one another.

"I don't know," said Shani. "I mean nobody saw him except for us. How could that thing sneak into a building or even come close to it without anybody seeing him?"

"Oh, come on. This thing could be able to magically turn invisible for all we know." Neither Shani nor Brex had a response. He was right. They *knew* nothing. At this point, all they had were theories.

Shani stood up straight, crossed her arms and said, "Maybe we should get more opinions on this." They all agreed to go find Lexi and Logan.

Once again, Brex headed toward the door and brought her camera along with her, hoping the chaos might die down. Maybe she could eventually get some work done.

*****

The stench of Anika's gym bags was getting too intense for Lexi to concentrate on homework. It didn't take long for her to decide that going outside to the park and working would be best, even though it looked like it was about to rain. Not an ounce of sun was peeking through those clouds, but she didn't mind, so she picked up her guitar, blanket, laptop, and book bag.

The amount of homework she had to do was overwhelming, but it was nothing that a cloudy day and a cold drink couldn't fix. She stopped at her new favorite coffee shop and got a large iced coffee with cinnamon. Then, she headed to the quietest park bench that she could find.

She spread out her blanket on the bench and unpacked her belongings, including vegan chocolate, and a ridiculous number of pencils. No one was around, so she thought it would be safe to take off her glove and uncover her scar. It would make it easier to play later.

Her list of assignments included solving problems for her calculus class, reading the first three chapters of her book for her Wilderness Literature class, and starting her three-page essay for her General Law lecture. Why was she taking that class? Anybody's guess was as good as hers.

Reading was her first task to knock out, so she sped through her book as fast as she could. The sooner she finished, the sooner she was able to take a break and play some music.

This time, she was going to work on the new song she was writing. She had never considered herself much of a songwriter. The last song that she wrote was in the seventh grade, and it was about a boy that she liked but didn't like her back. In the moment of writing it, she thought that it was the most brilliant piece of art that was ever created. Looking back on it, she realized that it sounded more like a toddler freestyling a muffled rap rather than an actual song, but she was tempted to try again.

So far, she had the melody down for the first verse. That was it, but she enjoyed playing it on repeat. Lexi lost track of time and eventually realized that she was spending more time playing the same eight bars than doing homework, and she couldn't care less.

Her phone buzzed a few times, but she ignored it. A few people passed by and gave her a smile, but more people were giving her sympathetic looks, thinking that she was probably lonely with no friends. Lexi viewed this as a good thing. At least they weren't giving her *dirty* looks. On the other hand, she also thought it was a missed opportunity since she didn't leave her guitar case open for people to drop money in.

About a half an hour went by when she finally decided to go back to doing homework. It wasn't that her classes were too difficult. If anything, they were surprisingly easy for her. They were just tedious. In high school, Lexi easily got straight As, but so far, her college experience consisted of too many boring gen. eds. that made her want to scrape her fingernails against a chalkboard right next to her professors' ears.

She took a much longer break than she was planning, but she justified it by telling herself it was "getting her head in the zone." The progress that she made on her song consisted of a few more chords, but no words yet.

Next, it was calculus time. She pulled out her text book and searched for her notes. She emptied her entire backpack, but no pad, which had all of her notes from class in it.

"Great." She mumbled, and she gathered up all of her belongings and headed back toward her malodorous dorm room. She was pissed until she realized that she needed food anyways. The iced coffee wasn't settling well by itself.

More sympathetic looks came her way when people saw her dragging her guitar behind her with wallowing self-pity expressions on her face, but people looked away the second Lexi came to an abrupt stop as her eye caught something she wasn't expecting to see.

A dark figure stood in the distance behind the entrance to the underground parking garage. More than half of their body hid behind the small brick building, but only for a fraction of a second before Lexi spotted them, and they whisked away, but a fraction of a second was all Lexi needed. She was able to catch something before the unknown spy completely vanished; something gold and shiny on their clothing. Was it the sun that she saw in the trees when she was running to her safety? Who was this person? Why were they watching her and why here? What was spying going to do? If they wanted to hurt her or steal back whatever powers she didn't have, why didn't they just come and do it? There was barely anybody around.

This person couldn't be a threat, but it still made her feel unnecessarily tense. She began walking toward them. Whoever they were, they were probably gone by now. For all Lexi knew, they most likely had the ability to vanish into thin air. She dropped her belongings, hiked up her maxi skirt, and started jogging toward the garage entrance.

Covertly, she ran around the opposite side from where they were hiding, hoping to surprise the masked sleuth, but before Lexi could reach the building, a four-legged creature cut into her path.

BARK! BARK! BARK!

"Whoa!" Lexi jumped so far back that she almost fell over. The largest German Shepherd she had ever seen stood two feet away from her and kept jumping on his hind legs, thinking they were going to play.

"I'm so sorry ma'am!" said the owner. "Roscoe has a bad habit of chasing people that run. He thinks it's a game." She held Roscoe's leash as tightly as she could and held him back with all her might, but he still seemed to be in control of their every move.

"Are you okay?" asked the owner.

"Yeah, yeah. I'm fine," Lexi answered, quite disoriented. Then, in the blink of an eye, Roscoe headed toward her school supplies that she had dropped. The teeth piercing out of his vast and lengthy jaw looked thirsty for a chew toy, and his eyes were locked on Lexi's calculus textbook. His owner kept restraining him from moving, but she was losing steam. Sensory overload was no joke to her. It was like her brain came to a complete halt, and that halt came with a painful pounding in her temples. The discomfort was probably coming from Roscoe's barking, but she tried to ignore it as much as she could.

Roscoe's owner managed to pull him away. A frisbee flew by, and his glowing yellow eyes followed its path. He dragged his owner in the opposite direction, and his barking surprisingly stopped.

It was then that Lexi realized her deep breathing abnormally increased, but as she saw Roscoe get farther and farther away, her breath slowed down, and her heart rate steadied at an orderly tempo. That beastly dog that ran her and her friends into that cave permanently heightened her protective instincts. Lexi liked dogs, but now she could barely come near ones big enough to knock her over. The worst part was, she knew it wouldn't pass anytime soon. More fears were about to pile up, and just the thought of that kept the tension in her shoulders, fingertips, and stomach.

The garage entrance was now vacant. Lexi searched and searched around the small brick building, but there wasn't a soul in sight. Keeping aware of her surroundings, she checked every corner of the entrance in case the unknown person dropped something, or left any evidence of being there. Only, before she could finish, she noticed something odd about the path her feet previously traveled, and it wasn't just the scent of lavender and roses bursting into her nose. It was also the feeling of her skirt catching onto something as her feet continued to move forward.

As she turned around, she saw a circle of colorful flowers surrounding the building that was not there before. Daisies, roses, lilies, and carnations beautifully bloomed as Lexi continued to walk. Stunned and unsure if this was her doing or not, she jumped away from the building and playfully walked in various dance-like motions. This was her wind-sweeping beach walk. By the flawless execution of the flowing pattern that followed her every step, she could confirm that the magic was certainly coming from her.

The ground continued to rapidly bloom with the fresh, colorful blossoms wherever Lexi stepped. The pedals softly tickled her ankles. All of the tension she felt was released into her magic. After a few moments of joyfully running in the grass, she glanced around, making sure nobody was watching her. Explaining how she was able to grow plants in a matter of seconds to the police wouldn't be the easiest thing, but as far as she could see, nobody was around.

"Just a few more minutes," she thought to herself. Curious, she placed her hands on the fresh, dewy grass. She concentrated as hard as she could and only thought about planting a new, green, youthful, tree. As she closed her eyes and flexed every muscle in her upper body, she inhaled as much oxygen as she could. The nails on her fingertips dug ever so slightly into the dirt, and as she opened her eyes again, a small evergreen tree sprouted before her. She had been aiming for a birch tree, but it was close enough. It reminded her of an undressed Christmas tree for dolls. Tiny green leaves jabbed her palms as she stroked it. It all seemed surreal.

All of a sudden, she heard faint voices coming from behind her. She stood up, brushed off her skirt, and gathered up her things. Anxious, she searched through her bag, hoping to find her phone, ignoring the fact that she had just planted an entire garden in a place that nobody is supposed to garden.

As she dashed through the park and onto the sidewalk, she pulled up Shani's contact. Surprisingly, she had two missed calls from her.

"Crap," she whispered to herself. She dialed back, but it went straight to voicemail, which was always a huge pet peeve of Lexi's. Annoyed, she threw her phone back into her bag, and picked up some speed. Her skirt blew fiercely in the wind as she headed toward Shani's and Asher's apartment.

.....

Asher, Brex, and Shani waited for Logan at the coffee shop next to campus. Logan had texted Asher a half an hour ago, saying that he would be there in ten minutes. Shani was the least impressed out of all of them.

By the time Logan walked in, Brex had already chugged her way through her iced coffee, while Shani and Asher weren't even half way done with theirs.

"Remind me why we are talking about this in public again," Logan requested as he sat down.

"Hello to you, too," Brex snarled. "We all wanted coffee, and it's completely dead in here. No one's listening." She sassily and loudly slurped what was left of her coffee, which was just melted ice at that point.

Logan defensively put his hands up in the air and said, "Fine. What do you guys got?"

Asher didn't wait a single beat before he blurted out, "You stole the powers of Zeus." Logan stared at Asher for a few seconds to take in what he just said. After he took a shallow breath, he tilted his head and eyes down towards the table.

"Okay. That makes sense." The rest were slightly relieved to hear his response. "Not gonna lie, I did think about that. I just thought it sounded really freaking stupid." They all shared a quiet chuckle. "What made you think this?"

"Well, while you were throwing around a dirty, old football last night, Shani and I made a few discoveries." Asher took out his phone and pulled up a video of him shirtless and facing away from the camera. A few seconds into the video two pearly white wings sprouted from his back and almost knocked the lamp over that was right next to him.

Logan was surprisingly calm and asked, "Dude. Are you supposed to be a bird?"

"That's what I said!" Shani exclaimed.

"Enough with the bird shit!" Asher shouted back.

"Interesting choice of words," Brex commented, not being able to help herself. Asher gave the impression that he was about to get up and walk out of the shop, but Logan interrupted and changed the subject instead.

"So, what was your discovery, Shani?" Logan asked. Without saying anything, she turned her head towards her water glass, and sharpened her eyes as if she were staring into someone's soul. At first, Logan was sure she was going to make it explode, but when a bubble the size of a tennis ball slowly and gracefully escalated into the air, even Shani was surprised. The bubble followed Shani's big brown eyes as she made it dance a few figure eights and balletic twirls. Before anybody could notice what she was doing, she pulled it right before her eyes and popped it with a petite whistled exhale.

"That's it?" Logan tried his best not to sound rude or cocky, but he was genuinely a bit confused. "I electrocuted an entire room, and you can pop a bubble? Come on there's gotta be something more and better—"

Before he could finish his sentence, Shani drove every drop of water from the glass straight into his face. It was like a miniature tsunami, crashing against the surface. Shani stood still and once again gave him her classic, terrorizing glare, while the rest leaned backwards, fighting back their laughter.

"Did that answer your question?" Shani didn't blink.

"Okay, yeah, yeah, I get it. You're like the queen and ruler of all things aqua, or whatever."

Brex handed him the napkins that were at the end of their table and sarcastically mumbled "You got a little something..." while pointing to his face.

"When did you learn how to do all that?" Asher asked.

"I may have stayed up and practiced a thing or two," Shani proudly and cockily stated.

After a few more laughs and wet napkins, they heard a little knock on the window. Lexi stood there, frantically waving her hand with a sizable grin on her face. They all gave little waves back before she ran to the main entrance of the shop and entered the building.

"Guys! You will never believe what just happened!" Before she continued, she spotted Logan's damp shirt and hair. "I would ask what happened to you, but do I want to know?"

Without a word, Logan scrunched his face and gently shook his head.

"Great!" Lexi was too excited to wait and hear the story anyways. She sat down and softly said, "I found out what my powers are."

"Really? That's amazing! We did too!" Asher replied, trying his best to sound only a little like a six-year-old entering Disney World. "What can you do?"

Lexi looked around to see if there were any plants in the room that she could somehow manipulate, but none were in view. "Well I can..." she began. Then suddenly an idea struck. She looked out the window and saw a branch starting to break off a small tree that was planted on the sidewalk.

Patiently, she waited for a few people to walk by and she mildly nodded her head towards the tree and whispered "Look over there." The rest turned their attention, while Lexi put all of her energy and focus into the injured branch. It was easy for her to feel the passion that she had for the earth. She didn't want the branch to be broken. It needed to be healed. The stress and negative strain floated away from her mind as she visualized restoring the snapped wood.

Her abdomen tightened, and her breaths became deeper as she watched the branch lift back into place and glow with a deeper and richer color than it was before. Impressed wasn't quite the word to describe how the rest felt watching the lavish repair. It gave them a comforting and astonished feeling as if they were watching a Christmas tree being lit up for the first time.

"Hold on a sec," said Asher, interrupting the moment of pure silence. "Aren't you an environmental science major or something like that?"

"Yeah. I know, it's weird, right?" Lexi responded.

Asher turned towards Shani and stated "Okay, there's no way this is a coincidence. You love the ocean and are now the Queen of the Seas or whatever, and then Lexi loves plants and the earth and is now a tree whisperer? Come on. How did *that* happen? This is a cartoon."

"Why are you asking me?" Shani asked defensively.

"Because if I didn't direct the question towards you, I would never hear the end of it," Asher answered without an ounce of regret.

"What's *that* supposed to mean?"

"Guys, come on we can't all fall apart now. Don't do this again," said Brex, cutting off the bickering.

"You're right. I'm sorry," said Shani, exchanging apologetic glances at Asher.

"Same," Asher stated.

Shani awkwardly stared at the table and fidgeted with her manicured fingernails before she spoke again. "But to be honest I was kind of thinking the same thing, and I'm not sure, but it must have something to do with each special ability being attracted to our personalities. In the explosion, the magic had to go somewhere and follow something."

The rest of the group looked at her like they were waiting for her to continue, but she couldn't tell if they were following what she was saying or not. "Yeah, I have no idea if that just made sense, but—um—yeah."

She brushed her hair back behind her ear and waited for someone at the table to respond.

"I mean, you gotta be right," Brex eventually said. "I highly doubt there's any other reasonable explanation."

They all politely and subtly agreed by nodding their heads.

"Okay, so who's who?" Logan asked. "My knowledge of these gods doesn't expand beyond the movie Hercules, so hit me."

"It's not a video game, Logan," Shani sassed "But I'm guessing you have the power of Zeus, Brex, we've already established you have Hades, I have Poseidon, Lexi might be Demeter? Maybe? Asher has wings now, so he probably has the powers of Hermes, but he could also be Cupid. Who knows!" She let out a few snorts, expecting the others to follow along, but instead, she awkwardly laughed by herself, while the others knitted their brows and looked away.

"You know what else I find peculiar?" Lexi began. "There were five of us that went into that cave, and there just happened to be exactly five different powers hidden down there? Really? That seems like a little bit too much of a coincidence to me too. Unless there's more down there."

Shani put her elbows up on the table and started biting the nails on her right hand. Even she was stumped.

"You're right. I think we should go back into the cave," she said.

For a moment, there was a brief silence until Logan broke the peace and said, "Are you nuts? We almost froze to death the last time we were there!"

"And this time we know how to get out," Shani responded calmly, trying to lower the volume in his voice.

"Shani's right," said Brex. "It's not like we're gonna be chased down by some crazy-ass dog again." She looked around the table, hoping everyone would agree, but strong enthusiasm was severely lacking. "Look, we don't all have to go..."

"No," said Asher. "We'll be fine. We should all go together."

After the five of them nodded their heads in agreement, they returned their empty coffee cups and headed out the door.

It was busier outside than it had been earlier. More cars driving, and more people on the streets. They avoided making eye contact with pedestrians or looking carelessly suspicious at all costs.

"I have an idea," said Asher. "I think Brex and Logan should go in by themselves, and the rest of us can cover up the door while they go in, so no one will see them. That way we can guard it too, and you can be in and out before the door freezes over again."

Brex and Logan shrugged their shoulders and exchanged agreeing looks.

"That could work," said Brex. "But I'm not really sure what we are looking for. Are we just going to see if that green stuff explodes again?"

"I guess you can just look around and see what you can—" Shani fell silent as she looked into the distance. A few yards away from her was the ditch that they escaped into while being chased by the giant dog. But there was no door, or at least none that she could see.

She ran towards the ditch to confirm that she wasn't going insane. The rest ran behind her to find the same thing she did: no red door.

"Of course," Asher said. "Why *wouldn't* the door magically disappear?"

7:

"What language is this?"

Asher started kicking at the ground. Maybe somebody covered it up with fake or new grass. He didn't want to miss a single thing.

"Maybe we have the wrong spot?" Brex suggested.

"No, it was definitely around here," said Lexi. "I remember. That tree has that weird, low, thick branch and that hill right there with a pointy peak. It was here. I mean, maybe we're not entirely correct on the exact square foot. Give or take a few yards, but come on! Regardless, somebody covered it up, or it disappeared."

Asher kneeled down to his hands and feet and pulled at the grass. Nothing was loose or too mushy. All he was doing was pulling pieces of grass out of the dirt, but Shani started quibbling with him telling him to cut it out, so he did.

"But...why?" Asher asked as he got up to his feet. "Are there more power, magic potion thingies down there? Or did we steal them all?"

"Whoever put it there, they probably just don't want people to know it was here," Shani added. "They might not know that we were there in the first place."

"Um, I don't think that's true," Lexi interrupted. She held up her hand like she was asking to go to the bathroom in an elementary classroom. "I'm sorry. I got all wrapped up in finding out my abilities I forgot about the other part." She looked around just to double-check that the stalker wasn't listening to them. "Somebody has been following me, and I think I saw them the night of the fire."

"What? How do you know?" Shani asked. "What did they look like?"

"I'm not sure. They were wearing a lot of dark clothing. I couldn't see their face, but around the time we saw that dog, I saw part of a silhouette of a person and some of the fabric from their jacket because it was shiny. It kind of looked like a sun. I saw them again in the park before they jolted outta there."

Lexi was anything but scared. She was primarily worried about scaring the rest of them into thinking that they were being stalked and in serious danger. Proving Shani's theory that somebody was out to get them was the last thing that any of them wanted.

"Do we think they're a threat?" Brex asked.

"No," Lexi responded. "They would have attacked me right when they got the chance, right?"

"Not necessarily," Asher added. "What if they need us to be alive to steal our powers back?" He said this with the confidence of someone who just won an academy award, but everyone stayed silent, giving him the impression that he definitely had said the wrong thing.

"I don't know why I'm just thinking of this now, but it's kind of weird that a big mystical-looking dog just happened to drive us into that cave isn't it?" Brex asked.

"What if he was trying to kill us by driving us in there?" Asher asked.

"Or wanted us to steal the powers for whoever he was working for," Lexi suggested. "What if the person that's been following me was working with the dog? Maybe they are trying to hurt us."

"Well, whatever they are trying to do, we can't trust anybody," said Shani. Then, Lexi suddenly stopped in her tracks. "What?"

"What if our scars have some sort of tracking device in them?" It sounded even more abnormal and crazy when she said it out loud. "Like, if we're using our magic, they can find us. I mean how else would they have found me? I didn't tell anyone that I was going to the park today. I just went because Anika was stinking up our room."

Logan overdramatically gasped and hunched over, acting like he was having a heart attack.

"I'm sorry, Anika? Anika is your roommate? Oh geez. I am so sorry. She seriously thinks everyone on the team wants to hook up with her," Logan laughed, but no one was laughing with him.

"Thank you for your condolences, but not the point," Lexi continued. She was about to ask what they thought of her theory until she realized that there was a flaw. "Wait. No, that wouldn't make any sense. I wasn't using my powers until after they left."

Lexi thought hard about what she possibly could have done that would make her traceable, but nothing came to mind.

"Whatever it is, maybe we just shouldn't use our powers at all," Brex suggested. "You know. Just in case."

"You're right," said Logan. "We also don't want anybody seeing what we can do."

The group exchanged eye contact with each other, implying that they all agreed, but Shani asked if they all complied anyways, and everyone nodded their heads.

They started walking back toward campus. It made Logan crack a little smirk. The last time they were on this path all together, they were running for their lives, but now they carried a little more confidence.

After a few minutes of walking, they came across the bar, and the burnt-down building. For the first time since the fire, it was utterly vacant. Not a single strip of crime scene tape was to be seen.

Brex took one look and said "It's time we pay this place a visit."

·····

"Are you sure you don't want us to come with you guys?" Asher asked as the girls were putting on their gear for what might as well have been the break-in of a lifetime.

"Trust me, this is a woman's expedition. Besides, it'll be too chaotic if we all go," Shani replied. She wore a thick black jacket that looked like it had at least ten pockets in it. The jacket held her pocket knife, flashlight, pepper spray, and taser. Being too careful was never something she believed in.

"Yeah, you won't be able to handle it, boys," said Brex, lacing up her black Doc Martens that she considered her "going out shoes."

Lexi walked out of Shani's and Asher's bathroom wearing black leggings. It was the first time any of them had seen her in something other than a long, flowy skirt.

"Hold it!" Asher jumped right in front of her with his hand up. "Who are you, and what have you done with Lexi?"

"Yes, yes...Lexi has legs...but just wait until you see me in shorts," Lexi winked, letting her hips fall from side to side. She whipped on her jacket and shook out her long curly blonde hair.

The three women stood together putting on the finishing touches for their mission. Logan couldn't help but notice that they looked like they were dressed to go to a convention that was just for the color black.

"Is all the black really necessary?" Logan asked.

"Yes," the three ladies all said at the same time, without even bothering to look up at him.

"Sorry I asked." He walked away and turned on the T.V. "Guess it's just you and me, bud," he said, looking at Asher.

"Yes, but you guys gotta keep your phones with you just in case we need you," said Shani. The boys rolled their eyes as she turned away.

The girls double-checked that they had everything they would need in any scenario. Weapons? They had that. Tools to break in through any door that was locked? They had that too.

"Ready, ladies?" Shani asked.

"Let's do it." Brex gave her flashlight a little flip and caught the handle.

"Everyone's phones are charged? We'll need to take pictures!"

Lexi reached out her arms to shove Shani out of the doorway and said, "Jesus, Shani. Let's just goooooo!"

Asher and Logan exchanged laughs and flipped the T.V. to Netflix. "What should we watch?" Asher asked.

"Actually, I invited Adam over to play some video games. You cool with that? I thought it would be fun. I also brought a little throwback." Logan pulled out the video game *Brawl* from his backpack.

"Aw, man," Asher laughed. "Hell, yeah!"

They played one-on-one for a few minutes before they heard the bell ring. Logan answered it, and Adam walked through the door. He hopped up over the couch and slapped Asher on the back.

"Ow. A little harsh much?" Asher teased. Adam gave him a little smirk.

"What are we playing?" Adam asked. Logan held up the disc cover to show him.

"Damn! I haven't seen this since like what? Elementary school? Get ready to be crushed, my men!"

⁕⁕⁕⁕⁕

The girls walked the entire route to the building. As they got closer, they tried to hide behind as many landmarks as they could. Their biggest fear at the moment was having the wrong person follow them. Their second biggest fear was getting caught by the cops. It would certainly be difficult to explain why they all had cult-like scars on their palms and were dressed up like they were about to rob Jeff Bezos.

They all jumped behind a thick tree trunk as Shani said, "Look. There's a cop car right there. We have to go around." Lexi beckoned them to follow her. The three of them casually walked across the street, acting like they were chatting and giggling.

Once they reached the sidewalk, they darted into the alleyway that was directly in front of them. The cruiser could have been empty for all they knew, but they didn't want to take any chances. They were now out of sight and beneath the shadows.

The time was almost one in the morning. On Sunday nights, the streets of Boston were at their calmest, but sneaking around was still precarious. The three of them had to be as quiet as possible and stay out of sight. They crawled on grass, hid behind walls and bushes, and finally reached the alley behind the Romanov Building.

"Anybody see an entrance that's in a darkish spot?" Brex whispered, looking around. Their backs were up against the dusty brick wall. Their clothing helped them blend into the dark shadows almost perfectly.

"I think I see a small window right there." Lexi pointed to a spot on the lower part of the wall that looked like it reflected a small portion of light. They walked over to it, still close to the wall. Lexi was hesitant to use her flashlight, so she placed her hand on the reflection. It was cold and smooth, and definitely glass. It was a window.

Lexi felt around for the handle. It was a sideways sliding one, and when she found it, she pulled as hard as she could, but it wouldn't open.

"It's either stuck, locked, or melted," said Lexi breathlessly.

"That's okay, we can just break it open. I have my flashlight," said Brex, preparing to make a compelling whack.

Shani put her hand out to stop her and said, "No! Wait! Somebody will hear it and call the police, or the police will hear it themselves."

Brex raised her eyebrows and let her eyes roll almost all the way back to her head.

"Okay, fine. You're right. Let's look over here." Brex squatted close to the ground and progressed alongside the bricks. Shani followed behind her while Lexi kept attempting to pry open the window with the flathead screwdriver that she brought.

Brex came to the end of the wall, but when she turned the corner, the perpendicular wall was brightly lit with a street light. They knew stepping out of the shadow would be too risky. Plus, there was no door, or window that they could reach on that part of the building.

"Damn it," Brex cursed. Shani pulled her backwards, so her head wasn't lit up by the street lights.

"Guys. I can't get it," said Lexi. She shoved her screwdriver back into her jacket with a disappointed look on her face.

"It's okay," said Brex. "We'll just have to go up and around." Shani and Lexi knew exactly what she was talking about. There were windows on the second story of the building. One of them was bound to be open. Brex was clearly scheming, piling on top of one another to reach one, but Shani decided to play stupid, hoping they would look for another way.

"What?" asked Shani and Lexi.

"Oh, come on, guys! What else are we going to do? It'll be fun! Just as long as we're quiet, no one will hear us or see us. This part of the building is completely dark. We're in an alley."

The three of them looked up to see if there was a broken or open window that one of them could slide through, but it was too dark to determine anything.

"We need the flashlight," Lexi called out. She started ruffling through her jacket to pull out her flashlight. Shani desperately wanted to argue, but she didn't want to come off bossier than she already was.

Brex shone her light for only about four seconds. That was all she needed. There was a window to their right that was completely shattered.

"Over there!" she pointed.

"Okay awesome," said Shani. "You ready?" she pointed her attention towards Lexi.

If there was more light, they would have seen the little color in Lexi's face drain from fear.

"Why do I have to be the one to go up?" The answer was obvious, but she didn't always enjoy acknowledging the fact that she was roughly half the size of an average human.

"Come on, Lex. We don't want to waste any time," said Shani. "Okay, so who's boosting her up?" She tried to point the pressure towards Brex, but the answer was, once again, fairly obvious. Only this time, it was Brex and Lexi giving Shani the "snake eyes."

"Shani, I'm five-three," said Brex. "You're a literal mountain."

"Ughhh. Fine!" She hiked up her pants and stretched out her arms. Brex spread her feet apart, preparing to spot the untrained acrobatic act, even though she knew that doing so was completely pointless.

The process of hoisting Lexi into the air started off as a disoriented catastrophe. Shani tried to grab her feet, but her squat was too deep to stand back up. Brex stood there with her hands out unsure of what to do before she finally said, "Jesus. Just face me, and I'll grab Lexi's hips."

Shani braced her wrists together for Lexi to have something to step on while Brex squeezed her palms around Lexi's petite waist.

"One," Shani began.

"Two, three!" Brex quickly finished. They both significantly underestimated how much easier it was going to be with the two of them lifting a ninety-five-pound girl, and Lexi went flying straight up into the air. Luckily, she was able to frantically grab the window sill.

"That—that was real smooth, guys. Maybe—maybe we should have brought the boys," Lexi stammered as she struggled to hold herself up. Shani was still holding her ankles, but they were now slightly above Shani's head while Brex stood there in awe with her hands moving from side to side, unsure of where to be.

"Sorry! You okay?" asked Shani.

"Yeah, yeah. I just gotta pull myself up without stabbing myself." Surrounding Lexi were shards of glass, pointing inwards. She used every bit of strength and adrenaline that she had to carefully haul herself up with her forearms. The throbbing pain in her arms didn't last long, but she was almost certain that she either tore or pulled a few muscles.

Finally, she got one knee under her stomach and in between her arms to pull herself through the window.

"Guys! I'm in!"

"That's awesome, dude, but are you okay? Did you cut yourself?" asked Shani.

"No! I think I'm good!" said Lexi, even though it was almost pitch black, and she could barely see anybody.

"Okay! Now go to the basement, or whatever floor that is and unlock the window to let us in!" Brex whispered in the loudest voice she dared to use.

Lexi pulled out her flashlight from her back pocket and switched it on. The building could have been old ruins for all she knew. It was colorless and covered in ashes. Most of the interior walls were made of brick, similar to the exterior, but Lexi didn't like the feeling that it gave her. The tightness and claustrophobic intensity invaded her personal space. Nevertheless, she moved along. Horror movies were always an activity that she could easily tolerate. How was this any different? After all, she was the one with the powers.

Some of the hallways were nearly blocked off from fallen bricks, but after turning a few corners and climbing over a few barricades, she found the staircase. If she had anything intoxicating in her system, she would have thought that this was the staircase to Hell.

Her feet scurried down the stairs as fast and gingerly as they could without falling. She didn't want to keep Shani and Brex waiting, and the sooner she could be in the company of other humans, the better.

At the end of the staircase there was a door. It looked as though somebody had beaten it down and tried to break in. Or maybe somebody was trapped inside, and they were trying to get out. That would make sense, but as far as the police knew, nobody was inside the building when the fire happened. Not only that, but the door looked like it was broken down from the outside, not the inside. The hinges were broken and the wood was tilted in toward the room, but she couldn't be certain about anything.

Lexi pulled out her phone to take a few pictures, and immediately after the flash went off, she heard a knock coming from behind her. She jumped so vigorously that she dropped her phone and flashlight. Now she was in nearly complete darkness, and the only reason she didn't let out a scream was because she heard a muffled, "Lexi? Are you there?" followed by the knocking.

"Really?" Lexi whispered under her breath. She could hear where the voice was coming from. Whether it was Brex or Shani, she couldn't tell, but it didn't take long for her to find the window. There was the tiniest bit of light coming from that area which she figured was a street light leaking from the small alley through the glass. She picked her phone and flashlight back up, and sure enough the dusty basement window was directly in front of her.

"Lexi? Are you okay?" This time she was close enough to tell that it was Shani's voice. Lexi pulled up what she hoped was a safe chair to stand on and reached for the lock, turned it, and pulled it open.

"Damn. You made it!" said Shani, looking surprised.

"Were you doubting me?" asked Lexi, indignant.

Lexi helped them down into the basement by guiding their legs onto the chair, while still silently begging for the chair not to break. Shani came down smoothly on her belly as her legs easily reached it. Brex's journey, on the other hand, had a few bumps and scratches along the way. She started off sliding down through the window just like Shani did. Only this time, she was interrupted by a car light coming towards the alley in the distance.

Her head and the rest of her upper body were sticking out of the basement window, looking like the building had fallen on top of her when she heard the car get closer and closer to her. She knew in an instant that she couldn't take any chances and threw herself into the room. Her arms didn't just release from the edge, they flew. The next thing she knew, Brex felt and heard the crunch of the chair shattering into multiple pieces as her feet crashed into it. Lexi reached out her hand for Brex to catch, but she missed by almost an entire foot. Naturally, Brex's legs scurried backwards to try to catch herself, but ended up falling straight onto Shani.

BANG!

They crashed onto the floor and laid there like floppy pancakes. Shani let out an airy grunt while Brex struggled to pull herself up and help her.

"Oh shit! I am so sorry, Shani! Are you okay?" Shani clutched her head in pain, but sat up and shook it off.

"Yeah, yeah, yeah, I'm fine. Geez, what the hell was that all about?" Brex grabbed her hand to help her up.

"There was a car coming, so I just kinda...threw myself. Sorry, I panicked."

"It's fine. That's weird, my head only hurt for like a few seconds."

"Yeah, just like your scar on your leg," Lexi added. "I guess it's a side effect."

"How did you know that?"

"There was no scar when we were changing in your room earlier."

"Oh." Shani was expecting them to lose it, but almost nothing could shock them at this point.

While Shani and Brex dusted themselves off, Lexi stood there frozen.

"What? Did I hurt you too?" asked Brex.

"No, it's...look behind you." Lexi pointed her flashlight at the wall behind Shani and Brex. Against that wall was a shelf that displayed some of the most beautiful artifacts they had ever seen, and somehow, they all looked untouched.

"Whoa. What are all of these?" asked Shani, reaching to touch the gold plate that stood up on a display stand. Its impeccable detail grasped the eye of anybody who had the privilege of seeing it. Its abstract design drew what looked like a human face. Whose face it was, they couldn't tell, but they looked happy, calm, and at ease. Right below the face, surrounding the bottom circular lining of the vase, were what looked like arrows from an archery set, only these ones were double-sided and had dark silver lining that popped against the gold base.

On the shelf below the golden plate stood a bright green vase with magnificent white paintings of creatures that resembled monkeys. It shared a shelf with long shell necklaces that looked like they were handcrafted along a Mediterranean beach.

"You guys think this is the place we're looking for?" Brex asked.

"So far, it seems so," Shani answered.

"What do you think this place was?"

"The website said it was just rented-out offices. I'm guessing this person just liked to collect antiques." They both snapped a few pictures before they heard—

"Guys! Over here!" Lexi whispered loudly. Her flashlight pointed at a trunk that looked like it could be a treasure chest owned by an elder who obsessed over the 1970s. It had a green base color that resembled the pigmentation of grass: deep, smooth, and blended.

"Do we dare?" Shani dramatically asked.

"We dare," Brex proclaimed without hesitation, but Lexi pointed her flashlight directly towards an unfortunate obstacle.

"Shit, it's locked," she said. Shani kneeled over to try to pointlessly jiggle it open.

"Maybe I could either pry it open, or I could try and pick the lock too." Shani ran her fingers through her hair positively hoping that she would find a pin somewhere in her thick locks. "I swear I put one in here earlier, but I—WHOA."

Without giving any warning, Brex hoisted a metal stool she found in the opposite corner of the room and belted it over the lock, snapping it open, but with consequences. The two metals crashing together created such a noise they immediately heard a large, violent dog barking in the distance.

Shani flailed her arms in the air as she loudly whispered "BREX!"

"Yeah, didn't think about that." Still holding the stool in her hand, she gently lowered it to the floor and placed it on the ground without making a single noise.

"Okay, we need to work fast now, and we really...REALLY need to be quiet," Shani exclaimed, dashing toward the contents of the trunk.

The dust-covered chest contained four items; two handmade blankets that were probably used once every other year when the heater broke, a set of old-fashioned gold silverware, and an old journal. The worn diary most likely held some sort of significance, for it was hidden deep under the thick blankets. The leather bindings had no markings of any sort, but it looked like someone rubbed a piece of sandpaper over it for at least an hour.

"What do we have here?" asked Brex, taking the book into her possession. She slowly flipped through the pages as Lexi and Shani double-checked the trunk, making sure that was all that was left.

"I mean this trunk could be pretty valuable," Shani said. "Maybe somebody wanted it bad enough to risk destroying it."

"Maybe they knew it wouldn't be destroyed if they did," Lexi said.

"What?"

"Look at all the fancy stuff in here. It all seems completely untouched. Somebody must have put some sort of fireproof spell thing on it."

Shani hated that her brain immediately slithered into a dark and negative space. "So, somebody'll probably be coming back for this stuff when it's safe. Guys, I really think we need to leave. We had our look around."

"Hold on, Shani," Brex said without looking up from the book. With her voice unsteady and her eyes broadened she continued to say, "You ladies might want to take a look at this." She turned the book to reveal a penciled drawing of a clock-like circle that looked too familiar.

"Holy...shit," Lexi daintily whispered. The three of them pointed their flashlights at the wrinkled page to get a better look. The familiar yet still unknown symbol was clear to them, but the rest of the page's content was still a mystery.

"What language is this?" asked Brex. "Japanese? Mandarin? Vietnamese? It looks like it's read from right to left. All of the blank pages are on the left side of the book. It's probably some Asian...or Hebrew—"

"No, I don't think it's any of those," said Lexi.

"What makes you say that?"

"I don't recognize any of these symbols." Brex and Shani assumed she was about to elaborate, but it took blankly staring at her for a few seconds before she picked up the hint to continue.

"I used to do a lot of henna tattoos."

"Of course, you did," Brex commented.

CREEEEK, they heard come from the ceiling. The three of them gasped for breath so quickly it made their lungs ache. As they looked up, and stayed as still as they possibly could, it happened again.

CREEEEK!

It was footsteps. They weren't alone.

"SHIIIIT," Shani mouthed. As they began to frantically look around for places to hide, faint voices could be heard in the background, but they were too far away for any of them to understand what they were saying.

While quietly tip-toeing around, Lexi came across what looked like a child's fort made out of twigs and dead branches. A messy, stacked pile of wood, which was probably once a desk with a bookcase attached to it.

"I mean, man, I told her it was no big deal, but she wasn't in the mood for listening," came a voice from the floor above. It was a man's voice. A squeaky, yet deep man's voice, and he was headed downstairs. But the worst part was...he wasn't alone.

Lexi beckoned Shani and Brex as frantically and as quietly as she could. The three of them jumped behind the pile of wood and killed their flashlights. The shadows under the wood protected them from being seen, but only if the men were dumb enough to not bring flashlights. Shani crouched to the floor in a downwards fetal position. Brex put her back up against a curved piece of wood and hugged her knees into her chest so tightly it was almost hard to breathe, and Lexi found an opening that made her appreciate her height like never before. She lay flat on her back right next to Shani and held her breath as the voices got closer.

"Women are freaking frustrating," said the second voice. As they came further down the stairs, the three of them could hear an odd sort of jingle sound as they walked.

Of course, they all thought. How could they be so stupid? They were cops.

"Would I have liked to get some beer on my birthday? Yes," the first cop said. "But am I going to make a big deal out of it? Not in front of her!" The two cops entered the room, and one of them immediately pointed their flashlight at the stack of wood where the girls were hiding, but luckily, their black clothing blended right in.

"Anyways," the second cop said. "It was probably just a raccoon, but we should take a look around just in case."

The three of them could hear the cops' footsteps strutting around in various directions. They were moving fast. A plan needed to be made, and it needed to be made quick.

"Wow, check out all this stuff," the first cop said. He was probably looking at the bookcase with the beautiful artifacts, which gave them just a few more moments to think.

"What do we do?" Brex silently mouthed to Shani. Shani looked at her, knowing exactly what to do, but she was too afraid to do it, and didn't even know if she could.

"I'm sorry!" she mouthed back. Brex couldn't help but feel scared and confused. What did she mean, "I'm sorry"?

Shani held out her arms, closed her eyes, and flexed her fingers into cat-like claws. Her body quivered as if it were about to explode. Then suddenly, the walls started to make an odd, rusty, screeching sound. Brex and Lexi carefully tilted their heads to catch a glimpse of the walls surrounding them. They were dimly lit, but the two of them were positive that they were moving. More specifically, expanding.

"Um. What the hell is this?" said the second cop, pointing his flashlight at the wall.

What could Shani possibly be doing? And then it hit them: pipes.

Brex was about to snap her head back to Shani with bulging eyes and a deeply dropped jaw, but before she got the chance, ice-cold water smacked her straight in the face. A massive and violent waterfall came rushing through the cracked walls as the policemen yelled "WHAT THE— LET'S GET OUT OF HERE!" Within seconds there was already a foot of water on the floor. The policemen dragged their wet feet through the river and safely reached the stairs. As they jolted back up to street level, the first cop mumbled something through his walkie-talkie. It sounded like a warning. More police or firemen were coming, and they were going to be there soon.

Still hiding, Lexi held her forearms in front of her face, but was still having trouble breathing. Shani lifted her head above the stack of wood to make sure the policemen were completely out of sight. She struck her hands back out to the side to stop the water from coming near them.

Brex and Lexi kneeled over, coughing up the water that accidentally went down the wrong pipes.

"Come on!" Shani loudly whispered. Still holding back the motionless waves, she ran towards the window while the other two stumbled to follow. Non-grip shoes were not the best accessory to wear when running on a wet floor.

As they fought their way to the exit, they noticed something was missing: *the chair.* What was left of it had washed away.

"HOW THE HELL ARE WE GOING TO GET OUT OF HERE?" Brex screamed. Lexi pushed her way through the two of them to peer out through the window above her. She spotted a vine growing on the wall of the brick building. She only hoped the fire hadn't utterly destroyed it, and it was strong enough to carry the three of them.

Lexi shot her arm straight up into the air, reaching for the vine as it grew longer and huskier than before. The tip of the vine sped quickly towards her scarred palm. She snatched the end and kept pulling the trailing plant, so Shani and Brex could catch onto some slack.

"Come on! Let's climb up!" Lexi cried, almost completely out of breath. Grasping the vine with wet hands wasn't the easiest task, but one by one, they used their long-lasting adrenaline to pull themselves out of the watery mess. Lexi climbed up first and checked to see if the coast was clear. When she saw nobody was in the alley, she grabbed Shani's hand and helped her through the window.

Brex was a little easier to handle, her adrenaline was pumping so rapidly, she popped right out of the window like a jack-in-the-box immediately after Shani.

"I don't like...being near...that much freaking water," Brex coughed, spread out on the ground and gasping for breath.

"You good?" Shani asked, helping her up.

"Yeah, yeah, I'm fine. We just...need to get out of here. Let's go."

They started running towards the dimly lit streets, staying out of sight as much as they could. Shani wrung out her hair, while Lexi stiffly attempted to walk comfortably with the rash she was quickly getting from her soaked pants. Brex couldn't decide whether it was colder to have her drenched jacket on or off, but it made her extremely tempted to use her powers for at least a little bit of heat.

"Shani," said Brex. "You know you could have put that circle around us before you burst those pipes, right?"

"Yeah...guys, I know, I'm sorry. I was just really freaked out." Shani admitting to her mistake and fear in the same breath made Brex and Lexi squirm in their stance.

"Couldn't you also dry us off or something?" Lexi asked.

"Do I give off the impression that I know how to do that yet?" Shani snapped.

"I mean, my phone should be fine. I was just worried about this," Brex said, pulling the old book out of the back of her pants.

"Holy shit. You got it!" Lexi yelled way too loudly.

"Hell yeah, I did. I would have knocked those obnoxious cops out if it meant saving this thing." She casually flipped through the pages again. A few pages were damp, but nothing was ruined and, miraculously, everything was legible.

·····

Back at the apartment, Asher, Logan, and Adam were miles deep into their video games. Logan was in first place, Adam was in second, and Asher was not happy about it.

"Come on! You definitely cheated that time!" Asher wailed to Logan.

"Asher, it's a videogame. You can't cheat in a video game, dude," Logan snapped in a young, nagging voice.

Still holding the remote control, Asher spread his arms and legs into a star position and let his torso flop down onto the couch.

"I have failed my people," he said dramatically.

"Your people?" Adam asked.

"Mario and Luigi, man. I rarely disappoint them."

Adam put a hand on his shoulder and said in a phony, sympathetic tone, "I think you'll survive."

BANG! BANG! BANG!

They all jumped out of their seats as their hearts skipped a beat. Someone was at the door, and whoever it was, they didn't seem happy about being there.

Asher ran to the door and peeked through the peephole. It was three drenched, angry looking women, waiting impatiently to come in. He opened the door and asked "What the hell happened to you guys? Or should I not ask?"

Both Brex and Lexi slowly turned their heads toward Shani, implying she was clearly the one to blame. Shani could sense their stares and stood there with her eyes closed, wishing the moment would pass by faster.

"Wow," Asher commented. "Some Charlie's Angels you guys are."

8:

"Protect them whatever you do."

It was pouring rain outside when Shani ran off to work. Unlike her usual arrival time, she was only going to be about three minutes early instead of twenty. She tried to calm down by telling herself that she was overreacting, and normal people were not like this, but that only brought her anxiety to a higher level.

Halfway through her walk, wind raced in an upward direction so brutally that it turned her umbrella inside out and pushed her forward, almost knocking her off her feet. She tried to make her umbrella turn back to its right position, but the intense wind managed to snap one of the screws and half of the dark purple fabric flopped down over the metal rod.

Shani hopelessly dropped her umbrella by her side, and started running even faster with the ice-cold rain bashing against her face. It was a bad day to be holding a backpack, a purse big enough to hold two gallons of water, and an umbrella that was now broken.

All she could think was, *Dammit, right now would be a great time to use my powers, but do I wanna get yelled at again? I did the right thing, right? Why were they so mad? I wouldn't have gotten mad. So bossy. I wouldn't have gotten bossy. Why does everyone always think I'm bossy? They should be less bossy! Oh shit...don't run into the door, Shani.*

Her head continued to scream until she finally reached the entrance to the aquarium. The instant a roof covered her from top to bottom and she was out of the hail-like rain, she crouched down and rummaged through her backpack to check and see if her books, laptop, and phone were all dry.

Shani let out an enormous exhale when she felt around the miraculously moistureless lining of her bag. She flung her backpack back onto her shoulders, and straightened up only to find a tall, handsome, young man, standing right in front of her.

"Whoa," she jumped back.

"Oh hey, sorry," he said. "Just wanted to make sure you were okay. You looked a little distraught out there."

"You don't say," she said sarcastically.

"Yeah," the man responded, clearly misinterpreting her tone. "I mean, you're soaked."

Not wanting to bother with him anymore Shani politely said, "Yeah, no, I'm fine. Thanks." She recognized him from the week before, but struggled to remember his name. He could see her processing the thought in her brain with a scrunched face and one shut eye.

"Seamus," he said, holding out his hand. "I don't think we actually got a proper chance to meet last week."

"Oh, no. We didn't, sorry, but I really gotta run. I'm gonna be late." She gave him an uncomfortable two-fingered salute, but before she could pass him, he jumped right back in front of her and mumbled something that sounded as if somebody were pulling stitches out of his forehead.

"Oh, wait! You've got something in your hair," he said. He put both hands at the tip of her shoulder where her wet hair was its messiest.

What it was, she didn't see. It could have been nothing for all she knew, but she stood there, horrified, and awkwardly walked past him in silence.

Did that white boy seriously just touch my hair? Shani thought to herself.

Before she reached the staircase, she heard the security guard, Al, mumble, "Kids."

For the next few hours, Shani shadowed tours, cut up a few fish, fed a few others, and cleaned some dirty tanks. The time was now three in the afternoon, but she was still scheduled to be there for another hour. After running out of things to do, she dreaded the rest of the time she had left there. She didn't do well with being sedentary. When she realized that she still had a two-hour lecture to go to after this, she became irritable.

"Let me see," said the doctor, looking around her office. "I have a few things to file. Why don't I send you the Google Doc, and I'll show you how to do it? Sorry, it won't be too exciting, dear."

The doctor spent twenty minutes showing Shani how to file expense reports. Shani was having a hard time hiding her initial facial expression that read "This conversation could have been summed up in roughly thirty seconds." Still, she was enjoying working for Dr. Carter and didn't want to make a fuss or disappoint her.

Shani sat there, typing away at her computer while the doctor was aimlessly wandering around the aquarium. The relief of not being on her feet anymore was glorifying. A breath of fresh air came rushing to her lungs as she leaned back into the cushioned office chair. Casually, her eyes followed Oscar, the office fish as he scurried around the ten-inch by eighteen-inch tank. Unfortunately for Shani, Goldfish had terrible memories. There was no getting any helpful information out of him. All he did was burp bubbles. If he was trying to say something, Shani couldn't understand it.

Ever since the weird and confusing conversation with Ilisa, she'd been too nervous to try to talk to him again. What good would that do? What if it was too dangerous to talk to him? Or what if he himself was the dangerous one? Still, she wanted to know more about him.

Where does the name Ilisa come from? Shani thought to herself. Eagerly, she pulled up Google on her computer and typed that exact thought into the search bar. The only problem was, she had no idea how to spell it.

"E-E-L-I-S-A, O-R-I-G-I-N?" she typed in, but Google assumed she meant to type in "Alisha." That was not right, but to Shani, the spelling made sense because he was an eel.

"I-L-I-S-A, O-R-I-G-I-N."

Bingo.

Her eyes were immediately drawn to the third top result that came up on the screen. "Top Five Boy Names of the 1920s in India." The scar on her hand, he recognized it. Why would a fish from India recognize this Greek scar?

She clicked on the link to see its meaning. "God is my oath" the screen read. Was he important? Did he have some sort of royal title? What connection did he have to Greece? Abruptly, she stopped reading, shook her head, and rolled her eyes at herself.

"Knock, knock," said a familiar voice at the door. Shani turned around to see Seamus standing halfway in the room. "Just wondering if you need anything." His awkward, closed-mouth smile made Shani terribly uncomfortable. It was one of those looks that she didn't appreciate receiving from men.

"I'm good, thank you," she politely smiled back.

"Okay." Tapping the doorway and scanning the room, he stiffly lingered and searched for words to say. "Well, I'll be down the hall if you need me."

Without even mumbling, Shani gave him a silent half-smile and turned back around as he slowly walked away. But then an unfortunate idea popped into her head. Desperately not wanting to, she had to try.

Shani stood up out of her chair and yelled "Hey, Seamus...actually wait a second."

He popped his head back through the door while almost running into her.

"What's up?" he asked.

"Just one quick question. Um...do you happen to know how long those moray eels have been here? The ones in the giant tank?"

Confused by her question, he hesitated to answer.

"The eels? None of them are more than ten years old. We had a few that gave birth to the ones we have in here now, but the older ones died a few years ago when I first started working here. And those ones, I don't know where they came from. Why do you ask?"

Completely unprepared to respond, Shani stuttered her way through what she thought might be an acceptable answer. "Uh, I just—I just have a project, thanks!" Without missing a beat, she plopped herself back down into her chair, pretending to do her work on her computer, stiffly holding onto the keyboard.

Unsure of how to respond to such an abrupt closure to the conversation, Seamus gave a quiet, "Yep" and proceeded down the hall.

Less than a decade, she thought. Ilisa had said there was a woman whom he knew from decades ago. He couldn't have been lying, could he? Swimming off like that gave her the impression that maybe he wasn't supposed to disclose certain information.

How Ilisa knew this, she wasn't sure, but she had to figure out who this woman was. Maybe she was like Shani. Maybe she had special abilities just like the five of them. Or she could be the end of their existence, or she could be the owner of the journal the girls found.

·····

On the other side of town, Lexi spent her Thursday afternoon shopping at the thrift store as a reward to herself for finishing her homework early. Her next gig was coming up in a few days, and she thought an Autumn-like headband would be appropriate for the occasion.

For this gig, the theme was "The Official End of Summer." The two songs that she, by far, was most excited to sing were "Summer Nights" from Grease, and "Wake Me Up When September Ends" by Green Day, even though Anika made it perfectly clear that those were weak choices by blatantly rolling her eyes whenever Lexi would practice them in their room. It only made Lexi more excited to play them.

The moment she opened the store door, she felt her phone continuously buzzing from her jacket pocket only to see a picture of Logan pulling up the tip of his nose on the screen, which he had taken and set as his contact picture on Monday in Morialsa's class without her knowledge.

"What's up?" Lexi asked, answering the phone. "And nice picture by the way."

"That truly means a lot to me. I'm glad you like it."

Lexi rolled her eyes and silently laughed while planning the next photobomb she was going to take on *his* phone.

"Question for you, little blondie. You have that VirtualDJ thing on your iPad, don't you?"

"Yeah. Why do you ask?"

"Well, I seemed to have run out of storage space on my computer, and I wanted to see if you were interested in mixing up a few of your covers for a party that I'm having at the frat house tomorrow night. You know, I just thought it would be cool. You're working on a new original song, right?"

Lexi wasn't used to people asking for recordings of her singing, let alone mixing them herself. She also had only been to one college party before when she was in high school. At that party, she made the mistake of getting drunk and high off weed for the first time without eating anything beforehand. Her dad ended up having to drive her to McDonald's at five o'clock in the morning while poking fun at her lame excuse for a hangover.

"A party? Sick. So, you're going to invite my music to this party but not me? Ouch, Logan. That kinda stings a little."

"Oh, yeah. I was thinking about inviting you, but I just haven't decided yet. It all depends on how I'm feeling tomorrow."

Lexi made a little scoff that was barely audible through the phone, but Logan could read her reaction perfectly.

"I'm kidding! You better be there. You and the rest of our new little posse. The fun will obviously not arrive until all of us are there."

"I'd be honored to attend and entertain such a gathering." Lexi unzipped the pocket of her purse where she kept her iPad mini. "Let me just check and see—" It was empty.

Her fingertips scraped across the bottom crease of the pocket where all the extra dirt collected. There was nothing there.

"Shit!" Lexi said under her breath.

"What? What's wrong?"

"I left my iPad in Morialsa's class yesterday. I remember, I—CRAP! I left it under the seat when I was—aw, shit."

Still rummaging through her bag, she ran out of the store and headed towards Morialsa's lecture hall.

"You good?" Logan asked.

"Yeah um—I'll put together a playlist for you. The recordings I have aren't the best quality, but they should uhh...be fine. I'm just gonna go look for it first. I'm sorry, but thanks. If it wasn't for you I wouldn't have realized it was gone!" She nervously laughed while pushing her lungs to take deep breaths.

"Hey, Lex! Don't stress, I'm sure it's still there. And don't worry, everything will be great. We'll have fun tomorrow night, and don't trip! The hospital will think your scar will mean you were abducted by aliens!"

"Yeah, yeah, yeah. Sick. Thanks!" Barely paying attention to what he was saying she tucked her bag under her arm, ran up the sidewalk, and kept her eyes straight ahead. She shoved her phone into her jacket pocket and tried to picture the shortest path to the lecture hall.

If she ran through the sketchy alleyway, she would cut off a few minutes, but regardless, the route from the store to the lecture hall was a few degrees uphill. It didn't take long for her to regret wearing her sandals from Walmart.

After catching her breath, she became close enough to her destination that it wouldn't make a difference if she ran or not. She dropped the bag to leave it hanging only over her shoulder.

If the iPad was still there, it wouldn't be going anywhere now. The doors to the hall were now in view. If somebody was about to steal it and run out with it, Lexi felt confident enough that she could trip them with a tree branch. Although, if it was gone, she'd be at risk of losing a lot more than just a DJ application. The pictures that she took of the journal the girls found were on that iPad.

Lexi thought that any normal person probably wouldn't know what it was unless they spoke the language that the journal was written in, but if the police found it, they might have the smallest chance of tracing the book back to the basement of the building that they found it in. Unlikely, but even the thought of that happening made Lexi's breath become a little bit shorter.

She was certain the door was going to be locked, and she would need someone to open it for her, but as she approached the sliver of glass on the classroom door, the iPad suddenly became unprioritized.

On the stage stood Professor Morialsa, tall and professional with his curly hair pushed out of his unshaved face. Right next to him stood Anika, poised and smiling with one hand on her hip. Something felt off. They stood there, just talking, until the Professor moved in closer to her. The way his chin tilted and his cheeks remained soft. It made Lexi's wrists twitch.

Lexi hid behind the door as much as she could, but she didn't want to miss a single second of what was happening.

Was he going to make a move on her? Was she going to make a move on him? Though his lectures were often useless and boring, Morialsa was a young and attractive man. Anika was tall, beautiful, and ridiculously tough on the inside and out. Could it be?

At the slowest pace possible, or so it seemed to Lexi, Professor Morialsa reached out his hands to touch hers. The familiarity between them was unmistakable. It couldn't have been their first time doing this, and just by the way that he moved his body towards her, Lexi could tell they knew they were going into dangerous territory.

Lexi pulled her head back away from the classroom. It wasn't a kiss. It wasn't sexual harassment or assault to Lexi's knowledge at least, but the iPad would have to wait.

⋯⋯

After the sun went down, Asher still had a few hours of studying to do before he went to sleep. His first deadline for his senior thesis was also due in a few days. It was just the outline that he needed to complete, and for some strange reason, he knew it was going to be the most difficult part.

He entitled his thesis "Can Somebody Create an Inner Monologue?" He read somewhere a few weeks prior to developing this title that some people do not have a vocal consciousness in their heads. If they want to speak to themselves, they must physically do it out loud. But would they be able to change that? He found it oddly intriguing, but the only problem was, he still didn't know where he stood on the theory and still had a large amount of research to complete.

A few hours went by, and most of his research was done, but when the clock struck one a.m., there was a faint yet abrupt noise coming from somewhere in his room.

Flickering Christmas lights. That's what he thought of when it caught his attention. His spine went from a small slouch to a perfect stack of vertebrae in a fraction of a second. Slowly and thoroughly, he looked around the room to see if it was a mouse or rat running around his room.

Putting his body low to the floor, he slowly and steadily breathed to keep the room as quiet as possible. The noise. It didn't sound like it was moving about the room, but it did sound like it was coming from behind the mirror or *from* the mirror.

Asher's large, circular, wall-mounted mirror gave off a cryptic reflection, something that Asher had never seen before. It was fuzzy. Almost like his bedroom was full of mist and dew. For a reason unknown, he felt some sort of odd force pushing him away from the mirror as he walked towards it. He couldn't accelerate no matter what he did, but he kept pushing forward one step at a time.

Only a few feet from his desk, he stood up straight in front of his mirror and stared deep into its inaccurate reflection. He couldn't see himself in the mirror. It didn't even show his room. All he could see were thin sheets of clouds and fog, swirling together with another blurry figure floating about, but he couldn't make out who it was. Seeing this, he wasn't nearly as frightened as he thought he should be.

Still standing motionless in front of the mirror, Asher could see the mirror getting brighter, but not blinding. The blurry figure was starting to come together, but it wasn't just one object, it was at least two. And as the image continued to sharpen, he could see that they were no objects. They were two human beings, and if he wasn't mistaken, it was one female and one male.

"Mur—rah—ruh," Asher heard them say, but for all he knew, they were speaking a completely different language.

"Huh—muh—nuh," He heard the gibberish again, but this time, he could tell it was coming from the woman.

"I don't know what you want me to say," he finally heard clearly. The woman was facing diagonally towards Asher, while the man had his back turned to him. Whoever the woman was, she had beautiful, curly, long, black hair, and she was wearing what almost looked like knight's armor. The man was wearing a black jacket and had his head completely shaved, though Asher still didn't know what his face looked like.

"Tell me, why is she coming here?" the man asked. "What does she want?"

To Asher, the situation suggested that the two unknown people couldn't see him, but why would he be able to see them? Why *was* he seeing them?

"She has to want something. She always wants something," said the frightened woman. "But I think this time, she wants a deal."

"We cannot make any sort of deal with that woman—that thing! She can't be trusted, and for some reason, everybody wants to trust her, but they will learn!" the man hollered, stepping closer towards the woman. The moment felt tense, but a soft sort of tension. As if it was familiar and she knew what to do next. Asher could sense a bond between them.

"I don't think we should be making any of these decisions alone. We need to ask for the others or anyone!"

The man gently took her by the arm before she could walk away.

"Okay, but we have to be careful about whom we trust. We don't want any more snickering around the kingdom." There was a moment of silence between them. Asher was tempted to ask them many questions. Who were they? What were they talking about? How could he help? What did they want? Although for a reason he couldn't comprehend, he felt as if he couldn't talk or make any noise at all.

In his peripheral vision, he could see the lights in his room dim. Everything seemed to focus only on these two human beings.

"Don't worry about that," said the man. "Just—just go back down the mountain and protect everyone. Protect them whatever you do."

The woman kissed his hand and turned to walk away out of the frame. Who was this group of people, and why did they need protecting? The man stood there motionless with his head dropped to his chest. He deeply inhaled before he slowly turned his body to face Asher, but before he could catch a glimpse of any of the man's facial features, the image was brutally wiped away by a rushing clump of fog. The mirror was once again an articulate blur, but this time it wasn't just the mirror.

His room was now filled with a blue steam as if he were in a fairytale, but before he could reach to touch anything or ask himself what was happening, he hastily replenished his lungs with air and stood up straight, shirtless, and covered in sweat in his bed.

As he tried to catch his breath, he rolled out his now sore neck and shoulders and drew his head back to his pillow. How could that have been a dream? It was all so vivid. Asher knew one thing; it might have been all in his head, but at least some of it had to be real.

9:

"Sorry. Typical Friday night."

The second Friday of the term was the hottest one yet. Every student on campus was dressed in the shortest shorts they owned and the thinnest shirts they could find. Most of the freshman girls strutted around in their favorite tube tops, taking advantage of being out of high school and not having to follow a dress code.

Thankful that it was finally the weekend again, Asher came home from his second and last class of the day and cranked the A.C. Tiny droplets of sweat wept from his forehead. He changed his shirt, kicked off his shoes, closed the blinds, and flopped down on the couch. More than anything, he wanted to crack open a beer and lie down to watch something good on Netflix, but to his dismay, he had three days of homework to complete that he had put off because of studying.

Yesterday, his Cognitive Psychology professor, Dr. Rhenata, assigned the class a five-page report on Piaget's Developmental Theory. She made the due date for Monday. On Wednesday, Professor Morialsa had them pair up with someone whom they didn't already know to complete a project about why some people still think that the earth is flat. Asher and Adam, of course, pretended that they didn't know each other and paired up to do the project together. Fortunately, for both of them, that project wasn't due until next week.

Senioritis was certainly kicking in, but Asher was determined to go out with a bang, so after a few heavenly moments of lying down on the comfy couch in a dry shirt right next to the A.C., he pulled himself up and reached for his backpack.

"HEY!" Shani screamed, jumping through her door. Their energy levels crashed together, and Asher didn't show any appreciation towards it. "Whatchya doin'? Don't you have a whole bunch of home-work to do?"

Rolling his eyes and regretting ever telling Shani anything about his academics, Asher responded "I was just getting to it, Mom. Thank you."

"Normally I would say something snarky back, but I am way too excited about this to hold it in any longer!" She jumped up and down and clapped her hands like she did when she was little after she had won every single school spelling bee.

"Hold on. If this has anything to do with fish, can I please just grab my beer first?"

"Rude," Shani responded, highly unimpressed. "But no. That's not even close to what I was gonna say. I got the prosthetic skin in the mail to cover up our scars! And it works really, really well. I just have to put some foundation on it." She held up her hand to show Asher. He could tell that the result wasn't exactly what Shani's dark brown palm looked like before, but it did look reasonably natural. If she ever had to hold up her hand to a stranger, they wouldn't know the difference.

"Haven't tried them on with water yet, but they are supposed to be pretty water resistant. You wanna try it on? I got everyone's shade of foundation."

Asher gleefully nodded his head and tapped the couch, beckoning her to come sit. He ripped off his Band-Aid and held out his hand while Shani cut out a small piece of the prosthetic skin. It was almost as thin as paper and completely opaque.

"Is Adam coming over later?" Shani asked. "You guys have that project together, right?"

"No. Actually I'm going over to the frat house later." Shani offered an inquisitive look on her face. Why Asher would ever want to go inside a frat house was something she would never understand.

"On a Friday night? That seems a bit odd. Do they still have rushes going on?"

"No, no. I don't think so at least."

Shani gently flattened the fake skin on Asher's hand and smoothed it out, hopefully attempting to make it look creaseless.

"So, he invited you to a party?"

"Yeah! Logan's gonna be there too." Asher knew what she was trying to imply, but he wasn't in the mood to lecture Shani about how uninterested he was in discussing the subject. "I think Logan invited the whole gang, so he's probably expecting you there too."

"The gang? Like the Scooby Doo gang? No. I don't think I approve of this."

Shani blew on his hand to make it dry. The make-up, the skin, the glue. The look was complete.

"What do you think?" Shani asked, bringing Asher's palm right in front of his face. It was as close to flawless as it could be. The foundation matched his skin perfectly, the self-made creases aligned smoothly to the real ones.

"Dope." He repeatedly opened and closed his fingers to see if it would come off or loosen up. "It feels a little weird, but I think I'll get used to it. Man, it's really sticking."

Shani prepared more skin for herself and for the others. Each cut became easier and smoother than the one before. She was going to be a master in no time, which she thought was a bizarre skill to have.

Before showering, and finishing her homework, she invited Brex and Lexi to pregame at her apartment. The three of them had their own group chat now, which was entitled "The REAL Charlie's Angels," even though Shani was aiming for "The REAL Power Puff Girls," but she settled. Both Brex and Lexi responded almost immediately, saying that they were coming. But the second after Shani told them what time to come over and that she had the prosthetics prepared, she received a text from an unknown number.

"Hey!" the first message read. Before she could ask who it was, they told her. "It's Seamus. Got your number from the boss lady. Just wanted you to have it. Ya know, just in case you need anything! See you tomorrow!"

Shani almost threw her phone on her bed. She knew exactly why he wanted her number and had difficulty believing that Dr. Carter would just give out her number when he didn't need it, and she definitely didn't need his. Reporting him to HR didn't scare her, but it wasn't something she wanted to make a big deal out of either. It's not like he'd been physically inappropriate with her, besides touching her hair, but that was just his cultural ignorance.

For now, she was just going to enjoy her night with her friends and at least attempt to forget everything that made her want to slam her fist into a wall.

·····

The streets were almost twice as packed as the weekend before. Cops were stationed at every corner with girls dressed in miniskirts and red lipstick, trotting right past them.

Asher, Shani, Brex, and Lexi got ready and pregamed at the 26 Main Street apartment. The legal drinkers devoured at least four shots of vodka each while Lexi elegantly sipped her favorite red wine that her dad bought for her as a move-in present.

Before they left, Shani taught them how to put on the new fake skin that she had bought for everyone. Lexi easily blended the skin into her palm and matched the foundation perfectly on top of the prosthetic skin while Brex, who rarely ever used make-up, used about three times as much glue as she needed to and blended the skin in a way that made it look like she had Play-Doh on her palm. Luckily, Shani and Lexi were able to fix it before the party.

Lexi switched from a Bohemian skirt to Bohemian pants and re-curled her already naturally-curly hair.

"What a difference," Asher sarcastically commented.

Brex borrowed a black, skin-tight dress from Shani, so they both could match even though Brex insisted on keeping her jean jacket and Converse sneakers. Asher changed into a long-sleeve shirt and switched to contacts, which he usually hated doing, but the last time he went out and got wasted, he almost lost his glasses on multiple occasions. This time, he was going to be prepared.

The four of them headed out, already feeling the buzz.

"Tonight," Shani began, sounding like a talk show host. "We are not going to worry about any of this magic shit. No talk of secret journals, or weird scars. Nothing!" The more she talked, the tipsier she came across.

"You feeling okay there, dude?" Brex teased.

It was as if Shani didn't realize Brex said anything until after a few dead, silent moments, Shani finally reacted by saying in her deepest voice, "Wha'?"

"Okay," Asher chuckled. "You're going to have at most one drink when we are there, okay?"

"Whatever, babe," Shani said as she playfully pushed his face away from her. "I just wanna daaaance!"

"Yeah, you once broke your ankle dancing sober. Forgive me if I don't have much faith in you."

Ignoring Asher, Shani threw her arms out to the side and ran towards the loud music and bright, colorful lights that were coming from the frat house. The acting bouncer let the four of them pass while collecting money from every other patron. Logan greeted them with a stoned smile and a beer in his hand.

"You guys made it! How've you all been?" Logan slurred while hugging everyone.

"Didn't we see you this afternoon?" Asher asked.

"Yeah, yeah, yeah, but I missed you, man." He pulled Asher's face over his shoulder where they stayed for a brotherly embrace.

The girls shared an adoring and teasing "aw," rubbing their backs and snapping a few pictures on their phones.

"Can't—breathe," Asher mumbled, but it took a few moments for Logan to acknowledge what he was saying.

"Um...HI!" Brex heard from behind her. She turned around to see a surprised Jenna, walking towards her with a dollar store shot glass necklace around her neck, and two space buns on her head.

"Hey, you! I should've known you were gonna be here." Brex walked around Jenna to slap her butt. Jenna took that as an indication to dance more sensually while Brex continued to stand beside her and snicker at her offbeat twerking.

"Yeah well, I sure as hell didn't know you were gonna be here! You haven't gone to a party since freshman year!" Jenna grabbed Brex's hand and pulled her to a spot in the living room where they weren't going to get trampled by six-foot soccer players, running to do keg stands.

"Logan invited me and..." Carefully, she stopped herself before she said, "the rest of us." Instead, she mumbled "...and a few other random...people...yeah."

"Hmmm, speaking of which..." As Jenna was seductively checking out somebody walking towards them, Brex peered over her shoulder to see Logan bringing her what looked like alcoholic sherbet punch.

"Heyyy," Logan playfully said in his deepest voice. "This is for you, milady." Quietly, Jenna pretended to say, "hi" to somebody and placidly slipped out of sight.

"Wow. Wasn't expecting you guys to have something like this here. Please tell me this is ice cream." She looked down into her cup with her cheekbones lifting to her eyes as if it contained a winning ticket for the lottery wrapped with chocolate bars.

"Technically sherbet, but close enough." They clicked their plastic cups together and lifted the bottoms of their drinks so high, they were almost vertical.

"Did Shani give you the skin stuff yet?" asked Brex, trying to not let anybody overhear her.

"Oh yeah, she did, but uhh..." He reached into his pocket and pulled out the skin glue before he finished his sentence. "She texted me an hour ago and said you have to put it on because apparently, you suck at it and need to practice." Holding out the glue in front of Brex, he kept an obnoxiously large and teasing grin on his face.

"As if you could do any better. You see, this is the kind of patriarchy that I am trying to destroy, but she makes a fair point, so fine." Brex grabbed the glue from his hand and followed him as he led her through the path of flickering, neon lights and awkward yet enthusiastic dancing.

By the time they reached Logan's room, Brex was convinced she had already bruised both her shoulders from shoving so many people out of the way.

"Sorry. Typical Friday night," Logan said as he opened the door. Everything in his room had harsh, dark colors except for all of his trophies, football flags, and a bulletin board of drawings that he had illuminated under a black light. It reminded Brex of the room she had as a kid before her mom insisted on her painting it a "less depressing color."

Brex picked up the scissors off Logan's desk and began cutting up the skin into what was shaped less like a circle and more like a crooked hexagon.

"Man, you do suck at this," Logan teased. Brex broke from her concentrated stare to give him a bitterly indignant look, staring into his soul.

"So sorry that my skills are lacking in the departments that don't involve Photoshop, Bob Ross." After spreading the glue smoothly and evenly, she took another glance at the black light gallery. One drawing drastically stood out to her. It was a bird's-eye view of Boston Harbor. Only the buildings were all pastel colors, and the ocean water was a lighter blue than the sky.

"I don't think I've ever actually seen one of your drawings before. They're not half bad." Carefully, she dabbed a small bit of the make-up sample onto Logan's prosthetic skin. It was about three shades too light, but Brex still convinced herself that she could blend it in to make it look natural.

"Sorry," she laughed. "I'll get Shani to find you the right shade."

Logan held his palm up to his face to get a closer look. It looked like a clay pancake that had accidentally been stuck to his hand in pottery class.

"Hah! It's okay. It's dark out there. No one will see it, and thanks. You never stalked me on my Instagram to see my work?" He put on his sarcastic shocked face and slapped his hand on his chest.

"Sadly, no. But I'm hardly ever on Instagram to begin with. So, no need to get offended."

Brex turned her attention to take another glance at the pastel sketch of Boston and asked, "What made you want to draw Boston like that?"

"That?" Logan pointed. "That was just to help my anxiety. I needed something calm. But I submitted it to the school paper last year 'cause I thought people would like it, and they did, so they printed it."

"They did? That's awesome!" Not that she was surprised at all, but she still wanted him to know that she was impressed.

"Yeah. You would have been able to see it if you were here last—if—I mean—" In that single moment, he regretted ever being able to talk. His head and fingers twitched with distress while his body temperature shot up at least five degrees.

Although Brex didn't even blink an eye. Her focus was still on her favorite image on the board.

"It's okay. Don't work yourself up. You think you're the first person to say something like that to me since I've been back? Everyone in the art department has a thing for gossip. I'm also not the only college student in the world who's dropped out." Brushing it off like it was no big deal, she walked away with a wide smirk that made her cheekbones look twice as big. "Let's go back out and actually be social."

Beckoning him with a slow and petite head tilt, she opened the door and immediately started awkwardly rocking her hips from side to side, offbeat to the music.

It was no big deal, Logan thought, but his heart rate still hadn't de-escalated. Yet he shrugged his shoulders and followed her straight out the door.

The music changed to an EDM song that almost everybody knew. The living room was almost twice as crowded, and there was now a two-by-eight-foot table that was hosting beer pong towards the side of the room.

Lexi drank her rum punch in the corner with Shani and Jenna. As a side effect of Shani's buzz beginning to wear off, she leaned up against the wall with her mouth closed tight and her eyes darting diagonally towards the floor.

"You sure you don't want another one, Shani?" Lexi asked.

"Noooo. I'm gooood."

"Smart choice."

Most of the time, Lexi wasn't much of a gossiper. It usually made her feel uncomfortable and awkward, but at this point, she was drunk enough to talk about politics, religion, money, and body odor all at the same time and be completely fine with it.

"Can you guys keep a secret?" Lexi asked.

"Juicy high school gossip that I'm too old to enjoy?" Jenna eagerly inquired. "Please, do tell."

"Weeeeell," Lexi second-guessed her level of intoxication that would assist her in moving forward with this conversation, but she desperately felt the need to tell someone. "What would happen if a professor slept with a student?"

Both Shani and Jenna were expecting to be asked anything but that question, but they proceeded to interrogate.

"Um, wow," said Shani. "Who is sleeping with who? And please don't tell me you walked in on two people banging."

"Not banging." Lexi kept her head down, hoping Shani wouldn't guess whom she was referring to. "I don't want to rat anybody out, but I think this is pretty ser—"

"Oh no," Shani interrupted. "You didn't see... Anika?"

Lexi stood there still without saying a word, which immediately gave Shani her answer.

"Lexi, who is Anika sleeping with?"

There was no point in hiding anything anymore. Shani would know what to do.

"I mean..." She scrunched her face, so her eyes were barely showing and lowered her voice so softly that she started to mumble. "Morialsa."

Instead of being shocked, Shani slowly lifted her eyes toward the ceiling as if she were thinking about what that experience might be like.

"Anika? And Morialsa?" Jenna asked. "What a cliché, a cheerleader and a professor?"

"That's a cliché?" Shani asked.

"It should be, it's kind of enjoyable to think about."

Lexi rolled her eyes, wanting the conversation to refocus.

"I mean...do I tell someone or...?" Lexi continued until Jenna cut her off.

"Is she holding something over you?"

"What?"

"I'm just saying. Do we really care about the sexy Brit-boy getting fired, or getting Anika expelled?"

As much as she disliked Anika, the truth was no. So, she shook her guiltless head.

"So," Jenna continued. "if Anika ever thinks she has something over you like the bitch that she is, you can prove her wrong. Only if you keep it a secret."

"Yeah, you're right," Lexi said. Anika had been desperate for what felt like months to try and get her to leave. Who knew what kind of nonsense she could get Lexi and her friends into? "Anika? Really?" Jenna added. "I know they're both consenting adults, but he could literally have anybody else in the school, and he chose Anika? And isn't it like the second week of school? How much of a ho is she?"

"I mean, I used to be curious about his kinks in bed," said Shani. "But now I don't even wanna know."

"Wowwww." Jenna's lips puckered like she was being kissed by a cartoon character. "The Amazon has found a twenty-five-year-old Jared Kushner."

"Ew," Shani snarled before the three of them shared a loud, intoxicated laugh that made a few people stop dancing and stare at them.

"What are you assholes cracking up about?" Brex asked, suddenly walking up and sliding into the conversation.

Shani grabbed her hand, leaned over to her, and snickered "I'll fill you in later." They subtly laughed into each other as they migrated their way to the dance floor.

Logan, Asher, and Adam all casually trickled their way back into the living room. Asher and Adam were playing a game of flip cup in the kitchen and taking tequila shots while Logan challenged his teammate, Kerry Gruber, to a game of beer pong. Logan lost miserably with six cups still left on Kerry's side. Usually, he was a fairly sore loser under the rare circumstance, but he promised his therapist he would attempt to improve his negative habit by smiling and encouraging the opposite player. In this scenario, Logan forcefully high-fived Kerry, but missed the first time and made him redo it. Then he awkwardly patted him on the back, but he whacked so hard that it looked more like he was burping a child, and Kerry almost let out a violent cough.

Nonetheless, they all met where the bass was strong and the energy was high. Jenna eventually escaped into Johnny Knight's room, not to be seen again. Brex couldn't blame her. Johnny was the tallest and, besides Logan, the most muscular player on the football team, and Jenna objectified men more than anyone she knew.

Time seemed to fly by for the next few hours. Shani wanted to be home by three in the morning, but when she checked her phone at 3:12, she decided she might as well wait until four at that point.

When Lexi finally saw her phone turn 4:03, she suggested they leave. Shani had to be at the aquarium in the early afternoon, and they were all, for the most part, sober.

Logan and a couple of the other frat's boys had migrated into the kitchen to raid the refrigerator and snack cabinets.

"You guys heading out?" Logan asked, as he saw them coming towards him.

"Yeah, I have to adult in the morning unfortunately," said Shani, hugging him goodbye.

"Next time, just crash here. As you can see, there's plenty of room."

"Eh," Brex mumbled. "We don't wanna overpower your bachelor pad with our strong femininity."

Logan knew she was being dead serious, but he laughed and acted like it would be no big deal anyway.

"You leaving already, Everly?" Kerry asked Brex. The only conversation she had ever had with Kerry was freshman year when he had asked her for a pen in their literature class.

"Uh, yeah..." she answered, confused as to why he cared. "I've been here for a while." His eyes were red, he was heavily breathing through his mouth, and his back was slightly hunched over. Not only was he smashed, but his eyes were bloodshot red, and he reeked of weed.

"You know, you were the talk of the art department however long ago it was now. Everyone was obsessed with you." He took a few stumbling steps closer to her before Logan slapped his hand on Kerry's chest.

"Dude, she's leaving. Let it go," said Logan in his shaky, stern voice.

Brex didn't seem to mind. She politely gave the room a smile and turned around with the others.

"We all thought you were like...killed." And the nerve was struck. She suddenly stopped and turned around. The look on her face seemed perplexed, but sullen at the same time.

"What?" she quietly asked. Until now, people asking about her disappearance didn't seem to bother her, but seeing her eyes fill up with animosity and fear worried the others, especially Logan.

All of a sudden, Shani felt something quickly heat up next to the bare skin on her leg. She looked down at Brex's hand and forearm. The color of her skin was bright orange with blotched patches of red. It was as if Brex's limbs were itching to explode with fury. Tension was rising, and Shani immediately grabbed Brex's hand with the hope that nobody would see, and Brex would calm down.

"Isn't that what everyone always thinks?" Kerry uncontrollably laughed. "Like in movies, when you disappear. Everyone always just thinks you're dead."

Air rushed into Brex's lungs in relief. She cracked an uncomfortable half-smile and said, "Oh yeah. I guess you're right. Well, surprise! I'm alive." She turned back around and started to head out the door once again with the others following her.

Kerry aimlessly wandered away with a beer still in his hand. The rest of the people in the kitchen stiffly looked away as if they had witnessed nothing.

Logan's anxiety kept him from thinking about anything else for the rest of the night. In a way, he felt like their friendship did blossom, but from another perspective, he felt more closed off from her than before. He didn't need to know everything from her past. Nobody did, but he wanted her to be able to open up to him and the rest of the group if she wanted to. Maybe she understandably didn't want to disclose to some drunk classmate that she barely knew, or maybe she didn't want to disclose at all.

10:

"And she's keeping track."

Brex dumped her school books onto one of the library tables far away from any of the windows that shined with sunlight beaming through them. While being hungover and dangerously behind on her art history and photojournalism homework, she also hadn't finished reading the untranslated journal the girls found, let alone deciphered it.

Once her laptop was up and running, she typed "impressionism with watercolor" into Google. Whether she was doing this assignment correctly or not was thoroughly unclear to her. For the last week, getting a full night's sleep had been a struggle, which made her doze off in a few of her classes. Staying out until four in the morning the previous night certainly didn't help.

After about a half an hour of offhandedly pushing her way through her art history assignment, she felt it was a good time to take a power nap. There was hardly anyone left in the library. What harm could it do?

She comfortably crossed her forearms together, laying them flat on the table. Then, right as she was about to doze off, a pair of boney, yet strong hands grabbed her by the upper arms.

"BOO!" a voice softly shouted behind her. Before fully processing what was happening, Brex's initial instinct was to headbutt this person with the back of her skull. Fortunately, for both of them, she snapped her head around instead to see Logan's obnoxious grin plastered to his face.

"You know I could light your hair on fire, right?" His facial expression went from goofily proud to slightly offended in half a heartbeat. "Haven't you ever heard the expression 'Let a sleeping dragon lie'?"

"Isn't it 'Let a sleeping dog lie'?"

"You wish it was a dog."

"Ouch." Logan sat himself down on the other side of her table while Brex wiped her eyes and brushed the hair off her face.

"You know it's Saturday, right? You can go to sleep," said Logan.

"No. No, I—I can't. I already asked for an extension on an assignment that was due Thursday. I have to finish it tonight. My professor is already taking ten goddamn percent away from me. I can't let it be any more. I stayed out way too late last night, and this hangover is somehow getting worse."

"Really? I thought you barely drank anything last night?"

"Well, you don't know what it's like to be this tiny, might I remind you."

Logan laughed and tried his best to show sympathy without making her uncomfortable.

"I'm sorry. Is there anything I can help you with? I mean we've taken a lot of the same classes."

Thinking of something for Logan to help her with only made her more anxious. It was as if she were trying to pull something out of her cramped brain with a rope, but it was stuck from the overcrowding. But she appreciated the offer too much to show that to Logan.

"Nah, it's okay. I just have a lot to catch up on, and—I gotta pace myself." She gave him half a smile and started aimlessly rummaging through her books again. "What are you doing in the library anyways? Don't you have like two classes this semester?"

"Again, ouch," he responded, trying to make her laugh. "I needed a book for my drawing class. And then I saw you, and to be honest, the more peaceful you looked, the more tempted I was to scare the living shit out of you."

Brex fought a laugh with all of the muscles in her body, but they couldn't take it. She quietly exhaled into a smile and tilted her head down to look at her shoes. Logan couldn't help but feel a bit of pride and relief rush through him, knowing Brex at least didn't find him completely annoying.

"Hey, have you figured out what that book says yet?" Logan asked.

"No. I tried, but it's definitely some sort of dead language that people don't use anymore, like Latin." She leaned her head down onto her planted fist but fought against her tired eyes.

"Why don't you let me try? I think my dad still speaks a little bit of Chinese. Maybe he'll recognize a few of the characters."

Brex didn't even hesitate for a second before she reached into her bag and plopped the dusty old journal onto the table.

"Be my guest."

Logan couldn't hold back the surprised look on his face. He knew Brex well enough at this point to understand her control issues. Now, she was going to give the book up like that?

"Why, thank you," Logan teased while slipping the journal into his bag. He zipped up his backpack and looked back at Brex. Something was off. She was looking past Logan's shoulder with an aghast stare. The color in her face was completely drained, and her eyes sunk out of her head.

"What?" Logan abruptly asked, but she didn't respond. He turned around to see what could possibly be wrong. Everything seemed normal until he spotted the T.V. It was silent, but on the screen was a fire. A building was burning down to the ground, and on the screen read "Another Tragic and Unexplained Fire Set to Cabin in the Mountains!" It was being broadcast live from the White Mountains in New Hampshire.

Brex broke from her trance and with a shiver in her vocal cords, she said, "We need to tell the others."

.....

Back at the Main Street apartment, Shani was making popcorn for everybody while the rest crowded around each other and shuffled through the book.

There were a few main conclusions that they were able to determine about the book so far; the pages were numbered, and it went to about 250 pages, but not even a quarter of it was filled out. There were numerous drawings, but only one of them they recognized, and whoever wrote in the book was left-handed. (Lexi recognized the smudges that lefties tend to leave when they write.)

"Okay," Logan started. "My dad said that this is probably Magadhi, but it's actually Indian. He's had a lot of clients there apparently."

"Indian?" Shani curiously asked.

"Yeah, a lot of people speak it, in fact. It's like an insanely ancient language."

Maybe Shani was being judgmental again, but she thought it might be a good idea to point it out anyway.

"Remember that eel I told you guys about? The one that won't talk to me, but told me about this person that he hadn't seen in decades?"

Everyone nodded, unsure of where she was headed with this topic.

"I looked up his name, Ilisa. It's Indian. I mean, think about it. They clearly both know what our scars mean. They're both probably eighty years old for all we know. This person could be who Ilisa was talking about."

"I mean that would make sense," Logan said, holding up the book. "That eel said they would probably know something about how we got our powers, right? It seems like this person has it all written down in here."

"I think whoever resided in that basement was a woman," Lexi said, trying not to be rude by interrupting. "I believe I did see a fancy hairpin all dusty on the floor when we were there, but I mean you never know, it's 2017."

Shani thought for a moment before remembering more of her conversation with Ilisa.

"Yeah, yeah, yeah!" Shani said, nodding her head and shaking her index finger. "He said this person was a woman!" She high fived Lexi from across the table.

"An Indian woman." Asher stated. "That narrows it down."

"Okay," Shani began. "I see your point, but there's—"

"Guys," Logan interrupted. "Look at this." He had turned to the back of the book. The last two pages on the left side. Logan read a list of almost a hundred different female names, first and last, but they were all written phonetically.

Written across from each name was a location. Each one was different from the next.

"What is this? How did we not catch this?" Logan asked.

"Look!" Lexi shouted. "At the bottom!" The bottom name nobody recognized, but as for the location, they did.

"Boston, Massachusetts," Lexi continued. "What if these are all different identities?"

"And she's keeping track," Brex added. "She must be running from someone."

"She wasn't just hiding in the cave," said Logan. "She was protecting it from whoever started that fire and had that crazy dog. But we got to it first."

"Wow. One hell of a job she did," said Shani, sarcastically.

It was all starting to make a little more sense now. Nothing made a perfect clicking noise in their heads yet, but the five of them sat there soaking everything in and scanning through more of the names written in the book.

"What's the name next to the Boston location?" Brex added, looking over the table.

"Ruth Lindy," Logan answered. He typed her name into Google search with "Boston" followed by it.

"It looks like she was doing something with publishing and marketing or something like that, but there's barely any advertising for her business. Just a few Yelp reviews, but I mean that might not even be her. I guess that makes sense though. She was trying to hide."

As Shani was scanning the list to see where the other locations were, she spotted a name that she vaguely recognized.

"Guys, look," she said. "Elise Patel. That's the name of the woman that died in the fire in 1937. From that article that I found. Remember?"

"Shit, yeah! Man, how is that a thing? How old could she be?"

Shani paused before she answered. She knew some hard-core convincing was about to be needed.

"I will bet you anything that it has something to do with reincarnation," she said, waiting for a chuckled reaction. It sounded even weirder coming out of her mouth than it did in her head.

"I'd buy that," said Brex, with a straight face.

"Thank you, Brex," said Shani loudly, aggressively presenting her hand to Brex. "It said in the article about her that she died in the fire. That's the only explanation."

"Wait," Asher stopped with his eyes pensively closed and his hand up. "I thought that reincarnation was like a...Buddhist thing."

"It is," said Shani, stating what she thought was obvious.

"But Greek mythology...I thought that was our 'real fate' or whatever you want to call it."

"I guess we'll still never know our true fate, even with all this knowledge, and trust me, I think that's going to be a good thing."

"Question," said Brex, wanting to change the subject. "How do we put this language into Google Translate?" Nobody answered. They were stumped.

"Are we going to have to hire somebody to translate this whole thing?" Asher asked. "There's no way any of us will be able to afford that."

Shani started pacing back and forth from the end of the table to the wall.

"No, no," she said. "All we have to do is highlight the parts that we think are important." She eagerly went to her room and came back into the kitchen with purple sticky notes. "Okay, what's first?"

Logan flipped through the pages while the rest of them propped their upper bodies on the tables, so they could get a good look at the book.

"Um...this page," said Logan, pointing to the page with the sketch of their scar. Shani ripped a sticky note in half and stuck it onto that page. They repeated the same thing for four other pages. The second one was a page with two identical blue crystals both impaled with hooked strings as necklaces. The third and fourth were the last two pages of writing before the blank pages. They figured this had the most recent information as to where this woman might be, or her latest discoveries, and the final page contained the sketch of what looked like a valuable, fossilized coin.

"Look at the border," said Brex, referring to the sketch. "It's a Greek crown. Ya know? The ones that they crowned the men with if they won the ancient Olympic games or something like that."

"Nice catch!" Shani exclaimed. "Now we just gotta figure out who's gonna translate this for us."

"Why don't we ask your dad if he knows someone? He said he has those clients, right?" Asher asked, looking at Logan. He looked down at the table as if somebody just asked him to drop and do twenty push-ups.

"Okay," Logan mumbled, putting his finger in the air. "Texting him a picture and asking one simple question was one thing. But you want me to actually go ask him for a favor in person?" The rest of them looked unimpressed.

"Is that too much work for you?" Brex teasingly asked.

"For me? No. For my dad? I might as well ask him to mow all of Iceland."

"Just tell him it's for a project. He's strict about you getting good grades, isn't he?"

Logan was never enthusiastic about asking his dad for help, but Brex made a fair point. His father might go a little easier on him if it was for school, but no matter what, it was still going to be like sticking a needle in his eye.

"Okay, fine. I'll print out pictures of this and go visit his office tomorrow morning."

"Amazing," said Shani. "We should also eventually try and find some videos of the fire and see if there's anything that we missed."

"Yeah and compare the two videos. Both of them. From the White Mountains and from here," Brex added.

"Great. Brex, you and I will do that. Lexi, do you still have those leaves you took from the building? Have you evaluated them yet?" Shani asked.

Similar to Logan's reaction, Lexi agonized saying the word "Yeaaah," while trying to act like it was no big deal.

"You sure?" Shani asked. "That didn't seem too confident."

"Yeah I just gotta...um...do a few things first."

"Alright," said Shani, barely disguising her confusion. "Let's keep each other updated."

.....

The next morning, Logan rolled out of bed, sore and unenthusiastic about moving any part of his body. Not just because of playing his rough, winning game the night before, but also because of his unfortunate meeting he was about to have with his father. He loved his father dearly, but asking him for favors always made Logan worry about their relationship. It wasn't in Shane Kwan's nature to compromise.

The father-and-son conversations that they had were never about girls, or feelings, or even Logan's mom. They were always about the future. It took a lot of convincing to let Logan major in graphic design. It wasn't until after Mr. Kwan looked up how much graphic designers could make in a year that Logan could even start sending in his portfolios.

Explaining his major to his father was also a challenge. Mr. Kwan couldn't wrap his head around the idea that Logan needed expensive equipment and technology if he was "just doodling." Logan didn't even bother telling him about the nude sketching class he had to take his junior year.

As he moped down the stairs, he noticed his frat brothers had left the house a mess after the game and after Logan had already gone to bed. Dishes overflowed in the sink, trash was everywhere, and on top of that, somebody had poured a beer in the corner of the living room and didn't bother to clean it up. It was just one of those moods that invoked him to leave a note on the kitchen table that said, "Wow. Clean up, before I get back, please!" And as he exited through the front entrance, not only did he slam the door as hard as he could, he rang the doorbell continuously for at least twenty seconds before he left just to make sure somebody would wake up.

He hopped on the train and headed to his father's office. While walking up the stairs to Kwan Legal Services he ran through what he was going to say over and over again in his head.

"Hi, Dad. How are you?...Good. So, I need a favor. I just need these random things of no importance...No that's stupid."

He thought it would be best to just wing it.

Knock, knock, knock.

Logan peaked his head through the office door.

"Son!" said Mr. Kwan. "Come on in." He seemed to be in a good mood. Better than usual.

"Hi, Dad." Logan tried his best not to give off the impression that he was only there because he wanted something.

"How's school going? You enjoying the nice weekend?" Logan's nerves started to get to him when his dad didn't put down the documents he was organizing to talk to him.

"Oh...it's great. Starting to get a little bit of senioritis though," Logan joked.

"Don't you worry. You'll go out with a bang. How was the game last night? Sorry I couldn't come."

"It was great. We won. Pretty easily too."

"Ahh. My son, the beast." Mr. Kwan gave off a radiant and proud look. Did Logan genuinely want to spoil it?

"Look, Dad. I uhh...have a little favor to ask," Logan said with his head down and his voice lowered. "Remember that picture I sent you of that language? I had no idea what it was? You told me it was probably that Mangahdi language?"

"Yes."

"Well, it's for a project, and it turns out I actually need it translated." He pulled out the pictures of the book from his backpack and placed them on Mr. Kwan's desk.

"What class could this be for?" asked Mr. Kwan. Logan's chest collapsed inward for half of a second when he realized he hadn't prepared an answer to that question.

"Uhh...Art History," Logan blurted out. "It's from a really, really old book, and I just need to know the meaning of it." Mr. Kwan didn't look like he was being disturbed yet, just confused.

"So, your teacher gave you this mysterious project. Didn't tell you what language or country it was from because apparently they don't know either, and on top of that they want you to translate it and don't tell you how?"

He could not have made the circumstance sound more awkward if he had tried. Logan thought the best way to get out of this crisis was to just play along.

"Yeah, I know. It's weird right?"

"I'll say," Mr. Kwan laughed. "These professors have you kids jumping through hoops nowadays. That's a good thing."

Shocked at his response, Logan continued to try to act routinely.

"Couldn't agree more, Dad." He quietly forced a shaky laugh. "So, you know people who can translate it, right?"

"Um, yes. I think Gina, my assistant, you remember her, right? I'm sure she learned a little bit about this in school. That's what she told me anyway, but it's Sunday, so she won't be here 'till tomorrow. We'll get around to it, okay?"

"Yeah! It's not due for a while, so no problem." Why did he say that? He could have said it's due on Friday or Thursday. Now, it was going to feel like an eternity until he got those translations, and the others will be anything but patient or pleased.

"But...didn't you have an Art History class last year, or something?"

"Oh...yeah. I have to take a few different Art History classes. Ya know there's just so much to learn."

"Really?" Mr. Kwan's reaction was less perplexed and more impatient. "Shouldn't you be taking more business classes for your major? I mean you already know how to do all of the...uh...painting, and drawing, and doodling stuff."

Logan was foolish to think he could get away with a single conversation with his father without him using the word "doodling" to describe his major.

"Yes. I know, Dad. I'm taking business classes, so don't worry." Logan slowly started to walk backwards trying to indicate he was ready to leave. "I'm gonna go now. Lots to do."

"Ah, go get 'em. And Logan, I'm going to try and come to your game next week, okay?"

Mr. Kwan was usually attentive when it came to Logan's athletic activities, but he would go through phases that usually revolved around work. He would regularly come to his games for a few months at a time, and then disappear for another few months with the excuse of "long meetings" and "extensive phone calls." Currently, his dad was in his "disappear" phase. Logan wasn't going to get his hopes up.

"Thanks, Dad. That'd be cool, and don't worry. I totally get it if you can't." They exchanged smiles, and Logan strolled out the door.

It was sprinkling by the time Logan came outside again. He waited under the four-foot by four-foot awning and ordered an Uber. Before he closed his phone, Adam texted him a few photos of the game from the night before that Adam's brother, Ryland, had taken. Logan opened up one picture to see himself the moment after he ripped off his helmet in response to winning the game. With the sweat, dirt, shining lights in the background. It was an Instagram-worthy photo.

He pushed the lock button on the side of his phone, but through the reflection of the screen, he saw something that he wasn't expecting to see.

A sliver of a human face was hiding behind the corner of a brick building and staring straight in Logan's direction. They couldn't have been more than twenty feet away from Logan, but by the time Logan turned around, they had vanished. Whoever it was, they were definitely following him.

Was it a man? A woman? He could barely even see what they were wearing. What was the point in following Logan? What were they trying to see or find?

"Hey, kid!" said the Uber driver pulling up to the sidewalk. "You getting in?"

11:

"Yeah, but they're probably long dead by now."

Another Monday rolled by. Being New England weather, the temperature dropped from eighty-five degrees to sixty-two overnight. About half of campus switched from their Boston Red Sox baseball caps to Patriots' beanies.

The lecture halls and classrooms were once again, all unlocked. Lexi was finally able to get her iPad back.

Wrapped in her new wool scarf, Lexi walked up to the door to meet the janitor who seemed to be opening the facilities for the public.

"Hello!" Lexi said to the old man, overly excited. "I left my iPad here the other day. Just wanna get it before somebody else does." She couldn't help but feel a little tense and nervous. It wasn't in her nature to lie or be rebellious, even though it wasn't close to being her first time.

"Oh...well, I'm supposed to clean a little first, but alright." The janitor slowly opened the door to let her in.

"Oh my God! Sick!" said Lexi, still using her overly dramatic voice, "That would be just amazing thank you!"

Speeding by him, she carefully used her peripherals to make sure he wasn't watching everything she was doing. She heard him typing into the security alarm before she reached the entrance to the lecture hall where she patiently waited for him to unlock the double doors.

"You sure you left it in here?" the janitor asked.

"Yeah, I'm sure. I left it under the seat in the front row. Fourth from the left. Here, watch me."

Lexi took off down the center aisle to the front row. There, under her usual spot lay her iPad. Untouched. Almost dead, but it was still hers. Everything was safe. Arrests, expulsion, and enormous amounts of fines were no longer on the table.

"Thanks! Sorry about that!" The janitor gave her a less-than-impressed smile as she ran back up the aisle and out the door. A few more steps, and he was out of sight. She pulled her phone back out to see if she got a solid recording.

While the janitor was punching in the code to the security alarm, Lexi had managed to carefully place her phone in the outer pocket of her bag with the camera already zoomed in and recording. It caught everything. The flip of her skirt, the violent sway from her walk, and the security code to the building.

.....

Later that night, Lexi set her alarm for one in the morning. She wasn't much of a night person, and at least a small amount of sleep was a must. Anika had been nowhere to be seen the last three nights, so she was, thankfully, not a problem. By one-thirty, her hair was flipped up into a messy bun, her jean jacket was on, and she was out the door.

Acquiring the information that she needed about the building had not been a simple or easy task. She found out that professors commonly came into the building in the middle of the night or early in the morning. Therefore, if the alarm system were to send any sort of notification to the authorities, it wouldn't be out of the blue.

Lexi had to pry that information out of her math professor by asking, "I was just wondering, but are we allowed to come in here after hours with you? Just in case we don't have time during normal hours?" The professor without a doubt thought she was trying to be seductive. She could tell by the way she made him look distraught and uncomfortable. But he answered.

Of course, students weren't allowed to be in the building after hours, but there was no way of distinguishing between a teacher and a student. All they needed to gain entrance to the building was the code to the security alarm and, unfortunately, a key, but that was no disadvantage for Lexi.

Before she left, she had cut a small vine from her bedside plant. She tested it to see if it was slim enough to crawl into a keyhole and if she had developed enough skill to thoroughly manipulate it.

After a few failed attempts, she managed to make it rapidly twitch a few times with a little bit of organic movement. It was good enough for her. For now, it was her only choice.

The only other obstacle she had to overcome was the cameras that pointed toward the two main entrances. The service entrance near the dumpsters was the only other way inside. It was cameraless and completely non-surveilled, which meant there was no security alarm keypad anywhere near it. She would have to run, but that's what the pants were for.

Before approaching the service entrance, Lexi went through the alarm code over and over again.

"Six-five-three-two-six...six-five-three-two-six... Six-five-three-two -six..." Not a single second was to be spared.

A few feet away from the door, she searched around to make sure nobody was watching her. The air was completely silent and motionless. Everything was set.

The entrance was dim, and the smell from the dumpsters was so severe, Lexi had to cover her mouth and nose with the collar of her shirt. She tried to move quickly while pulling out the cut vine from her pocket and sliding it into the golden keyhole.

It took a few tries, but Lexi prepared her running stance and planted her left leg straight behind her right. She pulled the vine in and out of the lock multiple times before the keyhole slit turned to the left, and Lexi heard the faintest *click*. It took a moment to register before she caught her breath again and sprinted through the door.

It was like holding a plank in gym class. Everything in her body felt numb. She didn't feel the pain of pushing her feet as hard as she could, and the moments lingered on for longer than she ever wanted them too.

It couldn't have even passed ten seconds yet, she thought to herself as she continued to gasp for deep but short breaths. Before she knew it, the security pad was in sight. It was beeping louder than she had expected it to.

She unflipped the protection lid and carefully, but quickly, typed in the code.

"Six...five...three...two...six." But nothing happened. It continued to beep. What could have happened? She was sure it was right.

"Oh, shit! Enter!" Lexi slammed her finger down on the enter button while her heart almost jolted out of her chest. It beeped three times, one right after the other, and then it stopped. It was silent.

"All this for some damn equipment."

She was in. Everything was fine and running smoothly, but her temples still dripped with tiny droplets of sweat, and her muscles still shivered from the blood pumping so fast. The shoes on her feet made emphatic yet squeaky noises as her size-five feet ran up the towering staircase.

The coast seemed to be clear. No lights were on, no human-made sounds were to be heard. The likelihood of a teacher's or janitor's presence was slim to none.

Lexi jogged her way to the lab while holding her phone with the flashlight on. "Room 22A" read on the classroom door sign. After taking one last look around, she used her free hand to try to push down the door handle, but it wouldn't budge. It was, of course, locked.

"GOD FREAKING DAMMIT! WHY DOES EVERYTHING ALWAYS HAVE TO BE LOCKED?"

She didn't want to use her powers again. After they all agreed that it couldn't be safe, but what else was she supposed to do?

The vine was still squirming so violently in her pocket, it almost jumped out. Was there too much magic inside? Was that even possible? The science behind magic was like a Monty Python film; confusing and weird, but who couldn't love it?

Sliding off her sweaty palm, the vine slithered into the keyhole. This time it struggled a bit longer. A few tiny leaves flew from the lock while Lexi kept trying to turn the handle. She ran through a few alternative scenarios in case her one and only plan failed, but nothing was coming to mind.

The small, dying vine needed to stay calm. Lexi took a break from pushing down on the handle and held the end of the vine that was sticking out of the keyhole. It gently vibrated between her fingertips, but only for a small portion of a second before Lexi sent tranquilizing signals through her skin. It felt like her soul connected to the green creature. Suddenly, she had full control. She opened her eyes, and the handle was already turned down for her, and the door was ready to be pushed open.

"Sick. You know, you're a lot stronger than you look. I think Imma call you...Ivy," she said, pulling Ivy out of the lock. After pushing the door open and flipping on the lights, Lexi pulled her phone back out to video record everything in the entire room. Each and every item had to be placed back exactly where it was left. And gloves, gloves needed to be worn the entire time. Luckily, she knew exactly where they were. Under the teacher's desk, bottom drawer, to the right. Not a lot of students remembered to wear them at the beginning of each and every class. Lexi was usually the one at the beginning of the lesson handing them out since Professor Terri had tenure and didn't care what the students did.

She snapped on her disposable gloves, pulled the burnt and ziplocked leaves out of her jacket pocket, and got to work.

First step: testing the leaves for chlorine. The probability of the law enforcement officers testing the crime scene for chlorine was fairly high, but who could *really* trust any government intelligence anymore? She grabbed a test tube and a D.R.D. tablet to test the chlorine levels if there were any; dropped a piece of a leaf, water, and the tablet into the tube; and shook them all together. If the water turned pink, it meant chlorine was the chemical used to light the park and that building on fire. But of course, the tablet dissolved, and the water remained clear. Lexi took it as no surprise, but there was no harm in double-checking.

The next few steps she took included testing for benzene, ethanol, methanol, and pentane. Each test included various mixtures of chemicals that forced Lexi to wisely wear goggles and a lab coat. They were long, tedious procedures that made Lexi become fatigued, but after every test came out negative, she grew frustrated.

There was one test, however, that she didn't think was necessary to take. But as she thought more about it, the result would make sense.

She scrambled for more test tubes and other equipment that she needed, but unfortunately, there was one ingredient that she was not excited about getting: blood. Lexi groaned while tilting her head to the ceiling and reached for an alcohol wipe. After disinfecting the tip of her finger and the knife, she gently punctured her skin until drops of blood came seeping out. Holding her finger above the test tube, she took a few deep breaths through her nose to distract herself from the pain.

There was enough blood in the tube to get a solid test. Lexi wrapped a giant bandage around her finger and washed the knife. Then, she dropped another small section of a burnt leaf into the tube and prepared to put the sample underneath the microscope, but when her eyes and microscope focused onto the bloody slide, she discovered something she wasn't expecting to see.

"Really?" Lexi whispered to herself. Then, she thought of an idea, but for this experiment, she was going to need some help.

·····

Brex was dead asleep under her down comforter when the clock struck three a.m. The vibrating sound of her phone woke her from the deep comfort she desperately needed.

Her eyes took a few seconds to focus before she could reach for her phone to see who was calling. Part of her was relieved that it was only Lexi. The other part of her wanted to reach through the phone to strangle Lexi for waking her up four hours before her alarm was supposed to go off.

"You better be dying," said Brex, answering the phone.

"Quite the contrary. I need you for a moment."

Brex rubbed her eyes and flopped her head back on her pillow. She was already annoyed that Lexi had woken her up, but now she wanted Brex to physically get out of bed and participate in human interaction before the crack of dawn?

"What? Why? Lexi, it's the middle of the night."

"Yeah. I know. How else was I supposed to get access to all of the equipment from the lab?"

Suddenly Brex sprung up straight in her bed, now highly alert and attentive.

"WHAT? Lexi you broke into the lab? How? What? Elaborate, please."

"Why do you think I was putting this thing off for so long? But to be fair, it actually wasn't that hard. I can explain when you get here. Don't worry. It's all good."

"Okay, fine! Which building is it? What room?" Brex used all of the energy she possessed to reach for her jacket and slip on her sneakers.

"Meet me at the back entrance near the dumpsters of the science building."

After taking one last exhausted breath and grabbing her keys, Brex brushed her hair out of her puffy eyes and let out a long, "Kayyy."

It was unexpectedly freezing outside. The unprotected skin on Brex's ankles started to burn from the wind striking against them. It was the first time of the season that Brex could see her breath as it escaped her lungs. Fire would've come in rather handy.

She reached the back entrance to see Lexi, patiently waiting in the doorway.

"You're insane, you know that?" said Brex as she stopped in her tracks. The puffiness in her eyes died down, but she could still barely see Lexi's luminous blonde hair through the fog and dark skies.

"I prefer brave, but nonetheless, come on! I don't wanna be seen." Lexi beckoned Brex to follow her through the door, and they proceeded down the hall.

"So, are you gonna tell me how you almost got yourself expelled two weeks into your college career?" asked Brex.

"Hey! We already broke into a building illegally and almost got caught, but didn't. And like I said, not as bad as I thought it was going to be. The security code was the easy part. It was unlocking the door that was the hard part, but if I told you how I did that, you'd be pissed."

Brex didn't need to look at Lexi to follow what she was saying.

"You used your powers, didn't you?" Brex politely inquired.

"Well, what else was I supposed to do? I can't afford the equipment, and it's not like they're just going to casually let me in to run tests for a crime scene they don't know I stole from."

Feeling sympathetic, Brex understood. It was hard to fight with her. She would have done the exact same thing if she had Lexi's confidence.

"I get it," said Brex, feeling amused by Lexi's solid defense.

"And it's not like this woman who's been following me has hurt me yet. If anything, she's our one clue to finding out if we are actually in any danger."

"Also true," Brex added. "You haven't seen her again, have you?"

"No," Lexi answered as they both approached the lab door that Lexi had propped open. "But who knows? Maybe she'll turn up."

Lexi led Brex into the classroom where she had tiny, chopped-up pieces of leaves spread all around the table.

"Exactly how long have you been here?" asked Brex.

"Ehh...about two hours."

Lexi's back was turned away as Brex's eyes finally awakened in bewilderment. "Ah, I see." Brex scanned the table to read all of the labels Lexi had written below every sample. "Why exactly do you need me here?"

Lexi took a loud, deep breath in through her nose, trying to put off answering her question for as long as possible.

"Weeeell...I need your fire," she finally responded.

Without any hesitation or exasperation in her voice, Brex responded by saying, "Why?"

Lexi was so relieved that Brex wasn't screeching through her lungs that she almost forgot that Brex still had no idea why she was needed.

"Uh...well...I kind of have a weird theory that might not make a lot of sense, but I really think it's the only explanation as to how the fires started."

As she patiently nodded her head, Brex said, "Okay. Hit me."

"Okay, so, I was thinking that the start of it was from some sort of chemical, right? But I've tested multiple samples for multiple different flammable chemicals, gasoline of course, but also chlorine, acetone, anything that has a flashpoint of less than a hundred degrees Fahrenheit, but nothing came up."

"So," Brex interrupted. "You think that there's a magical chemical that was sprayed onto the trees and bushes ahead of time?" Scratching her head and fiddling with her hair, Brex tried her best to follow along.

"I mean, no. Not exactly." Lexi reached for an untouched sample of unburnt leaves and held it in front of Brex. "I need you to burn a little bit of this. Just trust me."

Brex slowly reached her hand out to take the sample out of Lexi's hand.

"Okay," Brex said in a gentle and breathy voice. The sample was small, no larger than two by two inches and cut up into a perfect square. Just like a match, Brex snapped her right index finger straight, and a small bulb of orange flame popped up from the tip. Carefully, she moved her finger closer to the sharp corner of the greenish leaf. Slowly but surely, the leaf's edge turned dark red with smoke profusely emitting from it.

"Cool," said Lexi after she blew the smoke out. "That's all I needed."

Only about a centimeter of the leaf was burnt off when Lexi took it out of Brex's hand to compare it to another sample. After staring at the burnt, cut-up leaves laid out on the table for a few moments, Lexi stood there boldly and still, without breathing. Something wasn't right. She couldn't believe what she was seeing.

"What's wrong?" asked Brex.

"No. No, this can't be right."

Brex patiently waited for an explanation, worried that everything Lexi had just done was about to go to waste.

"Look at this," said Lexi as she pointed to a group of samples labeled "Burnt with Bunsen Burner." "Look at the edges. They're a mixture of brown and black. Now look at the samples from the fire near the park. They're bright red and orange. They all come from the same kind of tree, and dead leaves don't look like that no matter how long they've been dead for."

Brex couldn't help but continuously look back and forth between the samples. She was right.

"And my sample?" asked Brex.

"That's the thing. I thought your flames were going to have the same chemical reaction as the ones from the fire, but it didn't. All fire has carbon monoxide, but the fire that burned down the Romanov building tested negative for carbon monoxide, but you tested positive. I didn't even think I was going to need to test for carbon monoxide, but thankfully, I did. The flames that you possess, they're just...normal."

Brex was catching on, but still had to ask, "Wait. So, what are you saying?"

"I don't think the fire that burned down that building was fire at all. At least not from...well...planet Earth...I guess? It sure as hell isn't on the periodic table."

Trying to take in everything that Lexi was saying, Brex was having a hard time believing that there was such a thing as "fake" fire. Her motto was always, *If it walks like a duck and quacks like a duck, guess what? It could be a few other things but shut up because it's probably a fucking a duck.*

Before Brex could say anything else, a realization came to mind. A realization that brought her frustration and hopelessness, but at least it was somewhat of an answer.

"And you thought that if whoever did this was like us, then we might have a better chance of tracking them down? But now that we know they aren't, we're basically back to where we started."

Lexi silently and slowly nodded her head.

Hope all of a sudden drained from Brex's body. She could feel her exhaustion again. Her elbows fell onto the table as she rubbed her eyes and pushed her hair back.

"It explains why the police couldn't find any flammable chemicals at the crime scene," said Lexi. "There were none, and we...we're the only ones that know about this."

Pensive and distressed, Brex stayed leaning against the table with her fists against her forehead.

"But," she said without moving. "Remember the eel that Shani told us about? He got scared when he saw Shani's scar? It made her think there are more people like us?"

"Yeah, but they're probably long dead by now. Didn't he say he was like a hundred years old or reincarnated or something like that?" Lexi brushed her long blonde wisps out of her face and started to clean up her mess.

"We don't know that," said Brex. "But we do know that either this talking eel can't be trusted or those people can't be trusted—"

"It doesn't matter," Lexi interrupted. "This guy won't talk to her. She won't be able to get anything out of him."

"Well, maybe he'll eventually crack. You know Shani. She'll beat it out of him eventually. And besides, maybe somebody else knows something."

12:

"Are you seeing what I'm seeing?"

Lexi texted the group chat about her gig for that night. This time, it was at a new restaurant called "Bevanda," an Italian place with supposedly the best pasta sauce in all of Boston. Asher replied in the group chat, asking if they had cheese-filled pizza crust. The moment after Lexi texted the word "Yeah" Asher immediately replied with his R.S.V.P. without any more questions.

"There's no force on Earth that can come between me and my cheese-filled pizza crust," was Asher's catchphrase before he started taking Lactaid.

Brex helped Lexi haul her equipment to the restaurant. Luckily, it only took them one trip, and Brex dug out her giant suitcase to put Lexi's new speaker equipment in. After almost finishing assembling everything for her set, Shani and Asher strutted through the door.

"Thanks for coming early to help us guys," said Brex sarcastically. "You're real troopers."

"Hey!" Shani exclaimed and put up her index finger. "I had a lab report to finish that I basically had to pull out of my ass. You're lucky I didn't show up late to the show."

Every last cord was plugged in, and Lexi's guitar was tuned and ready. She warmed up in the bathroom and fixed her makeup while the rest ordered their drinks.

"How are we all doing tonight?" Lexi blurted into the microphone after she hopped onto the stage with her newly bedazzled guitar. The crowd responded with a polite clap except for the hollering from the table the others sat at. Asher even got up and did a little hip swing that was a failed attempt at twerking, but Brex slapped his right glute anyway.

Lexi started off with an acoustic version of "September" by Earth, Wind, and Fire. A great way to ease into the crowd. She slowed down the tempo by just a hair and added a tasteful syncopation to it.

"*Ah—Ee—Ahh! Say that you remember! Ah—Ee—Ah! Dancing in September...*"

The crowd was eating it up. Mainly because there was a group of old ladies in the front row that kept screaming "Knock those boys dead, baby!" They became louder and less articulate as they kept drinking. It made Lexi keep giggling while she was singing, but she didn't mind. She was just glad there was no fire burning down a building next door.

"Sorryyy," Logan whispered as he sat down in the booth with Brex, Shani, and Asher. "Had to finish a project and run to my dad's office."

"She's got plenty of songs left. Don't worry," said Brex.

Logan headed to the bar to order a drink, but had a hard time getting by the old ladies who were now waving their arms from side to side in the air and singing along to a song no one in the bar recognized, including the old ladies. They mumbled whatever came to their mouth first, but luckily Lexi's microphone was overpowering them.

"So," Shani started when everyone was seated and attentive in the booth. "What's everyone's updates?"

"I got the translations," said Logan, pulling out a brown folder from his bag with paper hanging from it.

"Amazing. What'd they say?"

"I don't know. I just got them." He slid the files out from the folder to see that Gina had written the translation on the back of the pictures, but on the picture with the necklaces drawn on the front, there was one paragraph on the side written in a smaller font than the rest.

Hey, Logan!

I was able to translate most of the words, but a lot of it was written in incomplete sentences. It seems like whoever wrote this was just scribbling some things down. Also, I believe they wrote some slang here and there that also was a little tough to translate, since it was probably written years and years ago, and it was probably written by a person who was from a different part of India than my dad. Definitely not the type of stuff that I did in college! Haha! Hope your project goes well! And good luck with football season!

- Gina

"Alright," said Brex. "So, what was she able to translate?"

Logan turned his eyes to the few lines written on the other side of the paper. About two-thirds of the characters had English words translated underneath them.

"Okay," said Logan, clearing his throat. "All she was able to translate was; Souls, Dublin, South Africa, Caribbean, Boston, Change, Not, One with Shiva, Immortal, Devil, and Broke. Or at least that's all she had on this page. Also, South Africa is crossed out."

Shani puckered her lips in confusion.

"So, she only figured out one phrase? 'One with Shiva'? And who's Shiva? That's not a name on the list." Shani flipped through the book to the very last page, and scanned to see if she had missed the name "Shiva," but it was a dead end.

"Hold on," said Asher, pulling up the Google app on his phone. After typing the name into the search bar, the exact result he was looking for immediately came up. "Shiva; also known as Mahadeva, is one of the principal deities of Hinduism. He is the supreme being within Shaivism."

"Wait," said Shani. "Shiva is a man? And he's a....Hindu god?"

"Isn't one of your dads Indian?" asked Logan.

"Yeah, but he doesn't practice any religion. I don't know anything about that kind of stuff." Shani pulled out a small notebook from her purse before Brex caught her attention.

"Shani, you were right. There's more than just the Greek gods out there. Shiva, I mean whoever he is, wherever he is, he's real. Logan, you said one of those characters was 'the devil', right?"

"Yeah," said Logan, catching on to what she was implying. "You think they're referring to the Christian devil?"

"I do."

Asher turned towards the stage Lexi was on. Now she was playing a slow instrumental song that made the ladies in the front close their eyes and hug each other while swaying back and forth.

"Just wait 'till Lexi hears all of this," said Asher.

"What does the rest say?" asked Brex.

Logan flipped over the second page with the sketch of their scar on it and read "Timer, Magic, Year, Beyond, Largely Enhanced."

"Timer?" Shani repeated. "Interesting."

Lexi strummed the last few chords of her current song and smiled while the whole bar cheered.

"Alright, thank you, everybody. I'm gonna take a quick break. I'll be right back," Lexi said into the microphone before hopping off the stage and heading towards the table in the back. "What did I miss?"

"Shani's right, and there's a Hindu God alive and working with this woman that's been following us," said Logan.

Lexi bit her lips together in a contemplative manner, nodded her head, and said, "'Kay."

"We still have the last two pages to look at."

"Oh, sick." Lexi rubbed her hands together as if she were being handed a Classic New York Cheesecake for the first time.

On the last two pages, Gina circled four different characters and labeled them "Dates." They read; January 3rd 2016, April 26th, 2016, March 20th 2017, and August 27th 2017.

"August 27th," said Brex. "That was the day before the fire. Move-in day."

"What happened that day?" asked Shani.

"Hasn't been seen in months," Logan read. "Wow, a full sentence. Unfortunately, that's the only one, but it also reads; Spell renewed, protected, yesterday, and in my box."

"So, we *would* call this magic?" Asher asked. The rest of them glanced at each other, searching for a response to that question. "I just didn't know whether we would call it superpowers, or magical abilities or...whatever."

"You know, I think I like superpowers better," said Logan.

"That's what I think!" Asher perked up.

"Oh my God, boys!" Shani said.

"Sorry," said Logan, snapping his head back down to look at the page. "It doesn't say anything else about whatever spell they're talking about, but it does say the word, 'protect', so maybe they're talking about a protection spell?"

Brex recalled the night they broke into the building.

"The trunk, and all those artifacts, remember?" she said. "One of us suggested that there was probably some sort of protection spell on those things because they were completely untouched. There was barely even any dirt on them."

Lexi hit the table then snapped her finger and pointed at Brex to say, "Boom."

"You think that she put...or renewed, or whatever that protection spell on those things because she knew someone was coming?"

"Probably," said Shani. "We already knew she was in hiding."

A few feet away, Lexi saw the restaurant manager giving Lexi a forced grin and a thumbs up, indicating it was a good time for her to get back up on stage.

"Gotta go," said Lexi. "My original is up next, so listen up." She hopped back up on the stage, full of bright, but shaky energy. "So... everybody," she said leaning into the microphone. "This next song is an original. So, I'm a bit nervous for this next part."

"WOOO!" screamed one of the old ladies in the front.

"YOU'LL DO GREAT, SWEETIE!" said another.

Back at the table, Asher leaned into Brex and asked, "Next time, do you think we should be at that level since we're her actual friends?"

Brex glanced at the ladies once again, waving their arms in the air, before muttering back to him, "Uh, ch-ya."

The first chord that Lexi strummed was flawless. It was about eight bars of instrumental guitar playing until she sang. "Flowers blew beyond the sky..." were her first lyrics.

Everything was proceeding smoothly until Lexi's hand started to shake. The notes were progressively getting louder, and the vocal range was getting wider. It was only natural that Lexi felt a bit of tension. The last time Lexi performed, a fire blew up the building next door, and she got unwarranted superpowers, but something caught Shani and Asher's attention, something odd and impossible to ignore.

"Are you seeing what I'm seeing?" Shani asked Asher.

"Ohhh, shit," he responded. The small cactus that was sitting on a stool behind Lexi on the upstage left corner was slowly but surely growing. Lexi's tension was causing the wilderness around her to subconsciously change, and without missing a beat, Asher clumsily lunged forward and raced toward the cactus to block it with his body.

Luckily, the cactus was in the shadows of the stage and hidden from part of the audience due to a curtain that hung from a window, but it made the whole scenario look as if Asher was inappropriately staring at Lexi from behind while leaning onto the stage with one foot. The people whose eyes and ears were on Lexi almost immediately switched their attention to her new stalker.

"Hey, buddy," said the guy right next to him. He wore his gray hair in a low ponytail and a leather vest with colorful patches, none of them being recognizable to Asher. "What are ya doin' there? The lady is trying to sing." The large man took a few steps toward him, towering over Asher's awkwardly unstable body, which was roughly two heads shorter.

"Oh um..." Asher tried to think of a way to stall, but his mind went blank, and beads of sweat popped out of his forehead. "I just wanted a different view. Couldn't see very well over there."

Cracking his knuckles, the man took this as anything but the truth.

"Hey! Jimmy!" he said to the manager who was working behind the bar. "This creep over here is trying to disrupt this young lady's performance! And I smell beer on him!"

The old ladies in the front began to "boo" as Logan rushed over to try to save Asher from getting his face turned inside out. Lexi could see the cactus start to sprout from behind his head, and when Lexi stopped singing and turned around to see what all of the fuss was about, the spellbound, spiked-covered plant quickly gave her the answer. Clenching her fist and gasping for a quick deep breath, she pulled her shoulders away from her neck, lifted her chin and watched the cactus return to its normal size.

"What's going on here?" Jimmy asked.

"Oh, nothing!" Lexi yelled. "It's okay! He's my friend!"

"He was looking at you like a piece of meat!" the man said.

"OKAYYY!" said Logan, trying to push Asher out of the way. "It's all a big misunderstanding. He was just trying to see if her...uh...wire was mixed up."

"Looks like everything's fine, Rick," said Jimmy. Rick didn't like that answer.

"You keep playing, lil' lady," he said before heading back to the bar.

Lexi slowly and unsurely placed her hands back on her guitar to return to playing, unaware if it was the best idea.

"Okay," she said, continuing to strum.

Logan and Asher returned to their seats while Rick refused to take his snake eyes off Asher.

"What the hell is that guy's problem?" he asked.

"Just ignore him," said Brex.

The four of them ordered more drinks while Asher finally ordered his pizza. Even though he was worried Rick was going to somehow spit in it.

The night carried on as Lexi continued to play, and the drunk old ladies trickled out of the bar. It grew quieter by the minute.

Buzzzz...

Shani jumped as she received a text message, and just by intuition alone, she knew it was from someone she had no interest in talking to.

"Ughhh," she groaned. "Why does this kid keep bothering me?"

"Who?" Asher asked.

"Remember that kid, Seamus, I was telling you about? The tall, scruffy guy who thinks that he's entitled to everyone and everything?"

Brex came to a screeching halt. She almost choked on her drink before she slammed it down on the table.

"Describe this person more," she said.

Confused, Shani responded "Tannish skin, messy hair, blonde."

"Oh, sweet God." Brex dropped her head into her hands while her elbows leaned against the table. "How do you know him?"

"He works at the aquarium. The pricky shithead won't leave me alone. How do you know him?"

"Jenna set me up on a blind date with him. We met up at Lexi's last gig. The night of the fire. Barely lasted longer than like ten minutes though. He was creeping me out. I unfortunately forgot that Jenna has the absolute worst taste in men."

Logan awkwardly twitched, knowing exactly who she was talking about. He hardly remembered what the guy looked like, but he decided to not add to the conversation.

"Thanks for telling me," said Shani.

"Of course," Brex responded. "But why? Couldn't you already tell he was an ass? You weren't considering letting him into your pants, were you?"

"Oh, hell no! It's just now I have more of a reason to punch him in the face if I need to." They high fived from across the table.

"If there's anyone who knows how to handle a mess like that kid," said Brex, "it's you." But as the last word escaped her mouth, her appearance changed from flippant to concerned and pensive.

"What?" Logan and Asher simultaneously asked.

"How long has he been working at the aquarium?" Brex asked, looking at Shani.

"I don't remember. It was like seven years or something like that. He's a bit older than us."

Brex silently looked down at her lap, still keeping the same look on her face, but they could tell too many thoughts were scurrying through her brain.

"And he just happened to be flirty with both of us?" she said, finally breaking the silence. "And he also just happens to be working at the same place as that talking eel man who probably knows more about our lives than we do?"

They could all see where she was going with these questions, but Shani wasn't buying any of it.

"You think he's involved with this somehow?" Shani asked before Brex gently nodded her head. "Oh, come on. He went on an awkward date with you before we got our scars, and I also got the internship there way before any of this happened. I just—I don't know."

Without hesitating, Brex responded by suggesting, "What if we were set up?"

Even though the rest of the restaurant couldn't hear what they were saying, the whole room sizzled with a significant decrease in volume. The mood was suddenly softer, and whether they wanted to admit it or not, they had to take what she was saying with concern.

"Okay," said Shani. "That's an idea. Although as much as I can't stand this guy, I just don't think it really adds up, but I trust you. I'm not sure how, but I will look into it."

Brex felt a great amount of respect from Shani. All any of them wanted to do at this point was follow their instincts.

"I mean," Brex continued. "Lexi and I were talking about how we think...we think somebody else at the aquarium might know some things. We were thinking it was going to be another fish, but in my opinion, it's definitely something to consider."

Shani gave a silent nod with a trusting yet gentle smile.

"Alright," she said, holding her glass in the air. "Enough talk. Let's drink up!"

•••••

The rest of the night was a blur. Not only because of the alcohol, but also because of how long Lexi's set was. She was only scheduled to play for two hours, but the manager asked her to keep playing for another hour and a half and offered to pay her double. Some of the song requests required her to pull up lyrics and chords from Google onto her phone, but the crowd loved it.

Brex walked into her room, humming and dancing to a song that she didn't know the title of and barely knew the correct lyrics to.

"Huh—dee—dah—rolly—molly," she sang while opening her door. She reached for the light switch, but nothing happened. The bulb must have burnt out. Nonetheless, she continued to flip the switch back and forth, hoping something would happen, but of course, nothing did.

Checking the hall to see if the coast was clear, she snapped her fingers to make a non-threatening ball of fire appear, floating above her finger tips. It would have been just as easy to turn on the flashlight within her iPhone, but she argued to herself that this way was much more authentic and lively.

She searched underneath her bed for her favorite scented candles that she wasn't supposed to have in her bin. It was labeled; *Men After a Shower*, and it of course smelled like a freshly showered man if he bathed with Aéropostale cologne.

With the flames coming from her fingertips, she lit the candle and placed it beside the picture on her desk of herself and her younger brother, Odin. He always teased her for her obsession with this candle. She insisted that one should be lit at the dinner table, which in a way, she knew was a little weird, but she usually just wanted to cover the smell of her mom's terrible cooking.

Suddenly, she heard her phone ring. Before she answered it, or even looked to see who it was, she checked the time. It was almost 11:30 at night. Who could possibly be calling?

"Grandma Martha," the phone said.

"Of course," Brex whispered before she answered her grandmother's call for the third time that day. "Hey, why are you calling so late?" She paused to let her grandmother answer, but was shocked and disheartened to learn what she had to say.

"Wait what?" Brex asked. "What do you mean?... What are you saying?...Why?...Is it really that bad?...What the hell am I supposed to do? Just not go to school?...Nobody else has a better credit score or something?...Yes, I understand....I'm sorry. Thank you for trying anyways...I'm sorry...I really want to go to bed... Okay, love you, bye." Devastated and nearly breaking into tears Brex let her body clumsily fall onto her bed.

It wasn't that she felt sad, just low and hopeless, but something else was off, and she couldn't put her finger on it. It wasn't depression that now caught her attention, but negativity, as if something had now been lost. She pulled her hands away from her head to see a sudden change on her scar. The arrow that was always pointing towards her middle finger on the left hand, was now pointing closer to her ring finger, as if the clock was now striking 12:02.

She glanced back and forth between her scar and the candle. It was so simple, looking at the magical flame that she created, she now knew exactly what that arrow meant.

13:

"At least make it a challenge."

"So, it's like a power-o-meter or something like that?" Shani asked. She and Brex walked to their classes, trying to keep their voices down to avoid eavesdroppers.

"Yeah, I guess you could call it that," Brex answered. "I was thinking something more like...fuel tank, but yeah, that works too."

"And the rest of us...we're all going to run out too?" Shani kept looking at the ground where she was stepping as if she were having an existential crisis.

"Yeah, I don't see why we all wouldn't. I'm surprised Lexi's hasn't gone down at all yet."

"Why do you say that?"

Suddenly Brex remembered the fact that they agreed to not tell Shani about the midnight break-in at the lab because of her predictable reaction.

"Not important," Brex responded. "But what *is* important is that we have no clue what gives us more power or what happens when we run out. Do we lose them forever, or temporarily? Does it hurt? I don't know."

They kept walking with coffees in their hands and people passing by them with no idea of the terror Shani and Brex were discussing.

"Okay, look," said Shani. "I think our best chance at this point is to keep our eye out for that woman. Maybe even set a trap for her or something. If she wanted to hurt us, she would've by now."

Brex bit down on her lip while internally laughing at the thought of setting a booby trap for a magical lady who secretly spies on college students, but it was hardly the time for insensitive jokes.

"Regardless of if we are able to find this woman or not," said Brex, "I don't think it's going to do us any good if we don't know how to use our powers. We need to defend ourselves. We should at least experiment to see what we can do." Shani couldn't disagree. Could she drown an entire ocean? Or stop a tsunami? Now that Brex put these ideas in her head, she needed to know.

"Ya know, I would really love to see Asher flying around Boston 'cause he would definitely try and act like he's Superman," Shani teased.

"Really? I always pictured him as a Batman guy."

"No, no. He likes *real* superheroes."

They both silently laughed into each other, attempting to cover their faces. "Okay all jokes aside, I would love to see how good of an aim I got. Ya know like have a target that I can throw balls of fire at." Brex subtly flicked her wrist as if she were throwing a frisbee.

"Oh! We can go under the Zakim Bridge. It's right next to the river in case you light anything on fire, and I can use the water to test out my powers and such."

In Brex's eyes, Shani was in over her head. Shani was the best student she knew. Was she really about to risk getting caught taking over the entire Charles River? The burnt-down building was one thing, but practicing magic, or whatever it was they had, outside and out in the open? Poseidon's powers must have congested her brain and put a burden on her frontal lobe.

"As dope as that sounds...don't you have a class at like eight in the morning?" Brex asked, secretly hoping she would say it was canceled.

To her surprise, Shani gave a shrugged chuckle and said, "Brex, I haven't slept since junior year of high school."

"What about senior year?"

"Running for President of the United States is less work than trying to get into a good biology undergrad program."

"Duly noted. I'll text the others."

*****

Evening arrived, but the time they chose to perform their conspicuous activities, it turned out to not be as convenient as they thought. A few blocks down from the bridge, a civilian was being put into an ambulance from their home with four police cars flashing their lights outside. The neighbors, who were about to tuck in for the night, were not pleased.

On top of that, the forecast reported that it was going to rain at around 10 p.m., and the five of them had decided to meet at 9:30.

"Why don't we just do this another night?" asked Asher.

"Because I am extremely impatient," said Shani. "And we need to practice using our powers wisely and not like freaking idiots. We don't know how long it's going to take for them to completely drain out."

The two of them walked side by side beneath the starry and misty night sky. A few of their classmates and acquaintances spotted them and grew curious as to why they were suspiciously lurking through the stagnant part of Boston on a Wednesday night. Asher exaggerated his peers' concern and was convinced at least a few were about to follow them under the bridge, but Shani paid them no attention. There was no point, and she especially was growing tired of the immature college students who still shared the same intruding behavior as teenaged high school students.

"Ehh...OW!" Shani mumbled as she forcefully scratched her bra line underneath her clothes.

"Still allergic to bathing suits?" asked Asher.

Before they left, Shani gave a roughly twenty-minute speech as to why it was important that she wears a bathing suit just in case she has to get wet or go into the river. Asher knew this speech included something along the lines of "a bass could chew off my sweater" and "the germs in the water aren't good for my clothing," but for most of her yapping, Asher was mumbling occasional responses while scrolling through Instagram.

"Okay, not all bathing suits are made of nylon, and this tag didn't list the ingredients," said Shani as her skin turned bright red.

"I'm pretty sure they are, and you really could have just worn something else."

"Yeah, but they make my boobs look good." Shani pulled her shirt forward to look down at her breasts. Asher didn't remember this part of her speech, so he looked down with her to see for himself.

"What are ya doin' there, perv?" said a familiar voice from across the street. It was Brex walking towards them with a perplexed, but teasing look on her face.

"We like boobs, okay?" Asher responded.

Brex gave him an audacious eyebrow lift as she joined their walk towards the river.

Suddenly, Asher felt a harsh drop of ice-cold rain hit against his cheek. He brushed it off and looked up into the navy-blue sky. The rain was early. For now, it was only mild, but it was about to get heftier.

"Shit," he said. "The rain is starting early."

"Eh. Whatever," said Brex. "That just means less people will be bothering us."

The patch of land that was underneath the bridge was about the size of a basketball court. In order to get there, one needed to climb down a steep pathway of dirt in between a few trees and bushes.

Underneath the bridge, the ground was sloped with the river meeting at the lower level. The only reason the community didn't consider it a beach was because of the homely, scattered patches of grass. Only about half of the rocky beach was covered by the bridge. The closer they got to the river, the more spirited and animated the waves felt.

Brex scurried down the dirty hill with Shani and Asher behind her. The decline was so steep, the three of them were prepared to clumsily tuck and roll down the hill instead. Behind a ten-foot tall cliff of rocks stood Logan and Lexi, occupying themselves with various gadgets and objects that were hidden within a pool of light too dim for the others to identify.

"What's all this?" Brex yelled over the wind and the violent waves.

Lexi pointed her flashlight straight into Brex's face and said, "You didn't think we were coming empty-handed, did you?"

"Yeah, have you met this chick?" said Logan, making a sarcastic, aghast face and pointing his thumb to Lexi.

"Apparently not," Shani chuckled, walking over and admiring everything they had brought.

Brex recognized a slingshot, an old but large Christmas wreath that was duct taped to a tripod, and the biggest squirt gun she'd ever seen in her life. Yet Logan carried one object that was unfamiliar to her.

"Is that a mini fridge?" Shani asked, referring to the unknown artifact. It was painted a matte black with a circular glass window in the middle. Lexi was convinced it was actually a miniature space ship that the government secretly put cats in.

"Yeah!" Logan answered "I got it online. It's portable for camping trips and stuff like that. I thought it would be fun if Brex and I had like a competition for who cooks food the fastest. There's quite a bit of turkey in there."

"I like turkey," said Asher raising his hand.

"Um, okay," said Brex, taking a few steps closer to Logan. "But I hope you're ready to lose."

Logan opened his mouth and shook his head while trying to come up with a smooth comeback. He let out one aggressive laugh and took one short breath before giving up on trying to be humorous and said, "Yeah, I know."

The night was growing colder by the second, and the icy drops of rain were falling more frequently.

"Fire is gonna be hard to maintain if the rain gets any worse," said Brex, covering her head with her hoodie.

Suddenly, an idea struck Logan. His wandering eyes looked up into the night sky, and he didn't even bother to hide his pensive facial expression.

"What?" asked Brex.

"Let me try something," said Logan, climbing up onto the rocks without taking his eyes off the few stars that were now barely visible. With rain drops dripping from his face, he shot his right hand into the air with his middle finger reaching the furthest, stretching to its full capacity. The veins in his neck bulged through his skin so prominently, they created shadows even in the darkness.

With a forceful grunt and flexed abdomen, Logan released his longest rod of lightning yet. Within a split second, the bolt pierced through the sky and evaporated the single sinister cloud that was directly above them. The rain slowly decreased to nothing.

"Holy freaking hell, dude!" said Asher without blinking.

"Sick," said Lexi with the same reaction.

"Zeus is the god of the sky, right?" asked Logan, wiping the rain off his face with his long-sleeved t-shirt, and climbing down from the rocks. "Did you guys seriously doubt me?"

The rest stood there in silence with a few shoulder shrugs and inquiring faces.

"Oh, never mind," Logan mumbled.

"Okay, somebody's gotta keep watch," said Shani. "We'll rotate, but I wouldn't worry. The rain looks like it's still coming down everywhere else. I don't think anyone is gonna be waltzing around over here."

"Alright, let's do this!" Lexi howled like a cheerleader drunk at the Super Bowl.

"Cool. I'll keep first watch," said Brex as she quickly climbed back up the hill while Asher was up to bat. He slid off his shirt before remembering what fall weather felt like. His pearly white feathers glistened against his brown skin. Although, he was starting to grow goosebumps. He shivered his way to where the land met the water when Shani screamed "Do some jumping jacks, you wuss!"

Without looking in her direction, Asher gave her the middle finger and sprouted his wings to sail along the surface of the river. Immediately he could smell the muck of the polluted water, but in a way, it was oddly refreshing.

Centimeters away from the rippling waves, Asher's stomach felt a cool steam rising from the water onto his skin, but he didn't care. He wanted the breeze in his face to brush against his shoulders and cheeks with more pressure and more friction. The tips of his fingers slowly dipped into the river, and the ice-cold water splashed the entire front of his body. The resistance started to slow him down, but he wanted to go faster. He tilted his head forward, flattened his arms by his side, and stretched his feet. His wings flapped as fast as they possibly could, pushing every bit of strength he had into the new muscles that sprouted from his back. After reaching a satisfying speed, his body spiraled in the air like a corkscrew with his wings wrapped around his body. To Asher's surprise, this caused him to pick up even more speed, and the top of his scalp felt almost as if it were about to catch on fire, but an ice-cold fire.

Finally, he reached the opposite end of the river. The trip was only a matter of seconds, but to Asher, it felt like a lifetime filled with wondrous, endless experiences. He stayed close to the bridge to avoid any unknown wandering eyes. Reaching into his pocket, he pulled out his LED flashlight and flashed it twice towards the rest, giving them the signal to begin.

At the opposite end stood Lexi with her slingshot and glow-in-the-dark bouncy balls. With her elbow parallel to the ground and her feet in a wide grounded stance, she released her first ball into the air. The noise of its take-off was silent, but its crash into the water was at a higher volume than expected. Asher's goal was to catch the bouncy ball, and he missed it by a landslide. He flew too fast, too far to the right, and the ball zoomed straight past him.

"We need a coach," said Logan.

"Have a little more faith in him," said Lexi, preparing her next attempt.

Asher double-flashed his light once more and flapped his wings with more force, trying to sustain his energy. Lexi stretched the band on her slingshot, but this time, she aimed slightly towards the bridge so the ball would fly towards Asher at a diagonal angle. If he were able to see with better depth perception, it would probably be easier to catch.

Asher's eyes immediately caught the glowing dot in the distance coming towards the side of him. At first, he thought he was flying the perfect speed in order to meet with the ball, but he quickly noticed where the ball was headed; directly towards the substructure of the bridge, and he wasn't going to make it on time to catch it. Almost immediately, he thought of an alternative plan, and he flew a few feet in the opposite direction.

"What's he doing?" Logan spat out. As the words were exiting his mouth, the ball bounced off the bridge's arch, and it flew almost effortlessly into Asher's palm.

With the ball in one hand and the flashlight in the other, he flickered his light three times as a sign that he had caught it. But he was close enough for them to witness the infamous catch, and they were already cheering.

Feeling relieved, Asher flew back to the miniature shore to return Lexi's ball.

"At least make it a challenge," said Asher, tossing Lexi the ball and shaking out his feathered wings.

"Oh, please," said Lexi, elongating her words. "That was just one. Wait until I bring my bow and arrow." Shani and Logan slowly turned their heads towards her in bewildered amazement, while Asher laughed off her comment and flew back over the surface, unaware that she wasn't kidding.

Until he became sore and fatigued, Asher continued to practice. A few balls he lost, but most of them he easily caught. One of them he snatched with his wing, but he neglected to mention that when he returned the ball to Lexi.

Next up: Shani tackling the water. Kicking off her shoes and sliding off her jacket, she stuck her toes right into the edge of the river. The ground felt rough on her feet. It didn't feel like soft and smooth sand, but suddenly they were connected. She could sense what the river was thinking, what its next move was. The calm before the storm. It was a sensation that took her by surprise.

With one tremendous and aggressive extension of her arms, she caused the biggest wave she could make to come crashing towards them. As it drew closer, its strength and size rose to its peak. All of the tension in her body extended from the crow's feet in her eyes to the tips of her curled fingers.

"You ready, Brex?" Shani yelled over the boisterous wind.

"Yup!" Brex yelled back. She prepared herself by copying the exact stance Shani put herself in. Standing a few feet away, Brex lit the brightest flames she could imagine. Her long black hair blew away from her face as the now fifteen-foot-tall wave was only yards away from her.

"Here it comes!" Shani exclaimed as she horizontally flung her arms toward Brex, causing the wave to continuously circulate around Brex's entire body like a vortex trying to suffocate her.

Brex pushed her arms out to the side, not letting the miniature hurricane drop one bit of the river on her. Alternating her head from right to left, she noticed her flames expanding with durability and the rotating cylinder of water slowly diffusing away from her.

"Oh, come on! I know you can do better than that, Shani!" Brex laughed, trying to spot Shani through the active water.

"Hah! Well, okay then! IF YOU INSIST!" Shani drew her arms closer to each other with the edges of the water reflecting her.

"Shit," said Brex, trying to not let Shani hear. But before the water came any closer to her, she inhaled deep through her nose and focused her eyes so hard on the water, the liquid almost evaporated with her penetrating stare.

Everything stood still. Brex and Shani were neck and neck. The circulating river stayed in the same tube-like shape, and impatience was no stranger to the rest of them, waiting for something else to happen.

"Did they happen to plan out how they would end this?" said Logan, leaning in towards Lexi.

"Nah, I don't think they got that far. Thank God this wasn't Asher doing this. That would have been a hell of a lot worse."

Asher stood at the top of the hill keeping watch with his arms crossed and secretly hoping that Shani would get river muck smeared all over her. Seeing her defeated was occasionally amusing to him, and always satisfying.

With Lexi's impatience spiraling out of control, she spotted a few vines growing on the side of the bridge and mumbled under her breath, "Hmmm...yeah enough of this shit."

While putting all of her focus on two of the vines, she reached one arm out at a time hoping to connect with the living green creatures. In an instant, they altered their focus to Shani and Brex. It took much less effort than Lexi thought. The vines wrapped themselves around the two magical bodies, forcing their arms down by their side. Brex's fire was immediately put out, and the river spat outwards, releasing all of its tension, but not without deluging Shani straight in the face and torso.

Asher stood at the top of the hill hunched over, hysterically crying with laughter.

"Wow. Turns out she did need a suit," Asher said to himself. "Too bad we forgot towels."

"LEXI!" the two hostages simultaneously yelled.

"What the hell was that for?" Brex asked.

"Sorry. This was just a lot more fun," said Lexi, still holding her arms out. But before she let either of them go. Brex managed to heat herself up enough that she started to burn the vines that were tightening around her. "Ow!" Lexi dropped both of them immediately. She wasn't expecting to feel pain when living creatures of the environment did.

"Sorry. Didn't know you were gonna feel that. You okay?" asked Brex.

"Yeah, me neither!" Lexi laughed. "I'm all good. Target practice anyone?"

Lexi took her ivy plant out of her backpack and placed it on the ground about twenty feet away from the wreath. All ten of her fingers reached toward the plant, causing it to grow taller and larger than any normal household plant. With one swoop of her left arm, she shot the tip of the green bullet only centimeters above the wreath.

"I'll take it." The rest cheered her on until Logan joined her by shooting bolts of lightning through the wreath as well. As soon as each of them got one in the circle, Brex would pull it further back, until she got bored and pulled it out of the way at the last second so they would miss every time. Neither Logan or Lexi were amused, but that didn't stop Brex from keeling over in laughter.

Asher still stood at the top of the hill, waiting for somebody else to take over on lookout duty, so he could get a closer look at all the action. The time was almost midnight. The only color that covered the sky was now black, and it seemed like the rest of the clouds in Boston were now at rest. As Asher checked to see if he could spot any rain coming down, he spotted something else before he could get his answer. Not one, but two police cruisers were headed in his direction.

"Shit...GUYS!" Asher yelled. "COPS!"

"Wait, what?" said Shani. "Where?"

"I don't know! I don't even know if they're coming over here, but we can't take any chances. Under the bridge!"

Logan kicked all of their belongings behind the rocks and the five of them ran towards the shadows of the bridge as they heard two cars parking and two doors slamming shut at the top of the hill. Sure enough, the cops had been tipped off and were coming to investigate.

Scurrying as fast as they could, they kept looking back to see if they were in the cops' line of sight yet. Luckily, they reached the bridge before the cops were visible.

"So, when she finally moved all of her stuff out," said a familiar voice, "she expected me to pay for the moving truck. Something about chivalry and how this is all pretty much my fault or whatever."

The three girls exchanged lethargic, eye-rolling looks. They would recognize those skull-splitting voices anywhere. It was the same cops from the building they had broken into.

"What if they come over here?" Asher asked. Their bodies were flattened against the graffitied wall, but if the cops were to join them under the bridge, they would be seen for certain.

"I have an idea," said Lexi. "But I don't think you're going to like it very much." She turned her focus towards the rusty ceiling where at least fifty different vines were growing and almost covering the underneath of the bridge. The second Shani spotted the green creatures, she knew what Lexi was thinking.

"Oh no," Shani whispered quietly underneath her breath, but she knew it had to be done.

"Whatever you do, don't scream." And with one aggressive arm gesture, Lexi wrapped one lengthy vine around each individual body one at a time, and hoisted them into the air with their backs flat across the ceiling. To Lexi's surprise the only one who gave just a little squeal was Logan.

"So, I got my mom living with me now. It's the only way I can pay for a house," said the first cop. "Except she can't go down the stairs, so I'm living in the basement for now."

"So, basically you're living in your mom's basement...in a way?" asked the second cop.

"No. I'm living in *my* basement, you dick."

"Okay, okay. I'm just saying it would be nice to not be the only one."

Their voices were now only a few feet away. Asher tightly closed his eyes and recited, in his head, the only three lines of the Lord's Prayer that he almost knew; *Thy kingdom come, thy Earth is done on Earth that it is in Heaven, Give me my bread, soup, and crackers, or something along those lines.*

"What was even happening over here?" asked the second cop.

"I don't know. Somebody just made a noise complaint. They said something about hearing kids screaming."

The two uniformed officers were now directly underneath them. The distance between their stomachs and the top of the cops' heads was now at least fifteen feet, but any sudden movement or noise would unveil their hiding spot.

"Why don't you go on one of those dating apps?" asked the second cop.

"Because the last time I went on Tinder, I accidentally swiped right on my ex-wife."

If Shani had her hands free, she would have smacked herself in the face and pulled down her skin in agony, but for now, an eye roll was unfortunately all she was capable of doing.

"Alright, there's nothing here. Enough of this shit," said the first cop as they slowly walked away and continued to blabber about something that had to do with uncomfortable, middle-aged sexual encounters.

Asher fought with every muscle he had in his body to not cough. It was only a few more seconds until the cops were up the hill and out of sight. Lexi was able to follow the two men with her peripheral vision. The moment after the cops reached the street level, Lexi slowly let them down, and Asher let out a brutal cough that lasted for over ten seconds.

Brex pulled down her hoodie, brushed her hair off her face and said, "I really don't like those guys."

.....

The next morning, Asher woke with a headache so intense, it was almost considered a migraine. He cracked his back, rolled out his neck and reached for his glass of water, but something was off. It wasn't pain that he felt in his left hand, but rather discomfort. The only part of his body that felt negative and low. He flipped over his palm to see a difference in his scar. Just like Brex's, the vertical line was now tilted a notch to the right. His magic was running out.

Asher was about to spring out of bed to tell Shani, but before he could even remove his legs from under the covers, he heard a violent knock on the door.

Shani barged into his room without waiting for an answer. The color in her face was drained, and her eyes were bulging with tension.

"Check your phone," she said, and without questioning her judgment, he opened his phone to see a long thread of text messages from their group chat.

The last text message was sent by Lexi saying, "We used our powers too much last night. We have to be more careful."

Shani sat down on Asher's bed, looked into his tired eyes, and said, "We're *all* a notch down now."

14:

"Can you hear me?"

Throughout the next few days, the five of them were cautious about how they used their powers. The only exception Shani made to the rule was at her Saturday shift. After noticing how immobile he was she asked a baby squid if he was hungry or not. She grew concerned and didn't want to overfeed him or starve him to death. It turned out that it was just the new harsh lights disrupting his sleep. Shani took control herself and removed a single lightbulb, hoping nobody would notice.

Asher only used his special abilities while hanging up his elephant tapestry that he'd been putting off doing since he had moved in. Brex however, was the most tempted out of all of them. The feeling of heat boiling underneath her skin was a remarkable sensation. Even lighting a match-sized flame helped release stubborn tension and anger.

At this point, the only way Brex was able to let go of any aggression was to take some pictures. Not for her portfolio, just for herself.

A few minutes before Morialsa's class was going to start, she found the perfect patch of dead flowers outside of the building. She plopped down on her stomach and rested her camera on the damp soil.

The sun was covered with a thin layer of weightless clouds. It was perfect. The sun effortlessly floated in between two twenty-story buildings, creating beautiful and blinding sunbeams. She propped up the most disheveled and bedraggled flower she could find. The sun burned from behind the dead flower, giving it a sharp silhouette until an unexpected eclipse stepped into frame.

"Hey, Ansel Adams," Logan shouted from only a few feet away. "You're gonna be late to class!"

"I can tell time. Thank you very much!" said Brex, still looking through the lense. "I still have five minutes, and it takes less than one to walk like a goddamn turtle into that torturous classroom, but I'm never going to get the shot right if you don't get out of my way."

Logan quickly took a broad stride to the side like a ballet dancer jumping over a giant puddle.

"What class are those pictures for?" Logan asked.

"Eh, they're just for me, and maybe for Instagram." Finally coming out from behind the lense, Brex, refreshed, jumped up into the air, wiping her hair off her face.

"Hey there, Brex!" said a voice from behind Logan. Brex squinted her eyes to see her advisor and photography professor, Mr. Noah, walking towards her. He was a short, bald, and plump man who ate a block of cheese and two pieces of bread for lunch every day. He had a limp in his left leg and made various, uncomfortable facial expressions whenever he walked, even with his cane.

For the past three years, he hadn't been the type of professor to walk up to a student and engage in conversation with them. Therefore, Brex was dreading whatever was about to come.

"Hello, Sir," said Brex, forcing a smile through her teeth.

Mr. Noah awkwardly took a short glance at Logan, but still attempted to behave in a casual manner.

"Um...would you be able to see me in my office at some point this week?" Mr. Noah asked. "No rush, just want to discuss a few...um...options with ya. Just a few things, nothing bad of course. Ya know, just college stuff."

By the look on her face, Brex knew what he was talking about, but still had no interest in continuing with the conversation. Disappointment sunk into her eyes.

"Of course. I'll email you," she said.

"Great, thank you. Have a great class now." Mr. Noah gave a quick wave that was more like a salute, and a stiff smile. Limping his way to the building next door, he finally disappeared.

"Do you know what that was about?" Logan asked.

"Oh, I'm sure it's nothing," said Brex, dodging the question. "Maybe just some senior thesis stuff. Ready for class?"

Logan knew she was probably either lying or stretching the truth, but it didn't matter. It wasn't any of his business.

"Hell no, but I got an entire Netflix series downloaded on my phone, so I'll survive, I guess."

•••••

Today in Philosophical Debate, the students had their second debate of the semester. Last week was their first, and it ended in disaster. Two freshmen were assigned to argue about whether or not the Matrix could be real or not. Professor Morialsa thought that would be a strong and generic topic to discuss, but was arguably wrong.

Ricki, a tall, lean, intelligent girl who always wore black hoodies argued that the Matrix could not possibly be real because everything that science has taught the world proved otherwise. Sancha, a short, but muscular girl who had a deep and raspy voice because of all the cigarettes she had inhaled, counterargued by answering, "You don't *know* that." She wasn't wrong, but since those were, for the most part, the only four words that came out of her mouth throughout the entire debate, it made the performance excruciating to watch.

This week, it was two sophomores: Greg and Lavender. Their task was to debate if technology is helping society, or is it doing more damage than good.

Being a stoner and compulsive video game player, Greg began his opening statement by reciting, "Video games were very important to me growing up." Most of the students had no idea where his point was leading, but Professor Morialsa couldn't have been more unimpressed. Five seconds in and the student who had skipped half of the classes already was headed towards a plunging grade.

"All of these games and like...I got really good hand-eye coordination now. Which really helps with—um—typing."

A few of Greg's friends sat in the back row, nodding their heads with their skateboards practically glued underneath their feet.

"What are the standards to get into this school again?" Asher asked, leaning over to Brex. Covering her face and biting her lip, she shook her head, wondering for at least the tenth time why she had taken this class. It was reasons like this that students had a hard time taking any of Morialsa's classes seriously. Putting an intelligent student against a video game addict was not his brightest idea, but he would never admit to that being his fault.

"Can I make my opening statement now?" Lavender asked with her hand not even halfway raised in the air.

"Go ahead," said Professor Morialsa. Greg took a few moments to process losing the audience's attention by staring past the mezzanine with crow's feet around his eyes.

"So, technology is such a wonderful thing to have. It saves lives, it helps people get work done faster. But whatever happened to kids having an 'I read 100 books' contest? Kids care more about having iPhones and a T.V. in their room than they do playing outside and reading books. And let's be honest, all of the kids' television shows suck now-a-days. At least we had the good Disney Channel growing up."

"You can read books on iPhones and iPads, you know?" Greg added. "And books kill trees anyways."

After Greg made his surprisingly truthful argument, the rest of the class prepared their questions.

"How do you think the government should approach this issue of not reading or being active enough, or should they even be involved at all?" asked the shorter Kaitlin or Katelyn of the two, sitting in the back.

"They definitely should be involved. It won't be easy, but if we work on changing the curriculum in schools and influence kids to be more inspired by everything that they see, then we can encourage them to write and draw or whatever they want."

"But you can do all of that with technology!" Greg interrupted. The class, including Professor Morialsa, was convinced that this exact response was going to be his counterargument to everything from now on.

"Okay, look..." said Lavender, firmly and assertively. "It is scientifically proven that there are things that we need to accomplish to successfully develop our brain and keep it sustained that we cannot

substitute with technology. Facetiming doesn't cut it when it comes
to human interaction. You need to physically see people in person in
order for it to be mentally healthful. Or physical human touch! Maybe
not a lot of people like to be touched, but scientists say that eight
hugs a day improves your mental health. There's just something about
connecting with other humans that sends an incredible amount of
endorphins to the brain. Like one big spark...or like...jump starting a
car. Can we really ignore all of that?"

Lavender carried on with her speech, but now every word that
she was speaking became a mumbled blur to Asher. He didn't take
her analogy lightly. Why did that phrase sink in so deeply? He kept
repeating it over and over again in his head. *Jump start, jump start,
jump start.* A chemical reaction, a spark, lighting a fire, all from two
different energy sources. Their scars. They were energy sources too,
right? If the two of them met...

Suddenly, Asher's curiosity and impulsive need for knowledge
clouded his judgment and overcame his common sense. He spotted
Brex's left hand, halfway hanging off her desk while her right hand was
occupied with a pen. Without thinking, he reached his left fingertips
to Brex's and connected their two palms together. It only took a brief
moment for the space in between their skin to light a small yet magnificent beam that created an absurd and abrupt sound. Almost as if
a tennis ball-sized asteroid had hit the Earth.

The two of them almost sprung from their seats in shock. Brex
clung onto the side of her seat where Logan sat next to her, and he was
just as confused as they were. Asher didn't picture what he thought
was going to happen, let alone predict that outcome. Nevertheless, he
never felt more idiotic in his life. When he looked up to see the entire
classroom, including the professor, staring straight at them, a majority
of them had fear plastered on their faces, but it mainly frightened
the students closest to them. They pulled their upper bodies away,
wondering if the alarming noise was anything fatal, while Asher and
Brex were at a loss for words.

"Sorry!" Asher awkwardly hollered. "It was just my phone. It gets
really bright and uh...weird...ringtone. Yeah." He was certain nobody
would buy such an unconvincing performance, but to his surprise, the

professor dramatically exhaled in distress instead of calling to investigate the unusual situation.

"Bloody hell, just turn it off and let's move on!" said Professor
Morialsa. "Sorry, guys. You can continue."

Slowly, and one by one, the students turned to sit straight forward
in their seats though their attention was hardly returned to the two
speakers in front of the bright stage lights.

"Um...as I was saying," said Lavender. "I think it's important to
acknowledge the environmental effects that technology has on the
world."

"Doesn't technology help us make Earth-friendly stuff though?"
asked Greg.

Taken aback by his sudden change in tactics, Lavender was finally
at a loss for words. She ruffled through all of her notes struggling to
find a strong counterargument.

Professor Morialsa let his head tilt, raised his eyebrows and whispered "Hm, maybe this *will* end before the end of the year."

·····

"What the fuck was that?" Shani quietly shrieked. The five of them
stood in a quiet corner outside of the lecture hall, keeping an eye out
for passing pedestrians walking in the cloudy, drizzling rain.

"Shit, I don't know. I'm sorry, I wasn't thinking," said Asher, re-
lentlessly rubbing his face. "To be fair though, I didn't think *that* was
going to happen!"

"Okay. Well, what *did* you think was going to happen?"

Asher thought about his words carefully before he let them slip. If
he incorrectly proposed his idea, even in the slightest bit, she wouldn't
stop treating him like an idiot for at least the next month.

"I was thinking it might..." Asher was suddenly tempted to demonstrate his idea by clapping his hands together and twiddling his fingers,
almost imitating fireworks. He instantly realized that was the wrong
demonstration to choose from. "I thought it was going to make some
sort of spark to give our powers like a boost or something like that."

Shani subtly jerked her head back, processing the possibility of Asher being right.

"Okay," Shani said, crossing her arms. "Let's see your scars then. Did it work?"

Brex and Asher shared a look of excited curiosity. They hunched over, closely facing one another as they peeled their thin, artificial skin from their palms. But to their dismay, their results were less than what was expected.

"No," said Brex, under her breath. "It's exactly where it was."

"But what if it was only for like a few seconds?" Asher asked. "We could try it again."

They all slowly nodded in agreement. "Okay, but not here, and let's get out of this rain," said Shani, grabbing Asher's arm and leading them towards their home.

·····

Back at the Main Street apartment, the five of them prepared for the worst to happen. They shut the blinds and filled a bucket with water just in case Brex lit the curtains on fire. They even pushed the couch against the T.V., but that was mainly due to Asher's anxiety about how much he paid for the new flat screen only a few weeks earlier. Brex took off her jean jacket as Asher removed his shirt and they took their positions.

"Should we like count to three or something?" Asher asked.

"Sure. Together," Brex responded.

Together, and without even blinking, they locked their eyes on each other and recited "One...two...three!" Their skin collided, but their eyes were now shut. Neither of them were eager for any more surprises.

"Uhhh..." They heard Lexi say.

"What?" Brex shouted, reopening her eyes. "WHOA!" Before her stood a flame that was taller and more dominant than anything she ever created before. It was at least five feet high and it carried all the way down past her elbows, but when she looked over at Asher, he stood there looking perplexed and wingless.

"What are you doing?" he assertively asked.

"Nothing! I just thought of having this big booming fire, and it happened. Hold on, I'll loosen up." She defensively lowered her right arm and slowed down her breathing.

What did she need to concentrate on? What was it that was transferring magic to one another?

Energy, she thought. *I have to give every last bit of energy I have to Asher. I'm so tense all the time that I'm taking it all up.*

She pulled her shoulders away from her ears, let her body go numb, and her jaw loose. In the snap of a finger, Asher's wings sprouted from his back, and he flew straight into the air, letting go of Brex's hand.

CRUNCH, they all heard as Asher broke through the sheetrock on the ceiling. His arms and legs were spread out like he was making a snow angel. His wings weren't able to save him as he quickly bounced back to the floor and fell onto his side.

"OWWWW!" Asher hollered as he cradled himself on the hardwood floor.

"MOTHER FFF—Are you okay?" Brex cried. "I'm so sorry!" They all rushed over to him as he groaned his way up into a sitting position.

"That's...not how...I pictured that going...either," Asher stated, trying to force fully-formed words out of his mouth. "I'm fine, I'm fine. I don't think the ceiling is though." All at once the five of them looked up to see an oval-shaped dent the size of a boogie board in the eggshell-painted ceiling. A few bits of spackle continuously fell from the demolished architecture, giving a "snowfall" sense to the living room.

"Or the floor," Asher mumbled as he lifted his behind to reveal two wooden floorboards that were now snapped in half.

"I'll pay for your security deposit," Brex shamefully muttered.

"I know I won't feel anything in like five seconds, but can I at least have some ice?"

While supporting Asher's back with one hand, Shani threw her opposite hand towards the sink, grabbing hold of the water she had poured. Before beckoning the liquid to her, she clenched her fist as tight as it would go, freezing every little particle and breaking it into hundreds of pieces.

"Brex, hand me that towel," she said. Brex scurried across the small floor on her hands and knees to reach for the hand towel that was hanging on the small island and tossed it to Shani.

As she wrapped up the chilling ice, Shani asked, "Are you bleeding anywhere?"

Asher looked and felt around his entire body and said, "No but my right wing kills." Brex veered around to examine the back of his right wing. One thing particularly caught her eye.

"Actually, you *are* bleeding," she said. Asher could feel her wipe her hand on his feathery wing. "The only thing is...it's blue." She held up her first two fingers in front of him, which now looked like she had dipped them in expensive, blue sparkly paint.

"Whoa," Lexi whispered. "Do we all have blood like that?"

"Not according to my uterus," said Brex.

"I'm the only one of all of us that has extra body parts," said Asher, rolling out his shoulders as he tried to stand up. "That must be why."

"I'll go get a bandage to wrap it in," said Shani. "But honestly, I think you should leave your wings out for tonight. I don't know what's gonna happen if you don't."

"What? Are you crazy? If I leave my wings out, I'm using magic. My powers will be halfway gone by tomorrow morning!"

It was a hard decision, and Brex didn't want to admit it, but Shani had a strong argument.

"Why don't you at least keep the bandage on for a couple of hours?" she said. "Just take it from there, okay? Also, where's the broom?"

•••••

It was one of those nights where a good night's sleep was out of the question for Asher. A few hours earlier, he had taken the bandage off his cut, and tucked his wings away, only a half an hour after the collision. Everything looked fine, but it stung, and felt sore. It was odd. Before, when his wings were spreading wide, he barely felt anything, but when they were gone, he couldn't help but feel an ache in his shoulder.

He took pain relievers, but he wasn't surprised when they did nothing. "Take for deep cuts on mystical wings" wasn't listed in the "Uses" section on the back of any pain reliever bottle.

Being impulsive was a habit that Asher was all too familiar with. And the two things that made it worse were 1) Shani giving him grief for it and then proceeding to boss him around on how to patch up the dilemma, and then 2) Having anxiety about it for the rest of the night. He couldn't help but think about the impulsive actions he had committed over and over again. It was embarrassing and uncomfortable to have every single person in class staring at him. But for some reason, the discomfort in his shoulder gave him a distraction for the night.

He flipped through Elise's journal, trying to look for anything they might have missed, even though Shani already had done so a few times. After a while, he turned to YouTube to look at videos of the fire in the White Mountains. Maybe they also missed a clue or two in these clips, even though, once again, Shani had already been watching them on repeat.

Nothing was working. Surprisingly, he finished all of his homework and studying. Therefore, boring himself to sleep with his useless psychology major wasn't an option. He tried pacing around his room a few times and doing yoga, which consisted of switching back and forth between downward dog and cobra because those were the only poses he knew.

Eventually, he slipped out of his room and tip-toed down the hall. Accidentally waking up Shani was a nightmare he did not want to relive. When they were fourteen, they had a sleepover in Asher's backyard. They both woke up the next morning to his automatic alarm clock that he had forgotten to turn off the night before at 6:30am. She didn't speak to him for a week.

He filled up a plastic sandwich bag with ice and pressed it against his shoulder. It felt relieving until he realized the freezing ice would keep him up all night.

"Oh, freaking well," he whispered to himself as he walked back into his room.

He gently laid down on his bed with the pack of ice between his right shoulder and the sheets. Oddly enough, there was something meditative about the burning ice pack numbing his skin. It wasn't keeping him awake. It helped clear his mind from every thought he had throughout that day. His eyes felt like they were melting into the back of his head until he heard something odd come from across the room.

Flickering lights, he thought. *It sounds like flickering lights. Wait.. .I've heard this before. I'm dreaming. It's another dream. I have to open my eyes.*

Just like the dream before, he was paralyzed and out of control. He tried to move his fingertips to regain control over his own body. After a few moments, he was able to move his head around and force his eyes open to see what was happening in his dream.

The entire room was a deep red color. Somebody was angry. He could sense it. He looked over at the mirror. Once again, it was filled with a cloud-like mist. He walked over to it with more determination than before. He tucked away his fear and anxiety and embraced himself with focus and caution. His dreams were evolving. Now, he was more in control.

Standing before the mirror, he could see something start to form, but this time, he could see that it was a room. A room that barely had any lighting and had dark-colored bricks for walls and floors. Somebody was in the room, but he couldn't make out what they looked like yet. The mist began to vanish as it revealed not a person standing in the room, but a snake, a pearly white snake with bright red eyes.

It barely moved, until it noticed Asher standing before it. With a gentle "hiss," it slithered toward him, but stayed in the mirror. Asher didn't know much about snake facial expressions, but he could tell that it was scared. He didn't know how he knew, but he did.

"Can you hear me?" Asher asked. Nothing happened. Either the snake didn't understand English, which would make sense, or the snake was looking at something other than Asher.

After a few moments of silence, something strange happened. The snake curled up into a ball, and the white, sparkly scales all blended in with each other. It was changing shape. The colors shifted as it grew taller and wider, and within a single breath, Asher could see a long blue dress draped over a tall, beautiful woman. Her hair was long and dark with perfect curls. She looked like she hadn't eaten anything in days. The bags under her eyes made her look older than she probably was.

She said nothing, but her face said everything. Instead of looking directly at Asher, she was gazing over his shoulder. Wherever she was, there was someone else in the room, and they were no friend to her.

Her chest expanded further and her breath deepened. Her eyes grew darker, and her face drained in color. She slowly started to shake her head and backed away, but as she reached her arms above her head, the image in the mirror slowly disintegrated.

"No!" Asher screamed as he reached out, irrationally thinking he could help her. "No!" he screamed once more as his body shot straight into the air, waking up from the eventful dream.

He was sweating a lot more than last time. The room looked dull compared to what he had seen in his dream. He sat on the edge of the bed with a melted bag of ice sitting right behind him.

All he could think was; *I gotta write this down. I gotta write this down. I gotta write this down.*

He knew he had an empty notepad somewhere. After wiping up his sweat with his blanket, he searched through his desk and found the yellow composition book. On the front, he labeled it "Dream Book." In his first entry, he wrote at the top "September 7th, 2017, Dream number one," and he proceeded to describe everything he could remember about that dream. Even the tiniest details, he couldn't risk forgetting anything.

His next entry read, "September 18th, 2017, Dream number two, more vivid, white snake with red eyes, turned into lady with the blue dress, looked malnourished, somebody tried to attack her."

The dreams were eleven days apart from one another. What was the next one going to be? *When* was it going to be? And how on Earth was he going to explain this to Shani without her having an aneurysm?

15:

"I think they would just be scared."

Wednesday evenings were the worst days of the week for football practice. If it was Wednesday, that meant nothing but conditioning and cardio with absolutely no break in between. Coach Corden insisted it be this way at the beginning of Logan's and Adam's sophomore year, and had kept his word ever since.

After the team's ten-mile run, they paired up to do partner sit ups, which lasted for almost a half an hour. As usual, Adam and Logan paired themselves up, yet Logan immediately regretted it when Adam felt the need to repeatedly call Logan a "wuss" after his hip spazzed and his sit ups weren't up to par.

"Kwan!" Coach Corden yelled. "What's wrong with you?"

"Nothing, coach."

"Then why is my so-called quarterback whining and crying?"

At this point, Logan was so used to Coach calling him the "so-called quarterback" whenever he was even the slightest bit of a disappointment that he felt numb to the ferocious insult.

"I'm not!" Logan defended himself.

"One more lap for the both of your flabbering mouths," said the coach before Adam threw his hands in the air not knowing what he said to deserve this, since he didn't say anything.

"A'ight." Logan nonchalantly rolled his eyes at Adam once more as they both stood up for another tedious run.

Lexi came walking over to the field with her dinner and homework to watch practice. The cheerleaders simultaneously practiced at the other end of the field, and Anika made a point to present her annoyance by glancing at Lexi and laughing and pointing it out to the rest of the cheerleaders. Even though nobody laughed along with her. She thrived off the mistaken illusion that Lexi was weak and Anika was stronger than her. It was Lexi's third time spending dinner, watching her friends practice, but it did give her satisfaction to see Anika so miffed.

For dinner, Lexi made a peanut butter and jelly sandwich, Caesar salad, and her favorite smoothie with strawberries, bananas, applesauce, and green tea. For homework: math. Although she was so far ahead in the class, she was preparing not for next week's homework, but for the week after.

"Hey!" Lexi heard a familiar voice from behind her. It was Asher walking down the bleachers.

"Hey! How's your uh...airplane mode? Did you keep the wrap on all night?"

"Nah, I couldn't sleep with it on. Everything's okay though. My arrow didn't go down anymore, but I mean it probably will in a few days."

"That's good at least. Brex feels really bad. I think she almost peed herself when she found out how much your security deposit was."

"Wow," they laughed together. Asher took a scan of the field to examine the current tension within the stressful practice.

"Coach being a dick again?" he asked.

"Seems like it. I think Logan pissed him off again. He just went on another lap. Second penalty lap, and it's only fifteen minutes in." Lexi took another bite of her sandwich when Asher's phone started buzzing, but after checking who it was, he ignored the call as if it were an unknown number.

"Who was it?" Lexi asked with her mouth still full.

"Just my brother."

Lexi swallowed with her eyes wide open.

"You have a brother? How old is he?" Being an only child, Lexi thought having siblings was an intriguing conversation topic.

"He's twelve. He's my half-brother."

Lexi waited a few seconds to hear more of the story before she realized she had to ask for it. "What's his name?"

"Pablo. He's my mom's second son with her boyfriend."

"Oh..." Lexi could tell he felt uncomfortable talking about the topic.

She held on asking any more questions until, without any persuasion, he said, "I don't really talk with my mom, and Pablo, he can be just kind of annoying."

With strong empathy, Lexi knew how he was feeling.

"Yeah, I don't talk to my mom at all. I don't know anything about her. She could have another family for all I know. I think it's better that way though." Asher was shocked by Lexi's breezy reaction to her absent mother. Her refreshing perspective on the situation was something that he'd been aspiring towards for a long time.

"Really? I was like ten when she left. How old were you?"

"Ehh...like a year and a half I think." She again displayed no negative feelings toward the subject, but Asher couldn't push away the guilt. He had at least spent a few good years with his mom before he saw her maybe once a year on Christmas. Lexi wouldn't even recognize her mom's face.

"Sorry, that sucks," said Asher.

"Oh, no. It's like I said, definitely for the better." Lexi finished scarfing down the rest of her sandwich and licked her fingers like they were expired candy.

"So, what do you think?" Asher asked, assured it was okay to change the subject. "Any of those guys on the team seem cute to you?"

"Cute?" said Lexi at twice the volume, "Oh hell, yeah! Boyfriend material? Definitely not. I need a good balance of testosterone. This? This would be way too much for me."

Asher fell into his lap to laugh and mumbled "Accurate."

"Hey!" Anika shouted from a few feet away. She marched towards them, quickly and indignantly. At this moment, if she even remotely wanted to destroy someone's soul, her swaying hips gave the impression that she could do it with the snap of her fingers.

"What the hell is she coming over here for?" Lexi mumbled in between her teeth.

"I know what you've been hiding." Anika stood with her feet apart and one fist on her hip.

There was no way. No way she could have found out, Lexi thought. *We tried so hard to be careful. How?*

Asher looked at Lexi, hoping she would know exactly what to say, but luckily, she was already way ahead of him.

"Hiding what?" Lexi asked, rolling her eyes, subtly throwing one hand in the air and talking with a wrathful, effortless voice.

Anika gave a bitter, sassy chuckle and said, "Don't play that dumbass game with me. You're freaks." She slowly turned her head towards Asher and finished her sentence by saying, "All of you."

"All of us in the school?" said Asher. "So, what does that make you?"

Anika was too familiar with peers insulting her for her to be offended by such a comment, but it was still amusing to Lexi.

"You wanna tell me why you guys set that building on fire?" Anika snarled. For a moment, Asher's brain went numb. He had to replay what Anika said over and over in his head at least a few times before he thoroughly processed it. The surprise came as a slap in the back of his head.

Lexi sat there with one lifted eyebrow when she mumbled "Huh?" She didn't know whether to laugh, yell, or smack her in the face.

"What...How...What in the hell makes you think that?" asked Asher.

"You know you should really put a lock on your laptop, Flannagan. I know you guys have been messaging back and forth for almost a month about the fire. And I don't know how you did it, but I know you were doing some sort of voodoo shit. And I don't know why you did it, but I'm sure the police would love to see these pictures I took of your computer screen."

Asher's heart started to thump so hard, he was feeling his heartbeat in places he didn't know was possible to feel a pulse. What did he say in those text messages? Did their conversations sound like they were the ones to blame for the fire? Was it enough to get convicted?

Lexi was taking the accusation surprisingly well. She laughed and stood up in an attempt to intimidate her even though Anika was almost two heads taller than Lexi.

"Trust me, dude. I didn't do anything wrong, and all of your evidence is off. How does anyone know that's my laptop? Or if that's actually my conversation. Those are easy to fake, you know? Plus..." she continued as she held up her phone to the side of her face. "I think the cops would be more interested in you and...what do you call him? Jim?" On her screen was a picture of Professor Morialsa caressing Anika's face and arm.

Only for a slight moment did Anika's eyes widen before she said, "It's completely consensual, and there's nothing in the rule book about a teacher dating a student."

"Ahh...well, you're right about something. There is no rule about a teacher dating a student. That is correct, but you're still seventeen, aren't you?"

This time, Anika stood there as still as a statue, with her face filling up with a deep shade of red against her dark skin. Asher was so overwhelmed with information at this point that he wouldn't have been surprised if he was being pranked, but he sure did find this whole situation entertaining beyond words.

"You said so yourself. You skipped a grade, but you haven't told him that yet, have you? Eh, it doesn't matter. A jury won't believe him. The school won't believe him. And they'll throw your ass in jail too! Which I think is unjustified, but hey...I don't make the rules."

Anika lunged at the phone, but Lexi's reflexes were an incomparable match for Anika's speed.

"Hey! What's going on?" said Adam, running over to the bleachers.

Lexi put away her phone and gave Anika a testing look to see if she had anything to say.

"Nothing," Anika groaned, shamefully walking away.

"Just some insecurity issues," Lexi said, looking at Adam.

"Dude, tell me about it. Sorry you gotta put up with her." Adam laughed as he didn't bother trying to hide his voice from Anika.

"Same."

Asher, still sitting down on the bleachers, finally burst into laughter with both of his hands covering his face and his eyes staring at the ground. He was in such euphoria from oxygen deprivation that he barely even noticed Adam was standing right in front of him.

"What's so funny?" asked Adam. "Lexi, you tell her off or something?"

"Or something," Lexi responded.

"Gotta get back to practice. See ya two later, and thanks for coming to watch!" Adam ran back to the field where an angry Anika stood, glaring in their direction.

"You took a picture of them?" said Asher, finally reaching reality once again.

"You didn't seriously think that I would walk away from a situation like that and not fully document it, did you? I was just waiting for the right moment to use it."

Wiping away his tears of laughter, Asher looked up at Lexi from his seat and said, "I wanna be you when I grow up."

Lexi gave him a little curtsy and queen-like hand wave before she sat back down next to him.

"You know, I really do feel bad about how insecure she is," said Lexi, "but that doesn't give her an excuse to be such a dick to everyone. Besides, little does she know that we are the last people she should be messing with."

.....

The next day, Lexi and Shani met up for their lunch break in between classes. Lexi filled Shani in on the entire "Anika Fiasco" in explicit detail.

"I cannot believe you did that!" Shani exclaimed "I knew you were a badass, but holy shit."

"Eh, she had it coming, but yeah it was pretty freaking sick," said Lexi, walking on the sidewalk with her coffee. The two of them walked towards the Boston University Bridge hoping to enjoy the nice weather while it lasted.

"Hey, it's been over two weeks since the beginning of the semester. You can request to change dorms if you want to. And if it doesn't work out, you, of course, are more than welcome to sleep on our couch if you really want to. It's not like Asher and I ever really do anything."

It was a tempting offer. Not that Anika was ever in their dorm to begin with, but the thought of possibly never being alone in a room with her ever again, made the sky seem a little bluer than before.

"I'll definitely see what I can do. I can't be the only miserable freshman in the entire school, but thanks for the offer. I'm probably going to spend more time at your apartment anyway though. Let's be real."

In a few seconds, the waves grew stronger, the wind drove faster, and the sun burned a little brighter. It was almost as if nature sensed their presence.

"Ahh! I just want the sun to stick around for this winter," said Shani. "I mean global warming and all, but still."

"Hey, Shani," said Lexi, finding no smooth way to slide into the conversation. "Can I ask you something? And you can totally say no, of course. It's not like it's any of my business. I really am just curious." Lexi scratched her head and looked down at her feet already regretting her request.

"Yeah, of course."

"What happened to Asher's mom?"

Shani wasn't surprised Lexi would ask such a question. It was only a matter of time before they all opened up about their families.

"Ah, well, she left when I think Asher was about ten. Asher was smart enough and old enough to know what was going on. He barely talked to his mom for like a full five years after that."

"What? Oh shit. Why?" Lexi wasn't sure if she wanted to hear the rest of the story, and she wasn't sure if Asher wanted other people to know. But what harm could it do if it was coming from Shani?

"His dad found out that she was pregnant with another man's kid," said Shani.

Lexi's jaw tightened as her eyes twitched. "That's so messed up," she responded after she had a moment to process the information.

"Ohhh yeahhh," said Shani, lifting her eyebrows and deepening her voice. "Asher was a smart kid. He's only met his mom's boyfriend like three times. They never got married and for all we know, they're probably in an extremely abusive relationship. I remember just being so confused. It was like one day his parents were the happiest couple

I've ever seen, besides my dads, of course, and then his dad was crying at the table as his pregnant mom walked out the door. His dad thought it was important that Asher knew the entire story. Not to make his mom the bad guy or anything, but he just thought he deserved to know. I'm pretty sure Asher doesn't even know his brother's birthday. He talks to him sometimes and will go to his soccer games, but Asher can sometimes have problems with closure. He knows it's not Pablo's fault, but I think it's probably going to sting forever."

Sipping the last of her coffee and lifting her chin up to the sun, Lexi's soul felt a little puncture wound. The story hit close to home.

"I told Asher a little bit about this," said Lexi, "but my mom left when I was really little. Like a toddler, or maybe I was younger. I don't really ask about it. I kinda feel lucky about it though. I've never felt the need to have a mom, which I know in a way sounds kinda weird, but my dad always did everything for me. Except for maybe the time he told me to YouTube how to use tampons and pads."

Shani laughed so vigorously, her coffee almost came out of her nose.

"Wow," Shani bellowed. "My dads at least gave me a book."

The two girls exchanged genuine and expressive laughter before they returned to their serious conversation.

"You know, I don't even have any memories of her, and my dad has barely even dated since my mom. I've always felt like that was just normal and I didn't need anything else, but I forget that some people don't always have the privilege of feeling that way."

"So...you don't know whether she's dead or alive?" asked Shani. Being asked such a question made Lexi feel as if she was thinking of an upside-down world. She never felt the need to wonder if that was a possibility, let alone try to find out.

"I'm sorry," said Shani after a few moments of silence. "You don't need to answer that."

"No, no, no it's okay. I just never thought about it that way. I always pictured her to be somewhere out there, maybe spending time with a new family or something. I guess that's just 'cause I knew it bothered my dad to talk about her, and I didn't want to upset him."

In a way, it felt good for Lexi to discuss a topic that she had un-knowingly buried deep in her soul all those years ago. In another way, it seemed odd to be talking about her absent mother in a manner that wasn't negative. How did that make her feel? It was unclear.

"I think Asher will come around," said Shani. "He goes to therapy every once in a while, but I don't think he talks about his mom all that much. He usually just goes when a teacher pisses him off."

Lexi immediately thought of the time when her dad made her go to therapy because she stepped on a teacher's foot in the sixth grade for giving her a "B-" on her report about polar bears, but she decided not to share that information.

"So, what about you?" Lexi asked. "Do you know why you were adopted?"

"I don't know much, but I do know that my birth mother escaped from South Africa during Apartheid when she was really young and then came here. Then she had me when she was also really young. When she saw a gay couple on the adoption list, she chose them immediately before she even met them."

There was a sense of pride that came with that story. Just like Lexi, she was beyond grateful for the circumstances of her life.

"You know, I get what you mean by not needing a mom. I mean, I had my Aunt Thoru who definitely gave me all the motherly love I ever needed. She doesn't even have that much money, but she bought me my first car. She's also the reason I met Asher. I'm a lot more privileged than I think sometimes."

"Wow. Really?" Lexi asked.

"I was too shy to ask him to play with me when we were both in our yards. I don't think we were even two. So, she held my hand and walked me over, and we played 'toss the bouncy ball' for an entire afternoon. Been best friends ever since."

"That is the most adorable thing I've ever heard," said Lexi, picturing toddler versions of Shani and Asher with Shani most likely critiquing Asher on his bouncy-ball tossing skills. "I wonder what our parents would think about our current situations."

There were a few brief moments of silence between them while they envisioned what their parents' reactions would be to their supernatural abilities, even though they both had pictured the scenarios countless times.

"I think they would just be scared," said Lexi. "They wouldn't be mad. They wouldn't try to send us to the crazy house. They would just be...scared."

As they tried to continue to walk along the bridge, the wind disagreed with them. The blustery air pushed against them, leaving them no choice but to cover their faces and shut their eyes as tightly as they could.

"Really? I didn't think it was gonna be this windy today," Shani shouted over the noise.

"I don't think it was supposed to be this sunny either," Lexi yelled back. She now regretted her decision of wearing her usual hippie skirt. One arm was covering her face while the other held her skirt from flying through the air and revealing her black booty shorts. The fact that the wind was ice-cold wasn't helpful either.

Then, an abrupt cacophony came out of nowhere. Not many cars were passing the bridge this time of day. Still, the echoing sound of a motor, or rather multiple motors crept upon them. They were getting closer and coming from behind them.

Shani uncovered her eyes for only a brief moment to see where she was walking. The sound of the vehicles convinced her to turn around and take a glance at the opposite side of the bridge. Three cars were zooming towards them, and Shani's stomach churned at the sight of their presence.

Each car was a different make and model. A red one to the right, a blue old junky one to the left, and a shiny black one in the middle. Shani didn't know the makes of the cars, but they were driving as if they were all together. Almost as if they were in a street gang. One was in the middle up ahead while the other two traveled behind, making a perfect triangle.

Something else was off about the mysterious cars. All in a half of a second, Shani squinted her eyes to sharpen her sight. Could that be possible? Was this real? No driver. None of the vehicles had drivers.

Shani processed all of this information so fast, she could barely hear Lexi screaming "SHANI" in her ear.

Before she could acknowledge anything that came out of Lexi's mouth, she felt Lexi violently pushing her out of the way. The driverless cars were coming straight at them, and they were not about to stop.

They missed the metal hoods by inches. If Lexi's skirt was any longer, the red car would have torn it off. All three cars daringly and carelessly crashed into the stone wall and briefly soared in the air before they all made their descent. But they did not descend alone. With the bridge wall, came around a hundred square feet of the floor breaking off and plunging into the water. Shani and Lexi tried to run for their lives and jump to safety, but they were too late. The top of a street lamp shook loose and struck Lexi in the back of her skull. Shani reached for Lexi's arm, but the floor broke beneath them.

Shani screamed as she saw herself and Lexi plunge to the surface of the water. As Shani drew closer, she tried to think of what she could do. Could she make the water disappear? That wouldn't help. Could she make the river catch them? That wouldn't be any better, but it didn't matter. She couldn't think that fast. Before she knew it, she and Lexi broke through the water and faded into the darkness of the river.

16:

"Just to make sure they're still alive."

Everything was dark, or at least it was before Shani drearily opened her eyes. How long was she out for? Did she pass out or black out? A small beam of light finally reached her eyes. In the distance, a blotch of yellow material moved fluidly through the motion of the water. She focused her eyes to see Lexi's hair covering her face. Lexi. She was still in the water.

As Shani rushed to her friend as fast as she could, she moved at an abnormal speed. Not slow from her lack of consciousness, she was fast. Her feet kicked through the water like a jet ski on the lake. Then there were her eyes. The more she focused, the clearer she could see. At first, she questioned if she were hallucinating or dreaming until she felt a sting from the bleeding scrape on her arms. It was anything but ordinary, but that wasn't the most peculiar part of it all.

There was a calming sensation that the molecules in the water were giving her. It was almost as if they were telling Shani that everything was going to be fine, and they were going to take care of her. Without a second thought, Shani opened her mouth to gasp for the breath she so desperately needed. Her breath...it was water. Water seeped in through her lungs and pushed back out. The river tasted foul, almost like dog saliva, but it felt natural, like a reflex.

"Whoa," Shani mumbled, hearing herself perfectly clear through the water, and watching the bubbles from her mouth float to the surface.

There was no time for admiration. Surrounding Lexi's head were liters of blood. Her blood. With an effortless push, Shani grabbed Lexi by the waist and shot up to the surface. The sun was still shining as Shani forced the upper halves of their bodies into the fresh air.

Without missing a beat, Shani immediately heard the shrieking sounds of humans shouting and screaming at the top of their lungs.

"Look! There they are!" she heard a man say.

"Somebody help them!" a woman with a baby cried.

As Shani pushed her way through the water, rushing to shore, a boy no older than sixteen dove head first into the heavy current. Visibly a trained swimmer, he freestyled his way to meet them halfway, but luckily and miraculously, they weren't far from shore.

"Quick! Help me hold her head up! Her head is bleeding," Shani shrieked, spitting out water. The boy flipped onto his side, cradled Lexi's head with one arm and frantically struggled through the waves, even though Shani was doing most of the work.

Tall and brittle trees stood where the river met the land. At least ten people were scattered among the trees, waiting for the three swimmers to arrive at shore. With the amount of adrenaline running through Shani and the boy, they could have easily pulled themselves up onto the grassy surface, but at least four blurry faces pulled them by the arms from the river.

"Please! Somebody call an ambulance!" Shani cried, reaching for Lexi.

"Already done!" said the woman with the baby. "Who knows C.P .R.?"

"I do!" coughed the lifesaving teenaged boy. "I can do it." He pulled his exhausted body to Lexi and checked her breathing. Nothing. No movement at all. He checked her pulse. Nothing.

Now vigorously shaking, the boy tilted her head back and lifted her chin to give her mouth-to-mouth resuscitation.

"Careful!" Shani breathlessly screeched, sitting on the other side of Lexi.

Two five-second long breaths, still no breathing. He moved to contractions. With straight arms and flattened palms, he heavily panted his way through thirty steady contractions, but there was still no pulse. Shani tried to concentrate. She could tell there was water in her lungs, but she couldn't focus enough to remove it. Even if she did get the water out of her lungs, she was still unconscious from hitting her head.

"Come on! COME ON!" Shani whipped her head back and forth between Lexi's motionless body and the pathway where the ambulance was to arrive.

Her body was back to breathing. He plugged Lexi's nose, took one deep breath, and inflated her lungs as much as he could. After the second blow, he moved back to her chest to repeat the process, but before he could...

SPLAT!

Lexi coughed up what looked like a liter of water. Her eyes still closed, and her body still lay flat on the ground. She arched her back, trying to gasp for as much air as she could.

As Lexi's head faced Shani, she let her upper body drop next to Lexi's, letting every bit of air and tension escape.

"She's okay!" a tall, round man said to the paramedics as they ran to the rescue.

Lexi finally opened her eyes to see Shani's tearful face looking over her. To everyone's surprise, Lexi didn't show any signs of fear whatsoever; rather confusion and concern.

"Are you okay?" Lexi quivered. "Is everyone okay? What happened?"

"We were hit and fell off into the river, but it's okay. We're okay. An ambulance is coming."

Instead of hope or relief coming across Lexi's path, fear was trapped inside of her.

"Shani, no," she whispered, pulling Shani close.

"What?" Shani's voice shook.

"We have to get out of here. It's a trap. Those cars, they were just to weaken us. If they wanted us dead, we would be dead. Whoever they are, they're coming for us. I can't get in that ambulance."

Shani knew exactly what to do, or more so, who to call. "Yes, you can," she said with determination shivering throughout her body.

"What?"

"Just trust me."

The paramedics spared no time. One paramedic was tall, one was short, and one was bald, and they all crouched down closer to Lexi than she wished.

"Can you tell me your name?" the tall one asked.

"Sarah Jessica," Lexi responded with no hesitation. Shani bit her tongue in relief that Lexi didn't add the name "Parker" to the end.

"Alright, Sarah," said the small man, yet with a deeper voice. "We're going to put you on the gurney, ready? Three...two...one!"

Lexi was expecting any movement in her head to overwhelm her with pain, but when her body left the ground, there was nothing but relief. That wasn't going to work with the paramedics.

"Ahhh!" Lexi faked, but Shani was too paranoid to realize she was faking. She was just as nervous as the paramedics were.

"Don't worry, just keep breathing." The only thing that Lexi was worried about was what on Earth Shani could be thinking.

"Can I ride with you?" Shani asked.

"You're family, right?" the bald paramedic asked, clearly trying to get her to say yes, even if it wasn't the truth.

"Yes, of course."

The bald paramedic threw open the driver's door and jumped in as the other two hauled Lexi into the van, and Shani followed. The lights and sirens were already turned on, and the driver gave no warning before Shani almost fell off the chair. But that was her sign. Her sign that it was time to execute the rest of her plan.

Shani hunched over, trying to act like she was crying over Lexi's conscious body, but she was careful to make sure neither of the paramedics in the back noticed that she was in fact texting Asher on her phone, which was somehow still working.

"SOS! Follow the ambulance that's headed down Storrow Drive! We will open up the door while you catch us! Now!"

Asher wasn't always the best at texting back right away, but they knew they had at least ten minutes before they reached the hospital. Shani's fingers bounced against her thigh until seconds later when Asher responded with "OMW!" Shani could sense that he understood the urgency, but what if he didn't make it on time? What if he couldn't find the ambulance?

"Is she going to be okay?" Shani asked, trying to give her best performance.

"Yes, she is. I'll make sure of that," said the short paramedic. "Her heart rate is at a surprisingly normal pace. You're a fighter, Sarah."

"I know. Thanks," said Lexi, trying to make her throat sound scratchy.

"Come on, come on, come on." Shani mouthed with tight lips. Shani was praying for traffic to slow them down at least by a few seconds, but the road was almost perfectly clear by the way Shani felt the van picking up speed. No turns yet. No motorcycles trying to cut in front of them.

Lexi couldn't keep her eyes off Shani. She knew she couldn't say anything. But what was going to happen to them? Did Shani have an actual plan, or just an idea that would eventually lead to a plan? The anxiety holding tight in Shani's temples and forehead gave Lexi a loose answer to her question, but there was nothing that Lexi could do to help. At least for now, but Lexi understood more than Shani knew.

Whooooosh!

Shani and Lexi felt something brush against the van.

"He's here," Shani whispered into Lexi's ear.

"Who's here?" Lexi asked. "Asher? Is that him?" Shani put her finger against her lips before the paramedics picked up on the strange wind as well.

"What in the—?" The short paramedic stepped through the doorway, closer to the front windshield, trying to find whatever was flapping against the van. "What's going on?"

"Um...I think—" The bald driver was about to say it had to be a bird, but before he could, the back doors slammed open.

"Ahh!" Asher screamed before the left door took him with it. "Ow! He was now squished between the outside of the door and the left wall of the van.

"Jesus!" Shani quietly screamed as she helped Lexi up.

"HEY!" The two paramedics screamed with confusion and fear. How did the van open? And what were they trying to do?

"Sorry!" Shani hollered before she made it look like she hit the large container of water with the head stabilizer, when in reality that wasn't going to make a dent in thick plastic. But she didn't have time to look for something else. She was the one to make the container explode, and it exploded right into their faces.

They were about to jump out before Shani noticed that something was off. Why wasn't the driver pulling over? Shani looked through the small opening to the driver's seat to see that something was wrong. The driver repeatedly stomped on the brakes, hoping the van would come to a halt, but they were still racing down the road.

"Oh, no," she whispered to herself. "Asher, what did you do?!"

"Asher?!" Lexi yelled when he didn't respond.

"I'm coming! I'm coming!" Asher yelled back. He pulled himself up and out of the entrapment, but still held onto the end of the roof where the van doors were supposed to be closed, holding onto it like an enchanted wheelbarrow that was spiraling out of control.

"How are we going to slow this thing down?"

"DON'T WORRY!" Asher screamed much too loudly. "I BROUGHT BACK UP!"

"Oh, Lord," Lexi whispered to herself as she and Shani turned to see Logan in the distance, ready to strike when necessary, or at least that's what they assumed since he stood there with too much confidence and his hands in the air.

"Get away from anything electric!" Lexi screamed as she pulled Shani up onto the gurney and before they knew it, the entire van was covered with blue and white sparks that would blind the naked eye. Asher had time to think through the process of closing his eyes, but not letting go of the metal. His hair stuck up and his face was every shade of red, but his hands didn't hurt enough to let go of the van just yet.

"Uh oh," Logan whispered to himself. It didn't work. No amount of electrocution was going to stop this van. "Please don't make me." He knew what he had to do, but it was risky, and it was going to take more than a single moment. On top of that, he didn't know if he could do it.

"Come on, Logan!" Asher hollered.

It took longer than his deep breath to gather up the amount of electricity and force he was going to need. Even with the activity pulsing throughout his body, he wasn't sure when the need for more power was going to end. The pressure in his heart was unbearable, but it was still a pressure he needed, wanted, and craved. But if there was any consequence to saving the lives in that van, there wasn't a single consequence that would stop him.

"LOGAN!" Asher screamed again.

The van was only about two hundred feet away now, and it was picking up speed. Instead of waiting a second longer, Logan instinctively shot two bolts of lightning into the van's front right tire. The tire that was closest to him. With the amount of stamina coursing throughout the one object, the tire had no choice but explode.

"Shit!" the driver screamed, almost falling into the passenger's seat, but it was working. Catastrophically, but it was working.

Logan didn't have time for a break. He needed to get the other tires off.

"Ahh!" His second attempt at ripping off the other front tire took a toll on him. It was almost as if his soul was being ripped out of his body from the skin of his arms. The loss of power was too much to overcome. As the van passed him on the road, he fell to his knees, knowing he wasn't going to be able to do it again.

"GUYS, GET OUT!" Logan hollered with every drop of energy he had left.

"They'll be okay!" Lexi shouted to Shani. "Asher catch us!"

Without any questions, Asher nodded and shouted "THREE, TWO, JUMP!" and with one foot each, their bodies left the metal vehicle and were thrown into the soft, yet strong wings that carried the three beings back onto the road before they tumbled their way to safety.

Lexi threw herself back to standing as if it was a reflex. She ignored the sore bones and muscles that stung like giant needles in her body. In the distance was an evergreen tree. There was only one option to save the three paramedics in the van. If the branches couldn't catch the van, it was headed straight for a rail guard.

"I'm sorry, tree," she wept as the muscles in her arm snapped with the tree trunk. In order for it to fall in time, Lexi had to push with it. One of the tallest evergreen trees that they'd seen in the city of Boston slapped down on the pavement so hard, it made a small, straight dent. The pavement crumbled into bits as the van was slowly caught by the branches and remained straddling over the trunk. It finally stopped.

"That escalated quickly!" said Logan, running up to check on his friends.

"We need to get out of here," Shani shouted. "Now!"

•••••

Brex ran up the sidewalk as fast as she could. Her phone was on silent until she noticed she had five missed calls from Shani, which she figured was usual for Asher to get from Shani, but not for her. She wasn't sure where she was anymore, she just knew if she kept running east, she would eventually land near Fenway Park, where they were supposed to meet.

"Oh, shit!" Brex loudly, but scarcely whispered to herself, out of breath. She saw the sign that said "Fenway Park" with an arrow pointing to the left. She crossed the street while almost getting hit by a minivan, and ran down the alley with the smell of hot dogs and cheap nachos shooting up her nose.

"Come on, come on. Where are you?" She searched around for familiar faces. Her jaw tightened together before she saw Logan lethargically drifting down the alley. Logan's eyes were puffed wider than a pillow. Shani, Lexi, and Asher on the other hand, had faces smeared with blood.

"Oh, God." Brex ripped off her jean jacket to clot at least one person's blood.

"Brex, we're fine," said Shani. "Our wounds are closed. We just need to not have blood all over us. Did you bring the water?"

"Yeah," Brex pulled out a plastic water bottle that was stuffed in the inner pocket of her jacket. "Come here."

The five of them stumbled their way into a small niche between two buildings across from the Fenway Park entrance.

"What happened?" Brex asked as Shani took the water and sprayed everyone down, trying to get them clean.

"Where do I start?" she asked. Shani filled everyone in on what they didn't know. Being the most uninformed, Brex remained confused even after Shani wrapped up the story.

"Wait." Brex shut her eyes and ran her fingers through her long hair. "There were no drivers in the cars?"

"No, none of them," Shani responded.

"But there had to be someone controlling them. Someone who knew where we were, but didn't want to come near us for some reason. But why would they want to do that?

"Why would they send something like that?" Asher asked. "Why wouldn't they hire someone, or why wouldn't they poison us somehow?"

"That's what I'm saying!" Lexi shouted too loudly before Shani shushed her. "I don't think they were trying to kill us. Whoever these people are know that it's going to take a lot more than that, and they know how to do it. They were trying to trap us or lure us to the hospital where they thought we would be."

"They need us to be alive in order to take our powers," Logan pointed out.

"That's the only explanation," Brex agreed.

"But why can't they come near us?" Asher asked again.

"We don't know yet." Brex began pacing in a circle and audibly breathing through her nose. "Let's just get you guys home. We shouldn't be out here."

"We should check if the ambulance is on the news," Lexi added. "Just to make sure they're still alive."

17:

"They're all screaming, but we can't tell why."

"Are you sure you don't mind me staying here?" Lexi asked while Shani tucked her thick blue sheets into the couch of the Main Street living room.

"Stay here for the rest of the freaking year, dude. I don't care. Neither does Asher. Ow." Shani continued to put in an unusual amount of effort to make the couch look presentable even though her arm still hurt from her tumble earlier that afternoon. But Adam was only a few feet away from her, so she was trying desperately to be discreet about it.

After fluffing the pillows, she grabbed fabric freshener and sprayed the cushions like she was forbidden to ever spray them again.

"You do know we are still in college, right?" Lexi asked. "I know I'm new to this whole thing, but I'm good with just my blanket, pillow, and a bottom sheet. That's how I like it anyway. I'm not a middle-aged mother that thinks the dessert forks should be placed outside of the main fork and not closer to the plate."

"Yeah. You're acting like my grandma, Shani," said Adam, standing on a ladder and slapping fresh spackle on the ceiling. "Man, what kind of basketball were you messing around with to make this big of a dent?"

Brex stood at the bottom of his ladder, holding the sides and footing it at the bottom. "Logan and Asher put sand in it as a metaphor for the 'Whose balls are bigger and stronger?' challenge," she said, mentally high-fiving herself.

"That sounds about right." Adam made his final clean swipe with his scraper and walked down the eight-foot ladder.

"Why exactly do you have all this stuff again?" Brex asked, helping him fold it up.

"We had this party at our frat house and—"

"Oh, that explains it." After the latest frat party Brex attended, she had a better grasp of how football players and alcohol mixed together.

"Adam, thank you," said Shani. "You really didn't have to. Venmo request me for the spackle. Okay?" She silently peered at Brex, implying that the money was in fact going to come from her. Brex sarcastically stuck out her tongue and gave her a thumbs up all while Adam wasn't looking.

"You want me to leave this here, so you can paint it when it dries?" Adam asked.

"Eh, I think we got that part covered, but thanks." Asher's wings were still not at their finest, now due to multiple circumstances, but Shani already felt guilty enough asking Adam to help with Brex's accidental demolition.

"Brex, you want me to walk you home?"

"Huh, I was gonna ask you the same thing," she said before she walked over to Shani and whispered "You sure you guys are okay?"

"We're fine," Shani softly whispered back. "Those paramedics were barely even bruised. No one's coming after us. And even if they saw something no one would believe them. I'll text you if not though, okay?" Shani smiled as Brex nodded, grabbed the bucket full of tools and beckoned Adam to follow her out the door, carrying the ladder by himself.

"I'm gonna order food for us," said Shani, pulling out her phone. "I haven't had time to shop. You want some wine?"

"Always," said Lexi, now trying to luxuriously lay in her new bed. Nothing was sore anymore, but her muscles were still tense and occasionally shaky.

All of a sudden, they heard the sound of bare feet scurrying through the hallway and getting closer to the living room.

"Di—fof—affholf 'eave wifout fayin' bye?" asked Asher with a toothbrush in his mouth.

"Yeah, where have you been?" Lexi laughed. Not only did he have toothpaste drooling from his chin and onto his shirtless chest, but he had gruesome nap marks on his forehead and shoulders.

He spat his toothpaste into the kitchen sink and said, "I kinda half fell asleep doing my homework. I haven't been sleeping too well for the past few nights."

"Don't tell me I have to take care of the both of you now," said Shani.

"You don't have to take care of either of us," said Lexi. "I'm fine. *We're* fine. Are you even fine?"

"I'm fine!" Shani defensively threw her arms in the air.

"You guys wanna watch a movie before going to bed?" Asher asked, falling onto the living room chair.

"Yes, please," said Lexi, pulling the covers over her. "I vote anything on Hulu or Netflix."

"Of course, anything," said Shani. The three of them snuggled into their cozy spots surrounding the T.V. after Shani made her famous homemade popcorn for everyone. "Hey, so...there's something else that I didn't tell you guys yesterday."

"You're not growing scales, are you?" asked Asher, stuffing popcorn in his face.

"Not exactly, but good guess," said Shani, giving him a sarcastic thumbs up. "No. When I was in the water, trying to help Lexi, I— I found out that I can breathe underwater. So, I have gills apparently."

"WHAT?" Lexi screeched, gleefully sitting up straight on the couch. "Sick! Elaborate more, please!"

Shani was almost blushing. "Well, I had this weird sort of instinct. It was almost like a message telling me that I was safe, and I could take a deep breath 'cause I really needed to, obviously. And you know what else? It was almost as if a spirit was telling me this. I felt...connected to another being. Somebody was watching over me—over *us*. It felt so empowering. I can swim really fast too. I'm no Aquaman, but still."

She ended up being the entertainment that Asher and Lexi wanted to watch. The two of them sat there with popcorn in their laps and eyes glued to Shani's beaming face.

"Sorry I didn't tell you earlier," she said. "But you know, other things came up..."

"I don't know what you're talking about," Asher joked before they all shook their heads in unison instead of laughter.

A few minutes into the movie, the three of them almost drifted into their own personal bubbles. Lexi pulled out her pencil that read "SAVE THE TURTLES" across it and worked on her biology homework while Shani was already making more popcorn, but secretly hoping she would be able to get away with hogging the whole bowl.

"So, is that douchebag still bothering you at your internship, Shani," asked Asher, now aimlessly scrolling through his phone.

"Ohhh, yeah," she responded. "The other day he said, 'You know, Shani, I don't know what your teeth look like because you never smile.' UGH!"

"He did not!" Lexi said, throwing down her pencil and book. Giving no regard to her homework anymore, all of her attention was on Shani.

"It gets sooo much better." Shani had to put down her beloved popcorn to prevent her spastic gestures from knocking it over. "I went to Dr. Carter about it, and she just said, 'Well I think that's just because you have such a lovely smile, dear.' Like are you kidding me? It's almost 2018! It's so disappointing hearing that coming from a woman."

Asher scratched the back of his head and rubbed the temples of his forehead, not wanting to tell Shani what she needed to hear.

"Dude, I really think you should tell your advisor," he said, pulling his body as far away from her as he could on his chair.

To both Asher's and Lexi's surprise, she didn't seem angry, and she didn't get defensive, only frustrated.

"Ughhhhhh," she moaned, immediately bringing her popcorn close back to her chest and shoving as much as she could into her mouth.

"I know how much you hate asking for help, but I think that's better than being sexually harassed at work and having your boss do nothing about it."

Shani took a few moments to finish chewing and think about what her response was going to be. "Yeah, you're right," she finally answered. "But what are they going to do about it? My advisor is a guy for one, so he's probably not gonna get it, and I have no actual proof of what he's been doing. It's not like he touched me. Well, besides the one time that he touched my freaking hair."

"Oh, Lord," Asher and Lexi both mumbled.

"To be fair he was trying to get something out of it, but it was a little aggressive and forward. But I'll think about it, okay? I just gotta give it a hot second and think about how I'm going to approach it. I don't wanna do anything stupid."

Both Asher and Lexi quietly and respectfully agreed as they put their attention back into the movie.

Trying to sneak his way through, Asher let his hand crawl over to Shani's popcorn bowl. Only a few inches away with his eyes still glued to the screen, Shani caught him before it was too late.

"Ow!" Asher whimpered after Shani smacked his hand away.

"Nuh uh," she said. "You had your turn."

.....

The next evening was the beginning of an amazing weekend. Logan held another frat party at the house, Shani wasn't scheduled to be at the aquarium the next morning, Brex finished her new portfolio early, and Lexi was headed to the Butterfly Museum to do research on her evolution paper that was due in a week.

It was around eleven o'clock when she walked out of her dorm and started her journey to the train. It was only the second time she had to take the train in Boston. The other was when she was eleven and took a school field trip to the Boston Museum of Science. Her one prominent memory from that train ride was when her friend Joey cried from stepping in gum and ruining his new sneakers. Lexi was the only one who offered to help him get it off, but didn't have any hand-sanitizing wipes for afterwards. Therefore, she had to go the rest of the trip with used gum residue on her hands. This time, she took precautions and stuffed a few single wipes in her handbag before she left.

Unfortunately, she only had a few hours to spend at the museum. Her last class of the week was at 3:45, and no matter how much she studied, she didn't feel that she was prepared for it, but that was a normal feeling for her.

The train didn't smell nearly as bad as she thought it would. Instead of the stench of sweaty sports bras, it smelled as if someone had over-cooked tomato sauce. She whisked down the stairs and reached in her pocket to get her wallet ready, only to see the train was down.

"Excuse me," Lexi said to the closest train attendant. "When do you think the train will be up and running again?"

"Hard to say, sweetie, but you can stick around for as long as you want to."

The man had to be at least twice Lexi's size, which made her feel even more uncomfortable on top of feeling violently angry with the way he was staring at her up and down. Instead of answering, she just focused her eyes on the ground and walked away as fast as possible. Being sexually harassed on the street was distressingly normal to her, but by a train attendant? That was a first.

Lexi hiked up her skirt and ran up the stairs. Just in case the creep from the train platform was following her, she turned the corner before she ordered her Uber. Uber said the car would meet her at the pick-up location in four minutes, but after seven minutes, Lexi was worried the driver was lost. There were too many occasions when the driver couldn't find her location, would quickly give up, and then charge her for it. There were few things that enraged Lexi more than stupid people.

The time was now 11:42. At this rate, she was barely going to have any time with the butterflies. To any other person, a few hours would be more than enough time to stare at colorful insects, but Lexi found the creatures fascinating. They could keep her entertained all day long. Her project was going to write itself.

Finally, she saw the gray Toyota Corolla pull up. With her fingers crossed, her head went back and forth between checking the license plate on her phone and checking the plate on the car. It was a match.

"Who are you here for?" Lexi asked, leaning over to look at the driver through the window.

"Alexandra?" the driver asked. He looked as if he were almost six and a half feet tall. His sandy blonde hair almost touched the top of the car ceiling.

"Perfect." Lexi hopped in the back seat as fast as she could. "Listen, since it's not too busy out, and I'm a little late, I would love it if you—" She stopped to notice something odd. The man wasn't moving. He didn't even look like he was breathing. Lexi could see in the rearview mirror that his eyes were staring straight forward without even a little twitch.

"Hey, are you okay?" Lexi asked, but before he could answer, his entire upper body fell straight forward onto the steering wheel, causing the horn to continuously go off. "Oh my God! Sir?" She frantically tried to pull him straight back up and unbuckle his seat belt to give him C.P.R. She stuck her two fingers on his wrist to check his pulse, but there was nothing. No heartbeat, no movement, just silence.

Oh no, she thought. *What could possibly be happening? This man didn't look a day over thirty. Could he really be having a heart attack?*

Lexi jumped into the passenger's seat and reached for the lever over the man's unconscious body to make his seat lie down, but before she could adjust him into the right position, she smelled something that almost made her vomit; something much worse than sweaty sports bras.

Where was it coming from?

Her question was quickly answered when she saw a thin layer of glowing blue steam coming from the car's ventilator.

The density grew by the second. Lexi's first instinct was to stay and try to save this man, but was this going to kill her? What if she held her breath? No, she needed to leave. She turned her body to reach for the car door, but her arm...it wasn't moving. Neither was her other one. Her vision blurred so intensely, she couldn't even see what was outside the window anymore. She was too late.

Everything faded from blue to black. The last thing Lexi could sense was the excruciating pain of her head hitting the door handle as she lost consciousness and felt the car slowly drive into motion.

*****

The day was now turning to twilight, and the temperature was dropping like an ice age covering Earth.

"Hey, it's me again," said Shani, leaving another voicemail on Lexi's phone. "We're all getting really worried. You said you would come over before your gig, and we're just looking around for you all over town, and I guess I'm just going to continue calling until you pick up 'cause I don't really know what else to do. We're headed to your gig at Bevanda now. Okay, bye."

The four of them quickly walked to Bevanda, barely stopping for traffic. They could see through the windows that the restaurant wasn't at its peak rush hour of the day, which gave Shani no problem with shoving open the front entrance door as fast as she could.

"Lexi?" Shani hollered as she quickly scanned the room.

"Shhh, Shani we can't draw attention," said Asher, trying to keep up with her agile speed as she raced through the restaurant. "It's too risky. We just have to look around, alright?"

Shani agreed with him, but not enthusiastically. All she wanted to do was look around and hope to see Lexi's face, but instead, she saw Jimmy's. The manager stood behind the bar, helping to make some drinks.

"Um, excuse me! Jimmy!" Shani hollered.

Jimmy gave a friendly, charismatic smile back while pouring what looked like a hard, frozen coffee drink.

"Can I help you?" he said as the four of them approached and surrounded the bar.

"Yes, please," Shani responded placing her hands on the wet, freshly washed counter. "Lexi is supposed to play here tonight, right? She didn't happen to come early, did she?"

"Lexi? No, she's not supposed to come in for another hour or so. Why? Is something wrong?"

"Um...no she—" Shani couldn't finish her sentence, all control was lost when the image of Jimmy behind the bar was whisked away and replaced with an image of Lexi fully submerged in a glowing, deep, green liquid.

"Ah...ha..." Shani tried to talk, but not a single word could be formed. And no matter how many times she blinked or squinted, the traumatizing image of Lexi possibly drowning wouldn't leave. Shani's shoulders shivered as she noticed something cold. Could Lexi be in another ice cave? She couldn't tell, but she kept her focus straight forward, hoping she could see more, but she was powerless. Whoever, or whatever wanted her to see this vision was in control.

Shani's knees and ankles struggled to hold her and collapsed as she reclaimed her own vision.

"Is she okay?" Jimmy asked as Brex and Logan kept her shaky body standing.

"We need to get out of here," Shani whispered to Brex. "We need to get to Lexi, she isn't here."

"She's fine," Brex said to Jimmy. "We just think Lexi...uh might not make it tonight. She'll explain later. Um...phone problems." She softened her voice and helped Shani regain her balance. "Come on, guys. Let's go. We gotta go."

The four of them turned to run out the door, but to their dismay, something large and round was blocking their pathway a few feet away from their exit. Asher bumped into a large, rock-hard body and jerked backwards as he scanned upwards to see an angry Rick, piercing his eyes through Asher's skull.

"Ah, sweet God," Asher whispered under his breath.

"What did you just say, boy?" Rick responded with beer flicking out of his beard.

Brex grabbed Asher by the arm and said, "He said he's very sorry for running into you, and we'll be on our way."

"I'll be keeping my eye on you while the little lady is up on stage tonight!" said Rick.

It was easy for Asher to just keep walking and ignore him completely. Shani, on the other hand, was not as much of a pushover.

"Okay, buddy! It's very nice of you to be concerned for our friend, but we got it," she said, marching up to him, giving him a condescending pat on his slightly bald head.

Brex's first instinct was to get the manager's attention. That was her usual reaction when bartenders threatened to throw her out of their bars. Although this time, it felt like getting an adult involved with child's play, but her patience was running dangerously low.

Jimmy was only a few feet in front of her when she made eye contact with him and said, "Hey Jim—" but suddenly, she was unable to speak.

It was like a three-inch thick sword struck clean through her scar. The pain in her left hand was so agonizing, she couldn't help but fall to the floor. Everything went blurry. It was almost as if her senses were completely cut off. She barely noticed how violently she was screaming as she connected to the cement tiles.

"What's going on?" one customer cried out.

"Call 9-1-1! They need help!" said another customer.

They? Brex thought to herself. *Please, no.* She prayed it wasn't true. With her teary eyes and clenched muscles, she fought her way to flip her body over to see Shani, Asher, and Logan all hunched over on the floor, clutching their scars.

What was happening? How could she possibly stop it? The pain wasn't diminishing. It wasn't becoming any more bearable. All Brex could do was squirm on the floor with at least four people surrounding her.

"They must've been poisoned or eaten something really bad," she heard a teenage boy say.

She had to get these people away from her. They had to escape before any cops or paramedics came, but how? A diversion. That was the only way, and suddenly her eyes locked with that dreadful cactus that Lexi had almost blown up the week before. How flammable were cacti? And how was she going to engulf it in flames without anyone noticing?

All she could do with her entire body glued to the ground was focus her golden eyes straight into the soul of the green, potted plant, in hopes her powers were developed enough for at least a small spark to ignite.

Now, at least three people were on the phone with the police. She could hear the voices of people struggling to describe what was happening to the authorities.

"They're all just...hunched over, and on the floor," said one middle-aged woman.

"They're all screaming, but we can't tell why," said another.

But Brex had to do everything she could to completely block them out. She didn't even blink as her forehead continued to tighten. The spark. It was almost there. She could feel it, and the pain; it was beginning its descent. Suddenly, she could feel her fingertips again. Everything was being overpowered by the flames sprouting from within her, and in the snap of a finger, there was a single crimson and amber spark that burst at the tip of the prickly cactus. It was now only a matter of seconds before somebody noticed, but in the meantime, the fire had already traveled to the satin curtains hanging from the window.

Oh no, Brex thought.

"Is that smoke?" said one of the middle-aged women. "Oh my God, it's fire!"

"Everybody out!" screamed Jimmy, and suddenly the paranoid, screaming bar transformed into a violent stampede.

One man tried to help Brex to her feet, but she gathered up enough strength to pull herself up. As her feet trampled towards the door, she spotted Shani, Asher, and Logan, fighting their way through the crowd. They were okay. They were going to make it out, but they still had to sneak away.

Logan was closest to the door, and he was the first one of them to get out of the building. He figured the majority of the sprinting patrons were either going to go left or right, so he made the executive decision of immediately running across the street, hoping the rest would follow.

Out came Shani. Logan's light blue sweater caught her eye. She fell a few feet behind and followed Logan to the cross walk. As they were about to cross, Asher stumbled out.

"Asher!" they both screamed, which caught his attention. Brex was the last one out of anybody to race out of the restaurant, or so she thought.

"Help!" Brex heard the second she passed through the door. It was the sound of an old woman screaming, and it was coming from inside. "Help!" she heard again. She almost tripped as she jolted back inside to see a table toppled over onto a woman who appeared to be in at least her eighties.

"Oh my God," Brex screeched as she ran over and threw the table off her. The fire was getting closer. They had to keep moving. "Here, give me your hand!" Brex yelled as she quickly pulled the woman to her feet. The second Brex put the small woman's short arm across her shoulders, the sprinkler system finally activated.

The ground almost immediately became drenched, which caused Brex to almost slip once again. Thankfully, she was able to catch herself and not break the fragile human she was helping.

"Mom! Mom!" Brex heard a middle-aged man holler as they finally exited the building. A tall, brunette man who was at least three times the size of his mother came running down the sidewalk, panting from how far away he got before he had realized he was missing someone.

"Really?" Brex screeched before she gave him a deadly glare, handed his mother over to him, and ran back to the closest crosswalk. The rest of them stood, anxiously waiting at the other side of the street.

"Thank you!" said the oblivious man as Brex ran away. Instead of vocally responding, she just gave them a sharp wave without turning back to look at them.

"Are you okay?" Logan yelled as Brex made her way to the opposite side of the street.

"Well, I just set a freaking building on fire, so no, but the moron forgot his own mom," she said as they continued to walk by themselves.

"What is with us and burning buildings?" Asher asked as he kept trying to catch his breath.

"Everyone's okay, right?" Brex asked.

"I think so," Logan responded. "What was that?"

"I don't know," said Shani, "but before whatever that was, I saw Lexi in more of that green liquid. She might be in another ice cave, but I don't know for sure. I think the screaming was some sort of signal to tell us she was in danger."

The rest didn't know what to say. What was their next move?

"Did you see anything else? If you didn't we have no leads."

The hopelessness filled Shani with guilt and anxiety, until she knew exactly what to do. "Damn it," she said. "Yes, we do. Follow me."

18:

"Do you have water?"

The four of them sprinted towards the aquarium with Shani's long legs moving the fastest. Brex kept calling Lexi and leaving voicemails with irrational hopes that she would answer. Logan repeatedly called Anika, thinking she might have some compassion to give him any information on Lexi that she had, but after leaving five voicemails, he realized he was sadly mistaken.

"Nothing," he said. "We have no other leads."

"I'm gonna get something out of this guy, I know it," said Shani. "I knew that creep was up to something. I had suspicions about him from the beginning."

"How are we gonna get anything out of him?" asked Brex. "I mean we can't just accuse him of that in front of people."

"Did you have anything better in mind?" Shani didn't mean to ask so aggressively, but it came off that way.

"Yeah, actually. Why don't we just ask him if he's ever even interacted with Lexi in the first place. As far as we know, he's only ever seen her when he saw her at the bar the first night of classes."

"Okay, yeah. Good idea," said Shani trying to recover from her unintentional onslaught.

They finally reached the doors. The sky was now a musty gray, and so far, time was not on their side.

It was almost closing time for the aquarium. Most of the patrons had already gone home for the day, and few people were exploring the main hallway, but Seamus was still nowhere to be found.

"Hey, Seamus is working today, right?" Shani asked one of the off-duty tour guides who was about to leave.

"Yeah, he's somewhere over there," he responded, flailing his hand around giving Shani the vaguest indication of where he might be.

"Uh...thanks, Mark."

The rest followed her around with Asher being the only one who didn't know what the guy looked like. They kept speed walking while making circles around the building until the sandy blonde hair and buttoned-down, striped shirt stuck out like a flashing, red light. Seamus stood there with a clipboard in his hand, gazing into the penguin exhibit.

"Seamus!" Shani yelled as she quickly approached him.

"Hey! What's up?" Seamus responded with too much confidence. "Oh hey, Brex. How's it going?" Suddenly he seemed intimidated with both Brex and Shani assertively standing in front of him.

"Hi," said Brex in a quite monotone fashion, without answering his question.

"What's going on?"

"Have you seen my friend, Lexi, anywhere? Shani asked, faster than usual.

"Lexi?"

"You saw her last month, remember?" Seamus shook his head, not catching on to what she was saying. "She was singing at that restaurant? Curly blonde—"

Her words faded off into silence the moment Seamus drew his pencil up to and behind his ear. It was white and read "SAVE THE TURTLES" along the side, just like the one Lexi was writing with.

"Where is she?" she asked quietly, but with shaking intensity.

"I'm sorry," Seamus responded. He seemed to genuinely not understand what Shani was talking about, but she wasn't buying it.

"You heard me. Where is she?"

"Shani, what are you doing?" Brex asked, trying not to move her lips.

"You know what I'm talking about."

"Shani, I really don't," said Seamus, trying to defend his ego by laughing at her anger.

"Don't fuck with me, Seamus. I know you know something." She took an intimidating step towards him as he tried not to show his awkward and uncomfortable fear.

"Something about what? And you're not going to scare me into anything either."

"There's no need to be a dick about it," said Logan, already growing tired of his toxic masculinity. "We're just trying to find our friend."

At this point, Shani was now getting closer and closer to Seamus as he started to take a few steps back, preparing to make a run for it if he needed to.

"Look, I don't know what your problem is, Shani, but I don't know what you're talking about."

It only took half a second for Shani to slam his entire body up against the penguin exhibit with full force and dilated pupils. Seamus couldn't hide his fear anymore.

"I've known. I've known for a while now," she said with her jaw clenched together. "I should have done something a while ago, but I'm not gonna be stupid enough to defend you any longer."

"Shani, oh my God. What are you DOING?" Asher hollered, trying to avoid touching her. No patrons were around to notice what was happening to come to Seamus's defense.

"Guys, he has Lexi's pencil. He took her. He knows where she is. Brex, tell them. Remember? We talked about this. You agreed with me. He's our only answer!"

Brex stood there stunned, not understanding what the correct response would be to the situation. They both agreed Seamus might be a lead, but their number one suspect? This was a new idea for Brex to wrap her head around, but what if Shani was right?

"Which pencil are you even talking about?" Seamus said before Shani gave him one more reinforcing shove up against the exhibit.

"Shani, let him go," said Logan, calmly.

"Why?"

"Shani, they were handing out these pencils at the Democratic midterm rallies from last week. Half of the city has these!"

Before responding, Shani took a moment to breathe and think about whether she wanted to acknowledge Logan's evidence or not.

"I'm still not buying it," said Shani, now with a softer voice.

"Shani, he's right," said a familiar voice coming from across the room. She jerked her head in various directions, still violently holding onto Seamus.

"What?" asked Brex. "What is it? Did you hear something? What happened?"

Brex hadn't heard what Shani heard. None of them did. They all looked at her with perplexed expressions, wondering if she was hallucinating. Shani peered over her shoulder to see Ilisa swimming still and staring at her with his bright yellow eyes. Throwing him away like garbage, Shani threw Seamus to the side and ran over to Ilisa without breaking one second of eye contact with him.

"What do you mean?" she asked, glaring deeply into the depths of his aquatic soul. Brex, Logan and Asher finally caught on to what was happening.

"That kid isn't a part of this. Trust me," he responded as quickly as he could.

"But how do you—"

"Just trust me! Now how do you know your friend is missing?"

"I saw her in a vision. She's in trouble. She might be suffocating." It wasn't just Shani who was close to tears at this point. It was all four of them. "But it was a little blurry. I couldn't really tell."

"Do you have water?"

"What? Water? Why water?" Shani had no clue what direction this was going to take, but she was growing more and more impatient by the second.

"Do you have water? You saw this vision when you were either bathing or drinking water, or touching it, right? You'll be able to see the vision more clearly if you're in contact with water."

He was right. The counter at the restaurant was wet from being recently washed.

"You need water? Shani, there's a fountain over there!" Asher said, pointing to a water cooler with paper cups.

Without any hesitation Shani sprinted to the water. She could see Seamus still, lying on the ground in agony with his phone up to his ear, but she didn't care. All of her focus was on the water. She lifted the nozzle, threw her hands under the water, and closed her eyes. Nothing came to her immediately, but she could feel it coming. It rose through her skin and into her eyes. There, she saw Lexi, still breathing underneath a green liquid, just like before, but this time she noticed another small detail; above the waterline, it was all white. Everything around her was steaming, but sparkling at the same time.

In the snap of a finger, she ripped her hands from underneath the water, opened up her eyes, and screamed "She's in an ice cave! We were right!"

"Which one?" Logan asked.

"I don't know!"

"How long ago did she disappear?" Ilisa snapped.

"A few hours ago," said Shani.

"The only ice cave that's that close is in the White Mountains. That's all I know. Go! I don't know how much time you have left! Go!"

The rest followed her as she charged toward the door, but not before passing Seamus who was just now hanging up his phone call, probably informing somebody as to what Shani had done.

"Crazy, bitch," Seamus mumbled under his breath as he stood back up. The only problem was he didn't intend for anyone to hear such an accusation. Shani, however, snapped her body around, took a few steps towards him, and punched him directly in the nose.

"Oh shit, that was a bad idea," she said, with the words stumbling out of her mouth.

"Run!" Brex screamed as they all sprinted out the door. All of the patrons and employees who witnessed the attack were so concerned with Seamus's wellbeing that barely anyone noticed the four of them charging for the main entrance.

Finally, after what felt like an entire college exam, they reached the outdoors where reality set back in.

"Where did the eel say to go?" Asher asked.

"The White Mountains," said Shani. "That's where the last fire was. It makes sense."

"How do you know we can trust him?" asked Asher.

"It's our only lead!"

"How do we get there?" asked Brex, panting from the unexpected sprinting.

"We can drive my car, but it's at my dad's house," said Logan, trying to get everyone's attention.

"Okay," said Shani, "Then how do we get to Logan's house? It's too risky to take an Uber. We gotta get someone we trust."

"Oh, I know," said Brex, holding her hand up and sprinting once again. "Follow me. Oh, and Shani, I'll continue to be annoying about the consequences of all that later, but you're a badass, and that was freaking awesome!"

·····

"Do you guys wanna tell me what you're doing?" asked Jenna as she was driving her car towards Logan's house. "And where's Lexi? Doesn't she hang out with you guys like 24/7 now?"

Shani, Logan, and Asher all stayed silent, hoping Brex would take the lead on this one.

"Um...to be honest with you," Brex started "Lexi's in a little bit of trouble." The rest glanced at her with wide eyes, wondering how deep into the truth she was going to pursue.

"Oh? Is she okay? Do you want me to go with you?" Jenna consolingly asked.

"No, no, no, no. It's fine." Brex's head felt like it was about to rupture. She was trying desperately to come up with a reasonable story quickly. "Her dad is having some problems, and we're just gonna go help him for the weekend. And we need Logan's big Hummer truck because he's...moving."

It seemed as if for a moment, Jenna almost bought the story. "So, you needed me to drive you there now? Last minute and late at night?" she inquired.

Brex thought it best to not say too many useless words and answered by saying, "Yup. Really last minute."

"Girlfriend kicked him out?" Jenna asked, changing her attitude about the situation.

"Yeah, yeah. I think so." Brex almost clasped her hands together to pray that would be the last question.

"My house is just the one up there on the left. Just park on the street," said Logan, reaching his hand forward to point to his house.

To a person who grew up poor, Logan's house would look like a mansion. It was no secret he had grown up around money. His house was painted a beautiful shade of eggshell white and was surrounded with trimmed bushes of varying sizes. The two pillars supporting the entrance to the doors, which were mainly made of clear glass, showed off the giant staircase, leading up to the second floor.

"Wow, that's a...that's a mansion," said Jenna, speaking for and expressing what everyone else had on their mind.

"Thanks. My dad has his own real estate law firm," Logan responded like an announcer who was tired of giving the same speech over and over again. "You guys wait here. I just gotta sneak in, and get the keys."

The rest of them steadied their initial movement with their inquisitive attitudes.

"Did you just say 'sneak'?" asked Brex.

"Well," said Logan, twitching his mouth, not making eye contact. "My dad really doesn't like me driving the Hummer, especially at night. Hence why I wasn't allowed to bring it to school, so I gotta just sneak it out. Don't worry. He won't hear a thing. I'm pretty sure he's asleep, anyways."

"Really?" asked Shani. "Then why are all the lights on?"

"Guys, we really don't have the time for this," Brex interrupted. "Logan, just be quick and careful, please."

"Right, right. Sorry. Just wait right here. I'll be right back." And off he went, skimming across the side of the trees, trying to blend in in case his father peered outside the window.

The grass was reasonably dewy from the mist in the air that night. Logan tried not to slip as he ran to the back door, completely hunched over. Passing the kitchen and first floor living room, he couldn't see anyone standing through the window. Now, all he had to do was pass under the downstairs bathroom window, which, for some reason, Mr. Kwan always insisted on keeping unblinded.

From this angle of the house, it looked as if nobody was in it, including the bathroom. Logan felt safe passing the downstairs window and walked up the stairs to the backdoor.

Reaching for his keys, Logan accidentally dropped everything in his pockets. His thick wallet tumbled down the few stairs that led back down to the grass. It made more noise than expected. For a moment, he held his entire body still to hear if his father was coming to investigate the noise, but nothing except the wind was audible.

After fumbling with his keys for a few moments to find the right one in the dark, he stuck his back-door key in the hole and opened the door. Now, all he had to do was get the Hummer keys from the key rack in the kitchen and somehow get the truck out from the garage without his father noticing.

The pathway to the kitchen was a short, but squeaky one. There were a few floor tiles that needed fixing in the hallway that connected the back door to the kitchen. He tried to avoid the places he knew would rumble at a high and long pitch, but also pushed himself to go as fast as he could. They were starting to run out of time.

The kitchen smelled like his dad's favorite curry, and his apple cinnamon candle was still burning. Mr. Kwan had to still be awake.

"Alright, yes," Logan heard his father say from a long distance. He couldn't quite tell where he was, and it wasn't close enough to be able to hear what he was saying clearly. All he could hear distinctly was the sound of CNN playing in the background on the T.V.

With little lighting, Logan spotted the keys he needed right where they were supposed to be. Taking a few steps closer to his goal and to his father's voice, he lifted the keys off the hook.

"Yes, I know. There were plenty of flakes in the courthouse that day. This can't all be Logan's fault." Logan was close enough now to know exactly what Mr. Kwan said, but what could he be talking about? "Which deposition was it?...And you're sure Logan filed it?...Dear God. We're gonna lose this case! I'm going to lose my biggest client!"

Logan quietly took a few steps closer to listen to a little bit more of the confidential conversation. Now he could tell his father was pacing around his bedroom. Every half a second, he could hear the smallest brush against the wood floors, which were probably coming from his slippers. "Look, I know. I'm sorry. Let's just worry about this next case, and then we will deal with whatever the consequences are. I'll talk to Logan later."

It was hard for Logan to react and keep moving. He stood still, stunned. What did he do? And what was he to do now? He had to shake himself out of it. Just like his father said, he needed to worry about what was happening now and worry about the rest later. Lexi needed him.

Now tip-toeing even softer than before, Logan headed back to the kitchen, but this time, he slipped past the back door, after double-checking it was locked, and through to the garage.

The door to the garage opened with blissful silence, but when the door closed, it let out one heavy piglet squeal. Logan felt the first thump of his heart pound through his chest. For a moment, he was convinced he wasn't going to be able to breathe for the next ten minutes.

Logan snapped his eyes to the hallway to listen if there were now footsteps coming down the stairs, but there was nothing to be heard. Mr. Kwan probably couldn't hear over the sound of screaming politicians.

The doorknob slowly slid through Logan's fingers. He flicked on the garage lights to see one of his most prized possessions. Zazu the Hummer truck that was named after his favorite "Lion King" character.

He stumbled down a few steps and flew into his car. Now was the time to move fast. Logan knew for a fact that his father wouldn't hear the garage door open. He had already tested that theory many times in high school when he would sneak out to sleep over his girlfriend's house almost every weekend.

The Hummer zipped down the driveway and pulled up right next to Jenna's car as Logan saw the other three jump out.

"Thanks, Jenna. Venmo request me for the gas money, okay?" Shani said as she ran to the passenger's seat of the Hummer.

"Will do!" Jenna responded. "Hope Lexi's okay. Keep me updated!" And she drove off back into the pitch black.

Logan watched his hands sweat as they gripped the wheel, hoping that he could keep his focus on the road and on Lexi.

"You okay?" Shani asked. "Did your dad see you?"

"What? Oh, no. I'm good," Logan responded.

"Alright. Good, let's go. We gotta get there fast."

19:

"We gotta total these cars before they take us out!"

The roads were nearly barren. Occasionally, Logan would see two parallel lights that were too bright for his sensitive eyes zoom past him on the other side of the road. Sometimes he would hear the sound of a cocky motorcyclist trying to pass the few cars that were on the dark highway.

For the first hour of the car ride, it was quiet. Shani would periodically give Logan an intimidating stare when he would be driving anything less than five miles over the speed limit. Then Logan would grip the wheel even tighter with his shaky arms and push on the gas pedal while his pulse increased. Everything about the situation was making him nervous. If they got into a car accident, Lexi would die. If they got pulled over and lost any time, Lexi would die. If he didn't drive fast enough, Lexi would die. The compulsive and puzzling state was making his brain go numb.

"Should we call Lexi's dad?" Brex asked.

"I don't think anybody has his phone number, and we don't want to worry him," said Asher. "We're gonna bring her back, and it's not like he could do anything." The tone in his voice wasn't convincing, but it still somehow soothed Brex.

"How we doin' on gas, Logan?" she asked.

"Only a few notches below full. We'll be fine." He kept checking his rear-view mirror to see Brex and Asher sitting in the back to confirm they were just as stiff as he was. If anything, he didn't want to feel alone. "What's our plan anyway? Do we have one?"

Shani closed her eyes and bit her lip before she spoke. "I think the plan is to just get Lexi and get out of there."

"And what about the people that are holding her there?" Brex asked, with a shaky and staggering tone to her voice. "What do we do about them?"

Shani dropped her head to the back of her neck and looked up to the ceiling almost on the verge of tears. It was unlike her usual reaction to pressure and sense of protection.

"If they are trying to harm us in any way, we have every right to do whatever we need to, but we have to be careful. If the police find any evidence of what we can do, we could be finding ourselves in worse places than where Lexi is right now. Who knows what they'll do to us."

"Why do you think they took Lexi?" Asher asked, looking out the window with his elbow propped up and his hand, smothering his mouth.

"Because it's a trap."

"No shit it's a trap, but why Lexi? They obviously know where we've been. They tried to kill you. They could have taken any of us in the meantime. So why Lexi?"

It was a moment they needed to ponder together. The silence between them triggered the extra adrenaline needed. They craved answers.

"Oh my God," said Logan, brushing his sweaty hair out of his face. "They didn't know who we were."

"What?" Shani asked, caught off guard.

"Today, at the restaurant. That pain we felt, we knew she was in trouble. So, we all have some sort of...paranormal connection, right? There must have been something that happened that day you two were attacked. The people who are after us had no idea that we took those powers. That's why it took them so long, and that's why they only attacked you. You said so yourself. They didn't want to kill you, they just needed you trapped, because they weren't prepared. They didn't know we existed. Ah, but shit. *Now* they know who we are."

The others stared at him, overwhelmed and impassioned. The pieces of the puzzle were finally pushing together.

"Shani, think hard," Logan continued. "What happened that day that was different? What did you two do to stand out?"

She immediately shut her eyes and took herself through that day. Her early morning class was canceled that day, and it was terribly windy. The two of them went on a walk across a bridge that they had never taken together before, but what did that have to do with anything? Besides finding out that she could breathe underwater, there was nothing out of the ordinary. Unless...

"Lexi's skin," she said, opening up her eyes. "It fell off. They must have somehow been able to track her down because her scar was bare and out in the open."

"But wait, no," Brex interrupted. "We've had our scars uncovered outside plenty of times before that. What made that time any different?"

"It has to do with something outside," Logan added. "That's the only thing that would make sense."

He was right. The process of elimination made the idea stand out like a billboard to Shani. The answer was right there, shining brightly into her eyes.

"It was sunny," she said. "Remember? Anytime we were outside and our scars were uncovered, it was either dark or rainy. The first night we got them, it was pitch black. The day Brex and Asher uncovered them outside the lecture hall, it was pouring when we got outside." The clarity astounded her. "That's gotta be it. There wasn't a cloud in the sky the day we were attacked. And remember, you guys said you were connected to me and Lexi somehow? The person who's tracking us is like us. They have the same scar. They have powers like we do!"

It was an odd feeling for them. On one hand, they were relieved they had more answers, but on the other hand, the answers still left them wondering how they were all going to survive. Only more questions were thrown onto their laps.

"Hey, guys," Brex spoke with a minor quiver in her jaw. "There's probably something I should tell—"

Asher aggressively grabbed her by the shoulder to stop her from speaking as he peered out the back window.

"Uh...Shani?" he said in his highest-pitched voice. "You said those cars that attacked you didn't have any drivers, right?"

"Yeah...why?" Shani responded, not appreciating where the conversation was headed.

"'Cause there are a few more behind us."

The terror that eased into the space around them resembled a scene in a horror film. The air surrounding them closed in so far it was hard to breathe. How did the cars find them? This time it was three SUVs. It was hard to tell, but it looked like one gray, one black, and the middle one was a neon cherry red. Asher squinted his eyes to make sure he couldn't see any silhouette of a human in any of the cars, but the longer he looked, the more certain he was that his eyes weren't deceiving him. No living beings were behind any of those wheels. They were getting closer and coming fast. This time, whoever it was controlling these cars picked more stable, higher-quality vehicles.

"Shani, take the wheel," said Logan as he stepped on the gas and turned on the cruise control.

"What?" Shani exasperated. "Are you nuts? Where are you going?"

"I'm going out on the bed. I'm gonna try and rip off the wheels. On the count of three, I'm gonna hop up and go through the back window, and you'll take over, okay?"

Feeling overly confident, Shani vigorously nodded her head in agreement.

"Okay. One, two, THREE!" Logan pushed himself up by jumping up onto his seat, grabbing the steering wheel with one hand, the head of his seat with the other, and dove to the rear of the truck with his arms leading and his head tucked down as far as it would go. Shani smoothly, but quickly slid her long legs in front of the driver's seat and took the wheel. Besides Logan accidentally stepping on Asher's thigh, it was a flawless transition.

Even with all the adrenaline now coursing through Logan's body, it was still a challenge to open up the pesky back window that was always getting stuck. He pushed his feet into the backseat, trying to not squish Asher against the door, and kept trying to pull the window open, but it barely wiggled.

"Goddamnit!" he muttered with his temper shortening and his patience growing weaker. Finally, after almost punching a fist-sized hole through it, he finally got it open. "Shani, keep picking up speed.

Zazu's a beast." And with that, he slid his arms and legs first through the window and crawled out onto the bed, closing the window behind him thinking he was being protective of the others.

"What the hell was that?" yelled Brex. "He's an idiot if he thinks he's doing this by himself." Slamming both hands on the window, she pulled with all of her strength to get it back open. Brex finally broke a sweat and felt her fingers starting to slide off the metal. Asher assisted by pushing the window from where he was sitting, but it seemed that Logan was going to be the last one through the opening. It was stuck, and it wasn't going to open again.

Logan tried crouching down on the bed of the truck but couldn't get a good view of the cars, so he fought to catch his balance and stand up while the truck was at full speed. Two of the SUVs were now approaching the sides of the Hummer. They were about to be closed in and almost completely trapped.

"Shani!" Logan hollered.

"Ah, shit," Shani muttered, now remembering how much she hated driving with the gas pedal to the floor. "I'm working on it!" All of her focus and attention was on the road. She slowly picked up more speed, feeling her confidence carefully rising, trying not to put cracks in it. The roads were, for the most part, straight on this section of the highway, but the street lights were becoming dimmer, and the night was fading into darkness.

Brex tried one more time to open the broken window, but she could feel her energy crumbling down, and she needed to save it. But before she lost hope, she looked out the side window and came up with an idea. She tied her long black locks with the hair tie around her wrist, unbuckled her seatbelt, and unrolled the right window.

"What the hell are you doing?" Asher shrieked, while the howls of the wind rumbled within the car.

"What am I supposed to do? The window won't open!"

Logan braced himself and took one long electrocuting shot at one of the gray car's front tires. He could see the whitish-blue color reflecting from the shiny silver lining of the wheel as the electricity and metal met, but the tire stayed as it was. This wasn't an old ambulance van. Whoever was after them learned their lesson, but Logan had yet to learn his.

After a few more strikes of lightning, something popped. He could hear something crackle and shatter apart right before a hunk of car parts scattered behind the car, leaving a trail of demolished metal, but the car...it kept moving.

While Logan continuously alternated his attempts to take out any part of the vehicle, any at all, Brex shoved her body head first out the window with her left leg draped over the truck door. She remembered seeing a ski rack on the top of the truck and kept reaching around for it while still holding onto the inside of the roof. It was difficult to see where the rack could be since the wind striking across her face forced her eyes to tighten, but after aimlessly smacking the rooftop a few times, she found the ski rack and grasped her soft but strong hands around the metal.

Her legs were short, and her skinny jeans were restricting, but she had to get the other leg to the bed of the truck. The sweat on her fingers made it challenging to confidently hold onto the ski rack, but with every flexor muscle in her hands, she stuck to the top of the truck like glue. Nothing was going to knock her off.

Her left leg swung around into the bed of the truck with her foot barely touching the floor and the top of the rim under her knee. Now all she had to do was put her right foot onto the rim of the window and extend her leg, thinking all of her weight would naturally fall into the bed. But when she shot her upper body straight into the air, the wind rushed against her so intensely, she let go of the ski rack and collapsed into the bed, straight onto her shoulder with nothing to cushion her landing.

"What the hell are you doing?" Logan hollered as he heard the loud thump and saw Brex trying to stand up.

"You didn't think you were gonna do this alone, did you?" she responded. With every muscle in her body connecting to one another and the dashing wind, she threw her arms out to the side and lit blinding and abounding flames that covered every bit of her skin, from her fingertips to her elbows.

"Asher!" Shani yelped from the driver's seat. "Keep an eye out on the cars. Help me navigate if a car's coming near me! Or just anything that's useful!"

"Okay, okay!" Asher wailed, trying to keep his attention span intact.

Logan stood on the driver's side of the car while Brex held her stance on the passenger's. Each one of Logan's arms extended out with chilling electric bolts, shooting out of each one. The right arm pointed towards the gray car that was getting closer to the truck's right side while the left aimed at the red car. Logan's stomach twisted in knots when he caught wind of each and every millimeter of electric energy was fighting to destroy what needed to be destroyed, but so far, nothing was working.

Brex took one aggressive swing at the driver's side window of the black car and shattered it clean with the strongest, most dense fireball she could throw. To her disappointment, it didn't slow down, not even a little.

"What are they even trying to do? Escort us there?" Brex screeched the moment before the gray car let go of its passenger seat door, almost taking out Logan as it swung right across his cheek. "Oh, ballsack!"

"How the hell did it even do that?" Logan screeched.

"What do they have in there? A canon?" asked Brex, covering her face while trying to keep her arms lit.

Whoever possessed these vehicles had complete control over them, but they had limits.

"We gotta total these cars before they take us out!" said Brex.

"Do these things have eyes?" Logan asked, still covering his face, ready to flinch at any moment. "How do they know where we're standing?"

"Does it look like I know?"

"We need Lexi! She could stop this without us!" Logan was growing faint. Every electrocution fuzzed his brain. His eyes closed for no more than a second and a half, but in that time, one of the side mirrors broke off and shot straight towards Logan's head. It was only because of the loud cracking sound it made that Logan was able to drop and duck in time to miss it.

"Ah!" Brex screamed while Logan wasn't looking. One of the headlights from the black car that was now almost parallel to the truck on the left side flew across the Hummer and struck Brex's waist as she tried to dodge it, immediately leaving a trace of blood on her shirt.

Without thinking, Logan's emotions revived, and he snapped his arm right at the black Ford, shattering its back window. Unsurprisingly, Brex stood next to him, trying to hold on to the side of the bed. Her eyes filled with a fuming, red light as each flaming limb shot colossal balls of fire directly at the steering wheel. The rubber melted before their eyes.

"Damn," Logan whispered to himself, but it made no difference. The Ford still didn't slow down. It didn't even swerve towards the edge of the road.

"They're not powering themselves!" Brex hollered over the raging wind. "It doesn't matter if we take out the engines! They're being fueled by whatever's dominating them!"

"Keep your eyes open!"

Pushing through their fatigue, Brex threw one fireball after the other, making significant dents in each vehicle while Logan tried frying the tires on each car. One by one, each car took its turn firing parts from its body. The two of them kept their focus sustained while they dodged each hunk of metal thrown at them until Brex caught the gear shift that soared toward Logan's head. She didn't even blink an eye as she melted the failed fatal attempt in between her fingers.

It took them a few more exhausting minutes to realize the lighter the vehicles got, the faster they could go. The black and gray cars slowly creeped up ahead of the Hummer.

"SHANI! GO FASTER!" Logan screamed at the top of his lungs.

"ASHER! WE NEED YOU!" Brex screeched through the stuck window.

"Go!" Shani hollered into Asher's face as she shut her fears away and pushed the gas pedal all the way down to the floor. The noise that the engine made being shoved into the red zone made her cringe, but just like her paranoia, she threw the feeling out of the Hummer, and it drifted away into the wind.

Asher rolled down the window, dove out head first before his wings sprouted before him. Everything moved faster than his eyes or his mind could process, but it was okay. In the blink of an eye, he landed straight on the front of the red car, denting the front hood and cracking the windshield.

His thick white wings spread out as far as they could, trying to fight the wind and slow down the car. They were almost strong enough, but they were close to blowing right over his shoulders. He managed to let the Hummer gain a few inches from the red car, but as the distance improved, the windshield popped out of place, slammed into the front of Asher, and knocked him into the air.

"ASHER!" Brex and Logan simultaneously screamed as they saw him tumble backwards.

Without thinking, Shani slammed on the brakes, causing the gray and black cars to race forward and trap in the Hummer on either side. The three lanes were neck and neck. The black Ford thought quickly, but not thoroughly. As it watched the Hummer pull back, it raced forward in front of Shani, thinking it could stop her, or she would crash into it. Either one would work. But instead, the black Ford slammed into the gray Subaru, and they uncontrollably tumbled into the side of the road. In a single breath, she saw the gray car nearly flip over the black SUV, but the second they hit the highway railing, they both burst into flames. The threats vanished in the blink of an eye.

All in one deep breath, Shani could see the flames out of the corner of her eye after she rapidly steered toward the right of the demolished cars. Shani's reflexes were strong, but they still had the red car to handle. And somehow after Shani had slammed her brakes just moments before, the demonic vehicle raced in front of her. Now, it was ahead of the Hummer.

Asher almost hit the ground before his wings caught the wind again. His vision blurred as he tried as quickly as he could to get back to the Hummer. The dizziness only lasted a few breaths before his next move was clear.

The red car was still in the lead. Shani could see its trunk squirming to come loose.

"That's it," she whispered to herself. "It's gonna hit us with the trunk." All she had to do was drive around it, or stay to the side.

She steered to the right, but the red car was quick and almost mirrored her movement. It drove right back in front of her in the snap of a finger. It was going to be harder than she thought, but to her advantage, the red car's trunk was still shuddering in its place. It was stuck. She still had at least a few seconds.

As sharply and as quickly as she could, Shani turned the car as far left as the Hummer could go, hoping to get some leverage.

"Ahh!" Logan yelled, unprepared for the abrupt action. He tried to catch himself before he fell backwards over the corner of the bed, holding himself up by catching onto the handle of the driver's side backseat door with his left hand. The wall of the bed dug into the back of his knees as he clenched his hamstrings and calves and held onto the top of the bed wall with his knees and right hand. The second his head hit the side of the Hummer, Logan saw, out of the corner of his eye, part of the red car's bumper flying directly towards his temple. Luckily, it missed his head by centimeters and audibly scraped against the side of his truck right under the tip of his scalp. Adding to the shock, the wind made it almost impossible to control any of the muscles in his body. The sweat on his hands certainly didn't help either.

"LOGAN!" Brex screamed.

Shani wondered what the loud bang and brief scream was. She looked into her side view mirror to see Logan struggling to hold onto his life. "Shit," she whispered to herself, lost as to what to do next.

"SHANI!" Logan screeched. "KEEP GOING! TAKE HIM OUT!" And she did so, trusting his judgment. His vision was morphed and disfigured, hanging by his legs. He couldn't tell which way was up or down or how far apart or close he was to anything, and somehow everything was going too slow and too fast at the same time.

Brex rushed over to help Logan to safety, but moments after she grabbed onto his clothing, the car finally released its trunk. The red hunk of metal flew backwards at the speed of light, and by following her impulses, Brex let go of Logan to straighten up, and brush the projectile trunk out of its course with the rushing wind of her fire before it even hit the Hummer. She could feel the weight of the metal, pushing past her. It missed the truck by inches.

Logan felt himself beginning to slip, but he was able to pull himself up enough to grab onto the ski rack while the other hand gripped the top of the roof. Brex rushed back over and yanked him up by his shirt, almost ripping it.

"I'm so sorry," Brex kept repeatedly apologizing for having left him. He tumbled onto the floor, hitting his head a bit too hard, but still managed to make his way back into a standing position. "Are you okay? I'm sorry. I'm so, so sorry," Brex kept repeating over the loud noise of the hasty wind in case he didn't hear her the first few times.

"I'm fine! I'm fine!" Logan insisted. "Let's just take this thing out!"

"The wind is too strong for my fire to reach that far! Hold onto my hand! Try to fry it as much as you can!"

Brex held out her left hand before Logan reached out his sweaty fingers and held on tight. Most of his fatigue had now faded away as his heartbeat pounded faster than it did on the football field. His arm drew back, preparing to channel all of his energy into one powerful bolt, but before his release, in the corner of his eye, he saw two enormous white wings swoop past him with gallant energy and graceful form.

"WAIT!" Asher screamed "I HAVE AN IDEA! SHANI! PULL BACK!"

Shani immediately pulled back a few feet away from the red vehicle. Just enough that it wouldn't compute what she was trying to do. Asher soared along the trees, still parallel to the racing vehicles, looking for a dead branch. It needed to be just the right size in order for it to work.

Up ahead, he could see a thick six-foot-long branch right in his line of sight, but from what he could see, it had no weak point. It didn't matter. He was going to have to break it off himself. There was no more time to waste.

Just like before, he charged straight forward, as fast as his wings would carry him with his arms leading the way like Superman. His fingertips spread wide open, preparing to catch the soon-to-be-dead, barkless weapon. He was tempted to close his eyes, but he wasn't cocky enough to be that dumb.

His skin meeting the tree was almost euphoric. Many moments were meshed into one. At first, he didn't feel the shards stabbing all the way through to the bone, but after he spun in a few circles, ruining his flight pattern, he could feel the moss meshing into the blood and the flesh from his palms.

"Jesus Christ," Brex whispered to herself and Logan. They could see Asher struggling to center himself while carrying what was probably twenty pounds of wood in his arms, but the pain soon released, and then there was nothing but unbreakable strength.

"BREX!" he called out. "WHEN THE CAR FLIPS OVER, LIGHT THE BOTTOM ON FIRE! THE WHOLE THING WILL EXPLODE!"

How the hell is he going to flip over an entire car? Brex thought. But she trusted him.

Luckily, Asher's adrenaline made carrying his weapon less painful, but for all he knew, he had no idea if it was going to work. "The front right wheel. The front right wheel. The front right wheel," he kept repeating to himself as he sailed directly towards just that.

Shani knew what Asher was thinking, and what she needed to do. The only thing she contemplated was if she was going to execute it or not.

While holding his six-foot-long weapon like a spear, Asher charged toward the car, hoping that the increase in speed would assist the vigorous attack. His eyes were locked on the target, and with one giant breath, he flew directly into the front wheel of the speeding car and stabbed the branch in between the pavement and the wheel, causing the car to tilt in the air just enough for Asher to flap his wings with one heavy thrust of wind. But to their surprise, the unexpected happened. The red car began to balance, just for a brief moment, but it all clicked. It was as if it had a complete mind of its own.

"BREX!" Asher screamed, not wanting her to miss the only opportune moment.

Breaking herself from her brief trance, Brex grabbed Logan's hand and shot her fire at the undercarriage. It was close enough to just barely reach it, and in that exact moment, Shani timed herself perfectly to swerve to the right and into the breakdown lane.

Right before their eyes, the car exploded into flames. Brex caught sight of a random car part flying toward their heads. Without warning, she grabbed Logan by the neck and pulled him to the ground. Logan ungracefully slammed his head against the floor once again, but they both successfully dodged whatever was coming at them.

"Brex," Logan muttered as Shani started to slow the car down, "Are you done beating the living shit outta me for the night?"

"I think what you meant to say is uh, 'thank you!' Geez," said Brex, relishing her sarcasm.

"You guys okay?" Asher asked, showing off his graceful landing onto the bed of the truck.

"I think we're both okay," said Logan, brushing off and examining his battle wounds.

"Let's get back in the truck before somebody else sees us," said Brex.

Logan took a few minutes to try to open up the back window, but it wouldn't budge. As a result, Asher ended up flying them back in through the window while Shani kept the car moving, and while Brex yelled at Asher for not thinking of that earlier.

"How did they find us?" Asher spat, trying to wipe off all of the blood from his hands.

"I have no idea, but we were right. It's definitely a trap," Shani responded.

There was an awkward silence before anyone spoke next. A silence filled with agony.

"How could we be more prepared than that?" Asher asked.

"We can't," said Brex. "But I think the thing we really have to worry about is the fact that this person, or whatever is after us, has unique capabilities, but the technology is advanced. They have some sort of soul. Logan shocked the hell outta those engines, and they didn't do anything. It was just by luck that they had any gas in them at all, or else we wouldn't have been able to blow up that little fucker."

Logan let Shani drive the rest of the way. He knew he would be too distracted by how he would pay for the damages to Zazu. The two things that made him cringe the most was the long scrape that ran along the right side of the bed and the left broken headlight that now made Shani twice as paranoid to drive the Hummer. If they were to be stopped by a police car, they would have serious complications, but luckily, they were almost there.

20:

"Humans tend to believe that there's just one answer."

The night became its darkest, though the moon was at its brightest. They approached the quiet White Mountains, looking for some sort of clue to bring them towards the right path.

"STOP!" Brex hollered to Shani as she stepped on the brakes. "Look!" To the right of the road, Brex spotted an over-the-shoulder bag that she recognized as Lexi's. It was dark purple and sparkly, but a pool of suspicion smothered the image. Something about it didn't sit right with her.

Shani immediately pulled over, and they all eagerly jumped out of the car. Brex was the first one to reach it, but didn't touch it. It sat there with a few patches of dirt smudged across it and a pile of leaves surrounding it.

"We should just leave it here," she said. "If they come back, we don't want them to know we're on to them. Plus, we don't know what the hell that thing is cursed with.

"Okay," said Shani, "Let's get moving." They proceeded down a pathway next to a mountain in what they assumed was the right direction.

"What are we looking for?" Logan asked.

"Um...I'm not sure. All I could see was the green liquid and the ice. There's an ice cave around here somewhere, I can feel it. I don't know how to describe it, but something in me is buzzing. I don't know where it is though, and I don't know what it looks like."

The four of them were running so fast with speeding heartbeats, they barely acknowledged the small sprinkles of rain falling from the sky.

"So, we have to look for another red door?" asked Logan.

"How do we know it looks like the one in the Boston Common?" Brex defensively suggested.

"I just said I don't know what it looks like," Shani snapped.

"It's gotta be at least some sort of conspicuous-looking entrance," Brex continued, ignoring Shani's attitude.

"Right," said Asher as they all started up a hill, going deeper into the woods. "Let's look for that."

"Anybody got a flashlight?" Logan asked.

"Just my fire," Brex responded. "But I'm not lighting that shit up near all these trees."

"Did we seriously forget all of the flashlights?" Shani screamed.

"Shani, don't do this right now," said Asher. Shani robustly dug her feet into the mountain with every step.

"What's *that* supposed to mean?"

"STOP ACTING LIKE THIS IS ALL ABOUT YOU!" Asher screeched as he got in front of her to stop her from walking. Logan and Brex also halted in their places, trying not to make eye contact with either of them. "You have really shitty, out-of-touch control issues. You are not the only one that wants to find her, and you are sure as hell not in charge here. Now let's just figure out how we can see better, and let's just move on and listen to everyone else because if we don't, we're never going to find her."

Asher snapped back around to begin his walking again, and even though they could hear the blended sounds of nature, the silence was painful. Shani stood there frozen with empty eyes. Asher had never raised his voice at her. Bickered? Constantly. But with that strength? Never.

"Hey, maybe this will help," said Logan, rounding up a basketball-sized lightning ball.

"Yeah, yeah," said Brex, grabbing his free arm, wanting to keep moving. Shani was the last one to get her legs moving back up the hill again. There was nothing that she wanted more than to forget everything that just happened. She didn't take embarrassment well, but she had to keep moving.

Logan's self-powered electrical ball gave them only a small portion of light. For the rest, they had to rely on the moon and Brex's flashlight on her phone. Her phone was the only one that hadn't died.

"LEXI!" Asher screamed. "LEXI!"

"Shhh!" Shani interrupted. "You could give away our position."

"LEXI!" Asher continued, ignoring her. Occasionally he screamed "ALEXANDRA!" just in case, but so far, they had no luck.

"Does anybody see footprints anywhere? Or torn clothing?" Logan asked.

"Not yet," Brex responded. "But if anybody feels a significant drop in temperature, it could mean we're getting closer."

There was nothing prominent or unanticipated in those woods, but in the snap of a finger, every thought, every sense, every feeling changed for Shani.

"Guys, she's this way," she said, pointing northeast up the hill.

"What do you mean?" Logan asked. "How do you know?"

A moment went by that filled Shani with trembling confusion, but also fear. These were new senses she was experiencing, and she wasn't sure if they were to be trusted. After all, she did see a huge pond up ahead. What if it was clouding her senses?

"I don't know. That's just...where we need to go."

The four of them picked up speed and ran up the pathway. The chilled wind gave them more energy and thrill. Now they knew exactly where they were going. Shani could sense where Lexi was, and hopefully that meant she was still alive.

Their violent pulses raced against the clock as their focus fixated on their pathways. Shani could feel they were getting closer.

"What was that?" Brex asked, with her feet stiffly glued to the ground along with the others. The earth. It vibrated like a chill shivering down a human nervous system, but it was petite, and quick.

"Earthquake?" said Logan. "Maybe a tree fell?"

"No." Brex could sense something beneath them. She couldn't distinguish what it was, but she could grasp no feeling other than negativity. "Guys. We—we need to run, and fast!"

Nobody questioned why. The four of them ran together as they felt the earth continue to pulsate and begin to split. They had never felt such an earthquake in New England before, but there was no question as to why it was there.

"It's gotta be some sort of booby trap!" Logan screamed as sweat streamed down his face. They all agreed, but nobody except Logan cared what it was. They just wanted to see if they could outrun it.

"Does anybody see an opening in the ground or anything?" Brex hollered, trying to avoid falling into the trap that was meant for them. The wind was now growing stronger, and the moon was losing its light. Nothing was able to bring Brex's heart rate back to normal.

"Guys! Guys!" cried Asher. "Look! I think I—"

The ground split open too fast for them to escape. They could barely hear themselves scream as they made their descent.

Wings, Asher thought to himself. *Why aren't my wings sprouting?* It was all too fast. By the time Asher's wings expanded to his sides, the five of them had landed on a flat, rocky, and dark floor.

It wasn't until a few seconds later that they realized what had happened, and that they were still alive. Logan took a tumble across the dirty ground that ended with him colliding into a truck-sized boulder that made him even more unaware of his surroundings.

All they could feel was pain, beating into their bones. Now covered in dirt, they struggled to find the strength to stand up and save themselves.

"Ahhh!" Asher screeched as he felt searing pain in his right arm. "Huys, huys." He fought to speak in a normal cadence, but his jaw felt like it had ripped off during the fall. Using his elbows, he crawled over to Shani who was in the process of wiggling her fingers to try to gain consciousness again. "Hum on, hum on. Up, het up." Trying to speak those words left him more breathless than before.

With little strength, he managed to gather enough adrenaline to sit up and put Shani's shoulder and head on his lap.

"Ash—" she struggled to talk without leaving herself in an uncomfortable amount of pain. "The—the—the." Her hand shook as she pointed up to the sky. Asher followed the path of her fingertip to see the opening of the earth closing before they could escape.

"NO!" he screamed, unable to move. After the small sliver of starlight was gone, they were in complete darkness. Not a sound was made. No crickets. No running water. They were alone.

Asher could feel more blood pumping through his entire body, giving him more energy to help the rest.

"Brex...Brex!" Asher cried after he felt Shani make her way to a sitting position. "Brex, come on. Where are you? Ahhh! We need your light!" All of a sudden, he could feel a fierce pain in his shoulder again. The wound must have reopened. It was odd. His wings had only been open for a fraction of a second before the collision.

"Asher?" Brex muttered, sounding dehydrated. "Asher, I'm—I'm over here."

"Brex—Brex, are you okay? Where's Logan? Did you see him?" Asher stayed on his hands and knees, feeling his way with his palms as he continued forward.

"Arhh. I think he's to my right somewhere." As the words left her mouth, she could feel the fingertips and nails of Asher's hand. They quickly clasped their hands together as they shouted for their friend.

"Logan?" they repeatedly gasped with what sounded like little to no air.

"Hold on," said Brex. "I think I can get something." With breathing becoming lighter and easier, she managed to clench one fist together and bring every ounce of her body's heat past her forearm. It started with a subtle steam, followed by a small spark at the tip of her knuckles. Eventually, the fire sprouting from her fatigued limb was bright enough to see Logan lying motionless a few feet away from them.

"Oh my God," Brex breathlessly muttered.

"Logan!" Shani squealed as the three of them frantically crawled over to him. "He hit his head!"

"We shouldn't have survived that, but we did because it was us. He has to be alive!" Brex almost burst into tears as she put her head close to his while being careful not to light any of his clothing on fire.

After a split second of silence, Shani was certain she heard a pebble toss across the floor behind her. Her subconscious acknowledged it, but she decided to ignore it until—

"You're right," said a strange voice coming from the dark. "He's going to be okay."

The voice took their breath away. Brex's fire extended far beyond her normal capacity for a brief moment. There was just enough light on the mysterious figure to see the face of an older woman, covered in dirt and holding a snapped tree root. She was scrawny, but didn't look weak. Although, her presence was unsettling to the rest.

"Don't waste your power," the woman said as she held out the plump stick to Brex. For a moment, Brex was hesitant to take it, but there was something trustworthy about the way the woman was making eye contact with her. The atmosphere was suddenly hopeful instead of malicious.

Brex slowly took the branch with her free hand and lit it with her ignited one. Everything seemed to be calm once more.

"You, with the wings," the woman said, looking at Asher. "You can help him. He can heal faster."

"How?" he asked.

"Your wings. They have healing abilities within them."

"The blue blood?" Shani asked.

The woman nodded before she said, "It's called ichor. It can heal you almost instantly."

Asher didn't have time to question her. Without much hesitation he looked back at his sprouted wings. The wound had indeed re-opened. Shani beckoned him to squat back down, so she could collect some of his blood.

"You only need a little," said the woman, coming a little closer to examine the process. Shani pinched the wound to scoop a daub of blood on the tips of her index and middle finger. "Into his mouth."

The ichor felt like wet Play-Doh in between her fingers. She tilted Logan's head back while Brex held his mouth open. Her fingertips gently scraped against his bottom lip as they saw a subtle glow illuminate his face and head wound.

Everything was still and silent as they waited for a result. Shani was about to give his lifeless body CPR until Asher felt Logan's fingertips twitch by his side.

"Shit," he said. "He's okay."

"Why didn't Asher's blood heal his own wound?" Brex asked the woman.

"Well, sometimes the most broken people help the ones most in need. And it's not as if his wound was deadly." They were all silent. Nobody could disagree with her.

"Who are you?" Shani asked. "Why are you down here?"

"Same as you," the woman responded.

"You didn't answer the first question."

"It's you," said Logan, gently coughing up dirt after he spotted the glowing sun on the side of her torn-up jacket. "You're the one that's been following us. Somebody was trying to kill you the night of the fire. The one with the sun jacket." The other three were so relieved that he was alright that they barely paid attention to what he was saying. Brex rubbed his back while Shani checked the wounds on his head, and Asher brushed off the dirt from his clothing.

The woman didn't argue. She made full eye contact with them, hoping to rope in their trust.

"I suppose my disguise didn't do. That was a gift. But never mind that. There's much to discuss," she said, "and I owe you all a long explanation."

"How about you start with your real name and why were you following us?" Brex asked. "Were you trying to trap us? Or hurt us?"

"No. I was trying to protect you...and me."

"Why?"

The woman's lips quivered, struggling with the choice of where to begin.

"Well," she finally began. "My name is Maya."

"Maya?" Shani asked. "I don't remember seeing that name on the list."

"You found my journal. Didn't you?"

Shani's cheeks blossomed into a bright red. She couldn't remember the last time she was so thankful for darkness. Yet, Maya's easing smile was anything but accusatory.

"I didn't put my real name on that list. I didn't need to, and you wouldn't have found it online either. I rented that room with cash. The owner owed me a favor. I worked a few odd jobs down there and lived there for the most part. I made sure no one could find me while I was protecting our Boston sanctuary."

"Maya," Shani stated. "All of those artifacts you had in your hide out...you're Queen Maya, right? The mother of Buddha?"

Shit, this woman is old, Asher thought.

Unsure of the correct response, Maya nodded and said, "Yes, actually. You discovered all of that just by my living space?"

"It doesn't matter," Shani snapped. "This is lovely and all, but now that we know who you are, can we please get out of here and find Lexi?"

"Shani," said Brex. "I have a feeling she really doesn't know how to do that."

"Well, why are we just sitting here talking, instead of figuring it out?" Shani stood up and walked across the rocky den while running her fingers through her hair and trying to keep calm, so she wouldn't inspire Asher to scream at her again. "What was that anyway? There are no fault lines in New Hampshire. And what even is this place?"

"It's his plan," Maya responded. "Moloch hexed Poseidon's trident to break open the earth when heavy weight passes over it. He's hoping that either you'll stay down here long enough to weaken you, or he has another plan in the sanctuary waiting for you. I'm not sure, but that's the only possible explanation. Because you are now alchelarcenists, he needs you alive."

"Alchelarcenists?" said Brex with a disbelieving tone. "As in like... magic stealer?"

"We didn't steal anything," Asher interrupted.

"And, Moloch?" Logan asked. "As in Satan?"

"In a way," said Maya. "And I know you didn't steal anything, but that wasn't always the case."

"Was it this Moloch guy that let a two-ton hamster loose on us during the night of the fire?"

There was slight amusement coming to her eyes as Maya said, "No. I did."

The minimal trust the four of them had put in her over the last few minutes was now in question. Even Logan, who was still barely standing up, took a step back from her instinctually.

Brex looked her dead in the eyes and said, "Maya, the only way that we are going to get us all out of here is if you tell us everything." They shared a tense glance for a moment, which reassured Brex she was on the right path. "And I would recommend you do it fast because Shani has yet to work on her patience or her temper."

"I am on your side," said Maya.

"Then prove it."

All eyes were on Maya. They waited there, standing and vigorously breathing through their noses.

"The Greeks were put to rest over a hundred years ago."

"The gods?" Asher asked. "They're dead?"

"Not quite. We were able to preserve them when we found out what Moloch was planning to do. We took away their powers, scattered them randomly across the globe, and preserved them in the frozen sanctuaries. The ice was to prevent Moloch from detecting them. And then we took their souls and divided them in half. We didn't think it was safe to keep their souls with their powers, and it is the only way we can wake them back up when it is time. Anyway, we put them into two amulets, and one of them, I am the protector of, at least for now." Her blotchy and bloody hands held the glowing, sapphire charm dangling from the chain around her neck.

"That's the necklace from your journal," said Brex.

"And enclosed in it are the souls of the gods?" Logan stated. "Makes sense."

Maya ignored Logan's sarcastic remark and said, "The other one is being protected, far, far away where he could never find it."

"But he did find yours, didn't he?" Shani inquired. "Back in 1937. It was your store he burned down. He tried to torture you. It was his fire...the devil's fire. He somehow was able to find you, or you were betrayed. He took your amulet, didn't he? But...I thought you died that night?"

Maya was impressed by Shani's intuition.

"That's right," she continued. "When he is especially indignant, his flames ignite faster and further than anyone can imagine. He can barely control it. Not that he cares. He thought he found one of our sanctuaries, but he didn't. It was one of our cover-up locations at the time meant to confuse him or anyone who was working for him. We constantly change guards and locations, but one of his followers, another alchelarcenist, stabbed me to death that night. She had stolen the powers of Hephaestus. She could materialize metal with the iron in her blood, and they killed the guard at that sanctuary the night she became one, but in my next life, I lived amongst the sea near the harbor in Boston. I was an eel."

"Ilisa," Shani whispered.

"How do you—"

"Yeah, I met him." She was eager to get this particular information out of Maya as fast as possible. "He helped us get here. How does he know everything about this whole ordeal?"

"Ilisa?" There was a sense of bewilderment in her tone. "We discussed him joining the Alliance; the ones protecting what needs to be protected. After I passed once more and returned to being human again, we pursued no such thing. He always reincarnated as an eel. He wouldn't have been able to execute his duties, and..."

"And what?" Asher asked.

"At one time, I had reason to believe he was the one to disclose our Boston Sanctuary."

Shani gave no reaction. Just silence, and the eagerness for Maya to continue.

"But he couldn't have," said Maya. "The only one that could communicate with him is Poseidon, and now you."

"But someone did betray you," Logan stated.

"Yes, but we still don't know who. Anyhow, that night that the Romanov building burned down, Moloch found me again and brought the same alchelarcenist follower with him. Her name is Kali. She looked like she had barely aged when I saw her again. When they found me, they wanted me to bring them to the sanctuary in exchange for not killing me again. I, of course, refused, but this time, I was prepared for them. I found a way to hex myself, so any mystical being wouldn't be able to touch me or my treasured belongings, but it got out of hand. Moloch fabricated an even bigger disaster. He almost burned Kali's face off, and he didn't care. His only follower from what I know, and he knows only his fire can permanently scar her. She also had the amulet, and I managed to take it back as she collapsed from the flames. But that wasn't enough. I thought the best way to get rid of the magic was to put it into humans."

"And along came us," said Asher. "You let your little pet loose on us. Where do you even keep that thing? How did you know he wasn't going to eat us?"

Shani, being a passionate animal lover, didn't appreciate creatures being referred to as "things." But she rolled her eyes, ignored it, and moved on.

"Baymour is a hellhound, and he does whatever I say. He knew exactly what he was doing. He was a gift from Persephone, and he hides within another cave in the trees. I've been following you to keep an eye out on you. I couldn't get near you just in case they ever found out where I was, or who I was talking to."

Now, the five of them all uncomfortably sat on the hard, rocky, and dirty floor. The rope holding them together tightened. Their trust in Maya was building at a steady, but slow rate.

"Because they didn't know we existed," said Logan.

Maya shook her head and said, "No. I don't believe they even found the sanctuary."

"How did they know where you were, but not the sanctuary?" Asher asked.

"I'm not sure, but I'm the only one who can open it. It's hexed. That's why it took me a few tries to let all of you in. I had to put some of my blood into Baymour's mouth, and he spat onto it as I instructed him to do."

"Ew," Asher mumbled with his lips barely moving.

"That must have been how Moloch was able to get into the sanctuary earlier. When he attacked me back in Boston, he must have taken some of my DNA, but it's uncertain."

"And Lexi?" said Logan. "How was she taken? Was it the same way Moloch possessed those cars to run Shani and Lexi over and then try to kill us on our way here?"

"The vehicles that tried to attack you must have been controlled by Kali. Her power has evolved to such great lengths. Anything metal, she can speak to. But to take away Lexi's consciousness? In the past they've used a sort of dust that's a combination between a lotus flower, scopolamine, and I believe a few other ingredients. I'm not sure what they call it, but it can make them take control of almost anything."

"Wait," said Brex holding her hand up in disbelief. "Scopolamine? As in the drug?"

"Everything mystical has a scientific basis."

The rest listened with their arms crossed and their eyes squinted. "You buying this?" Asher asked Shani.

"Yeah," she said. "But I just don't get—" Maya looked at her impatiently waiting for the question to be asked. "What are you doing down here? How long have you been here? And why did you not try to escape when we opened the fault line, or whatever you want to call it?"

"I followed them here. I saw her get in the car. I could see that the driver collapsed. Lexi was trying to help him, but she collapsed too. I knew they had found her. The car drove off, and I followed them. I had to switch transportation a few times, but I knew where they were going. Turns out, Moloch was already here. I didn't even know someone working for him had the trident. I've only been down here for a few hours. He must have thought this was the one place that would cloud your detection of her because of the ice, but he was clearly wrong."

The rest lost themselves in a pensive moment. Everything was more complicated and deliberate than they had thought.

"What does he want?" Brex asked. "I mean, he wants our powers, doesn't he? And he can't get them if we're dead. Why? What does he want with them?"

Maya lifted the corner of her lips and said, "I'm impressed."

Asher shot a sharp look around the room and raised his hands, trying to remind everyone that he was the first to suggest this theory, even though they couldn't remember if that was true or not.

"He's just trying to weaken you and find the perfect strategy to remove every bit of the gods in you, but did you ever wonder how to fill your fuel back up? How to make the arrow turn back center?" They stared at her blankly, giving her their answer. "It's because he knows the closer he gets to you, the stronger you become. He was the one who created this curse without the Alliance knowing when we took the Greeks' powers away. There are parts of his entity that are so powerful they could revive any being who needs it, unless it's too late."

"Wait," Logan interrupted. "Was Moloch injured during the Romanov fire? Was he bleeding or anything?"

Maya pondered for a moment before she answered and said, "I think so. From what I can remember, a part of the building fell on him as he was trying to escape his own fire. That's how I got to the sanctuary before he did, or if he ever did. He could have left behind a blood trail."

"What does it look like?"

"It's sort of a glowing dark red, but more thick than human blood. Why do you ask?"

In his mind, Logan drew an image of the picture Lexi sent to them the night after the fire.

"We saw some," he said. "Dammit. It could have helped us."

"Don't worry about it, Logan. We'll figure it out," said Brex. "And this is great and all to know, but Maya, you still haven't answered my first question." Maya didn't bother to play dumb, but she still felt hesitant to respond. "What does he want with our powers?"

For a moment, Maya's eyes lost most of the life in them before she said, "There are certain things that he needs in order to...transform our world in a way."

The vagueness in her words was unimpressive to them, but they kept staring at her, waiting for her to move on while their legs began to shake with impatience.

"If he can gain enough magic, power, and a few rare artifacts, he can expand the underworld farther than it's supposed to, and he can bring every living being on this planet into it, and they will have no control whatsoever."

With little articulation and a shivering jaw, Shani spat out, "He wants to turn the entire world into his own personal Hell?"

Maya responded with a single nod and turned her focus back to the ground.

"Wait, what is his reasoning for this?" Brex aggressively inquired. "How does that even make sense? He's not human. He's a mystical being. How would anything change for him?"

"He believes that it will cause less pain on Earth, and everything can be more under control...or more so *his* control. Or at least that's what he claims, but the rest of the Alliance deciphered his real plan long ago. If he expands the meanings of Hell he won't pass on."

"Pass on?" Logan asked. "He can die?"

"No, but his entity can disintegrate. The being that existed before him was Lucifer, but he grew too weak after hundreds of years. That's what modern medicine will do to the leader of death. He knew it would happen eventually."

I don't know how, but somehow he brainwashed Kali into thinking that his intentions were genuine and the right path to take."

"And you've been protecting these sanctuaries for over a hundred years?" Asher asked.

"Yes. Every few years, the Alliance...we switch places and move a few sanctuaries if we need to, and we'll do it at random."

"The Alliance," said Shani. "That's what you call yourselves? Who are they? Is there any way that they know where you are?" She glared at Maya, knowing precisely how she was going to answer such an obvious question. "Did you make plans with any of them? Or is there any sort of tracking device."

"If there were any of that, we would NOT be here."

"And the fire here a few weeks ago," said Logan, trying to alter the direction of the tense dialogue. "Who was on post that night? Do you know what happened?"

Maya held her hand out, indicating for them to not worry.

"Zara was the guard. She had just finished her apprenticeship for the Alliance, so she was fairly close to me, but she removed the alchelesters—"

"Alchelesters?" Asher asked.

"The physical gifts of the gods. Their magic. At least that's what Moloch called them. But she removed them before he came. She got word that he found her location a few weeks ago, but didn't have time to remove the cave. He found the cabin she was living in too. He burned down that as well...as much as he could find."

"Maya," said Brex. "Briefly, can you just explain how this whole thing works?"

"How what works?" she asked.

Brex struggled to find the right words until she said, "The universe, I guess. We've all heard a ridiculous amount of stories. Which ones are real? Are there other dimensions? Just...that kind of stuff."

"I can't *briefly* describe that, but I will tell you many of the stories you've heard are true. Although, it's a lot more complicated than that."

"How so?" Logan asked.

"Humans tend to believe that there's just one answer; one place that everyone goes to in the next life, but as I'm sure you've now discovered, that's not true. Living, breathing beings are destined for something far greater than something so simple. There are practically an infinite number of dimensions that beings can travel to. It's far beyond what any human can imagine. It's even too much for *me* to imagine. That's about as summarized as I can make it. And besides, you are still human. I don't wish for you all to know too much. It could drive you mad."

"I think that ship has sailed," said Brex.

"Please," Asher spat. "That ship has already made at least three circles around the globe by now."

Shani stood there, soaking in all of the information while aggressively picking at her scar. "Besides the sun tracking, how we fuel ourselves, and the power exchange," she said. "Is there anything else we need to know about our scars?"

"Specifically, the scar?" said Maya. "No, but you should know I had no intention of that happening when we temporarily laid the Greeks to rest. I'm still not entirely sure how Moloch created such a curse, but I do remember the night he forced the witches of Salem to help him. Kali, as far as I know, is the only other one, but there could be more. The Alliance...we don't communicate a lot. It's safer if we don't talk too much, or our conversations could be traced. We only communicate when we switch our sanctuaries around, and it's always at random."

Brex dug her fingernails into her scalp and forcefully ran her fingers through her hair. There were still many questions that needed to be asked, but so far, the answers weren't getting them anywhere.

"What if…" Asher began. "What if a bear or something came by? You know what I mean? Would it open the split back up? I could at least try to fly us all out of here."

"That's not gonna happen," Shani said with her arms now over her knees and wrapped around her legs.

"I'm still not in the mood, Shani, 'cause seriously, do you have a single thing better in mind?"

"Well, there's gotta be something. Lexi could be dead by now for all we know!"

"She's not," Maya interrupted with a slight perk in her posture. "She's just not. I can feel it."

They all believed her and convinced themselves they deserved the optimism.

"But how long until it stays that way?" Brex asked. She stood up and began to kick a few small rocks around with her dirty and torn-up Converse. After a few minutes, she noticed that the flames burning from the torch were dying down. Everything around her was a few shades darker than it had been moments before, but by using her sense of touch, she felt around for another root to pull from the earth and burn.

"I could really use Lexi's help right now," she muttered as she grabbed a hold of a loose, thick root and struggled to break it off. "Jesus—Christ—Shit!"

"Need help?" Logan asked.

"I'm not really up for toxic masculinity, thank you."

Logan had no rebuttal except for shooting Asher an indignant look before Asher shrugged his shoulders and left it up for Logan to fix whatever he had just made.

"Okay, fine," said Brex, finally giving in. "Just get over here."

Logan subtly shook his head before he tried to stand up, until something got in his way.

"Ahh," he sputtered.

"What?" Shani and Asher said together as they rushed over to help him. From where they were standing, it looked as if he had cracked a rib.

"Something just jabbed into my hip, and it definitely pierced through my skin." He went from sitting up straight to leaning to one side with one dismally weak arm.

"It's okay," said Maya, concerned, and walking closer to the group. "Just take it out, nothing will be damaged."

Brex's adrenaline now shot up three times its normal dose. Logan needed light. Getting a few splinters in her hands, she yanked out the branch with one clean pull. All five fingertips on her right hand wrapped around the bigger end of the wood, and the red and orange element grew twice as large as the light before.

"Okay, okay," Shani spat, with her hands flying around the front of her face, trying desperately to concentrate. "It's gotta be something in your pocket."

"Oh no," said Logan, quietly and discouragingly.

"What?"

"My key is in my pocket, or at least what's left of it."

While trying her best not to have a panic attack, Shani reached over to feel what she figured was the shattered plastic in his pocket.

"Okay," she said. "Is it still poking you? Can we just take it out?"

"It feels like it," said Logan as he already started to regret reaching into his pocket and taking out the car key as if he were ripping off a Band-Aid. Rather than screaming or cursing, he let out a long and aggressive grunt. Shani looked away as she rolled her eyes and recalled the time they had to take a block of ice the size of a ketchup bottle out of her leg.

"You good?" Asher asked.

"Yeah. It's fine, but ah motherffff—" He held out the pieces that were left of his father's car key in his hand. Luckily, it wasn't completely demolished. A small part of the plastic broke off in the corner, but the metal was covered in blood.

"Welp," Shani squeaked "it's out."

But then, the moment before he was about to instinctively put his key back into his pocket, an idea struck; an idea that he was already regretting.

"Oh, for the love of God," he said as he threw his hands into his lap and tucked his chin to his chest.

"What?" Brex asked. "What's wrong?"

The sour look lingered in between the wrinkles on his scrunched face.

"I know how to get out of here, but only if electricity can travel strongly through ground. To be honest, I have absolutely no idea if it does."

"Kind of," Shani answered. "But you'd need a really strong volt—" All of a sudden, Shani felt as if she could read Logan's mind. "Wait, you're not thinking of..."

"Yeah." Logan was almost in tears as he wiped some of the dirt off his face. "Come on, let's do this before I change my mind and before it's too late."

The five of them all stood up almost in perfect unison to watch Logan scurry around the earthy niche like a mouse attempting to escape from a cage.

"Which way was the car?" he asked.

"Uhh...uhh," Brex babbled as she closed her eyes and tried to retrace their steps. "We were driving northwest, and then we got out of the east side of the car...and the we, we mainly went straight."

"Well, we don't have a compass," Shani spat. "That doesn't tell us anything."

"Yeah, but we were facing um..." Brex turned around to point at the dirt wall behind them, "...that direction, and so it would be somewhere in the exact opposite direction."

Giving her a questionable nod, Logan turned back around away from them and lifted his dominant arm to grab hold of the cold, wet earth. He pointed his focus right in the direction that Brex recommended.

"What exactly are we trying to do here?" Asher asked.

Logan responded "I'm going to try and start the car and bring it up to the hexed fault line, so there's enough weight to open the split."

"And destroy your car, so your dad will kick your ass?...Can I watch?" Everyone, including Maya, rolled their eyes before meeting Asher's overenthusiastic gaze. "Sorry."

"Hold on," Shani screeched. She turned around to face the same direction as Logan with her finger up at her eye level. Her head was spinning so fast, she almost forgot to breathe. The wrinkle in between her eyebrows felt more strained than it already was when she closed her eyes. All she needed was focus.

Asher broke the silence by loudly whispering, "What are you thinking?"

"Shh! The pond. Remember seeing the big pond? We passed one. I'm trying to sense where it is. It's the biggest source of water that's close to us." She pulled some of the water from the earth to heighten her senses. A few water droplets touched her skin, and all of a sudden, the earth was telling her what she needed to know. With her eyes still closed, she reached for Logan's hand. As her skin collided with his, she drew his arm to the direction that her senses were taking her. "Reach this way. You'll have a better shot. And Logan, take my power."

"What?" he bickered.

"As in your left hand and my left hand. You'll be able to reach further and get a stronger voltage."

"Is this going to hurt her in any way?" Logan asked, turning to Maya.

"No," she said. "Just don't let go until you're ready."

They both shared a sudden rush of confidence as they grabbed each other by the hand, and Logan reached out before Asher interrupted them.

"Wait, wait, WAIT!" he screamed. They dropped everything to see Asher standing there in a panic. "We're getting ahead of ourselves. We still need to figure out how we're going to get out of here once the split is open. We'll only have a few seconds."

"You're going to have to fly us out," said Brex.

"Well, yeah. I figured that, but we have to do it strategically and safely."

"Um...okay," Brex grabbed him by the arm and ran over to the opposite side of the cave. "Asher, Maya, and I will be over here ready to fly out. The moment you hear it or feel it open or whatever, run over here as fast as you can. Logan, you come and grab a hold of me, and Shani get ready to grab a hold of Maya. And Asher, grab a hold of my scar for a boost. You'll be more than strong enough."

For a moment, Shani was hesitant to agree to having an older woman securely hold her up in the air.

"Don't worry," she said to Shani as she saw the look on her face. "I've lived many long and fulfilling lives. I'm stronger than you think." Shani let a gentle smirk wipe across her face. Shani still didn't know for sure, but she had *faith* that she could trust Maya. "And Asher," she continued. "Remember to get as far away as you can before you come back to the ground. We can't risk falling into the split again."

"Right," Asher confirmed.

"And Logan," Brex interrupted "Make sure the car goes past the split so it doesn't fall through too."

Logan nervously nodded his head and said, "Ready?" He turned to reach for his car once again, and connected with Shani and the magic she so powerfully possessed.

The sweat on Logan's right hand seeped into the Earth. A spark jolted from his body as he closed his eyes and pictured the car, sitting at the bottom of the hill with the brutal scrape on the side. He could sense the bolt of electricity creeping towards the hummer and crawling through the earth. It was working, and it was working fast.

Suddenly, Logan felt a sudden spaz jolt throughout his body. He could see a blurry vision if he kept his eyes shut. The car; it was being enchanted by Logan's influence. They were connected perfectly. The bond between them was almost hypnotizing. He felt the car engine starting with what felt like an instant explosion, and the wheels began to slowly loop around to follow in Logan's tracks. Then, unexpectedly, the image in his head wasn't an imaginary photograph anymore. It was real. The tighter he shut his eyes, the clearer the image. He could see everything the car was doing. If it was about to hit a tree, he could avoid it. If it was about to drive into a pool of water, he could swerve around it.

The power was rushing to his head. It was all profoundly thrilling. The Hummer's speed was increasing. It was only a few minutes away now. Asher, Maya, and Brex patiently waited a few yards away from them. It grew darker and colder, but Brex gave off enough body heat to roast a turkey.

Before they heard the engine, they heard the snap of a tree branch after the Hummer whisked through a mud puddle and brushed under an evergreen tree.

"Okay, you gotta slow it down now," said Shani, but he wasn't listening, or at least that's what it seemed like. "Logan," she kept repeating. He was in a trance, and it wasn't breaking. "LOGAN!" After the final scream, his eyes finally snapped open, and he pulled his arm away from the moist soil just in time for the car to drift towards the split, but it was quiet, and Logan lost his connection.

"Shit. Did I let go too soon?" said Logan before looking up towards the sky, but as he did, the ground shuddered. The moon-lit, starry sky expanded as the earth reopened once again.

"COME ON!" Brex screamed as she clasped hands with Asher. Shani and Logan refocused themselves and bolted towards the rest at full speed. The torch was fading, and the wind rushed against them, but the moment before Asher sprouted his wings the two resilient, fierce beings jumped into the arms of their saviors. Without breaking a sweat, Asher launched into the air with a cloud of dirt lingering behind him.

The sky was clear and straight ahead, but the split was closing sooner and faster than expected. Asher refused to show any signs of weakness. Nothing was going to slow him down. It was almost as if his wings were growing longer, fuller, and stronger as he flapped them harder and faster. They couldn't stop.

They were almost there, but not yet out. The crack was only a few feet wide now. If they didn't escape, they would be crushed. They could feel the loose dirt falling onto them. Shani's fingertips scraped against the rocky edge. The friction was increasing. She was sure they weren't going to make it until Asher gave one last swoop with his wings, then wrapped them around the four bodies surrounding him. The vibrant push saved their lives as the earth closed inches below their feet, and the loud slam echoed in their ears.

"SHIT! WE DID IT!" he screamed as he soared into the clear, fresh air.

"You have to land over there," hollered Maya as she pointed south, towards the darker part of the woods. Asher dove back down towards the ground, causing everyone's stomachs to twist in knots except, of course, his.

"Oh, my God. I'm gonna puke," said Brex as her scarred hand tightened around Asher's.

The end of the flight was near, and Asher felt confident about securely landing. But when solid ground was a few feet away, he over-estimated his deceleration. Their speed was still too fast for their feet to keep up. Shani was the first one to get her foot caught in the ground, which caused everyone to stumble over, tossing and turning until the inertia ran out, and they all came to a halt, spread out over the patchy grass.

"Sorryyyyy," Asher mumbled as he put away his wings and made his way to an upright position. "Is everyone okay?"

Shani and Maya mumbled their own stammered version of "Yes" while Brex and Logan groaned, trying to stand and give a thumbs up. Asher rushed to Maya's aid, unsure of what damage could be done to her aging body.

"I'm okay, I'm okay," she said. "We don't have much time. Follow me!"

21:

"Where are the others?"

"The entrance to the sanctuary is just over here," said Maya, hiding behind a tree and peering around the corner. "I don't think anyone's watching, but we have to be careful."

"How did they get her inside?" asked Brex.

"I'm not sure. They must have taken blood from me in Boston somehow. That's the only explanation I can think of."

Seeing that the coast was clear, the five of them proceeded to run into the patch of trees. They could see the damage the fire had done. Countless trees had fallen to the ground. Branches were empty instead of being filled with the beautiful, colorful fall leaves.

"Here it is," said Maya, approaching a pile of stones.

"Are you sure?" Asher asked. "Where's the door?"

Without any answer, Maya walked up to a pile of smooth, enormous stones covering a ditch in the ground. Making everyone nervous by climbing a few feet on the unstable rocks, she managed to reach the deepest part of the ground and squat motionless. The fingers on her hand spread as far as they could on a rock that looked just like any other. And within a few brief seconds, the boulders shook, making a noise resembling a miniature avalanche before they scattered and moved out of the way one by one. The others slowly and carefully made their way closer to see a round hole in the ground that showed a light glistening in the distance.

"Each member of the Alliance designed their sanctuaries differently," said Maya. "But we all have access to each one."

"Okay," said Shani, eager to jump in. "Let's go!"

"Wait!" The rest looked at her as if her head were about to spin off. "We have to be careful. Don't even breathe too loudly. I have no idea what hexes they've put in this cave. We don't even know if somebody else, besides Lexi, is still in there. Every single one of us has to be as attentive as we can be."

They all exchanged eye contact in agreement.

"Hey, but..." said Asher. "We all have powers. What can you do? How will you defend yourself?"

"I'll be fine," said Maya, stepping out of the way for Shani to go first because she knew she would insist on doing so.

The circular hole stayed open at about four feet in diameter, but to Shani, it felt smaller than it was. Squatting, she cautiously yet quickly made her way into the small tunnel, which immediately triggered her claustrophobia. It was like going down a slide with a rooftop on a playground. The ground was wet and sticky as she sat on the curve of the tunnel and squirmed her way through the darkness. In that moment, she remembered something she saw on the news about meditating when crawling through small spaces. Her nose tickled as she blocked out every bit of noise.

Use the diaphragm, she thought. *You're in a calm, open field.*

She was tempted to close her eyes, but there was barely any light to guide her through the area to begin with.

"Don't worry," said Maya. "It gets bigger a few feet in."

Shani wanted to move as quickly as possible, so she had no choice but to trust Maya's judgment. Her feet felt a ditch, but it was too dark to see how far down it was. Her triceps shook as she slowly scooted her pelvis off the edge. The drop was only a few feet, but her ankles still stung as she landed in the dark room that immediately made her feel oddly dizzy.

"I'm in!" she yelled.

"You go next," said Asher, looking at Maya. "I'll be right behind you."

Maya gave a quick, single nod and crouched down to follow Shani. Asher whispered to Logan and Brex, "Be careful. We still don't know if we can trust her," before he also hopped through the hole.

"You go," said Brex. "I got your back."

Logan gave her hand a small squeeze before he carefully lowered himself down into the darkness. Brex gave one more look around before she followed him. She could not shake the feeling that she was still being watched, and whoever was keeping their eyes on her was close by.

"Okay," she whispered as a way of reassuring herself she was going to be fine. Her Converse immediately got twice as dirty as they already were before when she stepped into the tunnel. Because of the isolated and disoriented feeling the silent darkness gave her, she pushed her way through the dirt as fast as she could. The slippery wet dirt only made her filthier the further she got.

"That's everyone, guys," Brex said, but as she waited for a response, the air only grew quieter than the moment before. The space vibrated with uncomfortable silence that rang in her ear. No one was there. "Very funny. Can we please go get Lexi now?"

It was too dark for her to be able to see the outline of a human body, but she still knew somebody was there. She could feel it, but now she was sure it wasn't any of her friends. They would have answered, and they wouldn't have left her there.

Calmly and gradually, she stepped one foot in front of the other. *Roll through the feet. Heel, toe, heel, toe,* she kept repeating in her head. It was the first solution that popped into her head that could possibly keep her calm. The slower her heart rate was, the sharper her senses would be, but everything was still. No noise was to be heard, until the silence suddenly and abruptly broke.

"Who's there?" she snapped, as she whipped her head around to see no one standing where she could have sworn she had heard a steady footstep. By now her eyes had adjusted to the dark. There were a few spots in whatever room she was in that glowed like scales on a snake. Brex took a few more steps towards the direction of the most lit area she could see, but again, nothing was to be found. Feeling that she might after all be more intact than she thought, she turned back around to travel in her original direction only to see the outline of a hooded man, standing at the other side of the room.

Instead of screaming, she pushed all of the oxygen out of her lungs, ran in the opposite direction and hid behind the first wall she could find. Although, her knuckles stiffened knowing she couldn't be hidden well. It was still too dark to know.

·····

"Hello?" Shani repeatedly shouted, speed walking across what looked like an open field. "Guys, where are you? What the hell just happened?" Nothing but grass and clouds surrounded her. If she looked into the abyss of any direction, she would only see where the sky and the ground met. It was daylight, but it was calm, and not even a breeze brushed across her face. She tried opening and closing her eyes a few times, but nothing changed. Was it real? It *had* to be real. The ground was touchable, and the air was breathable. Then she questioned what the word "real" meant.

"Oh, no," she said to herself. Her voice cracked, and the dry vocal cords shook with fear and thirst. "I'm already going insane. This is what Maya was talking about."

·····

"How the hell did I get back to Boston?" Asher asked himself as he walked down Main Street towards his apartment. The brightness of daytime shined into his eyes as he covered them with his arm and squinted to compensate. It was too hot for his jacket. He removed it and wrapped it around his waist as his head continued to fill with clouds. "Oh no. It's a trap! Shani? Brex? Logan?" He picked up speed and ran down the sidewalk. It was the middle of the day, so he figured sprouting his wings at this time was probably not the best idea.

In the distance, a few yards away, he could see Adam walking towards him. Adam was spaced out, as usual. His headphones were in, his eyes were glued to the sidewalk, but Asher slowed down to stand right in front of him.

"Hey, Adam," he said out of breath. "Have you seen Shani or any of the others?" But something was wrong. Adam didn't look up to see Asher, standing ten feet in front of him. He kept walking toward

Asher, still in his own world. He was about to scream Adam's name one more time until Adam didn't stop walking and smoothly brushed right through Asher's body.

Asher stood there, stunned. What just happened? *How* did that happen? A group of people sat on their stoop, talking just a few feet away from where Asher was standing. He ran as fast as he could to get next to them. All he wanted to know was if they could see or hear him, so he did the first thing that came to mind.

"AHHHHH!" he screamed, two feet away from the girl with red hair who sat on the lowest step.

None of them reacted. He was invisible. He was just an entity, roaming about, who meant nothing to anyone. He was left out. It was as if his worst fear were coming true.

.....

"What am I doing home?" Logan asked himself. He stood at the front entrance to his house, nearly paralyzed. His surroundings were vivid, but it still didn't feel like home. Something was off, but he couldn't tell what.

The door was closed behind him as he walked past the living room couch and the stairs that led up to the second floor. The first thing he noticed that was wrong was the smell. Mr. Kwan always liked to have the house cleaned with lavender-scented cleaning supplies. It was his wife's favorite, but the smell wasn't there. Their cleaning lady came in at least once a week. What changed?

He kept slowly walking towards the kitchen. Nothing about his atmosphere was euphoric. Everything was touchable. The rough, cream-colored wallpaper that always made Logan cringe when he touched it was still intact, but he wasn't sure if it was a detailed illusion until he noticed something missing from an old photograph.

"Mom," he whispered to himself. His mother was missing from the family photo of when Logan was an infant. It was just him and his father. "No, no, no, no, no!" He ran around to each room, looking for the rest of her photographs, but there were none.

His father always kept his favorite photo of his wife right next to his usual reading spot in the living room. It usually stood on the side table in the corner, but when Logan passed by, there was nothing there. She was gone. It was like she had never existed.

.....

It was dark where Maya stood. She had no idea where she was, yet there was still something strangely familiar about this place. The sound of waves crashed in the background, but she could see no traces of water. Moments went by before she noticed a different sound blurring into the background. It vaguely resembled the sound of two hands slowly rubbing together.

Maya slowly and quietly turned in circles to find out where the mysterious noise was coming from, but it seemed to be coming from all around her. As it grew louder and closer, it echoed throughout the space. Then there was one more sound added to the group, but this one was the most distinct of them all.

Hsssssss...

To her regret, she knew exactly what it was, and it was coming from right behind her. Trying hard to make no sudden movements, she slowly turned around with her eyes leading. And right there before her, stood a long, thick, white snake with deep red eyes. Eyes that could light a fire in any soul it possessed.

There was nowhere for Maya to hide. The only thing for her to do was step away, carefully.

"I'm sorry," she said to the snake. "I didn't mean to. Please don't." One by one, her feet stepped backwards, but the snake was only getting closer. "I know this can't possibly be real, but I desperately need to get out of here, and I need you to listen to me in order to do that. We are on the same side. I promise you. Remember?"

They began circling each other. The snake could clearly understand her, but it was testing her, and viciously teasing her at the same time. It was like she was trapped in her own nightmare.

•••••

Logan looked around in every cabinet in the house to see if the laven-der-scented products were stored somewhere, but he couldn't find anything scented at all, let alone anything lavender. He remembered a time when Mr. Kwan wore a bracelet that once belonged to Mrs. Kwan. He only wore it on special occasions, but Logan remembered seeing his dad put away the bracelet a few times in the bedside drawer on Mrs. Kwan's side of the bed. Maybe it was still there.

At this point, he didn't expect a lot, but he wanted to keep what little hope he had left. Logan booked it up the stairs and sprinted into his dad's bedroom. The light was already on when he ransacked the drawer to find nothing but a few old photographs and old birthday cards.

This wasn't his house. It didn't feel like his house, but where was he? It had to be a hallucination of some sort, but how could he escape it? And what was the point?

"Okay!" he hollered out into the open. "You're trying to scare me off? I'm facing my worst fears! What more do you want from me?"

•••••

Shani kept walking through her empty field. There was no end. She didn't recognize where she was. It was a place she had never visited, even in her nightmares. What confused her the most was why whatever illusionist created this place made everything so flat and boring. The environment gave her chills. It was like she all of a sudden had nothing in her life. She, who grew up with everything she had ever wanted, felt out of control, and abandoned.

•••••

Brex kept her lungs caved in. She'd been sitting still in a dark corner for a few minutes now. There was no movement, and no noise. It was time to move. Time to keep moving forward, so she could reach safety. She pushed herself up to a crouched position, looked left and right one more time, and slowly extended her legs fully straight. Keeping her chest up high and her eyes wide open, she took one step forward, and then another. After a few more seconds, she felt safe enough to run to her destination. Her Converse only made a few squeaky noises as her strong limbs pounded into the rocky floor. Her heart rate lowered as fewer drops of sweat ran down her face. The existing environment smoothly shook at a steady rate until the sound of a single pebble dropped from a few yards behind her, but it only encouraged her to sprint faster.

A small beam of light was only a few feet away now, but when she approached it, it was a dead end. Without being able to think of any other solution, she ran in the opposite direction. If someone was going to attack her, she wasn't going to be vulnerable about it and let them take her while standing still. No. They were going to take her while she was at her strongest.

Her asthma currently had little effect on her. Ever since her lungs could tolerate fire breathing through her skin, they were surprisingly more stable. Her reflexes grew sharper. If anyone came up behind her, she could penetrate their genitals faster than they could ask for mercy.

She almost lost the sense of time after running for a while. Once again, her vision became blurry, and she couldn't see the small boulder a few feet up ahead of her. Running straight into it, her left foot almost got stuck underneath the boulder as she collapsed onto her side in a daze.

It was all slow. Harshly falling onto her side only increased the feeling of being locked in a dark fairytale. As a reaction, her body naturally wanted to breathe heavier, but the deeper the inhale, the more her ribs stabbed her.

Her eyes slammed shut, irrationally hoping the pain would magically vanish. She flipped over onto her back, pushed her shoulders away from her neck to release tension, and opened her eyes, only to find a dark figure standing over her.

She tried to scream, but before she could, it faded into the darkness. The black shadow disappeared, like a video game character relocating itself. Every bit of her body lay there still as a mummy. Whoever it was, they weren't here to harm her.

*****

Asher speed walked like he was late to class. There had to be someone who could grant him some attention. Maybe that was the trick to getting out of here. He needed to find somebody to make his fear of being ignored disappear.

He passed by his favorite coffee shop and a few more familiar buildings until his legs gave out, and he had to take a break. Every bone in his body quivered with impatience and anxiety.

Maybe I didn't eat enough for dinner, he thought. *Or did I eat dinner at all?*

It was like being stuck in paranoid dream mode. Everything was out of his control. He relaxed by sitting on a random set of steps. Nobody could see him. Therefore, he wasn't going to get in trouble by being on someone else's property.

While his bony elbows rested on his knees, his head dropped toward the pavement as the sweat dripped down his face. It was daytime, and the sky beamed its usual New England fall weather; dreary and windy. After taking a deep breath in through his nose, closing his eyes, and lifting his chin, he reopened his eyes to see the dullness of his surroundings. The colors of the buildings. The polished lining of the clouds. Nothing seemed different, just dull. It felt like he was being mocked for his occasional depression.

Suddenly, he heard the door open behind him. He turned to see a boy of maybe twelve years of age skip down the stairs. Asher didn't take his eyes off him. The second the boy's feet touched the sidewalk, he turned around to reveal his face. It was Pablo, Asher's little brother.

"Pablo!" Asher hollered. But Pablo didn't respond. "Pablo!" he repeated. His little brother stood there, fidgeting like normal. He looked around as if he were waiting for someone, but no one was coming. He shrugged his shoulders and booked it down the sidewalk.

He was alone. Asher thought. *He was expecting someone, and they didn't come, and now he's alone when he wasn't supposed to be.*

·····

"I'm sorry," said Maya, "But please just listen to me, so I can get out of here. The boy is safe. I promise you. No harm will come to him!"

The white snake gave the impression that she wanted nothing to do with whatever Maya had to say.

It was just a false image, Maya thought. She didn't need to convince the snake of her sorrow and regret. She needed to convince herself.

"I can fix this. I can fix this," she whispered under her breath. As her eyes closed, she felt droplets of rain fall on her nose, then onto her cheeks and forehead. It grew heavier by the second. Even the cold air, blowing by her, felt low and dejected. She reopened her eyes to see a sullen, young woman standing before her instead of the bright white snake. The woman was silent and still, but her eyes said everything. She let the rain drip down her light blue robes as she turned and walked away into the dark, gray fog. Maya's hopelessness ate away at her, especially since it was a memory she hadn't thought of in a while, and she knew why.

·····

Logan remembered a diary that he kept in a box in his closet. It mainly contained notes to his deceased mother. He used to jot down a lot of questions that he wished he had gotten to ask her. It was his therapist's idea, but he stopped doing it after the age of twelve. He always justified the negligence by telling himself he was too busy with school and sports. That's what she would have wanted.

His closet was filled with items he hadn't touched or cleaned in years, but he remembered exactly where he had left that journal. Jackets, dirty pants, and old shoes he hadn't worn in three years went flying behind him as he found an old shoe box with old, torn-up books and middle school assignments that he had aced, but no journal.

It was only a few years before when he had stopped writing in it. He remembered exactly where he left it. He always remembered where he left anything. That was the only reason he could keep his room a mess. It was never a problem for him. Could he possibly be wrong this time? Maybe it was under his bed.

His stomach almost slid across the floor as he jolted towards the underside of his bed. This was mainly where he kept his old books and art supplies, but there was still a chance that it could be there. He threw the cover off the bin of books to see nothing but the *Feminine Mystique*, the last two *Hunger Games* books, and a few other novels that he thought he would be into but instead read the first three pages before deciding otherwise.

He wasn't much of a hoarder, so he knew it wasn't going to be in the basement. That was mainly where Mrs. Kwan liked to paint. She made it her studio, which to this day, Mr. Kwan still hadn't touched. He never wanted anything to be disturbed, unless Logan needed extra paint. Every once in a while, he would sneak down there and take a tube or two, which he always felt a little guilty about.

And then it hit him.

"Holy shit," he whispered to himself. "This isn't my biggest fear. It's my guilty conscience." He knew what he had to do.

Barely breathing, Logan ran downstairs and into the basement as he figured all of his mother's belongings were packed into boxes. The exact opposite of his real basement and what his father wanted. All of this time, he knew he should have been paying more attention to how his father was coping with his mother's death. Instead, his father just shook it off. It was the last thing he ever wanted to talk about.

He could see one of the clear boxes had a large stack of white sketching paper in it. He took it down so fast, it almost hit him on the head. Along with the paper he took out a few pencils that were still freshly sharpened before he flopped the bin down on the floor, and he began to sketch.

It wasn't his best drawing, but it didn't matter. All he needed was a genuine, tactful sketch of his mother. He needed to prove he hadn't forgotten her, that he *did* care. He cared about her and his father.

With all the determination he could muster, he ran back up to the living room and placed his sketch right in his father's favorite spot. Where the picture of Mrs. Kwan was supposed to be.

"Mom...." Logan started. "I'm sorry if you feel like I never bothered to know who you were. I just thought it would be easier that way. I didn't want Dad to ever see me be sad. I just thought it would make him sadder than he already was. I know I never really got to know you, but I think about you every day, and that will never stop, not ever!"

Logan couldn't remember the last time that he cried. It was something about this hallucination that made every chemical in his brain dance around in circles.

"Do you think I've been neglecting Dad?" He shoved his hands in his face, leaving his fingers and palms slightly damp. "I guess I just always thought that he was okay. He never told me otherwise, but now that I'm older, I guess these are things that I gotta ask him now. I'm starting to notice that he seems a little bit more distant than usual. I'm pretty sure it's because he feels guilty that he gets to witness me scoring touchdowns without you. Damn, Mom. You would have loved to see me on the field. You would have been so proud. I know what I need to do now. I need to be there for Dad. He's allowed to be sad, and I am too. I want him to know that he can talk to me about anything. I want to help him as much as I can. I don't want to be a screw up, but I know now that you would have been proud of me either way. I'm never going to feel guilty about that ever again."

He stayed there, crouched down on one knee. The foot he was sitting on already started to fall asleep. His head was glued to his knees before he ripped away and all of the oxygen was sucked out of his lungs.

"Logan!" screamed a voice. "Logan!" Maya was standing over him as he reopened his eyes back in the dark, rocky cave.

"Logan, are you okay?"

"What? Wha—?" His jaw was loose and weak. He saw Maya before him, but struggled to focus his eyes. It was like he was in sleep paralysis for a moment before he shook his shoulders and forced himself to regain control of his body and sit up. "Where are the others?"

He had to squint to be able to see through the depressing darkness. He thought he could see Brex's jean jacket on the floor, but he couldn't tell if it was on her or not.

"They're just over here, but we must try to wake them up! Just try talking to them and shaking them. They should regain consciousness."

Logan's eyes sharpened as he wobbled up to a standing position. His hands felt even grimier than before, and he could feel the blood pounding against the back of his neck, giving him a splitting headache.

Maya was already trying to shake Brex awake, but so far, she wasn't waking. She only lay there quietly whimpering and squirming as if she were having a terrible nightmare. Logan had to reassure himself that he wasn't going to be of any use to her. Maya had it taken care of. Asher and Shani needed his help.

Shani had collapsed behind a rock the size of a bedside table. Her legs stuck out, but her black jeans made it hard for Logan to spot her right away. When he eventually got to her, one of her arms flopped over her small waist while the other stretched above her head, profusely bleeding. It had scratched against the rock as she tried to catch her fall.

"Shani!" he screamed, as he gently held her injured arm. "Wake up! It's not real. None of it is. You're safe with me, and everyone else." Her eyes started to twitch, but it wasn't fast enough for Logan's satisfaction. "The room, it was hexed. Don't give in. It's just your conscience trying to get inside your head. You're stronger than that. Come on!"

Slowly, her eyes opened. Her head moved back and forth once she realized where she was.

"Am I—?" she muttered. "Logan, what just—?"

"You're okay, but you're bleeding."

"It's—it's okay."

"Are you sure?"

"Yes."

"Okay. Come on, we gotta help Asher."

A few feet away, Asher lay flat on his stomach. His hands were twitching as if he were having a panic attack. Shani knelt down to one side of him while Logan knelt down to the other.

"Asher!" they both yelled as they shook his chest and shoulders. Waking him was a bit easier. A ball of air shot through his nose as his eyes snapped open to see his friends kneeling before him.

"What the hell just happened?" he said as a few droplets of sweat ran down his face.

"The room was hexed," Logan said without missing a beat. He looked over to see Maya still struggling to wake up Brex. "Come on. We gotta help her."

Logan grabbed Asher's hand to help him up. He was a little too quick and aggressive, but Asher was still too dizzy to care or say anything. The three of them ran over to Brex's unconscious body. Her breaths were short, almost like she was crying and having trouble forming words.

"Brex? Brex, can you hear me?" Maya calmly asked.

"Wait, let me try," said Shani. She grabbed a hold of Brex's left hand and squeezed it. Nothing was happening in terms of flames or water sprouting about them, but wherever Brex was inside her head, she knew Shani was there. Her breathing regulated at a normal pace, and she didn't sound like she was in pain anymore. "Brex, wherever you are, no one is going to hurt you. I know that you're smart enough to know that none of this is real. That doesn't make it any less frightening, so you're allowed to be scared. We're all here. We're not going to leave you. Whatever happened, it's over now. You don't need to feel guilty about anything. It's all okay. Everything is going to be okay, no matter what. I promise."

Shani carefully and gently brushed Brex's long black hair out of her face. A hint of light shined on her skin, and it glistened as she slowly opened her eyes. For a moment, she just stared at the rocky ceiling, clearly not fully grasping what was happening. She looked lost, and then she looked at her friends as if she had no idea who they were.

Everyone stood there silent, everyone except for Shani. The only movement she made was rubbing Brex's upper arm, while still holding on with her other hand.

"I'm sorry," Brex finally said.

"For what?" Shani asked.

"I don't know, I just feel weird. We—we really need to stop passing out 'cause we need to go get Lexi, now!"

Besides Brex, not a single person was upset. They were all beyond relieved to see Brex conscious without any memory loss or serious injuries. They were all back, and they were one step closer to saving Lexi.

"Where is she?" Logan asked.

"She should be this way," said Maya. "The tunnel is just a little bit longer."

They all followed one by one through the narrow tunnel that was even darker than the room they were in before, but if they squinted hard enough, they could see through the little light they had.

Finally, they approached what looked like a door, but when Maya tried to open it, she was zapped by something bright and red.

"What the hell was that?" Asher asked.

"Dammit," Maya cussed, holding her electrocuted hand. "How many more spaces can this man hex?"

"Well, let me try it," said Logan, stepping up front. "I can't be electrocuted."

"No!" Maya held her hand up to stop him. "It's not that...um...exactly. If I'm not mistaken, the only way we can get through is if you give up some of your powers."

Asher looked at her suspiciously and said. "Why would you think that? And how could you come up with that solution so quickly?"

"It's a shield that's meant to weaken intruders. That's what Moloch wants. He needs you weak.

"Well then, why should we give it to him?" Asher's voice was now so loud it echoed throughout the cave.

"Asher, we don't have a choice," said Shani. "Come on. It won't drain all of our powers. Let's just all do it at the same time."

Asher was hesitant to cooperate, but his frustration was making him nauseous. He didn't want to trust anybody, but he was also adamant about not giving this man any more of his time or energy.

"Fine," he finally said. "On three."

"One," Brex began, "two, three." And in the snap of a finger they all placed their left hands on the iron door. A heartbeat later, the door gave one quick vibration as if it were being electrocuted before it slowly creeped open. They did it. They felt the cold breeze of chilling ice brush up against their tired faces.

22:

"Did anyone get burned?"

Lexi was barely visible from where they stood, but they knew it was her, lying deep within the hole. Foggy steam rose from the hypnotizing, green liquid. Everything about that room screamed jeopardy. They had to get in and out of there as quickly as possible.

"Come on!" Logan said, leading the way. The ice in this cave was twice as slippery as the other one. Brex had to catch herself a few times as she made her way to the pool. There lay Lexi with her arms and legs spread wide as if she were resting in a snow angel. Her blonde, curly hair floated through the small ripples, and her shirt was still filled with air bubbles. The tip of her nose was about an inch away from the surface. She wasn't breathing, but they could sense the energy expanding from her. She was somehow still alive.

"What is this stuff?" Logan asked, trying to imply that the question was aimed at Maya. "How do we get her out? It doesn't look like the stuff from the other cave."

"It isn't," said Maya. She knelt down to reach into the pool. Only her index finger extended towards the liquid. The closer she got, the more she shook, and when the skin finally pierced through the surface, it only took a single breath for the finger to prune. Or was it wrinkles? Even from a few feet away, the rest could still notice a difference in texture. "Moloch must have stolen this from the Underworld ages ago. It's the substance that Hades uses to contain the souls of those who have passed."

"Of course, he did," said Asher with his arms crossed.

"You four aren't completely immune to this, but if you get her out quickly, it shouldn't be able to reel you in. That's why Lexi is still alive, but she's stuck. She can't get out on her own." She stood up and brushed her wet hand on her dirty pants.

"Shouldn't?" Logan questioned.

"I could die almost instantly if I touch anymore of this, but if you can get her out as fast as you can, you'll be fine. I will make sure of it."

The tone in her voice sounded convincing enough, but it still was unsettling to hear that this liquid could have any effect on them at all.

"Okay," said Brex. "Shani and I will push whatever this green stuff is away, and hopefully she'll float closer to the top, and when that happens, Asher, you fly and pull her up by her shoulders."

"What do I do?" Logan asked.

"Stand there and get ready to catch."

The four braced themselves. They somehow knew if they were affected by this, it was going to be a sensation unlike anything they felt before, and it wasn't going to be in their favor.

Both Brex and Shani put one foot in front of the other with their arms extended out straight. Asher powerfully sprouted his wings and carefully hovered over the green pool.

"Brex, you push first on that side, and I'll pull on this side," Shani stated. Brex nodded before Shani continued and said, "Ready? Go!"

Brex lit just enough fire to create a wave that pushed the liquid into Shani's control. She could feel the green substance wanting to resist. It made sense. It wasn't water, but she was able to loosely manipulate it.

Lexi started to slowly spin as the waves kept pulling her to the surface. It was Asher's turn. He reached his arms to her shoulders, but the moment his skin touched the substance, something changed, and he couldn't identify what it was. He didn't feel weak, he could still see perfectly clear, but he was stiff and low. It was almost as if he wasn't in his own body anymore, and someone was sucking out his soul and replacing it with another.

"Asher?" Logan snapped. Asher could hear him, but he couldn't do anything about it. Whatever this substance was, it was ripping him apart, and fast. "Asher!"

He looked down at Lexi. Her eyes locked shut, with her face as pale as ever. He needed to fight for her. Whatever was fighting him, he could resist it.

"Come on," Shani whispered to herself. Asher could hear that too. They were all fighting for her. And with all of that energy, he pulled Lexi straight up in the air to safety.

Every one of them beamed with relief. Logan prepared to grab her before Asher said "Hold on. Nobody touch her before she's dry." Brex pulled off her jacket and wrapped it around Lexi as Asher slowly laid her down.

Just when they thought they would need to shake her awake, or give her CPR again, she snapped her eyes open and gasped for breath.

"Lexi?" Shani asked, trying not to touch her. "You're okay. You're okay."

"Do you know where you are?" Logan asked.

Lexi looked around at each of their faces, trying to figure out what her last memory was.

"What's going on?" she coughed. "Who are you?" she questioned, looking at Maya.

"There's no time to explain," said Maya. "We have to get out of here."

Asher tried to help Lexi to her feet, but she needed no such assistance. While still clinging onto her jacket, she sprang up into the air and started running towards the exit.

"Are you okay?" Shani asked while running beside her.

"I'm fine. I'm just cold."

The six of them were about to leave the sanctuary before Maya halted them to a stop.

"Wait!" she snapped. "Lexi, you have to hold your breath and close your eyes."

"What?" Lexi asked.

"The room we went through, it was hexed. If you hallucinate too, it's going to waste even more time, and trust me, you're not going to want to do that."

Lexi agreed, puffed up her cheeks, and grabbed onto Asher as he led her through the narrow tunnel. One hand was on her wrist, the other on the lower part of her back. He kept her close while they scurried as fast as they could. Lexi could feel her lungs burning as she yearned to breathe, but the rest kept reassuring her that they were almost there. She fought through it and tried her best to meditate as much as she could instead of going into hyperventilation.

"Step up," said Asher as he held her by the waist, hoping she could reach the rabbit hole exit.

"Just a few more seconds, and then you can breathe," said Maya from a few feet behind her.

Lexi clumsily reached around the cylindrical, dirty, rocky space before she felt the soft, wet grass. Her oxygen-deprived arms pulled her up to ground level while Asher helped push up her wet legs. The smell of dirt and old dandelions filled her nose as she once again took a painfully deep breath. The air was cold and she could feel her lungs pushing away all of her other organs. Asher followed right behind her before he pulled Shani up to the surface.

Finally, they all were all back to ground level. Lexi was now dry enough for everyone to throw their arms around in relief. They took a moment to catch their breath and decide what the next step was going to be.

"Thank you, Maya," said Shani.

"Do you have your vehicle?" Maya asked.

"In a way," Logan responded with depression and anxiety filling his throat.

"Good. We should get moving. We can talk more on the way."

They all helped each other up and assertively moved along. Brex grabbed two loose branches, lit them both, and handed one to Logan. Everything seemed awkwardly still and silent. Only the breeze and the crunching leaves could be heard.

Lexi felt like she was still trapped in a vivid dream. She compulsively touched her face, partly because she wanted to wipe off the messy, droopy mascara, and also because she wanted to double-check that she was truly still alive.

"Hey," said Shani walking beside her. "What's your meter at?"

"What?" Lexi responded, perplexed.

"Your scar. Where's the arrow?"

Lexi flipped over her left hand before she said, "Oh um, looks like it didn't go that far down. Guess you guys got there just in time."

"Um, Maya," said Asher. "I did have another question. I don't know if this has to do with anything or what it really means, but you might know—"

"Shh," said Maya, holding out her hand to try to stop them.

"What are we—?"

"Shh!"

The branches on the trees creaked with excitement. There was an unsettling energy that wasn't there before. Maya grew two inches taller when she heard a single crack come from the thick, long branch that reached out in front of her. Here was one last hex they had to overcome.

"Run," Maya whispered just loud enough for the rest to hear her. Logan was the first one to sprint before they all followed. He tried to aim for the pathway that would lead to where he believed his car to be.

By instinct, they all stuck together and followed Logan and his torch into what looked like the most reliable exit to take. Shani could feel the blood trying to pump through to her fingertips as they all ran in a clump. Lexi could feel her damp skirt stick to her thighs as she tried to pull it up.

Everyone's eyes were locked on the only opening they saw out of the forest and into an open field. They were just a few feet away now. Logan felt his football mentality kick in. He pushed his legs to run faster than they ever had in a game, and the adrenaline was indescribable until he saw Shani run past him with her long legs moving so fast, he could barely see them. They thought they were safe until a long, thick branch from a pine tree expanded itself out to rapidly thrust towards Logan's chest.

"Whoa!" he screeched as he dropped to the ground, dodging the aggressive murder attempt. His inflamed torch shot straight into a pile of mud, putting out the fire, but Brex wasn't so lucky. The violent, enchanted plant wrapped itself around Brex's waist and shook her so intensely, she accidentally dropped her torch. It only took a few moments for the dry grass and dead branches to be in flames, which almost burned Asher's front.

A swarm of trees threw their limbs towards the small crowd charging at them like a sword. Screaming filled the air as they all crawled and scratched their way away from the oncoming threat. The bark on one branch scraped against Shani's back as she tried to escape.

"Ahhh!" she screamed. She caught herself as she nearly fell to the ground but pushed to keep running.

The fire slowly grew behind them. The sparks crept in their direction as they sprinted away from danger. If Lexi's dress hadn't still been damp, it would have burst into flames.

Logan saw a long, thick, white tree branch aim towards his forehead before he shot a continuous, flashing lightning bolt straight into its core. It was more powerful than he thought it was going to be. The single bolt of electricity electrocuted the entire tree, but it didn't take long for it to revive itself.

"GO! GO!" Lexi screamed to the others, as she stopped running and turned towards the fire. They wanted to hesitate, but their trust in her was now instinctual. There was an overwhelming, deep anger seeping through these woods. She could feel it, coming from the ground, but it faded away the moment they stepped foot into the open field and only felt the danger in the distance. This magic Moloch had bestowed upon them was powerful, but Lexi needed to fight back before the threat followed them. It was her gift after all.

To her left was a smaller, but fuller-looking spruce tree. To her right was a taller, but weaker spruce tree. The larger one almost bent its trunk in half to reach toward Lexi's feet, but Lexi's agilely dodged it. With her anger, she shattered the limb into pieces, and the bark flew in multiple directions.

Grabbing a hold of the two trees, she pulled the tops down in hopes of snapping them off their trunks. Her arms shook with tension, from her fingertips all the way to her shoulders. With one snap, the two trees lost their upper halves. Lexi could feel the urge of destruction crawling up her spine, but she could see something further in the distance that she hadn't been expecting. The evergreens behind them were growing. Was this her doing? No. It had to be whatever this magic was. She had an idea, but it wouldn't come easy.

"Come on, Lexi!" Shani screamed.

The roots. That's all Lexi had to set her mind to. She couldn't see them, so she had to beckon the roots and plead for their assistance. Her palms faced up to the sky as she heard and felt the ground rumble. She had done it. They were listening to her.

Like a profoundly dark fairytale, roots spiraled from the earth over nearly an acre of the woods. They heard Lexi speak to them, and they were at her every command.

Stop this catastrophic brawl, she silently spoke to them. Lexi and the spirit of the earth were communicating, and they were becoming one. Using this much power and energy at one time took a toll on her body. She felt her heart strings pull away from her chest, but it was working. The dark brown roots grew thicker and stronger by the second. They outnumbered the assailants.

With a few whipping cracks, the enchanted roots wrapped themselves around the trees and pulled them to the ground. Everyone except for Lexi covered their faces with their arms and jackets to prevent any thorns or splinters piercing them. The attack caused the wind to blow faster and heavier.

A few roots spiraled up the tree trunks to rip them from the ground and snap them into pieces. Others wrapped themselves around the top of the trees like a maypole and crushed them into the ground. After a few moments, they could barely see anything happen. The forest was now covered in dusty dirt, flurrying about the air resembling fog. But then, all of a sudden, it was quiet.

Damn, Asher thought to himself. *How does she do it?*

They thought it was over until a small light sparked into something bigger. Instead of the leaves smothering the fire, they had caused the fire to grow. They could see the smoke rising from what now looked like the world's biggest beaver den. It was reaching higher and higher by the second while the flames grew brighter and hotter with every breath.

"Oh shit," Lexi said to herself. "Well, I just made that a hell of a lot worse."

"Shani!" Brex screeched "You have to pull the water from the earth and put this out! It's gonna burn down the entire mountain!"

Shani's face twisted in pain as she nodded her head frantically, and faced her palms towards the grass. The knots in her shoulders felt tighter than usual. She knew what she was doing, but no matter how fast she went, her conscience kept telling her it was too slow. The thought anchored itself in the back of her head. She *was* moving too slowly, and the intense shake of her arms and jaw were not helping.

Small droplets of water from the ground slowly rose into the air. It wasn't much, but she clasped her hands together as the water shot towards the flaming forest. It did nothing. The flames were too big. Shani kept trying, but she was running out of water. The lack of moisture in the dirt was going to turn the White Mountains into a desert.

The rest stood there helplessly. They were at a loss. What could they possibly do to help? Brex tried to connect with the inferno. It was her fire. Maybe it could hear her tell it to die down. But after a few minutes of closing her eyes and reaching toward the flames, she realized it was too advanced and now out of her hands. Only the real Hades could have such power.

"We need to call 9-1-1," said Asher, "We need their help! We need more water!"

"No, wait!" said Maya before she looked behind her. Nothing was there, but this time, the rest could hear and feel what she could.

Thump, thump, thump.

It was a quick and consistent pattern; like a giant's footsteps ready to tackle the kingdom. And then they realized, they recognized that feeling. They had felt that rumble before.

The flaming forest gave them just enough light to see what was happening behind them. Trees were flopping from side to side, branches were snapping, and it all crescendoed. Then suddenly, with an echoing roar, a shaggy brown dog the size of an elephant with glowing yellow eyes and a long fluffy snout, burst through the woods and onto the field. His chin drooled with saliva while his clawed paws dug deep into the dirt.

"BAYMOUR!" Maya screamed and pointed towards the fire. "Run, Baymour!"

And he did. His breathing made him sound like a bull running towards a red flag. His eyes locked on the crimson flames.

The rest stood there with troubling caution. Then Brex remembered he was a hellhound. He must be able to do something.

Even from yards away, he still looked titanic. His beautiful, soft fur ruffled in the wind and glowed as he jumped next to the growing fire. They could hear him inhale through his nose. It almost resembled a train whistling right next to the ocean. They couldn't predict what was going to happen when he exhaled, but when he did, it definitely wasn't air or water that he was releasing.

It almost looked like thick fog, but it was white, shiny, and spreading fast. Once again, the small part of the forest was being smothered, but this time the fire was dying down. Baymour only had to take one other breath until the fire was completely out. Everything was dark again as the smoke settled down. He didn't collapse with exhaustion, and for the first time he looked like the happiest dog on Earth as he turned around to see if Maya was pleased with his doings. She beckoned for Baymour before he ran directly towards her, and she met his wet, black nose in her hand.

"How did you know?" she asked him as he happily growled and gave her a closed-eye grin. The rest stood there astounded, unable to say the right words, or any words at all. He was ten times her size, and he was her pet. They still wondered what it was that put out the fires, but they didn't have time to ask or care.

"Thank you, you big...dog...person," said Asher, standing there so edgy that he forgot Baymour's name. "But we really need to go before we run into any other traps. Where's the car?"

"Uhhh," Logan looked around, not remembering which direction they were headed or even where they were coming from.

He scratched the back of his head and kept turning in circles until Brex finally muttered "Oh come on!" and reached into his front pants' pocket.

"Whoa! Okay, um..." Logan froze, not knowing how else to react.

"Got it!" Brex pulled out the car key and clicked it, but nothing happened.

"That was, uh, really close," Logan whispered, thinking nobody could hear him.

Brex started running to different spots of the field before she finally heard two small car horns and saw two flashing lights in the corner of her eye. She turned to face where it was coming from, pointed her finger, and said, "This way. Let's go!"

Everyone, including Baymour, speed walked toward the car. Logan couldn't take his mind off what the condition of the Hummer could possibly be. Was it even still drivable? The amount of money he knew he was going to have to spend on fixing it made his legs jiggle.

"Is everyone okay?" Shani asked as they continued to walk. "Did anyone get burned?"

"No," said Logan, "But we should get you some disinfectant for those scratches." Shani tried to look at her back over her shoulder, but all she could see were a few tears in her thin sweater.

"I still feel kinda weird from that stuff Lexi was in. What even was that?" Asher asked.

"It must be from one of his rivers," said Maya. "With any normal human, he would be able to suck any soul out within minutes, but Lexi is an alchelarcenist, so it was taking much longer for them to try to dissolve her, so they could steal her power."

"That's what we're called?" Lexi asked. "Alchelarcenists? Like magic-stealer?"

"We'll fill you in later," Shani whispered to her.

Brex lit one hand instead of lighting another torch. She had learned her lesson. They could finally see the Hummer. It was in rough shape, but to their surprise, it was drivable.

"Aww damn, Zazu!" Logan cried as he examined the long deep scratch across the left side of the car.

"We're gonna have a lot of explaining to do if we get pulled over," said Lexi.

Brex and Shani checked to make sure nothing was completely busted, so they could at least get home safely. Brex pulled her aching body into the passenger's seat, Shani and Lexi hopped in the back, and Logan jumped in the driver's seat to try to start the engine, but it took a few tries.

"Um, Maya," said Asher, trying to get her attention before he got in the car. "I did actually have one question I wanted to ask you."

"Of course," she responded.

He rubbed his palms against his pants before he said, "So lately I've been having these weird dreams. And they totally could mean absolutely nothing, but they were just really vivid, and...odd." Maya nodded, indicating he should continue. "Well, the first one, I saw two people. I don't know who they were, but the man was asking the woman, who was a curly brunette, why a woman was coming to meet them, but I don't know who this person was either. I didn't see their faces. Apparently, this man didn't trust this other woman."

"I'm sorry. I don't know who they could be. It's all very vague." Maya's crows' feet scrunched together in confusion. She had no idea who these people were, and Asher believed her. "But how many of these dreams have you had?"

"Just two."

"And what was the other about?"

"Well, both of them, I saw everything happening through my bedroom mirror. I don't know why, obviously, but the second one, there was this white snake. Her eyes were like deep, deep red. She didn't say anything, but it was like she was trying to."

"She?" Maya looked at him with concern, rather than confusion. "How do you know it was a she?"

"Because she turned into one. Into a woman, I mean, before I woke up."

Maya stood there silent with her eyes lost in the distance for just a moment before she said, "I'm sorry. I don't know what either of those dreams mean, but I can try to figure it out." But this time, Asher didn't believe her. Her voice lost every ounce of softness and her eyes twitched away from him.

"Okay," he said. "Thanks anyways."

"Got it!" said Logan as he finally got the engine to start. He had to zap it with his fingertip for a few seconds, but the ignition rumbled awake. "Let's go!"

"You didn't tell me about those dreams," Shani said to Asher as he got in the backseat.

"I'm sorry," he responded. "I just wanted to figure this one out myself for once."

Shani understood and tried to not let her control issues get in the way. She knew now, and that's all that mattered.

"How can we get in contact with you?" Brex asked Maya as Brex climbed into the car.

"It's not safe to do so yet," she said. "I promise when it's time, I will find you."

"Do you need a ride back?" asked Logan.

"No, thank you. I will ride back with Baymour. Besides, all of my belongings no longer reside in Boston. We don't know where we're going yet." Baymour gave her a wide grin and wagged his gargantuan tail, making the grass shiver in the breeze.

"You can ride him?" Brex asked in disbelief.

"Of course. I trust him more than anything."

"Thank you for everything," said Shani, smiling before she saw Baymour scoop Maya up onto his back, and before they knew it, they gracefully rode off into the deep, dark woods.

"Alright," said Logan, putting the Hummer into drive, "Let's get the fuck out of this place."

23:

"Unless it's too late."

Tree branches kept hitting the cracked windshield, which made Logan flinch every time. Although his paranoia about the car being in any way damaged wasn't nearly as bad as it was before. He started preparing himself for the punishment he was going to get, which he knew was going to be worse than all of the punishments he received in high school combined.

Shani, sitting in the middle of the back seat, went back and forth between caring for Lexi and caring for Asher. He still felt weak, but Lexi kept sliding away, trying to hint that she was fine.

"Is anyone going to talk first?" Brex said, keeping watch in the front passenger's seat, growing tired of their constant awkward silences.

"I'll talk," said Lexi. "Thank you, guys. I'm sorry about all of this."

Asher responded "You're sorry that a maniac demon is trying to delete the concept of time? I think we forgive you, or at least I do."

"He's not trying to kill us. He can't," said Shani. "His little procedure won't work. He knows what we're capable of and who we have behind us. He's scared. It'll buy us some time. We'll be safe for a while."

After a few minutes, they approached the road, even more bumpy and rocky than it was before. Not a single street light was in sight, but Logan squinted his black eye, which he had no idea how he got, in hopes of avoiding any more reckless barriers along the way.

"Do you wanna tell us what happened, Lexi?" Logan asked. "How they got a hold of you?"

There was a sudden rush of guilt that sprinted through Lexi. After the series of events, she almost forgot about the innocent man who died because she decided to get into that car. She told them everything, and all of the dots connected.

"Maya was right," said Shani. "It was that dust stuff that she was talking about."

"Lexi, none of that was your fault," said Logan, taking a few glances to look at Lexi in the rearview mirror. "But you're entitled to feel what you feel. I would be reacting the same way. The only thing that I can tell you is that it was one hundred percent not your fault."

Lexi responded with a single resilient head nod. "I'm just not up for the crap that's gonna be in the news. It's gonna be so much worse than the ambulance," Lexi commented.

"You know what I don't get?" said Asher. "This demon, or whatever, man, wants to live in a world where no one dies, yet he's taken lives. Lives of innocent people, and that's terrifying. What happened to the afterlife just being the afterlife?"

"We're gonna have to fight," said Shani. "I don't know when, but it's going to happen. Or else, it'll be the apocalypse."

Logan began to pick up speed. At this point, Brex felt safe. She was in the car. No one was following them, but she couldn't help but still feel a panic attack about to explode through her body. The nausea was too overwhelming to contain and stay silent anymore.

"He doesn't care about saving people's lives," she said with a faint crack in it. "He just wants control. That's what people like him, sociopaths, want. And I know what you're going to say...sociopaths are humans. But that's probably how humans become that way; from creatures like him."

There was something different about her in that moment. A vulnerability that they hadn't seen before.

"Is something bothering you? What's on your mind?" Logan asked. For a moment, he thought she wasn't going to answer. She kept her focus out the window.

"There's something I should...fill you guys in on. And I'm sorry I didn't tell you this before, but I didn't think it was safe to tell anybody. I wasn't sure if I was still in danger or not."

The others' throats tightened up. What else could be more dangerous than their current situation, and were they able to take on any more jeopardy? One by one, they looked at Brex with comforting and consoling eyes. Brex couldn't see them, but she could sense their energy and care.

"January of sophomore year, my parents were at our candy store in Meredith. They've owned it since before I was born. My little brother Odin; it was his turn to help them out that day. I thought it was just going to be any other normal day, but something...happened. I was with Jenna. We hadn't seen each other since Christmas break began. I got a phone call from the police. There'd been a robbery. An armed robbery."

For a faint moment, the others lost their breath. And naturally, their eyes closed in hopes they weren't about to hear what they dreaded the most.

"The video tapes didn't catch his face. It was just one guy with a revolver. He shot my dad three times, my mom four, and Odin twice; in the back as he was trying to get away. None of them made it."

Logan took the risk and pulled the Hummer over to the side of the road. All he wanted was to give her his full attention with no distractions.

"He was only fourteen, and it was all my fault." The pressure pushing through her face became so unbearable, she could hardly see, and her breaths were becoming shorter, and more staccato. Tears uncontrollably rolled down her cheeks.

"What do you mean, Brex?" said Shani, placing her hand on the back of Brex's chair. "This couldn't possibly be your fault."

"Because I was supposed to be at the store that day with my parents. It was my turn at first, but I wanted to go see Jenna, so I asked Odin to switch with me. He'd be alive today if it wasn't for- it was supposed to be me."

Shani remembered hearing about that story on the news. Brex's name wasn't mentioned, but she thought she ought to keep that to herself seeing that the tension in Brex's body was rising. The skin on her upper limbs were starting to smoke. Logan instinctively grabbed them in hopes it would somehow keep her feeling safe. His hands started to burn, but he wasn't letting go.

"Hey, we are going to do whatever we can to find this guy and take him down," he said. "And you're not endangered anymore."

"You don't know that," Brex whispered with the little air she could muster.

"What do you mean?"

With the deep and audible inhale through her nose, they could all sense that this wasn't the most painful memory to recover, but rather the most daunting.

"Detective Schwimmer, he was the lead detective on the case. He doesn't think it was just a robbery. He found illegal substances in my parents' house. I didn't know about it, but he thinks it might have to do with the black market. It might have been a revenge attack of some sort because the robber; he didn't take all of the money from the register, not even half of it. So, it might have been a cover-up, so the police would take a wrong turn during the investigation. There might be someone out there that's trying to hunt me down and kill me, and it's not Moloch."

Out of all of them, the most paralyzed was Logan. Growing up without a mother who loved him with her whole heart always made him feel incomplete in a way, but to lose every single person in one's family and then be in fear of receiving the same fate? That was something he hoped to never understand.

"That's where I was last year," Brex continued. "I inherited the shop, but it had been barely profitable for the past few years, so I sold it to pay off my parents' debt, which left me with essentially nothing. I've spent the past year and a half waiting tables, going to therapy, and living with my grandparents. After this summer, I decided that my therapist sucked, and I thought it would be a good time to go back to school, but a couple of weeks ago, the administration called, and my financial aid fell through. So, the likelihood of me returning to school in January is slim to none. I guess that's it. I think that's everything." Brex tried hard to laugh off her tears, but she only shoved her face in her scraped-up palms.

The others sat there, at the edges of their seats to be as close to her as they could be without completely overwhelming her. Being completely silent, they let her shiver with anguish for as long as she needed to.

"Jenna's the only person that knows. I deleted all of my social media, and made sure my name was out of the news just in case."

"Why didn't they put you into the witness protection program?" Lexi asked.

"They said it wasn't necessary just yet. Just as long as I laid low, I should be fine."

"Should be?" Shani spat. "That shouldn't have been good enough for them. Brex they should have taken every pre—" Instead of continuing to pointlessly bicker with herself, she stopped to think of a better argument to make. Blaming the police was useless at this point. "Brex, I'm so sorry. We can't even imagine. You were better off protecting yourself before you were able to set an entire restaurant on fire anyways."

Brex gave a genuine smile with a small, quiet laughter and said, "Yeah, I forgot about that."

"What the hell did I miss?" said Lexi.

"Let's just say..." said Shani as she comically put her hand on Lexi's shoulder. "We're gonna help you find other places for your gigs."

Lexi was the last person to let a little laughter out. Although a few tears were still being shed, they felt safer and more connected than ever.

"I'm sorry, guys," said Brex. "Logan, you didn't have to stop. We should really get out of here." With that being said, Logan gave an encouraging head nod and started the car. Once again, the beaten-up Hummer was on the bumpy road. "We should all make a pact. From now on, no more secrets. Especially when it comes to safety. We protect each other."

Lexi immediately agreed by putting her hand in between the two front seats. The others piled on with Logan being the last one and struggling to bend his arm and find the stack of hands while keeping his eyes on the road. Brex playfully pushed his hand away and said, "Bitch, keep your hands on the wheel."

The rest of the car ride was mainly filled with silence. Shani and Lexi fell asleep on each other while Asher quietly thought about what Maya said referring to his dreams. Was she telling the truth when she said she didn't know what they meant? Did she have any reason to lie, and if so, why? What puzzled him the most was the meaning of the mirror. To his knowledge, the mirror in his bedroom was just an ordinary mirror from Walmart. It had to be metaphorical, but that was the only lead he had.

Brex and Logan sat in the front seats, quietly listening to country stations. Brex leaned her head against the cold glass window in hopes of falling asleep, but she could barely even close her eyes. Every time she did, she saw Lexi lying there, trapped in that green fluid. Her mind unwillingly scrolled through different scenarios that Brex tried desperately not to think about.

What if they didn't get there in time? What if they weren't able to fight off everything that Moloch threw at them? All she knew was that she was not looking forward to being alone in her room while miserably failing at trying to get some sleep.

"Hey, guys," said Logan. "I'm just gonna quickly stop at my house to leave my dad a note." He could hear a few moans and groans coming from Shani and Lexi. He could even see Shani's long arms stretching to the ceiling through the rearview mirror. "Is that okay?" Everyone either nodded or mumbled "Yeah" as their response. "I just wanna request that he kick my ass after football season is over."

The Hummer pulled up to Logan's driveway once again, and Logan reached into his glove compartment for a sticky note and a pen. Before getting out of the car, he scribbled a few words onto the paper while leaning against the steering wheel. He ran up to the front of the house, slammed the note onto the window of the door that said, "I have Zazu, I'll explain later, and I'm sorry for screwing up. I love you."

Shani watched him approach his house and said, "Did you guys notice he was acting kinda weird after getting his car tonight?"

"Yeah," said Brex, "But I don't think we should pressure him. He'll talk to us eventually. I think we've had enough stress for one night."

·····

The time was almost four in the morning when they drove back into Boston. Logan checked the tank. He was running low on gas, but before they could reach the station, they passed something unexpected.

"They're still there?" Asher said, looking out the window at what was now a crime scene surrounding Bevanda. The yellow tape encompassed almost the entire block, but there was no more smoke from what they could see.

Logan was eager to eavesdrop and said, "I'm gonna park in the lot a few blocks away, and then we should see what's going on." They all agreed and continued on their way.

After leaping from the car, they scanned their surroundings for any cop cars that might be watching them. Asher pointed out one that was parked on the other side of the street, but they didn't see anyone in it. They tried to act as casual as they could by not running or looking around.

The bruises and cuts on their faces were almost gone, but as soon as they were out of sight from the cruiser, they used the inner part of their clothing to wipe off as much dirt as they could.

The smell of smoke was still in the air. They began to wonder how much worse it got after they ran off and left the building in flames.

They walked along the side of the building on the sidewalk of the restaurant's cross street. Reporters and police officers were too busy talking to other people to notice they were there. The only voice they could point out was Jimmy's giving a statement to who they guessed was a reporter.

"They've been here for hours," they overheard him say. "All signs point to one person starting this. The only person I've seen that's had any aggression towards another patron here." Their hearts skipped a beat as they held their breath, waiting for him to continue. "His name is Richard Harson. He goes by Rick. Good guy, but always had such uncontrollable anger issues. He was here that night. I bet he just lit a cigarette and didn't wanna be blamed."

Without missing a beat, Asher smacked his face as hard as he could and pulled down every bit of skin he had on his head.

"Okay, I know that man is crazy," he whispered. "But he didn't start that fire."

"Yeah, but what other choice do we have?" said Logan.

"HEY!" said a deep, booming, male voice from across the street. Before looking to see who it was, or who they were talking to, they all immediately knew it was a cop wondering what they were doing, and they were right. "What are you kids doing here? This is a crime scene, and it's four in the morning."

"Sorry we just um..." For the first time in a while, Shani was afraid of authority. "We were across the street when the fire happened and wanted to see what was going on. We've just been partying all night, and we're on our way home."

The officer, who was over a full head taller than Shani, looked down at them with a curled lip and one squinted eye.

"Did you see anything you wanted to report?" he asked.

"No, nothing," said Lexi, keeping her voice down in hopes Jimmy couldn't hear her. "We didn't see anything."

After a deep, sleepy breath, the officer said, "Alright, but I don't want you kids loitering around. So, run along now."

They immediately did as they were told without hesitation. They could see from the corner of their eyes the officer returning to the scene behind the tapes.

As soon as he felt they were safe enough to talk again, Logan said, "I have an idea. I wanna make just one more stop." At this point, they did not have enough energy to contradict him. They followed him around the park and up to the remains of the Romanov building, which surprisingly didn't have caution tape surrounding it anymore.

"Logan," said Lexi, "I know what you're thinking, but there's no way it's here anymore."

Ignoring her, Logan kept looking around, hoping she was wrong.

"It could be," he said with a faintly aggressive attitude. "It's worth it to look just in case. And besides..." He intertwined his fingers, put his palms to the back of his head, and closed his eyes for a brief moment. "Something that Maya said has been bothering me, and I can't let it go."

Suddenly intrigued, the others silently joined in, looking for the evidence of Moloch's injury.

"Remember when she was talking about this stuff, and she said that there were parts of his entity or whatever that had the power to give us more magic? The next thing she said was 'Unless it's too late.'"

"Well, yeah," said Shani without looking up. "If we get stabbed to death, I don't think any magic could save that."

"But I don't think that's true, and I don't think that's what she meant." Logan's feet froze to the ground as he continued to recover his memories of what Maya had said. "She never told us what happens when we run out of fuel. Did she?"

The others didn't like where the conversation was headed, but they stopped searching and planted their feet as well to listen to what he had to say.

"Moloch wouldn't create something that was in any way merciful," Logan continued. "I don't think we should be abusing what we have. I think Maya was actually saying if we use up all of the power that we have before we find the essence that we need—"

"We're going to die," Brex whispered before everyone turned to glance at her. Everything in the air flipped upside down. The crickets were still chirping, the wind was still blowing, but they couldn't hear any of it. They could barely feel themselves breathing. All of their senses went blurry until something caught Asher's eye.

"Guys," he said, standing over a crack in the sidewalk with his eyes facing downwards. "I think I found something."

The others rushed to him, silently hoping for the best. Something glowed from below. It resembled the skin on Brex's forearms when she became tense and angry: red and compelling. As Shani drew closer to it, the more her power radiated.

"Is that...?" said Shani as she fixed her eyes on the red substance that remained in between the cracks of the concrete. It wasn't much, but it was what they were looking for.

"Okay," said Brex, preparing herself. "I think on three we should all put our hands over it at the same time. Hopefully, it'll be evenly distributed." Without taking their eyes off the sidewalk, they all mumbled in agreement. They weren't hoping for their heartbeats to skyrocket again that night, but this was nothing compared to earlier.

Everyone's knees took a cautious bend, and their left arms flexed with energy shooting out of every fingertip. Brex took an audible inhale through her nose and said, "One, two, three!"

Before they even touched the ground, they could feel the spirit and strength thrust into their blood. They only needed half of a second before they absorbed what fuel was left. In almost perfect unison, they all slowly removed their skin from the concrete, only to find their arrows lifted by just a few millimeters.

"It's okay," said Asher. "It's something. It's better than it was before."

"Guys, I know we've said this like countless times by now," said Shani. "But we really need to be serious about not using our powers unless we absolutely need to."

"Agreed," said Brex as they all took each other by the hand to stand back up and walk away.

"Hey," said Shani to Logan and Brex. "Do you guys wanna stay at our place tonight? I honestly just kinda feel weird walking away from you two after the night we've had."

Brex smiled, looked at Logan, and said, "I really don't wanna be alone tonight."

"I've honestly never wanted company more," said Logan as he wrapped his arm around her shoulders and headed off to the Main Street apartment.

24:

"He still doesn't get it, does he?"

"Anybody hungry?" asked Shani while Asher and Lexi were at their small living room table with Lexi's lab equipment. "I think I'm gonna make some home fries."

"I'm in!" both Lexi and Asher said at the same time.

"So, what are you looking for exactly?" Asher asked as Lexi looked into her miniature microscope that she had borrowed without permission from the school's lab.

"Well, remember how Maya said that thing about Kali? When she attacked her last month, she didn't really look like she aged over the past eighty years. We know we can't possibly be immortal, but I just wanted to do some tests and see if Maya is right in her theory that we probably just live for an abnormal period of time. I mean, maybe Kali is under some curse or something. I don't know."

On one slide there was a sample of Lexi's fingernail from her left index finger. The other was taken off Adam from the day before after she convinced him that she needed a male sample of nails to see if it helped better as a plant-growing serum than a female's fingernail did. She also added to the fib by telling him that Asher's and Logan's nails were too repugnant to test, and his were the cleanest ones that she saw.

"I'm just going to look and see if Adam's sample is as immune to deconstruction as we are. I mean, I'm pretty sure I already know the answer to this, but I would just like to make sure Maya is telling us the truth."

Asher didn't blame her for questioning Maya's judgment or intentions. He stood out of her way as she continued her experiment.

Lexi steadied her tube over her sample as she put her slide under the microscope. Everything looked normal. She put one single drop of acid onto her fingernail and kept her eyes focused through the lens. Nothing happened. She adjusted the lens several times, but there were still no reactions. She tried putting a few more drops onto the slide, but just like she had predicted, there was no effect.

Now it was time for Adam's sample. Once again, she steadied the tube filled with acid over the slide after she carefully placed the sample under the microscope. Everything looked normal until she let a single drop of acid fall onto the nail. The cells immediately started to disintegrate. It was just as she suspected.

"Looks like we're gonna join the Tuck Everlasting family unless we figure out how to get this scar off," she said as she started cleaning up her equipment."

"I think we can still die if we get shot in the stomach, dude," said Shani as she cut up her potatoes.

"Can we stop talking about this, please?" Asher mumbled as he messed up his hair and rubbed his hands all over his face. "And don't even think about bringing up Maya right now."

"What's your issue with her?" Lexi asked. "I wouldn't be here if it wasn't for her."

"I know, I know." Asher didn't regret what he said, but he still wanted to get his point across. "There's just something about this whole Alliance thing that seems fishy to me. Like maybe they're not telling us everything. And to me, Maya could have avoided a lot of this. She didn't have to put these scars on us. And why didn't she at least give us her phone number or something to call if we need help? Like, come on. She could've—"

Suddenly, Asher was interrupted by Lexi gluing her eyes to the T.V. The news was on, and it was about Lexi's Uber driver.

"Marshall Declan has been reported missing. He was last seen driving his gray Toyota Corolla around Southie, Boston, working his shift as an Uber driver," the newscaster spoke. "He's 6'3" with blonde hair and brown eyes, and according to his records, there was one passenger whom he picked up but never dropped off."

Lexi's heart stopped beating while she sat on the floor in front of the T.V. There was a brief pause before the reporter kept talking. It was the longest pause of Lexi's life.

"Eighteen-year-old Kendra Smith was brought in for questioning a few hours ago by the Boston P.D. after they found evidence that Declan never dropped her off at her home."

"Wha—" Lexi exhaled. "I don't understand."

"But according to Detective Rodgers this is not enough evidence to warrant her arrest. We will have updates for you soon. In other news, grand theft auto is on the rise—"

Lexi couldn't take it anymore. She aggressively pushed the power button on the remote. After a few moments of sitting there as still as a stone, she turned back to Asher and Shani and said, "Someone is wrongfully going to jail because of me."

"No," said Asher in his deepest voice. "It's not your fault. You didn't kill that poor man, and just—no. We won't let that happen. You heard what they said. They can't arrest her. And after everything I've learned about this asshole, there's no way anybody is going to find this poor Marshall guy. No body, no crime. She'll be okay."

"Why do I have the feeling that Maya had something to do with this?" Shani asked as she stood still, staring at the T.V. and shaking her head. "How did she even know?"

"She had to have hacked into the application," said Lexi. "She's had plenty of time to learn how to do that." She gathered up enough energy to pull herself onto the couch to remain in a slump. "How is his family going to get any closure?"

Neither Shani nor Asher could come up with a good response.

"Promise me that we'll figure it out?" asked Lexi, turning her focus towards the two of them.

Shani smiled and walked over to the couch to sit right beside Lexi. Asher followed.

"Asher?" Shani said, making eye contact with him. "Still don't trust Maya?"

.....

Sunday morning rose. Shani walked to the aquarium, and it was the only trip there that she didn't dread. She was, in fact, a little excited. After punching Seamus, she had a new, bold image of herself. She was proud that she had stood up for herself, and couldn't wait to not feel so belittled when she walked through those doors. She regretted nothing.

Her new self-assured attitude had her noticing things that she hadn't noticed before. The exterior design of the building was exquisite and eye-catching. The abstract and slanted rooftop and the long walls of glass that displayed the exhibits on the inside beautifully complimented the view of the deep, green, mucky ocean. And today, the sun had the most beautiful shimmering light spread across the surface of the water. It was almost as if it were welcoming Shani to the new day.

She passed the patrons outside, walked through the door, and said, "Morning, Al," to the security guard at the front desk.

"Morning, Shani," he responded, already regretting agreeing to let her back into the building.

Shani took her sweet time, collecting everything that she needed to. Her locker was stuffed with filled notebooks that likely made no difference in her job. Besides being pestered by Seamus on a routine basis, the only thing that she was certainly not going to miss was the smell of that tragic locker room. If the day janitor, Paul, ever needed to call out sick, the locker room's stench would grow so bad, that the patrons would call the police on the aquarium, and it would get shut down immediately.

It was a fairly dead day. No field trips were scheduled. No new employee orientations were scheduled. Shani hadn't even heard a single child scream since the moment she stepped into the building.

The Giant Tank looked especially substantial that day. During the past few weeks, Shani thought a lot more about the size and the mystery of the ocean. It was overwhelming, and she loved it. She felt more connected to the ocean now than ever.

"Oh, Shani. You're still here," said the voice of Dr. Carter, catching Shani patiently loitering in front of the tank.

"Dear me," said Shani, with more sass than she thought she had. "Am I not even allowed to be in the lobby of a public area?" Dramatically, she placed her hand on her chest and leaned her upper body down to meet the doctor's height. She knew what the answer to that question was even though it was never specified to her, but that's precisely why she asked in the first place. How could she be doing anything wrong?

"Uh...oh...um no, it's fine I guess. I'm really sorry we had to let you go. You know it's what was best. Do you think you'll be able to find another internship before the semester is over?"

"Already got one this morning at the Wildlife Alliance, but it's not until next semester. So sorry not sorry that I punched whatever his name was in the face. It felt good. You should try it sometime."

Dr. Carter wanted to get out of the conversation more than anything, and Shani was living for it. She had never seen Shani act this way. The doctor's stiff face froze as her neck shrunk into her chest. Without saying a word, or even making the smallest murmur, she gave one solid nod and waddled away. It had been a long time since Shani had that sort of attitude. Using her assertive voice to scare away enemies instead of her friends made her feel more powerful than ever before.

As she was about to pick up her hefty bag, Shani heard three small taps on the glass behind her. She twisted her body around to see Ilisa swimming, still with a blank expression on his tiny face.

"Did you finish him?" he asked with low and sullen energy.

"What do you think?" Shani answered.

"He's just going to keep coming back, and with more people."

"Yeah, well, while he's trying to be a coward and hide and try to figure out how to drain us all from the world, I got school to finish, and grad schools to apply to." She wrapped her scarf around her head and readied herself to awkwardly wave goodbye to him.

"Did anyone get hurt?" he asked before she could leave.

"Not any of my friends, thanks to you. Honestly, I don't know if we would have been able to save her without you. So...yeah. Thanks." Ilisa gave her a subtle bow without making any eye contact with her. "You know, I still don't trust you, and I don't even know if I fully trust Maya, but I know we're probably going to need your help again in the future. So, I hope you're up to the task." He finally locked his yellow eyes with hers, slowly nodded his head, and slithered away.

"Hey," said Logan, walking up from behind her. "Thought you could use some help."

"Thanks. I think I'm good actually. I didn't have a lot of stuff. It's not like I was really that important around here anyway, but it feels kinda liberating being released from this place. I felt so awkward and judged."

"Welcome to the club."

Although Shani knew Logan was content with his strong personality, she did empathize with his current self-deprecating humor.

"How'd things go with your dad?" Shani asked.

"Well, let's see. While I was working at my dad's firm, I missed a deadline for a huge case, by a lot, for a recurring client. And now they don't want to use our services anymore. So, his business could fail. And all because I was an idiot, and I misread a deadline."

It was worse than she expected. How was one to respond to that? She wasn't sure, but she knew she had to say something.

"You're not an idiot. Far from that actually," she said with a comforting smile. "No, an idiot would be someone who punches a guy in the face after she throws him up against a wall at her location of employment that she needs in order to graduate and get into grad school."

Logan covered his mouth and bit his lip, fighting against his rising laughter, but it was too powerful for him to handle.

"Okay, that was anything but idiotic," he said. "That was awesome. That guy is gonna be more terrified of you than I am."

"Seems like he already is." Shani had a crooked smirk smeared across her face as they both looked over to Seamus acting like he wasn't secretly watching her with his bruised nose and eyes.

"He still doesn't get it, does he?" Logan asked, studying Seamus's discomforting behavior. "Why are some men so clueless?"

"Have you seen how some teachers teach sex education?"

"Fair point. How pissed off do you think he's gonna be if I just do a little bit of this?" Logan playfully and repeatedly poked her belly, pretending to sensually tickle her.

Only a little embarrassed and self-conscious, Shani tried and failed to quietly contain her laughter. "Oh my God, Logan cut it out! Hah!" she giggled as she frantically whisked away his hands.

"Let me take you out of this hell hole in style at least," Logan said as he pretended to seductively wrap his arm around her neck and headed towards the door. But before they completely vanished from the building, Logan shamelessly made an effort to turn to Seamus when he knew he was looking and give him a "thumbs up" with a teasing and devilish look in his eyes.

"You are such an ass," Shani chortled, throwing his arm down.

.....

The financial aid office was usually filled with kids who needed to pay off fines for getting caught with weed in their dorm rooms. For Brex, that was most of her freshman year, but today she had a meeting with a financial aid officer whose name she did not know. All she knew about this woman was that she was so petite that she looked like anyone could easily snap her in half if they were up for the task. She had fire-orange-red hair, and she was probably the crankiest woman Brex had ever met.

"Do you know how much you owe the school?" said the woman.

"Honestly, no," Brex responded with her hand and forearm already supporting her entire head.

"Too bad we don't have any more scholarships. I know there are a few out there that are specifically for kids with dead parents." The way that this pompous woman said the word "dead" with such little life or compassion didn't surprise Brex, but rather irked her in a way that only her little brother ever could.

"You dropped out in the middle of your sophomore year, correct? In January of 2016?" the woman asked with her eyes struggling to read what was on the computer.

"That's correct," said Brex. "I'm just trying to figure out if I should finish the semester or not. Or if I can switch to online classes?"

"That deadline passed a while ago. No more students are allowed to switch or drop classes without financial consequences."

It was a frustrating moment where Brex felt as if nobody in the room was on her side, and everyone was against her wellbeing and hopeful intentions.

"Okay," said Brex looking down at her fingertips that lay on her lap. "So, how much money am I going to owe if I finish just this semester?"

The woman silently scanned her screen before she scribbled what appeared to be a few items down on a sticky note. As she reached over the desk to hand it to Brex, the woman gave her a gruesome yet unnecessary stare that told Brex everything she needed to know about what was on that sheet of paper. She was not going to like it, she was not going to enjoy her time to come, and after she read the number, she realized she was right.

"Well that was more than I thought," said Brex, subtly crushing the paper in her hand and staring lifelessly at the wall. "This includes my financial aid?"

"Your financial aid was different when your co-signer was your father. Now that it's um...Zackary Weber, your grandfather, the financial status has changed. He makes more than your father did apparently. You know how this works." The annoyance and irritation in her voice not only offended Brex, but had her confused to the point where she couldn't hide it on her face.

"So, just because my grandfather makes a little bit more money than my dad did, I don't get enough financial aid? And you just don't happen to see how messed up this is?" Brex rhetorically asked.

The woman was almost disgusted at her reaction.

"You'll be able to arrange it, so you'll only have to pay around three hundred a month." All Brex could think about was the likelihood that this woman had never forked over a student debt payment before in her life.

"I don't think this scenario is the appropriate time to use the word 'only.' Also, that's on top of the student loans that I'm paying right now from the first time I attempted this shit."

Brex was expecting a privileged and ignorant scolding from this woman, but to her surprise, she rolled her eyes, gave a smirking, silent chuckle, and turned back to her computer as if Brex had already left.

"Thank you for...whatever this fucking was, lady. I'm gonna deal with this shit later, and I'm gonna do it with someone who actually cares about the students' future and wants them to succeed."

Brex casually walked out of the office as if she were walking out of any ordinary situation. She made no eye contact with the administrator and slammed the door behind her before she could hear any of the administrator's response. Enough was enough.

The fury and indignation blew away from her peculiarly fast. Instead, she felt confidence and ease. A hinted indication that she should have released that compressed ferocity a long time ago. She reached for her phone, eager to tell someone of the news.

"Hey," Jenna answered on the other side of the phone. Brex Facetimed her at what was clearly a bad time, considering Jenna's eye make-up was smudged all the way down to her cheekbones.

"Hey. You doin' okay?" Brex asked.

"Yeah, yeah, yeah. Just doing my usual nap."

Brex would have believed her until she saw the face of Kerry Gruber roll over towards her on her bed, also looking slightly unconscious.

"Are you sure this isn't a bad time?" Brex smirked.

"No. It's fine. It's fine. What happened?"

Instead of an answer, Brex pulled down the corners of her mouth with hesitating eyes. It was all that Jenna needed.

"Babe, I'm sorry," she said, standing up out of her bed and walking out of her room.

"No, it's okay. I'm technically just an obnoxious second-semester sophomore. It's not like I got that far anyways. I love this school, but it's not what I need. Also, that's not even really the main reason why I called you. Um—" She rubbed her forehead, wondering how she was going to phrase her next sentence. "You're alone now, right? Kerry back there is dead enough?"

Jenna quickly looked around before she eagerly said, "Yeah, yeah. Why?"

"I told a few people." Jenna needed no more than Brex's vague statement.

"Really?...Why? Are you sure?" She brought her face closer to the camera with her eyes squinting harder.

"I just...needed to. I don't wanna feel so alone about this anymore. I love you, but I need more people to know just a sliver of what I am feeling and what I need. I'm sick of hiding things."

All of a sudden, her focus shifted gears. The number of secrets she'd been hiding from Jenna was unbearable to think about. It wasn't something that struck her as significant or frankly bothersome until now, but there was nothing that she could do about it.

"Yeah?" Jenna impatiently asked.

"Oh yeah, well...it's just time to move on and not be a baby about everything anymore. I want everybody in my life to help me when I need it and with this huge life transition. I just want to be honest with people."

A proud and content sensation overcame Jenna. It had been one of her biggest concerns over the past year and a half. Now, her hyper-awareness and protective sensibilities could be at rest.

"I'm glad. I just want you to be okay. And out of curiosity, who did you tell?"

"Uh, it was Lexi, Shani, Asher, and um...Logan." Brex pretended like she was tired and couldn't remember if she told Logan or not.

"Ah, I see," Jenna said with a satisfied smile. "Lexi and her dad doing okay?" For just a split second, Brex was running through what she had told Jenna a few days earlier.

Lexi's dad was being kicked out in the middle of the night, and you all needed to go and help them move all of his stuff, she repeated to herself as she rubbed her eyes clean.

"Hah, yeah," Brex casually responded. "Everything is good. He's living with her grandparents now. Lexi's been talking to him a lot the past couple of days. He's been doin' alright."

Feeling that the conversation was about to wrap up, Brex looked down at her feet and added one more topic to the conversation.

"One more thing," she said. "I think I'm gonna go back to therapy too."

For a moment, Brex could tell that she was in a sense worried, but there was a small sign of relief as well when Jenna's deep breath turned into a light smile.

"Are you sure?" Jenna asked. "I just remember all of the negative things you told me from last time."

"Everybody benefits from therapy. You gotta find the right therapist for you. Or else you're just fucked."

They shared one more small yet joyous laugh before Jenna added "Hey, I'm happy you're doing better."

It felt relieving to hear that somebody noticed and acknowledged her progress.

"Thanks," Brex said quietly. "And thanks for being there for me. Love you, I'll talk to you later."

"Love you, and don't worry," Jenna said with a small wink. "I'll give full deats later."

25:

"What do you think? Business partners?"

The beautiful outdoors that next Wednesday influenced almost every student to run late to their classes. It was the perfect fall transitioning weather. Every caffeine addict had a hot coffee in their hands. The leaves finally changed to all of the burnt red and yellow shades on the color wheel. A few of the leaves had already made their way to the ground. The students and teachers took their time enjoying kicking around the colorful piles, and stepping on them to hear and feel a satisfying crunch.

Brex and Lexi comfortably sat on the curb outside of their lecture hall with their backs leaning up against the stone wall and their legs fully stretched before themselves.

"So, you're really going to leave?" Lexi asked.

"I have no choice," said Brex. "My grandparent's credit has gotten too low, but still somehow they make too much money, and mine sucked to begin with. My parents didn't leave me with enough money, and I didn't work enough to pay the tuition in advance. The only thing that I can do is finish the semester with a goddamn bang, and that's about it."

Lexi took her time, finding the right words to respond with. Money was always a significant aggravation in her life too. She understood the compromises people had to make, but this situation seemed especially unfair.

"Good thing you're smart and you'll easily be able to get by without a degree," said Lexi. "What is your plan anyway?"

"The only thing I can do: start a photography business." There was no second guessing. The confidence burst from each corner of her smile.

"You're gonna kick ass and put every other photographer in Boston out of business, you know that?" Brex casually shook off the compliment, but remained lighthearted. "Actually, you already have your first customer. I need new flyers for upcoming gigs. I was thinking of doing pictures that are more rocker-chic-type. What do you think? You and Logan wanna put together a poster for me?"

Touched by Lexi's encouragement, Brex sarcastically rubbed her chin, pretending to think about her offer. "Sounds tempting. How big of an order were you thinking? First time customers get 50% off, you know?"

"No way! I'm paying full price, and that is my final offer!"

The two of them jovially snickered at each other as three other figures jumped in front of them.

"Secrets don't make friends," Shani quickly spat out. "What's so funny?"

The two seated girls suddenly remembered what the conversation was about.

"I'm officially leaving school," said Brex. "And the likelihood of my return is slim to none, but mainly leaning towards none."

They weren't surprised, but still showed no lack of disappointment.

"But!" Lexi positively added. "She's going to open up a photography business, and I'm going to be her first customer. Sick, right?"

Brex could see on Logan's face that the news hit him the hardest, but he knew Brex well enough by now to know that she was the type of person who hated people pitying her. All she needed was the type of encouragement that Lexi was giving.

"That's amazing," he said. "You'll obviously crush it. What's the first project, blondie?"

"Well, actually I was just telling Brex that it should be put together by the two of you. I need a poster to advertise my gigs. I was hoping to get the best photographer and graphic designer that I know to do some collabs." Lexi ended her sentence in falsetto.

Logan immediately had his answer, but it was amusing for him to watch Lexi clasp her hands together in front of her face, her fingers glued to each other as if she were begging for a trip to Disney World.

"What do you think? Business partners?" Brex asked, reaching out her arm for a handshake.

Cracking a smile and trying to temper the blush in his cheeks, he reached his hand out in return and said, "Let's do this," as they exchanged a firm, effective handshake.

"Great!" Lexi shot up to her feet, bringing Brex along with her.

"It's 7:56. We should get going," said Shani, paranoid.

"Yeah, yeah, let's go, let's go! So, I was thinking of something like a bright red theme. Also, do you think I should straighten my hair? I think it would bring a whole new image to my brand—"

Asher slowed down his steps and fell behind in the moving flock.

"Hey, you guys go ahead. I'll be right there. I just wanna make a quick call," he said as he pulled out his phone.

"Alright," Shani said quietly and nodded her head. She saw the pensive and empty look on his face, but she had a guess as to whom he was calling.

The four of them turned around the corner as Asher heard a sweet young voice on the other end of the line.

"Hello?" the voice said.

"Hey, buddy. How you doin', Pablo?" Asher comfortingly asked his brother.

"I'm good, just playing some video games. Gotta leave for school in a minute. Why are you calling? Do you need Mom?"

It was like a needle pointing in the back of his skull and chest at the same time when Asher heard that question.

"No! No, I wanted to talk to you. You know, just see how you were doing. Is school going okay?"

"Eh, same old school. That Bobby kid won't stop picking on me though. My teacher even called his mom, and he still won't leave me alone."

Asher recalled Pablo mentioning a kid named Bobby a few months before. He couldn't help but be bothered by the fact that he hadn't talked to his little brother more about bullying. He knew for sure that his mother wasn't doing anything about it.

"Well, you tell Bobby that your older brother got you a skateboard for Christmas, which makes you a lot cooler than him."

"I can barely even ride it."

"I'll teach you more when I come home, okay? Does that sound fun or lame?"

"That would be awesome!"

Asher could hear the sound of his video game controller hitting the ground and the noise that the T.V. made when one loses a game in Mario Kart.

"You really wanna?" Pablo asked with his pitch rising a full octave.

"Of course. You need to learn from the best. I'll talk to you later, okay?"

"Okay. Bye, Asher. Love you!"

"Love you too," said Asher before he hung up the phone. It was the easiest phone call of his life, and yet he felt his soul soar.

"Hey! Ready for class?" asked Adam, playfully jumping right next to him.

"Wow. You're energized for somebody who skipped Morialsa's class all last week."

"Don't worry. I'm a new man now. I am ready for my debate today with whichever one of those hot, California Kaitlin girls I'm up against."

Asher laughed with only a small tickle in the back of his throat.

"Who were you on the phone with at eight in the morning?" Adam asked.

"My little brother."

"You have a little brother? You never mentioned him, or at least I don't think you did." Adam gave him a little nudge, trying to get more information out of him.

"Yeah. His name's Pablo. He's twelve and really smart. He's my half-brother. From my mom's second marriage. He's the best."

·····

"GOOD MORNING, CLASS!" the professor hollered, sounding a bit more cheerful and British than usual.

"Every. Single. Time," whispered Lavender in the front as she rubbed her forehead.

"How are we all doing today? Are we ready for today's work?"

There were a few naive freshman girls who sat in the front row every class, still intrigued and somewhat blinded by the professor's appealing physical features. They never even bothered to breathe and realize the lack of his organization and teaching skills. Plus, the fact that his "philosophy" class would often turn into a "political" one that revealed which students were dumber than most.

"Adam? Kaitlin? Are you two ready?" he presumed.

The two of them exchanged captivating smiles as they both confidently took their paths to the stage.

"Awesome. State your names, the topic you'll be debating, and the side you'll be defending."

Adam reached out to shake her hand before they started, while Kaitlin popped out one knee and held out her hand almost as if she expected him to kiss it, which he almost did but backed out of at the last second. Instead, he firmly shook it for a split second longer than he should have before she almost had to pull away from him. They exchanged one more smile and began their debate.

A few minutes into the discussion, Logan glanced over at Asher to see him compulsively biting his nails and staring down at the chair in front of him.

"Hey," Logan said, giving him a gentle, consoling, back-handed tap on the shoulder. "I don't like lying to him either. We'll tell him eventually. Don't worry."

"Really?" Asher responded, wholly disbelieving his last sentence. "I doubt it. It's not like this is going to end any time soon." He noticed the look on Logan's face, implying that he didn't like to be reminded of that fact. "But don't worry. It's fine. It's not like we're the only ones. Like I'm sure Brex really wants to tell Jenna, and I'm sure Lexi wants to tell her dad. But it really doesn't matter. We are all safe, and that's all that's important."

Logan agreed as they exchanged one more back-of-the-hand fist bump.

"And that's why I personally think that if you are forced to pick one," Kaitlin said, wrapping up her opening argument, "You should choose to leave the train on its path and kill the five people instead of switching the levers and killing just the one. We don't get to play God."

Asher covered his agony with his fingers spreading over his mouth and whispered "God, let this torture be over soon."

EPILOGUE:

October 1st, 2017

The crash of the tumultuous waves was the only thing that kept Kali calm. She lay still but in excruciating pain on a cold, wet bed. The less she moved, the less pain she felt. The repetitive sound of the ocean water dripping from the rocks tested her patience. Her breathing became heavier, and her heart kept beating faster and faster. She was stuck here. There was nothing that she could do to escape.

The oceanside cave never lit with daylight. It was always dark. The smell of the growing mold mixed with seawater made her nauseated. It was torture, but she was getting used to it.

All of a sudden, there was a cry coming from the distance. Not a human cry, a cry of wind. Wind that pierced through the sky like a needle. She recognized the sound immediately. After it got closer to her, and a rush of heat soared through the room, she knew it was Moloch, coming back from wherever he might have been.

The crimson flames from his body plunged through the hole in the rocks before he gracefully landed on the damp sandy floor. His dark skin was still red for a few moments even after the flames died down, vanishing into the air.

"It's not healing," said Kali instead of a greeting. Her voice crescendoed as she continued to express her pain. "It's been weeks, and you said it would heal."

The tension and fierceness in her face reflected the anger and frustration in her voice. The entire left side of her body was still burnt by Moloch's fire, but it wasn't a normal burn. It glowed. It glowed like the moon in a lunar eclipse.

"Don't worry," Moloch replied. "It will heal. You are only an alchelarcenist, and this is the only thing that can permanently scar you, and you were still powerful enough to handle those kids, weren't you? I wouldn't complain if I were you." His fingertips stroked her red, bumpy face. It was as if she were wearing a mask. The burn smothered her left eye socket and traveled down in between her eyes and to the side of her nose. Feeling lethargic and stiff, she gathered up enough energy to throw his hand away from her face.

"If you say that to me one more time, I'll shoot a goddamn arrow straight through your throat. There's been no progress. Even you can see that." They locked their aggressive eyes together. Moloch couldn't help but acknowledge and feel some of Kali's anger. The gray in her eyes brightened as she looked deep into his soul.

"It's because you're weak," Moloch said in the most monotone voice he could produce. Admitting this drew disappointment into his veins and onto his face. Kali was his, and she had failed. *He* had failed.

"THIS IS YOUR FAULT! Every plan that you've implemented has failed. Why did you even need to bring the rest of those idiots to the mountains? We could have drained her from everything she possessed. And then you tried to kill them, when you could have just waited. Your plan was flawed!"

"My apparent attempt at killing them was just to slow them down. I underestimated their strength *and* their intelligence. Which is exactly what you're doing right now. You're being foolish."

With her lightning-fast and agile reflexes, she grabbed his arm, but his strength overpowered her, and her injuries weakened her. He used her weakness against her and snapped her arm down onto the wooden bed.

"I'd be very careful, Kali." His voice was unnervingly calm. He wasn't angry, just assertive, and as much as he tried not to show it; concerned. "You're going to need help. You can't risk making the same idiotic mistakes again. I need you to be as healthy as you can be. You're still technically human."

"You were the one who left me there." Kali refused to look at him anymore. Discontented, she turned her head away to watch the mucky ocean water drip from the wall. "And I don't need any help."

"I wasn't asking your permission, and what could possibly be the harm in creating more people like you? We could create a whole army."

"We can't," Kali forcefully shouted, still looking away. "We don't know where the other sanctuaries are. We have nothing that we need to create more alchelarcenists. No people, no magic. What the hell can you possibly do?"

Moloch walked away before any of his true anger appeared in his countenance. Being around Kali did nothing but remind him that he was getting further away from his objective.

"There are two options," Moloch began. "One; we can convince those bastard kids to side with us. That might not be too hard. They seem like they'll believe anything. After all, they probably trust Maya."

"And what's the second option?" Kali asked, finally turning her head back to look at him. Suddenly, she was intrigued.

Moloch cracked a twisted smile and said, "Well. We could also just use the rest of the alchelesters from the Gods' cauldron that you were created from." He stayed turned away from her, but he could feel her shifting directions.

"What did you just say?" She held her core tightly enough that she was able to pull herself to an upright position. "You've had the rest of the alchelesters from that cave and you didn't tell me? Where the hell are you keeping them? Why didn't I know?" Her voice was now so loud it echoed throughout the rocky walls.

"There was no point in you knowing." Moloch found slight amusement in her reaction. For almost a hundred years, he had been keeping this secret from her, and she never knew.

"And why is that?"

"Because you would have wanted all of the powers that cave held, but none of those powers wanted you. That's why you only manifest one ability." He took a few steps closer to her, making sure she was giving her full attention to him. "When I created you all those years ago, there were two other alchelesters in that cave, but you attracted only one. The others had to go somewhere, so I took them for myself. You're powerful, but not passionate enough to receive them all."

Kali trusted Moloch. Not because she wanted to, but because she had to. That didn't ever stop her from questioning his judgment.

"How do you know this? How do you know that's even possible? Those witches created the alchelesters, not you."

"Because...one of those kids has two of the Gods' powers inside them, and they don't even know it."

Acknowledgments:

I started writing this book in the fall of 2019 after trying and failing to write another novel, which to be honest, I can't even remember what it was even about. While developing this crazy story over the past three years, I also wrote *The Other World*, and *The Tunnel*. And if you've been a faithful supporter of mine (first of all HEYYYY, love you, thanks!) but also, just an update, my sister, Taryn is on page 40 of my first book and she claims she read the first page of my second book, but do we really believe her? I'll give her ten bucks if she can name it. NO CHEATING!

Anywayyy...I'm so happy that I can finally share this story with all your beautiful faces. As always, I want to thank you first. You could have spent your money on anything else, and you probably should have, but there's no going back now so yaaaaayyy!! Also, thank you to my dad, Doug for editing yet another book of mine. Thank you to my stepdad, Dan for designing this amazing cover for me. Thank you to Sam who was the very first person to read the first two chapters of this manuscript and told me that it didn't suck. I seriously would have dropped everything if it wasn't for her enthusiasm. Thank you to the rest of my family and friends who always put up with me, even though I have to put up with them as well so I guess we're even.

Lastly, thank you to Brex, Logan, Lexi, Shani, and Asher. My children. The next two chapters of this trilogy are going to be a wild ride, so buckle up, 'cause not wearing a seatbelt is illegal. (Don't worry I'm already regretting that joke as you are reading this.)